KU-399-532

USES AND ABUSES

by the same author

SEMINAR ON YOUTH
THE STANDARD LIFE OF A TEMPORARY PANTYHOSE SALESMAN
SODOMIES IN ELEVENPOINT

ALDO BUSI

Uses and Abuses

Journeys, Sleepwalkings and Fool's Errands

Translated by Stuart Hood

faber and faber

LONDON · BOSTON

English translation first published
in Great Britain in 1995
by Faber and Faber Limited
3 Queen Square London WC1N 3AU

Phototypeset by Intype, London
Printed in England by Clays Ltd, St Ives plc

A CIP record for this book is
available from the British Library

ISBN 0-571-17054-4

Men, with their brief destinies, scan only a small part of life
with their existences, and rising up disperse like smoke
assigned only to that tiny part each encounters by chance
while they wander here and there . . .
the blood that circulates in the heart, that for men is
thought . . .
. . . the nerves . . . the nails . . .
the tears . . .
the crystalline sky . . .
. . . and the light hurled at them.

Empedocles, *Purification*

'MAKE ROOM! Come on!' cried the priest Don Palanca, elbowing his way through the hedgerows of roses and women that led right up to the altar – he treated both species like a single nettle and the nettles were delirious, offering buds and blouses until they pricked him in the hope of greater blessings.

The house in Borgosotto where I lived more than thirty years ago had a little concrete courtyard and so I had no roses to pluck for Saint Rita's day and carry to the parish church of San Pancrazio. That day all the boys and girls went up to have their roses blessed in the Romanesque church. It was a disorderly procession and a more cheerful one than usual; people made their way politely up the paths, each with their bunch wrapped in newspaper or butcher's wrapping paper. From the top of the churchyard I saw all these relations of mine among them and heard the bursts of mock imprecations from the old women and the laughter which brought closer and closer to me the scent and colours of a recurring festival. On the hill itself, however, was a spread of thick bushes of little pink and white roses – these were the ones I took into the church, sucking the blood and pulling the thorns out of my fingers with my teeth. Inside there was nothing really visible yet to look at – it is only a few years since the frescoes were brought to light and the place properly restored. From the walls a saint's or a friar's pale profile emerged here and there, looking like the paw of some animal or other, and there were no vestments on the high altar, a tiny Roman chariot laden with little red lights.

My little roses were so fragile that I had to be careful because the petals came away if you merely breathed too close. Once a woman said to me that they did not count for the blessing, you didn't take dog-roses into church, you needed real roses. When they had been blessed the petals were put away in the chest of drawers or in the sideboard in a glass jar or in a big sweet dish and you took one for a headache, toothache and women's hot flushes. You floated them in a glass of water or a cup of camomile, then with your finger you pushed them right in and sipped the liquid and swallowed the petal down without chewing it –

like the communion wafer. People who didn't entirely believe in this, on the other hand, used them for poultices for bruises. They got better right away. One day when I was pretending to have a sore head I borrowed a petal from a neighbour – maybe it would do something for me even if it was something nasty – but nothing happened: it couldn't get rid of an ailment I didn't have, nor could it make me have one I didn't have already. I would have liked to experience the same sort of thing as the others. Perhaps it really was the fault of the little wild roses, which because they were the wrong kind did not yield the desired effect on an ailment invented out of a desire for communion at all costs. If I had got to the point of being indebted for a petal I could make myself indebted for a few roses, but I was unhappy at having to give up the little roses within my reach. What a pity that the rites of men were so rigid that they excluded a whole variety of roses which – pretty or not – could be easily plucked by anyone who had no others, they pricked you a bit at first but then you were free to throw them away before you got home. But the rite doesn't free you, it ties you down entirely – right down to the sweet-dish. I had asked for a loan of the petal because I would not have known how to formulate my request differently – I remember once my mother had asked a neighbour for 'the loan of a potato' and gave it back to her a few days later. And so that year I began to feel my way: where I saw buds I turned up and said: 'Will you lend me a few roses, I want to see if the petal that has been blessed will have the same effect on me as on the others.'

I added that I would let them have the roses back as soon as I could – I had not the slightest idea about how or when I would be able to do so. They all said:

'It's early yet – and there aren't many this year.'

If I had just asked them for some it would have been easier because as it was, Saint Rita came, the afternoon came, and I was still going here and there to no avail because no one gave me roses. How could a boy get it into his head to ask to borrow roses? Wasn't there something deeply dishonest in that? Something ambiguous, mocking? I awoke suspicion like a thief in broad daylight when everyone is at home, or like a detail you could make neither head nor tail of in the whitewashed frescoes – once after a storm which had brought down flakes of plaster from the ceiling a little tail appeared, and then a hoof and a crest like a dragon's, just inside the side door.

I was left with Tannamori, the old woman who *lived* for roses and of whom it was said that she had the finest rose garden in Montichiaro. Few people were allowed in to see it. The whole house was surrounded by a very high wall and it was common knowledge that the old woman had never plucked a single twig to offer to anyone, relatives included. And she was someone who caused talk because she had never turned up to have them blessed, she grew them and let them die, convinced that she alone was intoxicated by a perfume which sometimes invaded the houses even at night and caught breaths accustomed only to what came from the chamberpots under the beds. I would try the impossible.

The ancient gentlewoman did not allow me to enter the big door to the garden. She shouted querulously and an old handyman came to take her place at the spyhole, careful to cover up as much as possible so as not to let me squint inside. He asked me what I wanted that I had to pull the bell so hard, and I told him it all in one breath, some real roses to carry up the hill to have them blessed. He looked at me dumbfounded by the astonishing offence. He did not come back and I could already see the irregular lines of people climbing up the slopes through the blackberries and the hawthorn bushes with bunches high in the air, kept safe in their arms like newborn babes or already elevated like a shrine, and I said Goodbye Saint Rita. At the last moment the spyhole was pulled open and the black bony arm passed three to me, one at a time, pale violet and magical. She did not say a word. It was a hasty gift and didn't even give me time to sign my imaginary promissory note as someone in debt for roses.

It is difficult to remember some things now. I see the open door of the little church and a lot of people outside because they couldn't all get in, I hear my short breath as a tardy pilgrim, there is a cock too on the threshold which goes off in search of worms among the motorbikes and bicycles leaning against the apse, the beadle's mule, and I remember myself with the roses in my fist as if they were a prize or a whip and my eyes looking round for that woman who had criticized my little wild roses. I feel an even more perfect change taking shape in my anxiety to at least experience the same things as other people. Benedictions do not generally take long. Now, or so it seemed, I was as of right taking part in the shared consecration. I played alone till evening, maybe playing at runnning from the church to the cross on the very top of the hill. The roses ran with me, they shook their petals in the wind; wherever they fell, I fell with them. I brandished them like lances. With those remaining petals nothing could happen to me, they would protect me from any evil influence, and even from myself, for taking on debts that were beyond the means of my gardens.

At dusk I arrived where I had to get to the year before – at the dusty briar with the little wild roses. I remember very clearly that dusk behind the little thorny aphid-covered branches because I remember very clearly that instead of picking them carefully I broke them off in handfuls, in a rage and frenzy to honour my debt speedily. When I got back home the three real roses did not have a single petal, I had scattered them by dint of whipping the air which was full of bogus guardian angels; not even with my immense will-power could I manage to believe in the same things and feel them. There was always a sort of inhuman little wave that swept me back just when I was sure I had managed to deceive myself entirely. I felt I had myself been lent to someone who had neither asked for nor deserved me and who nevertheless – there being no other repository – returned me to myself, to my impossible hunger for conformism in swaddling clothes, and to my pride as someone defenceless when confronted by his own truth and with his back to the wall, without the support of a nice little superstition to share with the others even in May, when it is beautifully sunny and if everyone has a headache you feel like getting one too by shamming just to be able to think sometimes of an inaccessible pronoun like 'us'. Then in the door-ring, seeing that they would not go through the spyhole, I left in return for the three real roses nine little wild roses and on purpose a few tiny drops of blood and went off with my fingers spread out because in this way my skinned hands hurt me as much as possible and no more.

And from then on it has always been like that, at least thrice, what a fool, because of impossible credits not granted but imposed at the very moment when I took them upon myself, thinking to myself that they were unalterable pledges. I know everything there is to be known on the subject but can do nothing about it just the same. I only hope that things are better for a boy today; I have succeeded in doing away with half the rite but the other half has remained roosting inside me like a wet chicken proud of its galloping consumption and of the keen wit that comes from putting up with the cold far from the nest. I could not do more even if, in any case, there are no such things as real roses.

I am talking to myself on a train to Lugano:

'Not only do real roses not exist but very soon not even roses in the absolute sense will exist. Just take a look – you won't see a thicket of wild roses even if you pay for them on the scale of a conference on nuclear fusion. The herbicides – like the yellow flags on the banks of the vanished ditches – vanished. There will be about three of us who notice. And May is no longer the month for roses but for a mass of rotten stuff that doesn't open to the full. And at your age with your new income, May becomes the month for income tax returns and your declaration of love to your childhood will inevitably be taxed and will be transformed into a declaration of love taxed at the going rate. There is no abuse that is not destined to have to come to terms with a base rate of 19 per cent and in the end, since it has become 50 per cent, you have to produce two abuses to enjoy one: one for the State and the other – the one that is left – for yourself. Like with two lovers: if you admit that half of each belongs to the State you can say that one of the two never really exists. I must constantly produce my double to have a simple unity – in many cases I have actually to triplicate myself. How many infringements will I need to make *others* – that is the indispensable minimum – into *myself*?'

It is a day in late September 1987. I am on my way to an Italian Swiss TV studio to record an interview on my recent arrest in London (indecent acts in public, oof!).

'... that lustful bigot, Sergeant Plod, who was making the list in the police station of the objects in my Peruvian shoulderbag,' and me putting a condom under his nose saying: "You forgot this, mind I want it back." And the other two who had picked me up in a lavatory in Oxford Circus after three days lying in ambush because I really did not believe that the City of Westminster had introduced *pretty cops* to catch homosexuals who take a good look out of the corner of their eyes – and very occasionally with both hands – at their neighbour's cock . . . the other two, as I was saying, who take me, somewhat repentant because of my subtle arrogance and the fun the operation is causing me, to a police station and then into a room to take my fingerprints and I ask at the end if it is possible to have a photocopy. 'Why?' asks the extremely ugly plain-clothes policeman who headquarters think is 'pretty'. 'To hang it up in my living-room of course!' I say, and Sergeant Plod looks askance again and hands me a biro to sign with and then cleans the handle with a rag, making a disgusted face as if I were spreading the plague, so I say to him: 'Just wait, I'll put that in the first chapter of something or other' and he says: 'What of?' 'Of a book obviously. Do you think I get myself arrested to amuse you? To give you a reason to draw your salary in a way that is such a disgrace to the European community? And now I can also tell you who I am!' The embassy, newspapers, interviews. At the first trial I plead not guilty and don't give in and leave bail of five hundred pounds as a guarantee that I will come back for the real trial and I am already hoping for a rich mass-media harvest with a jury of twelve of lady-pensioners and fishmongers and they had to settle for a little huggermugger affair, all fixed beforehand by the lawyers, and disappointed, instead of giving battle, I limit myself to winning the case but without getting costs and seeing the two plain-clothes policemen who at the end humbly greet me by nodding their heads. I would have killed them in an embrace but above all I would have smothered in kisses Plod, the blondish one, grey-eyed, with a washed-out look, the face of a communicant, paid to hate by order, the beast bred by Thatcher, the hooligan of irrationality which is turned into order and form – still, he has had it too somewhere or other like everyone else and without enjoying it.'

(It will never be transmitted.)

I take the opportunity to visit the Thyssen collection. Ten

minutes queuing, ten minutes of the lakeside avenue, ten minutes for the visit, and that's that. What interests me in museums are possible covers for my books. I can eliminate forty fourteenth-century ones, a hundred from the fifteenth century and a thousand from the Renaissance to the Impressionists without finding anything interesting. But I am enchanted by the poster outside a fish restaurant: 'Ladies! Royster with an oyster.'

From Lugano I take the train back to Milan and from there a plane to Brussels.

That way I have a bit of time to master the material given me by the Icelandic consulate, because before agreeing to the Swiss interview I thought: 'Since I am in Lugano and have to go on to Belgium I might as well end up in Reykjavik,' and since I wanted to go there without money problems I proposed a reportage to a weekly magazine. The free trip and the reward for the journalistic service that goes along with it are excuses to myself, traps I set off wherever you set foot in my bedroom from which you wouldn't get me out again. I invent flattering offers to myself – I make myself accept and propose them as if they did not come from me and so I feel I am crushed in the grip of an obligation – which is to transform death into writing, and since for me writing is movement and rhythm and never sedentary nor *thought out*, here I am by magic forced to leave my chair and my bed for some country or other where I can find a chair as quickly as possible and collapse into it and shut my eyes and draw new sighs of relief – until the hand mechanically slides towards the outside pocket of my travel-bag, touches the round end of a biro, feels the outlines of a notebook and then, as if I were digging them up by the roots from hard, resistant earth, I extract both of them with the determination of an old-fashioned dentist. Here we are again, the vice is returning to bubble in my veins, it takes over the veins of other people, it makes them flow towards it, it drains and floods them, ties in knots and undoes them, irons them out and creases them, and out there is weather of some kind to be described or it is already departure time and by good luck I have not seen any of what I ought to have seen. Because once your dream is shattered one reality is as good as another. It is from the climate that I draw my conclusions, not from what I know.

But what perhaps really urged me to propose a reportage on Iceland is the certainty that up there I shall feel myself to be geographically alienated, and in this state of disorientation I shall insert – like a flood of lava bristling with strange lichens of the mind – a certain growing sense of alienation I have as a Lombard-Venetian Italian which takes away my breath when I go slowly and realize how split are the civic consciousnesses of my nation. The north and the south of Italy are not like the north and south of Germany or the north and south of France: they are two peoples and two mentalities which are increasingly separate and inimical to each other. And then, seeing that they are both Italy and neither of them is Italy, what is my nationality now? And what is *theirs*? Who is an *Italian* today? What could anyone do today to be patriotic without being first and foremost antipatriotic where half of his own country is concerned? Not to mention the South Tyrolers . . . And then obscurely, I make the choice to go off to some place where – did I have a choice – I would not go of my own volition, to pay tribute to the only classical language left in the West – Icelandic, the language of immensely boring sagas which although set down from the twelfth century on go back to the first Norse settlements of the ninth. I have never felt sympathy for conquistadors and for all the trials connected with conquest which are supposed to make a real man, yet anyone who goes off to conquer a sterile piece of land covered with ice excites my curiosity more than the Iberians who go off to discover America and – along with everything on God's earth and above it – discover Indians and parrots, ready for the reasonable price of a few shots from an arquebus to imitate them in almost every respect. I would have imitated the native peoples and the feathered inhabitants and instead of setting up the cross would – if at all – have made it into a plough and banished the missionaries, the nuns, the Portuguese kings in exile, and kept only gallows-birds and flamenco dancers. To pay homage to the obstinacy of a language which has remained unchanged down to our day and which within its own syntax has coined all the neologisms necessary to confront the technico-conceptual expansion of the age seems to me sufficient reason enough to face a voyage to a country which instinctively does not attract me (except for the enchanting stretch of ocean that separates it from England). But how many discoveries I have made by getting the better of the pillow and bedside rug that says: 'I like it/I don't like it.'

My only worry is that there will also be a photographer to meet me at Heathrow – but suppose it was he instead who thought I had to meet him? So much so that I said to the huge number of deputy directors and directors of the vice-deputies at the weekly *Epoca*: Send anyone so long as he is talented, if he is talented he will above all be obedient.

Waiting for me at Brussels airport, amid the fumes of smog and the 18,000 employees of the tertiary EC who press forward like locusts the colour of London smoke to fly off towards the week-end on wings that are charged to their respective countries, is floury Signora Oo of the Italian Institute of Socialist Culture: the lady is very agitated, enthusiastic and Craxian to the last. I am put in a luxury hotel surrounded by military personnel (a marriage in some aristocratic Jewish family is being celebrated) and am left there because I am tired and want only to go supperless to bed. An appointment for tomorrow. I have time to get my keys, to take a stroll to the lift, then I hand the keys in again and go over to the reception room (everything long: dresses, vases, faces). I nibble here and there, say good evening here and there and at the first cries of *busii* . . . directed at me take the first umbrella haphazard from a kind of copper flowerpot and go out. After wandering about for two hours I don't know what to say about Brussels apart from the fact that it is there, that there is the king and there is no use asking why. The French language has introduced a completely new verb, *bruxelliser*, which means to rob a city of any identity until it is turned into a scarred urban conglomerate. The walls and the citizens are alike. In a station on the Métro there is a priest playing the organ who as he plays is stamping with all his might to cope with the little rock band in the shop opposite, 'Miss Pakistan', which sells Indian things and new Delhi tapes at full volume. The organist lives like a man possessed in this stretch of the underpass which is full of statues of saints and madonnas, pews, candles and holy posters: a poster on the wall says: 'Think together of your dear departed: collective Mass 190 francs.'

In the morning as I am shaving, still under the influence of the tapestries and candelabras, the carpets and crystal chandeliers in the hotel, I have a desire to see the remaining queens. It must be a sort of little hors d'oeuvre to the brilliant conversations which await me with Oo – from the second floor which is lined with velvet I hear a chatter of little fans: Oo must have arrived at the reception and is asking for me. Indeed she was asking the porter who comes from the Marche if he is going back to vote in Italy. In her battered car we are off to Antwerp, where I have to give 'the lecture' at eleven in the morning. Pouring rain in Belgium. Oo says it is a big boost for her prestige to have persuaded me to accept, admits she has never read anything of mine, but she had gathered from an interview that I am a porcupine and this set her off. She is taking me to Antwerp just as other women at this moment are taking their poodles to the fashionable hairdresser. And she says nothing about the money agreed on – not much, but of it there is extremely little sign. Besides Oo, who is such a chatterbox and so heedless, drives like crazy. Moreover her car has such useless brakes, and tyres that are so smooth, that I don't know whether we shall get onto the subject before we end up in the morgue. One of the two windscreen wipers is broken – hers – and every so often she asks me: 'Can you see anything from your window?' and if I say No she swerves out and overtakes on the right, gets back into lane sounding her horn, and finally risks overtaking properly, that is to say on the left, that is to say blind. Of a car that was a little slow to move over she said with annoyance: 'I bet it's a woman driver.' My safety belts have been gnawed by the teeth of a dog, there's no point in my fastening them. If at least it would stop raining – she says she is a little short-sighted too, but doesn't wear glasses because they make her look ugly. Oo is mad, a schoolgirl, absentminded, and one can't even say she is crafty – and perhaps, in spite of her salary, she too is in the red because she puts all her good intentions into everything. She knows all about the life, rebirth and miracles of Anna De Craxi and the Baudouins. Perhaps her ruin is that she wants to imitate them.

'. . . And Paola de Liège is still cuckolding him?' I ask.

'No – not any more. You know, her age . . . I always see her at my hairdresser's.'

'Is she still very beautiful?'

'Extremely. You know,' and she does something with her hands on her cheeks, pulling at them, 'she has become splendid again.'

'They must have grown-up children.'

'Oh yes, the oldest one is lovely. Just like his father, Alberto.'

'And does he cuckold her?'

'Does he cuckold her? Twice over. He's a rabbit on the loose, that man! He's had all the shop-girls in the Rue Royale one after the other.'

'A real gentleman of the old school.'

'I think so too. Besides, let's be truthful, a husband who doesn't play tricks on you, who doesn't get up your nose, is as deadly as DDT. If your husband doesn't make you angry and you the wife play the woman about the house, however much china *en vieux Sèvres* you are surrounded by, what are you to do all day? That way at least with jealousy everyone is talking about you, they invite you to cocktail parties to talk about you behind your back but near enough to for you to hear, you stay part of the circle, that's it.'

'It's nice to learn such Latin things about the Belgians, I didn't think they were capable of it. The first thing of Baudelaire's I read was *Pauvre Belgique*. But then fortunately a bit of the EEC came here.'

'But Fabiola has tea at half-past four exactly. Every so often she sends for the singers from the Scala when they are on tour. They play all sorts of wrong notes on the cups with their teaspoons! They're very democratic, the Baudouins. But I've never seen Fabiola at my hairdresser's.'

'Maybe she goes to another one.'

'But there isn't another one in the whole of Flanders. She will sweep them all away. Poor thing, she has so few of them.'

Oo manages to become heated even in the fog and damp.

'And what do people say about Queen Juliana and her daughter Beatrice?'

'Oh they are the most loved of all. The Baudouins are loved too but less than them. Have you seen the kind of permanent waves they display? When they take photographs of them they have to sacrifice a bit of chin to get in the whole head – it doesn't matter, the chin is double, naturally. Then Juliana has been close to her people at every moment in her career, wars or no wars, colonies and colitis.'

The queens of the great dykes.

'I'd like to interview them. If I have to interview other people than myself, I may as well begin with the queens. So long as they aren't English.'

'Ah, the English royal house doesn't even know where the British people are. It knows they are out there somewhere, but the farther off the better. If the English weren't so huffy as if they had something nasty under their noses they would have cut each other's throats. They prefer unemployment and slavery, but never to show the world that they are losing their phlegm, which is that of snobs who have been written off.'

'In fact the English royals are not loved, they keep them on to boost the circulation of the gutter press. Everyone despises them, apart from the fucked-up middle class, but their real support they get precisely from the ordinary Labour voters who detest them but don't buy the paper if there isn't a little royal scandal on the front page. A real queen doesn't care whether she's loved or not. Elizabeth is interested in the cash, not in love. Juliana happens to be loved, and perhaps since she is loved it matters to her too.'

'But Juliana is an exception – she is someone who opened up her safe every time it was necessary. In Birmingham it's different – all the English might die but they would manage to rear a fox in a lab just to be able to hunt it immediately afterwards. They have nothing in their heads – apart from the shape of their heads. Fortunately there's this Diana, always hunting down children with AIDS. She takes a great interest in condoms in prison – and in seals too, I believe. But maybe that's someone else.'

'The Swedish royals – Gustav – and the present one, big, fair-haired, who goes to the theatre by tram and without escort – they may be great rascals but they certainly are able to open things up. But what about you and your relationship with the Socialists – not that I want to know your business – '

In fact Oo is not interested in politics but only and exclusively in making propaganda for the Italian Socialists, a very loyal lady absentminded enough to give more consistency to her credo (for which she gets 8 million Italian lire a month) and she talks and talks, and organizes and organizes, and always comes to the same conclusion: with Craxi Italian culture abroad saw its greatest expansion since the Medicis but now with that surgeon Andreotti – he's good too, Andreotti, but would you like to take a bet? Do I know the Roman fixers, the Milanese tribal chiefs, the leftwing Socialists of Pescasseroli? And so on along the motorway to Antwerp through industrial fog and acid rain, Oo, distracted but well informed, drove on talking and thinking of something completely different while I brought up the subject of money – the money agreed for this meeting and which she was supposed to give me on the nail on arrival – and she says, oh, there's a lot of interest in your novels (not one of them has appeared in French), you will see what a lot of people there will be at the bookshop, I'm sorry, but the money hasn't come through yet. (But isn't money, according to Léon Bloy, the blood of the poor? I'm not all that poor.) With such a partner it is a real triumph if anyone manages to work out to the last detail his chances of getting loaded. What the Socialists give you is at most a little flag to fly on a pier, and sometimes they come alongside with an empty hold and sometimes with a full one – and it isn't clear whether you can keep the little flag because it is a present or only because they weren't watching for a moment.

I give this lecture vehemently, shouting to give myself the feeling that the little room is full. My theme is one of the most academic and most taxing: the romanticized literary study of myself as writer and man (?). I think that even I would manage better with some medieval subject: the psychoanalysis of the smile that kills with reference to the reign of Pope Luciani, or something with one of these greenish-Lacanian titles like 'Time and the Temple', that is to say 'Gnostics, agnostics and agnition with reference to the Templars and ravioli.' The public in the room: three daughters of immigrants from Southern Italy and various shopping baskets.

In Brussels the head of the Italian Institute whom, to be brief, I shall call Professor Gardella, on Sunday, under a weak watery sun, very kindly took me to look around two flea-ridden open-air markets. Gardella's hobby is numismatics, and at Christmas time he gives the consuls, the ambassadors, the interpreters (his *friends*) silver tongs for Brussels sprouts or sugar lumps. Since I went to Antwerp in a private capacity I ask him which are the fashionable writers most often to be found in Italian embassies abroad.

'To Athens I invited Montale, Sereni, Berto, but he already had cancer and turned it down, Buzzati and then Domenico Porzio who told me a wonderful story about Montale at the dinner in Stockholm with the Swedish royal family on the occasion of the Nobel Prize award. They were talking about the fauna of poetry, I mean to say, the poetry of fauna, and he said that, being from Liguria, there were a lot of squirrels in the woods. Everyone was listening in ecstasies as he described the life of this little animal when he began to say that they were very good to eat – wonderful meat – although the fur was very hard to pull away from the skin – not like rabbits . . . Such a panic.'

'And did you invite Mastronardi, for example?' I interrupted.

'No – a question of logistics, you see,' which must be a formula for saying: 'You know, only pure establishment figures.' Then he began to run down the Socialists and speak well of the Christian Democrats. So much for the cultural courage Italy shows abroad with its taxpayers' money – mine included – and I, whether Italy wants it or not, against my will or not, am part of the *national* patrimony and am certainly much more special than any politician or stylish writer who is going the rounds now. Does one need a dinner jacket to upset the cultural bureaucrats' plans? I'll have one made. Do you need patent leather shoes to say to a distinguished public of top people: 'Human beings of either sex, you are dead!' I shall buy them. Can one not be marginalized without being integrated? Then I shall give you all a shock.

At the airport in that hateful place London I pick out my photographer a mile off – a big blondish bearded fellow, skinny, with the feigned modesty of someone who does nothing to be likeable and smiles pro forma and, my God, I think, wait and see, he'll be called Baby or Rudy or Chippy, who feels he is someone and takes everything else for granted: one of those types with whom I could go off to one side in the sacristy only if I were a Catholic and, having taken communion, had taken him on as an extra penance. My association is not entirely unfounded: fiddling with his bits of apparatus (pompously exaggerated for the job) and without deigning to see in me – and in none other than me – his employer, he comes out with his having done thirty-three trips in the wake of Pope Woityla, not even as if it were a reference. Having spotted the type I lose no time:

'In practice you have always photographed elephants, *campesinos*, people with snot in their noses, the kiss for the earth, the council chamber, altars in the style of rock concerts,' and I do not conceal an undertone more of irritation than of irony, irony being a sugar-tongs used by those who take bitter coffee, of which I feel he is not worthy. And from this moment there springs a reciprocal distrust which will lend to our spiritual retreat a touch of functional torture. But it is clear that I have to deal with someone convinced of having to feel offended, and he will be too, but I don't know who he is, I don't follow other people's travels so much, but I do know that he will have to go click from time to time, an equerry expert in exoticism to whom I ought – according to the contract – to mediate my other-worldly thoughts on what I see and to whom instead I display my annoyance. Was Callas never engaged in order to submerge her voice in 'the loud clangour of the sonorous trumpets/ of the drums and the barbarous instruments' (Ariosto). I skim the pictures in the weeklies as I do the titles and the articles so as not to read or see anything else and then suddenly it appears that there are photographers to whom they dedicate exhibitions and journalist opinion-makers.

We each travel on a different side of the plane. The only thing that concerns me is the possibility of a dive into the ocean – big and wide below us – and that he might be the usual lucky one who is saved and tells the story of what happened. And thereby – seeing that he is a Roman from Palermo – the conflict not only between north and south but between the cosmic and the prelatal is becoming sharper – the photographer, by dint of taking pictures at religious services, has ended up by going to them and gives off a little odour of incense *Pour Homme*. It is the discovery of a deeper acrimony where apparently there is a merely superficial one that makes bearable – or at least less boring – a trip to Greenland which, not by chance alone it seems, must be identified with the Ultima Thule of the Greek and Latin accounts, that is to say the frontiers of the world. What is bringing me imperceptibly but inexorably to the verge of hysteria is his boring Roman version of a monsignore, his expression of deeply felt participation when he hears a sung Mass in the distance, which he has not understood just as he has not understood what I have said or left unsaid. He finds it more and more difficult to restrain himself, is really communicative when he pretends that he has understood nothing, that he, this impertinent fellow, is just as important as me on this assignment. Prejudices. Refusing to play the game of *Who's Who*, I gradually bring out all my professional diffidence or human failings, such as they are, only in order to involve his fishy person, which he takes to be a personality. He falls into the trap and thinks that my antipathy is *real*. Of course it is, because on one side or the other one has to take things to extremes, but it is also fruitful for our tandem, back to back, for our enforced double act. When we get out of the plane and take a taxi we are both buttoned up like two spies from enemy countries rendered incapable of not playing a double game so as to play one at least.

I ring the Italian consulate: no one. In this case we can say that north and south are unimportant and that they are consubstantially Italian, singly and together, that is to say – absolutely nonexistent.

'But you know it's dificult to take photographs here,' says Candid-Camera of his own accord. 'If you're on the trail of a story, an event, you know what it's like – but here! Like this! There's nothing.'

'They can't always have a Reagan–Gorbachev summit, and in that case I wouldn't have come. They're capable of focusing all the attention to themselves with peace as an excuse. Besides, listen – the only big event in Iceland now is that I am there, that's all. Iceland is a backdrop and as for you who are standing in front of all this – me and Iceland – no one sees you at all. How shall I put it? You don't count – that's it. You count in so far as you stand aside so as not to create distortion in the image you take of me.

It's simple. There is nothing to discover. We are trying to discover a discovery which either I shall make or no one else makes, and you least of all. And it will be a discovery even if there isn't one – the important thing is that it must be me that doesn't make it. That's clear, isn't it?'

Candid-Camera doesn't follow me, he giggles and begins to say his bit:

'But you see in Central America . . . the guerrilla warfare . . . the marches . . . the danger.'

' . . . the dead in the streets, the toucans, the ten-year-old prostitutes . . . the heads displayed by the hair – severed. Danger? All manna.' I am trying to depress him. 'Here with me it's harder. Take the geysers – do you know how many thousands of times they have photographed them? And the volcanic rocks. Here there's one challenge after the other for a photographer . . . a writer can always get by – suppose he writes ten pages on a hold where the fishermen are throwing away the bits when they clean the fish – a hold full of scales, heads, fishbones and bright brown guts, eggs and blood as thick as mucus . . . purple milt, guts purulent with plankton . . . what can you do about it with your official six-colour stuff?' I am lying to console him, spurring him on to a new state of receptivity which had been left on the immaculate robes of His Holiness the Spinning Top and never handed back. And then I think: 'The people on the editorial board put us together on purpose. They want modern reportage under the banner-headline of schizophrenia.'

'But with a story, some event . . . a journalist like you . . .?'

'Listen, let's split up. Let's go on our own to track down the darkness. And, please, I'm not a journalist yet. In more normal times when there was still some respect for teams of two they would have sent me Caravaggio or Parmigianino – not you.'

I have come because what tempted me above all was the surrender of darkness to the prose of my style. To describe darkness in depth, the primeval dark. The darkness which is the coping stone over a social settlement in an impossible land. But at four in the afternoon, while still in flight, the light was vivid and I had been deceived by people who tried to dissuade me from coming here because it is always dark.

Thanks for the advice – I have been in Helsinki for too many days of total light, light that was incapable of setting – and I wanted to plunge into the opposite situation. Because I feel like a mobile monument visiting all the other immobile ones, aiming to stand up the better in my own footsteps. To become a piece of darkness in a dark city excited my lurking imagination. And I didn't even have time to say to him: 'Hold yourself in readiness, for if the lady-president isn't on some whaler I want to interview her. Obviously it is all an excuse for you to take a photo of me with her – she's very keen on it,' before the taxi drives into . . . Reykjavik.

Reykjavik is one of these little (laughing) towns where the moment you have set foot in it you ask yourself: 'What now?' All the great feats having been done here – by the officials of the Danish kings to their allies, to themselves – I have decided to come to Iceland (by dint of justifying myself some good reason will emerge) to carry out the only heroic act possible here, given that from the eleventh century to today one million two hundred and fifty thousand people in all have managed to survive and sometimes to prosper – to give this land that is naked as when its mother bore it a coverlet of words. To do so I shall make use of some scraps of its landscape seen from the window of the plane: not snow, not eternal icefields, not displays of the aurora borealis (it's not the season) but an endless cradle of tufa streaked with a hard green moss, a green of vegetation that has managed to pierce the lava and naughtily displays the colour it has succeeded in snatching from the congenital extinction which did not want to see it on the face of the land. But I shall also put some quilting on the roofs of the little houses with their whorish reds, their coquettish greens and screaming purples like lips thrust out at the tourists and businessmen at carnival time – and here, the chosen city for congresses, there are more businessmen than ordinary men.

In the hotel a gentleman of about fifty with a velveted stomach and the chain of a watch coming out of his pocket, patent leather shoes, a well-tended bald patch, a square face and uneasy eyes, is going up and down in the deserted hall, twisting a jewelled ring on his little finger.

'Portuguese?' he says, smiling at me with great amiability, slipping into the lift along with me.

'No, Italian.'

'Ah, Italian, Natta, Berlinguer, Occhetto. Here on business?'

'No, I'm not. What does Natta mean?' But we have arrived already.

'I am the only Icelandic Communist you see, I live up in the north in a castle,' he says, following me down the corridor. Not that I don't like him, on the contrary, but all this unasked-for information alarms me. Wouldn't it be simpler . . .

'And you are here on business?' I ask out of pure courtesy, having reached my door, half resigned, half thinking of public morality,

'No, oh no,' he exclaims gaily, doing a kind of hop, 'I am expecting a lady! My wife! I am marrying her!'

And I – just so as not to give the impression that I was expecting something very different – say:

'And you can't contain yourself, is that it? My compliments and best wishes.'

'Thank you, thank you,' he says grasping my hand, sketching a little bow and turning down the corridor opposite.

'She's Brazilian, ah!'

I put down my baggage, look through the curtains on to a white building wall, transparent glass, and go down. I get into a taxi which hasn't time to take a run-up when it has already arrived in the centre of town, after passing the famous little house of the summit all lit up in the evening. So there is night and day here too as in most places and the darkness is as fleeting as everywhere else. The centre is contained in a handkerchief with trimmings of modernity in glass and cement and a few expensive neoclassical initials at the corners. The signboard of the daily national paper *Morgnungblad* is lit up on a little square smelling of fried fish, the main street not more than three hundred metres long, with the chemist's, the post office, the record shop, the most famous bar and two dives. End of the walk. I go into the most famous bar with a couple of customers eating pizza with cream. I had imagined I would find an atmosphere thick with sailors. Silence apart from the din of a little jazz on a guitar and a trumpet from the next-door room. They are playing this evening, a little local concert. No one looks at me, no one looks at anyone. I always knew what I would find here – exactly this.

'You are Italian,' says a young man in Italian.

'Ciao, yes, of course. Sit down. But I heard you talking their language – do you live here?' And I give a sigh of relief, at least I can chat with someone.

'Yes.' He takes a chair. 'Oh, there are a few of us here with pizzerias and restaurants – at least twenty. I'm from Genoa.'

'Did you come all this way to get work?' I say, pressing him further.

'No, no. Women,' and he shakes his head in resignation. 'All the ones I know came here for the women.'

'Ah. Do you know if Vigdis Finnbogadóttir is here or away?'

'Well, her car was there this morning.'

'What do you mean her car was there?' I say. 'I'm talking about the president.'

'Yes, her car was parked outside as usual.'

'Outside?'

'Yes, of course. In front of the parliament. A dark black Mercedes. Outside on the left.'

'Dark?'

'Yes, neither white nor green. A kind of stippled grey. Myself I think it's because it is secondhand and they didn't spray it well.'

'Nice to meet you, Bruno.'

The parliament house is in fact a cottage like so many others round about, and there will be parking space in front of it for a Mercedes, a little Fiat and a jalopy belonging to a vendor of roast chestnuts and that's all. Bruno – not much more than twenty-three, unassuming, with the lively but not brash look of a good lad – a bit of a cowboy where passion is concerned since he does not seem to like any topic that does not deal with women or horses, although he talks about the horses with passion and of women with great patience considering the mad things they make naïve and sentimental boys like him do. He explains to me that it is in this bar that it is chic to start up prodigious weekend booze-ups when young and old from the outlying districts and from the little towns round about descend on the capital (the centre) in order to blur in vodka the fatigue of every Icelander's average working day – thirteen hours, and the old-fashioned kind. It is obvious that having to overcome such daily toil over centuries of frost and lava leads to nationalistic feeling and various kinds of cultural protectionism and that the national language is a real government cult. Cult of the written language, I mean, not only the spoken version, not a televised one: the two television channels do not carry more than three hours' transmissions a day, made up largely of American films which combine spectacular qualities with modernity in their subject matter (I will see two on cases of hysteria in the army and the madness of war and a piece on Justice as a civic trap for the good but incautious) and which are an aid to learning the English language, the only xenophilic concession – one due to political and technological necessity. The cold outside is dry, healthy; I say goodbye to Bruno, we promise to meet again and I have before me a long blue phosphorescent street, deserted, without traffic: and now? Who knows whether I shall manage to put an arm round a puffin, the penguin-like bird which nests on an island south of the capital, or if I shall experience the polar intoxication of an islander in bed (out of doors is unthinkable) or if I shall at least succeed in meeting the lady-president.

The country gentleman who is expecting his Brazilian bride tomorrow is for the moment in the drawing-room of the hotel ready to waylay me. I think that before I arrived he had already worn out the receptionist, the porter and the night-porter. He has a lively look as he comes towards me, worried, like someone who has a great need for some well-meaning ploy of his to be revealed.

'Yes, she is arriving tomorrow from Rio de Janeiro,' he says, taking me by the arm, 'She is very beautiful, is just forty and has two daughters – '

'And all three are arriving?' I ask amazed – this is the country for women and you mean to say he is importing them from abroad?

'Yes, all three – can you imagine? One more beautiful than the next – the little ones, one is about fifteen and the other twenty. But I have to confess something to you – the black Mercedes out there, I have hired it and she doesn't know. It's the same one as I turned up in two months ago when she came to have a look at things and get matters settled. And something else she doesn't know is that the castle and all the furniture is in pawn. I didn't have the courage not to lie to her, that is to say, I lied outright – '

'My God, if I were you, if that was what she assumed and it comes out that – '

'But you should see how beautiful she is. She is a woman of great class, very educated . . . The first thing she wanted to see was the heating system and she was so upset that it only half worked. You see I can't possibly heat the whole house – only one wing. What do you say – will she forgive me? Will she marry me? Because she has made marriage a preliminary condition you see – I'm going to be a flop again – '

'But listen, if she loves you – '

'As far as that goes all three love me – in fact the little girls – ' he twists a handkerchief round his fingers nervously. 'The trip is all at my expense.'

'Well, I should hope so. It's going to be quite a problem. But aren't you going to bed? Good-night and good luck.'

'How am I supposed to sleep in this state? Don't you see I'm counting the minutes? You should see her bearing – such a temperament! I trade in timber with Germany – and you?'

'I don't. Good-night.'

'Are you married?' he says invincibly while I am waiting for the lift.

'I'm not.'

'Oh, married bliss! You're missing out on a lot. This is my fourth. And then I have two grown-up daughters,' and he winks at me.

Next day I begin to ring the Italian consulate – no one ever there. They're all the same. There's never anyone there not even if you go there yourself. Who knows who picks them – and in Brussels the ambassador is Saragat's son, in London he's Bottai's son. And what does a person do who is not *son of* . . .? If he's a cousin he has to provide the milk, if he is a brother-in-law, the cereals, if he is a nephew he sees to mild sentences for Italian crooks and if she is an aunt she is the guardian of Bacchelli's memory – the only one who does not aspire to a refund from the State for the so-called entertainment expenses. Oh the number of cocktails on their feet, sitting, leaning, that every nation has to provide for its representatives who do its entertainment and have as their cultural points of reference Eco, Pavarotti, Zeffirelli and Strehler!

But let's come back to ourselves – ourselves and Iceland, this country I am inventing. I leave my room late in the morning and hear a tornado of female voices cursing in the corridor. They come closer, a door is banged over and over again, someone imploring in English, curses in Portuguese: it is the lady with her two daughters. The three of them in front as if they had already repacked their suitcases or had not even opened them, and him behind, the fifty-year-old Icelander, massive and sweating, half suited, half pyjamaed, and in slippers. The fiancée tall and skinny, the fifteen-year-old (who must be twenty-five) squat and broad, the twenty-year-old (maybe thirty) hardly any taller, all three plain-looking half-castes, dressed with cleavages and fringes fit to make one giddy or cause an arctic shiver, and him taking them by the arm, holding them back, begging them to at least give him something back, but what I don't know. 'Oh, darling, these are for the inconvenience,' says the oldest of them, waving in the air with one hand the watch and the diamond ring which is already on her finger.

'I need the two thousand dollars to pay for the timber, please, please,' the man whimpers and seeing me sighs. 'Juanita, Juanita, Juanita!'

'We're not staying here a minute longer even if we have to camp at the airport. Liar! Swine! Crook!' I translate as best I can.

The three half-naked oldish ladies disappear, the scuffling noise of the man's slippers begins again wearily. I slip back into my room, there is no need for me to contribute as well to this his final humiliation and realization of the true nature of the three aspirants. But he, I was expecting this, knocks at my door. I open, he pokes in his big head, which is incredibly scented, and says:

'Did you see what smashing women! Now I am really broke – you couldn't – '

'I have paid in advance – I'm sorry. I'm sure you'll manage to deal with things – the truth that comes to the surface is the spice of life.'

'And now what will I do?' he says, looking out at the sports hall, which is beginning to be busy.

'It's not up to me to tell you – but begin from the beginning again. In any case there's no use arguing with fate. If you like tall, beautiful, educated women, with kids in tow and South American into the bargain, that's the price you have to pay. Alone. Or at most with those directly involved.'

'But I didn't even get anything. You understand? Nothing! And I paid in advance for the wedding dinner! Nothing! Nothing!' And with his hand he points to his little finger and his waistcoat pocket. 'At least give me a hundred dollars.'

'Let's make it fifty,' and I take out my pocketbook and give him the notes just to get him out of my sight.

He slips them into the pocket of his dark green jacket trimmed with gilt braid.

'Of course, that ring – '

'Oh that's the least of it. I keep the real one in the safe. Poor Juanitas, imagine how upset they will be.'

Because when he was shouting 'Juanita! Juanita! Juanita!' he was calling them one by one – you understand? He certainly wasn't the kind of man who lumps people together.

I break into the inactivity of the day which is spent in walking about alone and listening to vain ringing sounds on the phone. Everything, but everything, must happen here indoors: no bushes, trees catalogued as property of the nation so scarce are they. I have already seen everything at least four times and never once the inside of a house. Except for a request for eye-drops at an old chemist's I have not exchanged a word with anyone. I went to the restaurant where Bruno works but he is off-duty. I went round all the bookshops, the gardens, the woolshops, all the bars – all deserted – and there was nothing parked outside the parliament apart from the flagstaff from which the flag had been taken down. I experienced twenty different winds and that was enough.

In the late afternoon in the hall of the Holiday Inn the girls at the reception do not shake their hair, which is of every shade of blonde, because they wear it short, and carefully unevenly cut, razor-layered, but they open wide their eyes, which are not blue at all but dark brown, when I ask point-blank:

'Excuse me, but where do people make love here? I mean the ones who aren't married?'

The young woman says nothing and asks her neighbour for help; her only reply is to take up a pen and ask:

'Do you want to be called, sir?'

'You see – there isn't even a clump of trees, a few bushes, it's hellish cold.'

'Breakfast is from half-past seven to nine, sir.'

In comes Candid-Camera looking down at the mouth.

'Not found anything interesting?' I ask him by way of saying good-night or goodbye.

'If only there were some trail to follow, a story, an event – '

'If you like I'll give you a geopolitical rundown on Iceland: eighty per cent of the economy is based on fishing and the fish-curing industry that goes with it and the rest on the export of electrical energy and agricultural products. The inhabitants have gone to bye-byes by now – two hundred and forty thousand (not more than eight of them out and about) of whom ninety-one thousand are in Reykjavik, fifty thousand round about and the rest here and there – a lot of them there – where I'm not going to go. Second city – up there in the north – Akureyri, fourteen thousand inhabitants. Religion – Protestant. Some say it was a meteorite, others that it was an outburst of anger by a volcano – the island, I mean. Not one tree with a big trunk – only a few skinny pines or firs. Fields – out of the question. Ancient monuments – none. Archaeology – unthinkable, everything is rebuilt from generation to generation and only since wood (this too imported) has been prohibited by the national building commission as the basis for building – that is to say fifty years ago – have there been *solid* buildings. Before that – tufa which crumbles away every two or three generations. Of the twenty per cent of the economy that is not taken up by fishing there is seven per cent sheep-farming, mink-farming (exported already boned), a few hens and several thousand dwarf horses used for riding and for the table. Parties: three which I can't tell you anything about because they are as alike as peas. There is no right-wing party, because here you have either made it or you haven't – in any case you can't do a big act in a double-breasted pin-stripe suit at thirty degrees below. A NATO base which everyone looks askance at and which everyone bows down before because the USA is the chief commercial partner. Eight hundred and forty salmon caught in Reykjavik alone in 1987. Prison population: a hundred or so, the usual good lads inside for smuggling beer, alcohol or tobacco. Violent deaths including road accidents: an average of three or four per year. No case of rape, no pornography. And here,' at this point I look him straight in the eye, 'people – from the fishermen to the women who clean the herring – do something that some people will find extraordinary: they read. They read and buy an average of two, I mean two, books per month per head. Which comes to a global publishing output of six million volumes a year. Education: fifty-four per cent of the men and fifty-two per cent of the women go to school up to twenty and half of them up to twenty-eight. Students abroad: this year two thousand eight hundred. Africans here – fifty-two. I know – you can be sure I'd find out right away about the Africans. I just have to take a look around to see whom I can rely on.'

I explain to him.

Yesterday when we arrived by taxi (3,350 kroner for fifty kilometres or so – that is about 100,000 lire: single room – 38,900 kroner, but in the morning along with the coffee you can have a brioche with reindeer meat balls – the well-marinated kind) I had the presence of mind, given the little difference between single and double, to propose sharing a room with separate beds. All his prejudices rushed to his head and he almost feels ill: 'But you know I need to be able to think etc,' whereas I don't and, since I don't think, would have nothing else in my head than to jump on him; and what for me would be an act of charity for him becomes a mortal threat.

Seeing that he is thoughtful, perhaps absentminded or perhaps searching for some argument, a credential which might strike me (apart from a punch on the nose), I say to him point-blank, simply to raise the temperature:

'Excuse me but do you suffer from phimosis?'

'No. Why?'

'You look to me the type to have phimosis. But it's really not important. Good-night.'

'Perhaps it's best.'

'Tomorrow morning – everyone does his own thing, please.'

'And no one,' as if coming back to his obsessive thought, 'no one has ever taken the liberty of saying that I have to be more receptive.'

'For your own good, my dear, for your own good. The people on the weekly perhaps don't know it but I have inserted photography in my prose.'

'Ah, if I'd known I wouldn't have come,' he says, getting up with a disconsolately offended air.

'Be a good fellow – I could maybe say this to you – not you to me – and I would have come anyway because you or someone else is all the same to me. The same but not equal.'

'You – a journalist – to a photographer! You don't grasp the importance of the image!' he blurts resentfully: it is a whole philosophical category that he feels is threatened.

'Go on – it's better that way. We're not forced to like each other. Tell the truth – I bet you did an album of photographs of the Pope.'

'Certainly – ten thousand copies sold.'

'I could have sworn it. For some Pious edition. Ah! I bet! And can I ask you something?'

'Of course,' he says, perhaps thinking that now I shall readjust my skilful scorn for him and his category of polluters of the light.

'I have to ask you, otherwise it's like having a fish-bone in one's throat – what about your wife – why did you get married?'

'You really can't find any good in me!'

'It's just that – always on the move, never at home, the distance, the temptations,' I flatter him, but I know that types like this are too slow-witted to notice that they have been tempted and obviously believe only in 'a full relationship' with tenderness, getting to know each other, personal hygiene.

'Look, it was me who took that picture of Aldo Moro in the boot of the Renault,' is his only reply, like the dowry a woman without means brings in marriage.

'A whisper from the Red Brigades?'

'No – I was passing, I saw a lot of people, I had my camera with me. A photo that went round the world.'

'Well, that was lucky. I mean to say. It was a great photo. With him so withdrawn. So photogenically thin, his drawn face, bloodless. And then I bet you think black and white is much better? Certainly to have to listen to him for forty days – a character like that – do you remember the singsong he had in his voice, it must have been an unrepeatable experience for his captors. My God, what can three days with De Mita or Piccoli be like? I'd shoot myself first.'

From my room – a two-storey gym with a plume of steam – girls with highly coloured body stockings bend and twirl, sometimes I see nothing but legs, at other times only the bust up to the neck, because on the big windows there are sun-blinds drawn down haphazard on both floors. With their whole body I can see only the two teachers of gymnastics or gymnastic ballet, and the one on the first floor is platinum blonde, completely metallic because of the blinding light. She unscrews herself from her body while she twirls round three times, a red and black top, her hair held in place by an elastic band (distance – a hundred metres, but everything that is coordinated movement moves my heart to a closeness which is that of the skin); the one on the second floor has bright chestnut hair, a strip of blue sponge on her forehead, a black body stocking, an authoritative way with her arms, which at times are thrust out like swords and then allowed to fall down in a gesture of didactic exasperation. Both are beautiful, and I stay and watch them till the lights go out one by one, and then I see all the ballerinas full-length as they go down the corridor to the ground floor: little girls of thirteen or so, fifteen at the most, a wavelike motion of ponytails which electrify the semi-darkness and then they go out on to the street and begin to walk away calmly and disperse. Not a single parent at the door. Try to do the same in Italy at ten at night and then see how many girls are left at a quarter past ten. Or if you are a normally pleasant-looking woman who isn't sedentary try, like a friend of mine, to cycle from Mantua to Verona to see what has really changed in man–

woman relationships in the last two thousand years. I pull the curtains.

I forgot to tell Candid-Camera that Vigdis Finnbogadóttir is the first woman in the world to be elected president of the republic, that she naturally comes from the theatre, that she has translated Genet's *The Maids* and other plays, that she was elected in 1980, beating by a hair's-breadth the last of three male candidates, that she has a daughter, now fifteen, adopted when she was divorced in defiance of everything and everybody, that she studied at the Sorbonne, and that in the photographs as a young woman she is breathtakingly beautiful. I say this because I saw her in a recent photograph with the Spanish royal family – in the Icelandair house magazine – and she seemed to me to have got a bit plump. It may have been the windblown dress, obviously silk, obviously old Vienna, or else it was the fault of the photographer . . . Then I take the phone and say so to him, hoping that in the meantime he has just fallen asleep.

'But I couldn't care less about photographing the lady president even if she were dancing naked in the street!'

'Well, yes – naked in the street – think of the headlines. And let me tell you again, you don't have to photograph her, but her with me. Neither of us naked for the moment.'

If he manages to get to sleep it is just because that is his nature. I have done him the favour of letting him have all the other essentials drawn from the various sources in my possession. That Finnbogadóttir wouldn't be be much in favour of the sentimentality typical of women without a portfolio – and it is for this reason that ever since secondary school she was the most courted of all, because she was very witty in matters of love and quick and daring in her replies. And that the sources repeatedly report on her correctness of language, her knowledge of and punctilious defence of Icelandic, and how much this question of the mother tongue was perhaps what clinched her electoral victory over candidates too much in favour of communicating in English or Danish to outstrip her. The language spoken by the Lady is said to be appropriate and clear, an elegant and empirical setting forth of concepts and problems, and cultural loyalty synchronous with the roots of her nation and her active life, without hyperboles or political obscurantisms, without too much rhetoric, in short the supreme mastery of true orators. But what is certain is that they can't have much to hide. And that she proclaimed the need to maintain the national language as a measure of unity between people and respect for their country. And that she is a specialist on the *Edda*, a national literary monument – like the *Divina Commedia* in Italy – set down in a labyrinth of versions and variants and that she knows everything about scaldic poetry – whereas with our prime ministers it's a big deal if they venture as far as collecting relics of Garibaldi.

Nationalism understood as a cult of difference, as the right to continue to be what one is so as to be able to understand what others are like and so to cooperate in combating any form of imperialism which would reduce everything to a hegemonic mush which has no taste except a poisonous one. The only nationalism that isn't harmful either abroad or at home cannot be based on the moment-to-moment calculations of ideological particularism – only the far-sighted neutrality of a real language can be the glue that creates a *nation*. At least to begin with. And I am here with an Italian who instead of saying 'biglietti' says 'bijetti' and perhaps thinks that it's me that can't talk properly at a booking office. Why do I feel myself more of a foreigner at Avellino than in Copenhagen and why is someone from Lecce more subject to racism in Como than in Belgrade? The alienation that impelled me to come to Iceland as a whim cannot have its real origin in the fact, which I do not ever wish to take into consideration, that a few hundred kilometres from home in *my* home I no longer know where I am. *I* become an insecure and ill-received identity which must continually look over its shoulder because of a social code (I might almost say a liturgical one) which it does not know, which it will never manage to know in time and become one with – an identity which will have to content itself with moralistic folklore, the demagogy of Southern Italians, with television populism made up of gags and television news in dialect? A code which above all is a threat to life itself and does not confine itself to good or bad manners in a book of etiquette about how to walk properly . . .

These questions, at two in the morning, exhaust me but not

enough to soothe my state of glandular excitement. I amuse myself for a while with things in my head, I recreate bodies – images like those of adolescence – I think that tomorrow morning the most sensational news in the *Morgnungbladid* (which I shall not be able to decipher) will inform the population that in the night Miss Hilda Ithrottaleikvangurdottir of the Society for the Protection of Animals tried to steal the puppies belonging to the Minister for Fisheries and, caught with her hands in the tin, was sentenced to bait his hooks for the whole weekend.

A sensation of a sensation from the past – of rain that has already fallen borne up to an immeasurable height and made to fall again, and I noticed that the rain here is different, oily, it has difficulty in running down properly from one's clothes, that they will remain stained for ever. Water that stops flowing under bridges, that does not want to go in any direction, that has difficulty in running, like a spread-eagled corpse bumping against watery corpses in front of it strengthened by surges of water with arms and legs of foam. The surges are greasy and turn like spits that have been over-oiled, foaming on their surface against a grey and purplish sky. The noise of the rain is unchanged – in my half-waking state you believe you are thinking, whereas when you detach an element of thought to look at it against the light, it is as if of its own accord it frays between your temples and you see that the whole thought was a kind of dream, that it cannot be traced back to an otherwise rational expression. Mosses like green emery paper, drains all round the crumbling house on which I am climbing in precarious equilibrium, losing my hold, feeling that my strength is exhausted. There is a deep channel between the houses, which are apparently of cork, blackish and afloat; the channel divides the two houses into which I continue to move, without domestic gear fortunately, and there's also an unresolved legal problem because of a bit of land which others are claiming – other people whom I have never seen. I feel that I have a right to my house – that goes without saying – plus a room which, in fact, is part of their house and which they don't want to let me have. Without that room – which they deprive me of every day and keep moving about – I am lost because I don't know what to do with my house. By itself without that external room it has no sense. I grope and go out and in until I find myself in that same room which is not entirely mine and once there my real house, thanks to the continually changing perspective of the room that moves about in the house that isn't mine, begins to be desirable. When I reach it and from inside can no longer see it from outside it loses all its attraction and I start again on the route that brings me back to that room – where will it have run off to now? – from which I see and hear my own house.

I am still dripping with rain, I have slipped into an attic when there was no need to, I have made my way through a brightly lit labyrinth of obligatory passageways, and must immediately confront another attic further up still. I begin to climb up, grasping at protruding and slippery bricks, and hope that it will be the last attic. I catch hold of the window-frames too, which give way under the weight of my body, often my hands are full of rotten wood and I am always on the point of falling into the void. The channel below is calm, it allows rubbish to run away at a constant pace into a brook; it is raining non-stop. The tiles are black, broken, they conceal an immensely long blind rat, I can see its tail of pink hairless flesh, its head is always turned in another direction. In the cracks in the walls a bright green herb grows. I remember that the peasant women used it to wash out the bottles before pouring in the new wine, that glass-green herb along with sand from the ditch removed any incrustation. I am tired, I should like to find shelter as soon as possible and dry myself and draw breath, but the moment I sigh and try to sit down there is a new attic to be reached and the mysterious necessity which orders me to clamber over it is mad and inexorable – I still have not arrived at anything except my nature – that of a haphazard climber.

For months I have been having this dream, and the only thing worth noting in my view is that, except for myself, whom I do not see but of whom I am aware, and the flayed tail of the blind rat, there is no real being to serve as a yardstick of what is happening in this scene. And the neighbours, whether defendants or prosecutors: I hear protesting and voices and annoyed voices but no one has ever materialized each time I cross into their room which I have found once more. And that I shall never have peace; each time I am in one place I want to enjoy the view of that place as if I were opposite, looking at myself. But dreams have everything to lose by being interpreted, they end up relinquishing their secret substance and becoming the interpretation one gives of them.

And at last it is time to wake up, to sell off one's nervous system to some political system or other. The important thing about putting up with the days is that the nights are made up for a hundred times over. That is why I do not give tuppence for daydreams because I manage to throw out of the window as they are born all my projections of reality as what it is not, because I think there is nothing less imaginative than our daydreams; I dream only in the old-fashioned way with my eyes shut and if possible at night and whenever I can allow myself to do so. You may say that I never sleep when I am sleeping, or that I sleep because it is indispensable for dreaming. I would not exchange my untransmittable nightmares, which often leave no trace in the memory, for all the communicable and satisfied pleasures of this world. The night of my brain which is in jeopardy shut up in itself, in which *I* consider myself to be the equivalent of a seismograph registering the cracks in the void of existence, is my only guiding beacon. I feel a great love and tenderness for my sleeping body, passion and compassion, and for this reason when I have made love to someone I have remained for hours watching him sleep without ever disturbing him, without ever inserting myself. A dreaming body is already perfect in itself, unless it is he who seeks you, groping in his dark for obscure happy memories of the previous day. I do not believe it has ever happened to me either in one sense or the other. But I have shamelessly enjoyed watching someone sleep, especially if there was a fly hovering over the tip of his nose and perhaps penetrating into the sleeper's dream with the hum of a propeller come to tickle him under the hangar of an armpit. Then I waited for that same fly to come and hover over me.

I must admit that this trip has gone to my head a bit, for the moment I am awake I have royal thoughts – the legacy of an oneiric distillation in which Vigdis the Beautiful brandished a swordfish in one hand and a parchment in the other and shouted, transformed into a ship's figurehead: Of the Nibelungs I am the muse, while Eleanora was only the Duse.

'Hello?' I say to the porter's desk. 'How can I find the telephone number of the president's office?'

'Wait and I shall look.' It is a male voice: the men here speak an English so dense and guttural that it puts all my vertebrae into tension and sends waves of heat through me. 'Look – here meantime is the number of Vigdis' secretary.'

'You mean Lady Vigdis, the president, I imagine.'

'Is that not what you wanted?'

'Yes but I thought – Excuse me, but why do you call her Vigdis?' I mean how dare he? The same repugnance as the crowd gave me by shouting 'Sandro, Sandro' to the President of the Italian Republic – exactly the same crowd as then in the football stadiums threw fireworks, shoved and stabbed, and the moment it was outside in terrifying throngs, ganged up and overturned cars and beat up passers-by. And this whole herd of animals on the loose, taken one by one, were all good, decent, honest fathers of families who – this is the point – call the President of the Republic 'Sandro' and not, as would be fitting, either 'Your Excellency' or not call him anything at all. For this reason I felt piqued by the familiarity this boy had assumed.

'But everyone calls her that – Vigdis. She's *our* Vigdis, isn't she?'

'Of course, I'm sorry – I misunderstood, I'm sorry, I didn't understand.' Because he said it with such spontaneity that he disarmed me. And he gives me two numbers – one for Vigdis Bernadóttir, the president's secretary, and the other for the real Vigdis – but there is no point in ringing the official residence because it is shut for repairs.

'Nyow – nyow,' says a child's voice on the telephone.

'Hello? is that the president's secretary?'

'Nyow – nyow – nyow.'

'Is your mummy there?' I try.

'Nyow – Nyow,' and then. 'Mummy!'

'Hello. Yes, I am the president's secretary. What can I do for you?'

In short: an appointment the day after tomorrow at midday.

She cannot promise because on Thursday there is a meeting of parliament but in principle it should be possible to get half-an-hour out of the president. I thank her. Since we are speaking English she doesn't use some polite formula as in Italian but leaves me speechless with a humble thank you.

As is usual when one talks to various ministries and institutions at home: calm, quiet, polite, and above all grateful to the citizen who has allowed the civil servant to make himself useful.

Because the countries you go through help to understand the country you stay in. And what point would there be in coming to Iceland only to see Iceland? And as has been said: the true journey is the homeward one.

On the list in the guide to the city, the list of events, the month of November stands out. In November nothing happens, which together with the hoped-for darkness was the panacea for an absolute contemplation of nothing, a sure antidote to any temptation to travel-literature exoticism. There are swimming-pools in November but only because they can't be closed: the hot water is free and now I see that the whole countryside is lined with medium-gauge pipes which come and go, crisscross, interspersed every so often with a low building for separating the water from the steam. The water with its slightly sulphurous tang is very good, I would even say interesting. I have a taxi take me to the cemetery. Candid-Camera is with me. Once in the cemetery I burst out laughing: since there are no admirals here (the only existing army is the Salvation one) all the stones are low, small and made of tufa, a few of marble (imported), and naturally there are no trees but bushes which skeleton-like grope their way down the gentle slope. The photographer stands next to me. Every so often he decides on a different path from me. I count the flowers in the five or so acres: three red carnations, four yellow chrysanthemums, two white carnations.

I go to cemeteries to understand from the monumental masonry the nature of the chimeras of the city of the living who remain behind. This one here pleases me – it is all in proportion to Homo sapiens: a flat 2 m × 0.70, the essential. Candid-Camera photographs little or nothing, nothing goes click in him. Naturally it is not the nothing that I understand. For him *nothing* is really nothing. Certainly with a chorus of serfs with abnormal chests and little thin legs everything would be much easier, snub noses, dwarf sisters – Andeans.

'Are there seals here?' he asks me.

'Yes, nun-seals. Up north. All at prayer.'

He goes off once and for all and I go back alone on foot. I see him in the distance taking photographs in the direction of the storage tanks for collecting the hot water from the natural springs by which the municipal heating is fed. I like more and more the volcanic valley bottom of my indifference to 'nature', I like the thought of walking on splinters of the tertiary age, I like the phantasmal origin of everything once you apply 'science' to it. I was afraid I would come across birches – they distress me beyond words, ever since once upon a time I was obsessed for kilometre after kilometre by the same birch-tree which pursued my train from Helsinki to Leningrad. My curious feeling about the 'green' of that period has never been resolved. So I walk on and on with rare passers-by who never for a moment commit the error or gaffe of abandoning themselves to the immodesty of giving you a glance. I reach the harbour, the unexpected blue. I might say: 'At the very moment when the fishing boat *Raufarhöfn* was unloading its catch and all the men of the crew, their solid thighs covered with yellow plastic leggings . . .' The fishing boats are there but they are not unloading anything. And moreover in the night I shall not even see the light of an offshore fishing boat. I go back to my hotel because I have a nostalgic feeling for my little girls on two floors.

My favourite gym teacher – the one on the first floor, the canary blonde – this evening is wearing a white T-shirt on top of green pants with white dots. She seems in a bit of a hurry, poor thing, she must have a life to live too; and what if one day she decided to satisfy the whim of getting fat, how can she with this kind of work? Her pupils twirl and twirl again and stop for a moment as if they were holding their breath; there must be a mirror on the wall. They look at themselves from head to foot and then fly away. But it is not an evening for innocent looking: I go out again, here I am again at the centre again, now I know it by heart. At the Laekjarbrekka restaurant the tables are occupied by two girls, a woman and two girls, two girls and a man, a girl by herself. I eat two first courses, I'd like to have a chat with someone. Nothing doing. A bottle of white wine: the equivalent of 34,000 lire. This is what a de luxe life must be like: having a great time round the void to pass the time because the little thing you would really like – a chat with the delicate lonely redhead who is desired by a grilled sole – is not on the menu or is unpriced, does not let herself be dazzled by the luxury of a propitiatory dance in order to find her wishes for some secret desserts granted. And once again I turn the pages of the *Icelandair Review*: cod fillets fastened together at the tail to dry, instruments for deep-sea fishing, the completed construction of the airport at Keflavik; a lumpy girl with a little pointed hat and curls as hard as iron exhibits a salted cod with pride and seems to invite one to 'Buy salted cod – very good.' And then ships, cargoes, some ancient bowls, the old open-air parliament – the Althing – to which the inhabitants repaired up to two centuries ago to make known the new legislative arrangements and to make marriage contracts, and it seems that from the review a fishnet is thrown at the reader to make him recognize an enchantment, the enchantment which I do not feel and for which I feel no need.

It is not always necessary to love a country, it is enough to respect it. Besides that is why I came here – to discover its existence. In itself. And all the faces are beautiful, in the street and on the page, they inspire energy, confidence (in themselves), detachment, an indecipherable sensuality not easily interpreted by the foreigner. The total absence of any gesture or attitude that speaks of prostitution. The young people beautiful and useless as always, as everywhere, as they ought to be, concentrated on themselves: males with powerful jaws (chewing on smoked herring down the centuries). The women (who here keep their own names even when married) all very beautiful when young, tall, with an air of a vestal manquée, an actress manquée, a Miss World manquée. In a pastry-shop I am served – but no, it is a mini-self-service – by a waitress with features of snow that no sun would manage to melt, a real Brunhilde, a wise woman from a saga who does not wish to be watched and has learned to distance any indiscreet glance like mine. Simply disappearing into the little room at the back from which every so often a lock of her mass of hair appears, which is cut across, sculptured down towards the middle of her back, of a blonde that is a little oily – but, what shall I say, proud because it is the oil from work.

Back in my room – the young woman at reception says to me: 'If you want to find out about love all you have to do is go to any discothèque, sir. On a Saturday.' 'Do you pick them up there?' 'Pick them up, sir? We go there to dance – there's no picking up or setting down. Although now that I think of it . . .' 'Think of it – do think of it. Good-night.' 'Do you want to be called?' 'I could undertake to wake all the clients every quarter of an hour, I sleep so little.' 'Why?' and she looked at me out of the corner of her eye, pretending to shake her short hair – a constant noise like reconnaissance planes or heavy traffic at a subdued level. I look out on to the balcony, buffeted by an icy wind, four layers of cloud each of which follows its own celestial course: nothing. Neither in the heavens nor on earth. A drunk man elegantly dressed and without an overcoat reels up the hill. And it is only Tuesday evening, it must be an apéritif to Saturday's witches' sabbath. There is a process at work – shamefast and perennial, a pulling at the frozen and unending rope by proud people, gathered round their family nucleus, behind these windows, a way of keeping themselves to themselves so as not to squander precious energies which tomorrow will serve for another excavation, another digging operation, a raising or lowering. In the stern, amid the frenetic activity of all enforced repose, the wait to pull on the kilometre-long nets, even if by motor, adds to the accumulation of waiting across the centuries with arms ready to spring into action and the curtains to contract in chorus. And the calms, the storms, the tempests, the breakers came to tear away, to smash, to confuse their minds which were homeward-bound and their bodies drawn down into the waves. Death before its eyes, the shark hurled itself at the boat and seemed to laugh each time it escaped capture – and seemed to laugh even more once it had been ripped open because it showed all the eggs it had in store, waiting to kill or be killed with the choleric indifference of wild animals. And in the bar in the centre – a cup of horrible coffee priced at one thousand six hundred lire – a Scots fisherman was talking to himself, brutalized by loneliness and melancholy, which isn't the way things used to be – the harbour districts have become sad since AIDS, the time waiting for embarkation isn't fun any more. Breaks in the voyage have become another reason for anger.

More advertisements in another magazine: 'Fresh fish from the uncontaminated arctic waters of Iceland'. They must make them come here specially and if they are not already distilled at the frontiers with the international waters they will separate them out – straight ahead or over there into quarantine – nasty stuff!

I wake up with a start: Beowulf, Breca, Egglasefa! I had been dreaming up a whole army bent on becoming a saga, all lined up one behind the other with their chain-mail (sheeps'-wool mixture) coming down to their knees so that . . . Voice Off Screen on the fringes of the dream: 'Do you Scald them first?' I say: 'No, I serve them as they are, Fred.' Fred? And in the morning the bus I have booked arrives for me and the photographer and from one chill blast to another here we are on our way to the geysers. If you are among geysers you are bound to find hot water. I shall not linger on the further pattern of the war of words between me and Candid-Camera. I look out of the window: the landscape will be duly lunar like the bus, which is narrow and somewhat tatty – in fact we notice after going fifty kilometres in blinding sun that it is only a little pullman, into which twenty of us are packed, among them two old ladies, one who keeps her little mouth in a perpetual simper and the other who has hers always open in a fixed and naughty smile because of her dentures which must be extra-large. The guide starts to talk: about the four hundred kinds of winged creatures which migrate here, nest, and pursue other activities which are truly typical of winged creatures and few others. He won't stop because he really knows everything: from the quantity of electricity exported to the number of ponies, from the religions (here they are almost all Lutherans) to the animal fodder, all imported apart from the guts of fish and sheep, to ancient customs, to the pilgrimages of the Icelandic scalds to the courts of Europe.

No one listens to him. A champagne-coloured pony with a punk mane and unique equine sex-appeal. We stop to look at a crater 'ten metres deep'. The last to form in Iceland 'five thousand years ago', while there have been any number of underground movements and eruptions, the last in 1984, and each time death and destruction for hundreds of kilometres with villages evacuated. So there was not only the surrounding ocean to contribute to the pride of these brave people who have survived – and survive well. Volcanoes have set themselves down there in case anyone should have thought for some decades that they had nothing to enjoy except chilblains. Then we make for Thingvellir, the prime minister's summer residence – a long house he doesn't even live in all of, only half. Lakes and any number of pinnacles of distant steam. We even see a clump of young pines – a rarity. And then there we are at Geysir, where everything erupts a little and not very well, apart from a little geyser alongside the most famous which is 'old and tired by now', the guide tells us. We stop to eat in a kind of canteen for tourists: soup made with Knorr cubes and unappetizing bits of fish (Second Ice Age) for the main course – fifteen thousand nine hundred lire. But first we betake ourselves (to betake oneself is a verb that makes me laugh a little but every so often it too has to take a little air, poor thing) to the Golden Waterfall, the Golfoss, so-called because of the unfading rainbow. The twenty crones from another bus with its still walking dead come along with us. My two little old ladies look like two malignant little witches: since the photographer took a picture of me – I almost ordered him – they smiled at us, no doubt they have taken us for a honeymoon couple. I say so to him and he makes a face like a man of the world – profoundly disgusted with *savoir faire*.

The waterfalls keep him busy for quite a while, I watch to see if some old woman falls in, they all go to the brink of the abyss to collect little silicate pebbles. Just imagine: witness of how twenty old women all together take each other's hands and, swaying to and fro, gradually pull themselves up to the top of the ridge, take a step more and – whoops: all fall down! And Candid-Camera could at last photograph his story, his event of the year. How much all those things which are so tiredly sensational have tired me out; but it is the usual story, people, nothing has ever happened – not yet! Look for instance how snobbish that rainbow is:

perforce it has been there for a hundred years to be snapped! Look in what a tired way it leans on the rock that is most swept by the cascade, how stoical it is about that sharp needle from the violent jet that tickles its left palm. And we arrive at the geysers, which are fenced off because there were tourists who wanted to feel with their hands whether the water was hot – and each time all hell broke loose because the nearest hospital is ninety-four kilometres away. Some people even went in up to the elbow. They say they were all – every one of them – Americans. I am thoughtful for a moment.

I go close to the hole with its soft violet shades and the water gives out a low visceral roar. It spreads out and then once more comes together in the central hole, it spreads, gurgles, walks about a little, amuses itself, begins to make me lose patience, and then it grows and grows, concentrates itself, begins to pulsate and breathe powerfully and then, ah the coward, scuttles away in all directions and begins again. The little geyser makes fun of you a little. Then a sudden restlessness, unusual, and all at once all the water is sucked towards the same point. 'Get back!' the guide says to me casually, and slowly, majestically, the bubble gets bigger as if emerging from the breath of a master glassblower. It grows wider, flattened at the sides, and a first puff, then a second stronger one and the third spurt, mother of pearl and then suddenly milk white, ejaculates high in the air and I begin to jump with joy and begin to shout 'Hurrah, hurrah!' as if it has managed it, and then little spurts and nice dribbles rain down all round and I stand there, almost forty, stamping my feet and looking round with an uncontainable desire to do ring-a-ring-a-roses as if I were a member of one of those horrible international choirs For Life and World Peace. And I stay there, worried, excited like a slightly naïve porn-film director, to see the scene over again two or three times, and every time seems to me to be the first time, this mighty vagina that ends up by becoming a phallus is killingly funny. Then suddenly dusk descends, sleet on the road, snow on the mountains, the headlamps of the few cautious cars, the very rare houses ghostly in the light that is taken brutally from the sky. Darkness. A void in which I wrap myself like a pig, rolling down into the craters and leaving hanging on each sickle of lava a shred of my mental flesh. I arrive at the hotel with a desire to have sex that leaves me dazed. The little old woman with the rosebud mouth & company I discover are in the room opposite. They throw me a prudent smile, that heart-shaped mouth, even if toothless, gives a twist as if to say: 'No, not this evening, young man.' The open-air sculptures of Asmundur Sveinsson are swimming in my head like dolphins – totemic, *nithstengur* or *shoots of shame* into which the ancients uttered curses at the gods and created wizards: half wind half thunder, shouting out the cry contained by the stone from which they are sculpted.

'Did you vote then?' says Candid-Camera on our way once more to the centre to meet Vigdis.

'No – did you?'

'Yes, before leaving. Why didn't you?'

'These referenda seem to me to be an insult to the Italian language because of the way they are conceived. A national disgrace.'

'What is all this about language? Photography yes. Of course, all you need is a story, an event . . .'

'But you duly photographed the geysers didn't you? And the one of me from the back must be good. A great idea. But I bet you were only pretending. So tomorrow, at the president's. Is your cock too small?'

He laughs – he is loosening up.

'What does that matter?'

'People whose cocks are too small usually have a CV exactly like yours. I swear.'

Since we are a little early we take a little snooze – I spend all the rest of the night writing preliminary notes and questions: 'Many thanks for the honour you do me by receiving me. I shall not waste your time,' and even: 'Have you five minutes to spare, Signora?' No, that won't do, ask her about her lovers, if she has any, if she has had a lot, and if it isn't just by chance that she has learned so well to appear on the national and international scene without ever making a gaffe. I shall not ask political questions: official information here is completely at one with the truth in the streets – there is no point in wasting time. That she is 'very popular' as many people tell me is a fact, that she was a hit in Italy is another. It would have been different if I had to deal with Thatcher – since the conversation will be carried on in French at the express desire of the lady herself, had it been Thatcher I would have started: 'Madame hommasse . . .' And the questions, cut out the most impertinent one: 'Signora, how have you managed to reconcile love for contemporary theatre with Christianity? Do you take a lot of aspirins?' Or even: 'Would you feel fit to run a government if one day Iceland needed to stage an army?' – cut out 'stage': she may be the most brilliant Icelandic actress but she is still just an ordinary citizen. Don't exaggerate.

But, my God, how is it possible to do an interview with someone you find so nice because she doesn't make herself desired? Talk about cooking? about flounces and furbelows? And, for goodness' sake, don't ask her anything about AIDS, it's here as it is everywhere, and particularly when they have just had a referendum on mass screening and the country has said Yes and the health services are preparing for the task. And drugs? Bruno, that addict for the Icelandic summer and horses, has already told me: five in the whole of Reykjavik, a widespread check-up by the police and social banning of the few cases there are, marijuana-smokers and cocaine-adddicts included – there are about ten of them. Average amount confiscated in a year: 18 grammes apart from the big coup last month with two Colombians who had 450. But everyone knows about Colombians – you only need to read their passports and, if there are no partnerships involved, they even open their pillowcases these days. Please don't ask stressful questions about *other people's* sexual freedoms – here you don't need to advance your own and then not know what to do about them. Bruno again: 'Not more than eight arses available in the whole of Iceland.' 'And do they manage to have a good time?' 'Under a lot of stress – always in discothèques, very effeminate, always dancing. Very much under stress. Here everyone goes dancing at the weekend, they are all in high gear because of the vodka; and they leap on each other on the spot, I've seen them myself, tremendous screwing. But it's simple – they go to her house – if a girl is more than fifteen or sixteen she takes them to her bedroom and the man can stay all night. In the morning he goes away saying good morning to the parents, who think nothing of it, they did the same in their day!' He is here because he got to know an Icelandic girl at Nervi in a discothèque, she naturally didn't beat about the bush. Let's go back to my parents' place, she said to him, and Bruno who hadn't grasped that she meant Landkotsún, a few kilometres from here, not wanting to look as if he didn't have his feet on the ground . . .

Another question: 'Your great grandmother, Madame, died at a hundred and your mother was over eighty, so you should have half a century left – would you perhaps have a decade to spare to come and rule Italy? At least long enough to shut down all the private TV stations and at least one surplus national one, give a thorough shake-up to the whole area of cocaine-heroin, rid us of our juvenile unemployment (3,500 posts unfilled because of lack of labour, even highly specialized labour, last month), install effective systems of industrial de-pollution, raise the quality of courses and the number of students, in other words to teach what *language* means, beginning by putting things and names and names and things together again, the citizen to the State and the State to the citizen.' 'Do you think I am too polite?' 'Is the price to be paid for a woman president of the republic too high or is it reasonable? And the galloping inflation, Madame? When I think that for the price of an evening snack I can buy myself a jumper I feel like eating the wool.'

From a window I see girls getting ready to shave men and boys: it is a State girls' school, they are learning to be barbers. Just look how he's bleeding! Let's go in. 'Yes, of course,' says the man, swallowing as the razor is raised in the hand of a radiant girl, all freckles and hair clips in her honeyblonde hair, 'in the morning we come to be guinea-pigs, they do our hair and shave us free, they learn their trade and in exchange we give them a little of our old pensioners' blood.' 'It's all right for them,' a boy with a fresh cut on his cheek whispers, 'they've got the point where they begin to respect statistics.' 'I'm sorry?' I say. 'Yes, of course, eighty for women and seventy-four for men. It takes him all his time to get home with his aftershave. But what about me – I'm just nineteen?' The barbers listen and continue unabashed to make a lather and shut the men's mouths with their shaving-brushes as we go round the stools.

Then we go into a supermarket:

A cucumber – 3,150 lire

A clove of garlic – 1,740 lire

1 onion (a nice big one, I have to admit) – 1,500 lire

If you buy the cucumber for various pleasurable purposes you have a bargain, in all other cases you've been had.

'How much do they earn a month in the country of geysers?' I ask.

'Boh!'

'I'll tell you: labouring jobs a million and half a month, as an agricultural worker or clerk half of that. Thank you for feeding me my lines.'

Candid-Camera shrugs and here we are in front of the Stjornarrathith or seat of government. We go in. A wait: ten minutes because in front of us there is a woman smoking nervously and turning the pages of a fashion journal. Vigdis receives people even to talk about their personal problems, just imagine. But the formula 'Madame la présidente' seems the most fitting, because it sums up, subtracts, gives the proper stress, and since one is dealing with a woman, sprays a touch of feminine grace as well as of politics *tout court*.

And Vigdis Finnbogadóttir receives us, sparkling, very slim and tall, a warm hand-clasp, very *charmante* in her grey/black suit with little velvet bows and lots of beautiful buttons behind such as I hadn't seen since Tunis. She has a frank smile and naturally in the preliminary exchanges I ask her permission (I repeat it) to take some photographs.

'Oh, then can I dash out and comb my hair?'

I am deliberately embarrassed and she, slipping through a little side door to her small but very elegant office, disappears saying: '*Vous savez, je ne suis qu'une femme, au fond.*' She reappears exactly as before.

'Madame, which foreign dramatists did you stage in the theatres you managed until a few months before becoming president?'

'Ionesco, Beckett, Sartre, Giraudoux, *La Folle de Chaillot*, which I translated, and then Fo, who is very popular, you know.'

'All very worthy authors.'

'And in those days courageous ones. But you want to know this sort of thing? Interesting – no one ever asks me.'

And every so often she shows her profile, turning her head carefully towards Candid-Camera who takes a picture – discreetly, but so urgently that I am afraid the lady will get a little distracted.

'Then I translated Arrabal, whom I really love.'

'You see in the preservation of the integrity of Icelandic the means of preserving the integrity of its people – is that not so? Can you explain it to me more clearly, because I don't know any politician in Italy who has any idea how much the economic success of a country is bound up with the culture of the language as a factor making for national unity.'

'But that is obvious! What is a nation if not a group of people who talk to each other and transmit thoughts to each other formulated in accordance with a linguistic convention? Almost all Icelanders have more than a good smattering of a couple of foreign languages, but they are all conscious that the introduction of a *foreign* word inevitably brings with it the irreversible surrender of a *thing*, of a *national* object, whether modern or antique. And we are in a country that is too thankless for us not to go at it and force it to produce – all of us closely united for the same ends. We cannot afford the luxury of too many options; everything before it becomes superfluous must pass through the filter of prime necessity. Since lighting is necessary everywhere, just like water and gas and heating, there is not a single house in Iceland that is less well equipped than any in the capital. And that entailed considerable efforts from the nation in the last twenty years, and considerable loans from abroad, which we honour and will strenuously continue to honour. Then perhaps we shall take the next step. With due respect for the thrift taught us by our parents.'

'May I say that I find you extremely feminine, certainly you do not resemble Margaret Thatcher.'

'That's for sure! That is to say, I mean, I had not thought about it, it seems obvious to me.'

'To be feminine or not to look like Margaret Thatcher?'

'To be feminine. You see, women's best friends are other women and men's are women. Why should a woman ever begin to mimic what she *thinks* a man is – certainly she can only get it wrong – just because she has a position of power? Why should she ever aspire to power if she sets out on the wrong foot? A woman is always a *woman* and even more so if she is in power. In fact to begin with she is chosen precisely for that reason: if people know she is an ugly copy of a man in women's clothes they would not even vote for her, don't you think so?'

'Apart from being an intellectual, an economist, a president of the republic, you are also a beautiful woman – don't you feel that you are a rare species?'

'In that case Iceland, presidents apart, is a magnificent zoo. But do say so – by electing me the Icelandic nation has paid tribute to the memory of their mothers and wives who waited a lifetime for a boat to come home. And meantime, I can guarantee you, did not sit with idle hands. Here women work as much as the men, feminism doesn't come into it, it is a feminism with historical origins, as old as the country itself.'

'But beauty is not something one wins by conquest.'

'Ah my dear, you are still young – you'll find out that you're wrong.'

'Do you ever cry?'

'Yes, at weddings. I weep buckets. Why shouldn't I the moment I am moved?'

'Have you close men friends?'

'At least five men and as many women to whom I can tell anything, but everything.'

'For example?'

'From the new power plan to my weakness for white roses.'

And the conversation continues nice and sparkling for another half-hour until I realize, seeing that she does not make up her mind to dismiss me, that perhaps it is up to me to relieve her of the awkwardness of dismissing me. And that is how it is and suddenly after I kiss her hand stormily she says to me: 'Tell me about your novels.'

Then I have an idea.

'Madame, would you mind posing outside meantime?' I ask with every seductive wile because there is a wind blowing that would shift even menhirs.

'Oh, that's the end of my hair-do. Tell me the title again? *So . . . So . . .*'

'*Sodomies in Elevenpoint*, it is coming out in January. You will be even more *ravissante*, Madame.'

'You think so? Ah you *messieurs* from your part of the world, you are so intelligent. European men are so intelligent, no one has ever not respected me or undervalued me because I am a woman. I spent some wonderful days in Rome. I even visited the Pope.'

Candid-Camera lights up. We go out on to the courtyard, I feel like taking her arm. Indeed I hide my hands behind my back to resist the temptation.

She says to me: 'You know my *chef de cuisine* comes to me from a Lord, a very old family, and my daughter who is always in the kitchen listens to the cook with what I would call greed because he knows so many old words which she then brings me. And I never lose an opportunity to put them back into use: they are perfect, functional, they have a historical patina, dignity and timbre, they seem to have been specially forged, why not put them back into circulation? Of course one must not be fanatical about things, least of all about purism, but it takes very little to be philological and pleasing, don't you think?'

'And the dress you are wearing, where is it from?'

Madame restrained her smile a little and then with the most severe kind of presidential flirtatiousness says: 'From Paris, promise not to write about this: I have just told the journalist from *Bunte* who came in before you that I buy my clothes in Germany.'

And overflowing with my own brand of rosewater nationalism – the only possible kind because not only has Italy never been made but it is one of a whole number of Italies – I run to the florist, have seven white roses, five white carnations, sprigs of white daisies with thick green foliage and three red roses put together and urge the shop-girl to deliver the bunch immediately.

'What did you whisper almost in her ear so that she seemed thunderstruck and then burst out laughing?' asks Candid-Camera while we are waiting for the luggage to be delivered at Linate airport outside Milan, to set his seal on our mutual embarrassment at having to say goodbye after such a long silence.

'Nothing special,' I answer. That is something I want to keep to myself.

Every time I go on a journey I travel a good distance backwards. Lobsters have that funny way of orientating themselves thanks to their posteriors where their sense-organs are scattered, but you can't say that they walk backwards – they walk with their own idea of forwards and in their own way, to one side and then, if you watch them closely, diagonally. But they move forwards and never back; besides it is possible that they do not have geographical categories and therefore the confused way in which they walk is order itself applied to a non-existent goal. They bump into their goal by chance – that's it, and once they have reached it know that it is a goal that continually travels backwards (that is to say, forwards) over all the various stages that brought them here and not somewhere else, inconceivably there and decisively there. Travelling to Caracas in December in the grown-ups' womb: a plane under the belly of the blue air. For example: who was I, who do I think I was at 'Thirteen' I murmur. But is that really so – and then? *Thirteen* exists? Was I really that age? Even I? And what now? Shamelessness is when you make a great effort to overcome a new horror and to find words and appearances for men who walk in and out of the years as they run past; in certain attitudes human silhouettes seem stripped of any defence. Faces set in an expression of astonishment or rarefied fear by the moment of orgasm. I have not spoken of it before, I have not wished to recall my adolescence, perhaps it is the last free zone unaffected by the ink which sweeps aside any decorum. To write is to profane and memories written down are memories lost.

Why do I practise auto-profanation? I do not know. I draw on the last reserves out of the need to feel once more the deceptive flavour of innocence. I call it that for the sake of convenience, but at that age I was already suffering so much that the pain had burnt away any innocence. So from the village I set out on my bicycle down the avenue lined with horse-chestnuts. It was always August. I cannot be mistaken because in those days the seasons had an outline as sharp as a snapshot and then there is that story about the dust raised by the drought because only the main road was tarred. You ate the dust raised by other people's bicycles. Some of them are already dead but I don't know who. There was a youth of my age whom once, at the river, I beat up because he wouldn't toss me off among the reeds and then he did it for me, and it was the first time that I ejaculated somewhere that was not in bed at night. The first time I was tossed off was by another boy: this one was the builder's lad who mixed the lime and sand with a spade, the palm of his hand was wrinkled and I can feel once again its clumsy movement on my sex. I only pretended to do it in return, to touch his, he didn't matter to me. My God, how long it lasted! I felt that something was arriving within me from far-off lands and the stages were infinite and infinitesimal. I remember a flood on a clump of nettles and in the hollow of his hand. I must have been stuck there for twenty years masturbating over that memory. The boy, who ended up dead in a mixing machine in a quarry, has lived on with me for all these years and I never knew what he was called. He was squat, I remember, and had not even had it off yet. I talk about him to myself for two reasons: because the onanistic spell has been broken and because in breaking, it hurls me into a state of remorse that I never returned the pleasure to that boy whom I had given a bloody nose with a punch. But the truth must be different: perhaps he was someone who was waiting for me along with a couple more to beat me up, and it is possible that finding him by himself I wanted to let him see that everything is much more difficult when it is one to one. He had long hair full of tufts covered with chalk – look how his eyebrows powdered white emerge suddenly from the clumps of clouds. But I haven't yet reached the bar where I was going to take over from my father – a takeover that could last three hours or three weeks. In the bar there was the little radio alongside the toaster.

A writer always has a spare life when he decides to gamble with his own; often, in the bottom of the drawer, lies not so much something as someone who has been put on in front of a mirror and then folded away. There is no need even to rummage: it is the first life you come upon the moment you put your hand in. Everything has stayed just as it was. The illusion is perfect, it clings to the only possible reality of the past: the past you meet today and pretend it is not your contemporary as it is to all intents and purposes because your past has not remained there somewhere but has grown up with you and you are its shadow – not vice versa. I feel a certain shame at saying so but that is how it is. Of myself in those days I have a memory of extreme solitude – what am I doing there on top of the hut of a ticket office at the playing field? Why have I left the bar and am standing up there like a sentry? Why do I turn my head to see if a customer might have arrived and then turn it back face to face with the full sun; to whom am I making these signals? Was I on the lookout for someone in particular, a player, the keeper's son, a brother of his? Was I jealous of something going on between two friends I loved deeply? I was passionate and arrogant, egotistical and solitary. But desire was all-consuming – the desire to undress someone at the back of the bar. Sensual desire was already cleft by love because in those days I was madly in love with Giacomino in *Seminar on Youth*: I loved him, whom I could not have, whose mere nearness paralysed my limbs and tongue, and I was going about ravenous for sex with someone, anyone else. This then led me to have sex with men and to love women; up to the age of twenty I tried to love the man I made love with and to make love with the woman I loved, then I gave up for good. There is nothing special in this. The majority of people whom I have known are the painful and unacceptable memory of a scission, memory buried live which tries to stand up as long as it can. It would seem that in order to become adults the rule applies to everyone that one only pretends to grow up. I have arrived at the bar and put the bicycle against the railing with the wistaria and the wallflower – a smell of sprayed paint because a little further on is

Puddu's body-works and the smell too of fresh water because on the other side of the street, in front of the bar, there is a whole green expanse, a field full of streams. The smell of the water is like the smell of a ranunculus stem broken off as I walk along deep in thought. (I am breaking off here because contemporaneously I am writing a *love* letter to Someone, someone with a typical actor's face in photo-novelettes, rather long well-lacquered air, and (naturally) blue eyes; from what I can gather he is a commercial traveller in spare parts for biplanes, or perhaps in leatherware: end of letter.)

At thirteen there was a need to upset the isolation of the bar, it was like being shut away in an open prison. And certainly it was from there that I perfected the instinct to keep myself company on a big scale. In the glass of the door, with the radio turned up full, I felt an exciting pleasure in seeing myself dance – I danced rock-and-roll alone, then there was the cha-cha-cha then the twist, but my dream was to figure-dance the tango with elderly ladies or at least with girls of my own age. Now in the door with the mirror I canot see my own skinny figure contorting itself with a certain symmetry; I see premonitory splashes of ink which come together for a moment, then I see sequence after sequence, I get glimpses of pages overprinted with the ungraspable fleeting impression of a rhythm. Without knowing it I was writing the life of the dancer I would not become in the material that is most like the wind in its fleeting transparency: a mirror. The most grandiose spectacles at which I have ever been present I set up with rudimentary tools but brought them to a peak of technical refinement thanks to the psychic ruminations implicit in any improvisation. There was a thick black cotton blind with brown and white stripes which cast enough shadow on that wing of the door to shield the glass so that I could see my reflection in it and satisfy my intoxication with myself: the screen. Since there was gravel outside if anyone arrived they would never catch me by surprise in some impure act of loving myself totally and in secret a few steps from the public street. Yet once a woman unexpectedly pulled aside the blind and caught me a prey to that mysterious hallucination which sucked the blood from my face and in which I reached somewhat funereal states of ecstasy of total communion with myself and my latest exhumations whatever they might be: I do not think I was ever so ashamed before or since, as if taken by surprise while one is turning one's own corpse upside-down to force it to stop breathing, pulsating, beating time.

The bar was so out of the way and so little frequented – apart from the midday break when the mechanics from the Fiat garage came, some of them with their little pots which they heated up on the gas in the back of the bar – which was not only my private dance-floor but a cavern of sex. There was quite a coming and going of men of every age so that inevitably one day or other they ended up behind the coffee-machine and undid their buttons. I remember that in those days erections and penises were one and the same thing – they were never the result of manual stimulation – the excitement was the cause of the rest, not the effect of something preceding it. I was rarely satisfied with a state of excitement that did not refer to me and me alone. If a mechanic got into a state of excitement because he had felt the need to talk about women first of all I pretended not to notice. In this sense – in this sex – the elaboration in fantasy of other people's thoughts was a flux of which I was more jealous than of the influx that flowed in somehow or other. There was no possibility of having me while pretending to be satisfied with me because of a desire for something else impossible. Either I was the impossible rendered possible or it was better to have nothing.

They are very rare, those lovers who while making love with you do not even know that they are thinking of another person or persons; you are no one and you feel it. This after ten minutes have passed or ten years; and you forgive it and go on fucking so as to be forgiven in your turn.

I remember the son of the rag-merchant who also sold roast chestnuts; they lived in a cement hut with cardboard in all the windows, the boy hadn't been to school, he had tawny hair, an oblong and irregular face, he looked like a Red Indian with freckles. They said he had a bigger prick than anyone else, even if to me it never seemed that he had a bigger one than mine and besides his was a little bent at the end. He always came to the bar; with the excuse of bottling the wine we went down into the cellar and there we even tossed each other off two at a time. He was called Putanelo and I always felt superior to him because he was dirty and in his house there was a rank smell. He was nice in a crooked way always with this prick in his hand – he exhibited it, even at work, he too was a labourer, and my last memory of him is him opening his toothless mouth and pulling at the plastic tube to bring the wine up for the demijohn. Feeling of remorse here too, I treated him with gentlemanly contempt and told him it really was time that he put the tube down into the first bottle. The remorse becomes more intense: I saw him again for the last time fifteen years or so later, by chance at the tobacconist's. He had emigrated to Belgium and on seeing me he almost threw his arms wide open and I took a step backwards as if we had no memories in common, I greeted him in a lukewarm way and asked how he was, he had even more teeth missing, he was wearing a dark suit, he had the same damp smell offset by a popular aftershave lotion. Then he had a fatal accident, they may even have told me but I don't remember. But perhaps he didn't die. If he lived here now I would adore him, I would do everything to convince him to go to a dentist. We always become good just a tiny bit too late. Also because, thank heavens, no one would any longer be able to put us to the test.

There were two mechanics as well, one of them engaged and the other newly married, who took it out standing, leaning on the grating of the big window to see if anyone was coming. I began to touch it for them from the other side of the table on which they had laid out their handkerchiefs as a tablecloth: I would stretch out a foot from which I had removed the shoe. They told me to give over, then up against the inner wall, they begged me not to make them come because that evening they were going courting or wanted to fuck the wife and fuck her all night. Sometimes, following a whim, I even took them at their word. In the pan they had an omelette every other lunchtime. Once the miracle happened; the fiancé bent down and took mine in his mouth. I fainted and he had to slap me a couple of times. He was terrified, he slapped me and tried to remove the splashes from the art nouveau showcase for the loose sweets, the luxury ones, they had liqueurs, were rectangular.

Then that summer there was a procession of sons of Southern carabinieri, sons of airmen from the military camp at Ghedi or youths waiting for the bus that ran between Remedello and Asola. There were two women too who came from far away in the countryside and on Thursdays and Fridays rented a room in the village and, when business was done, counted the money to see who had earned most. I remember that one of them insisted that I should go and see her, her and her daughter as well, who was my age. One day she had lit a cigarette, she had made me sneeze by blowing the smoke in my face and when I got my eyes open again she had her legs open and was eating a piece of fried salt cod and she had no knickers on. I looked at it for a while but more out of politeness than anything else: I couldn't wait for the electrician with the squint to come; he came to adjust the coffee-machine every week because he didn't dare tell us that that was not his trade. He was the proudest man I had ever known after myself. One day he took my hand and put it on his overalls – dry, washed-out overalls with no smell – and put into my hand, bending two of my fingers, the tag of his zip. I didn't do even a third of what he wanted from me and he stopped coming to rob us for a repair he was incapable of doing. There was a period when, for reasons that I do not remember, a paraplegic adolescent in an invalid chair was left there for a good hour, and one day being fed up with listening to sounds I did not understand and mumbled conversations that had neither beginning nor end, I took his out and began to fondle it. Down there he was like all the others – better in fact. One day I realized that he was holding back to have a longer orgasm, as if he were insatiable, so I took out his scrotum as well and began to lick it underneath. Well, if he doesn't die on me right away it will be a miracle. And a sin too because that person is still living but I am sure that since those days life has never had in store for him anything more beautiful than this expedient to keep him quiet both during and – above all – after.

But here we are: the right music has come on on the radio and I am already in front of the false mirror on the door. Whole afternoons could go past without seeing even a dog come in, I danced till I sweated, then my appetite was inexorable. I got through five slices of toast with ham and cheese, which cost more than what went into the till. On those days when no men came by I masturbated for an average of two hours; when I pulled down the shutters at ten o'clock it felt as if it would be better to stay holding on to the handlebars than to mount my bike. In the morning, I had five rolls with my coffee. I was exposed to a solitude that was incredible and hungry, hungry in the power and the frenzy to shake myself with orgasms more and more, as intensely as I could. These were not only tossing-offs, they were mad crusades to blunt the impetus of a brain that seemed to contain another and then another and another again, like the prancing of a charleston superimposed on a cha-cha-cha crossed with a waltz. That glass in the half-light was really a transparent coffin and why does one profane a transparent coffin? I don't even want to imagine why.

Far less do I wish to resist it: because of the pleasure of doing it. And to give another push to the instinct for survival, which is already to some degree supplanted – trampled under foot. I do not know to what extent the pleasure in doing it is tragic, or if it is only an animal desire to challenge oneself, to flush oneself out, to cut the ground from under one's own feet. There were braggarts ready for all kinds of things in exchange for a scrounged ice-cream. I never offered a Penguin free to anyone in exchange for sex – having got to know things one at a time, I already knew their price one at a time, which is the indispensable condition if one is not to put a price on those things which either cannot be paid for or do not exist. Apart from the son of a Sicilian carabiniere no one ever tried it on, I believe – he actually demanded a cassata. He had wide loose shorts and a big testicle always stuck out somewhere; they called him 'the donkey that got among the sheep', he had a prostatic secretion which, had it had some sort of taste, would have done very well to pour on crushed ice. One day at the river, seeing that I had cut myself in the foot and was losing blood, they said someone must piss on it to disinfect it. He let himself be persuaded, then he pulled his prick out of his underpants and pissed on me, scoring a direct hit on my bleeding big toe. I spent several years tracking him down in cellars and bars, in the hope of taking it out for him, it seemed to be the only intelligent thing about this donkey. Then he attended a school for magicians, reading cards, coffee dregs. Even in those days he kept on braying: 'No, no, no. It's a sin.' He prophesied hell for others and kept paradise for himself and, just to come well he was capable of torturing me, denying himself for weeks because I denied him the cassata. He always gave in. He became an important magician. I was looking for someone who would repeat for me what the mechanic had done and I had no peace. If I think that not so long ago someone's dentures got stuck on it and that, playing things down, I handed them back to him with refined indifference. Then I realize that time has passed since these days and how much of that peace has gone under the bridges of my hunger for male genuflections. Caracas.

The girl from the travel agency is behind the barrier, waving a board with my name, unexpected among the heated faces which crowd together in the airport entrance hall. Guendalina has a thin slim figure, a red hair-clip (a butterfly with a wingspan of at least ten centimetres) in her carroty hair which is in unintentional disorder. She makes me get into a ten-year-old high-powered car, too long for me even if I had to park in the air. The cars, if I look around, are all like this: huge American imports at second or third hand. And falling apart, with big areas plastered over and never repainted. It is getting dark.

'Be prepared – traffic going to the centre will be heavy and it can take an hour or two. It is because a pier on the bridge linking the airport to Caracas is collapsing and every day, just as they feel like, they close one lane.'

'What do you mean, "just as they feel like"? Do you mean that one that goes over the pier?'

'One day yes, the next day no, like the lottery. And then what difference would it make? The whole pier was crumbling away and no one had noticed. Now at least they have noticed, later they'll see to it. If it is fate . . .'

'You mean the bridge could collapse from one moment to the next?' And I wonder whether apart from the flight among American rubbish and carcasses, this phrase could be used as a metaphor of the state of the Hispano-American republics whose bridge with Europe and the United States consists of billions of dollars of unhonoured credit which keeps on its feet more than one dictatorship graciously baptized Miss Democracy whereas, to all intents and purposes, it is a decrepit matron.

'Exactly, but everyone thinks some other time will be the unlucky one when they are already somewhere else. The bridge was the idea of President Pérez Jiménez in 1953, before that you went up and down the hills, down there – can you see them? – four hundred bends, half a day and more for a few kilmometres. This bridge is all thanks to the exploitation of the oil at Maracaibo. Now Maracaibo is run down, things aren't going well, anyway, people have noticed some difference between when they were going well and now. Here it's a big deal if things go at all.'

In a tunnel for a quarter of an hour, we advance by centimetres, half-suffocated, in a noise of scrap-iron, of bits of cars dragged along the tarmac. Guendalina speaks an Italian that has a marked Southern cadence; the butterfly has slid down on to the back of her neck. 'Do you know that up to the beginning of the Eighties a dollar was worth one or two bolivares at the most? Now you need thirty and inflation does the rest and petrol is so dear here, yes, more than a dollar a litre, just think? There you have the advantages of having petrol in your backyard – even Volkswagen has shut down and shortly we'll install gears in mules. Look at that car cemetery over there.'

'And the average salary?'

'Anyone who has one doesn't get more than eighty dollars a month.'

'How do you manage?' I say, and what I mean is 'How do you survive?'

'In fact we don't manage even though the crisis has been less acute for a year now.'

And after I don't know how long, the car – she drives with the face of a rodeo rider, cursing and making rude gestures if they try to overtake – comes on to the accursed bridge wished here by President Pérez Jiménez, the dictator whom at least three taxi-drivers – getting on in years – will in the coming days call by his popular nickname 'El Cerdo' – the pig.

'Here we are,' sighs Guendalina, whose grandparents were

from Palermo, one of the two hundred thousand Italians who emigrated or were born here.

'In what sense?' I ask, staring at the hundreds upon hundreds of similar jalopies like giant beetles jammed in on every side; in the case of an emergency there wouldn't even be room to open a door.

'We are at the critical point. Just think if the bridge were to split in two at this moment! What a slaughter! But this evening things are better than usual – they are letting the pier crumble a little more but to make up for it they let you go over a lane and a half.'

'Just as well. You're an odd person. Allow me,' and I hand her the butterfly which has slipped down on to the seat.

On the road, every hundred metres or so, a broken-down car, with a boulder under the wheel to block it because we are on a slight slope, people preparing themselves with a tired air, without any particular signs of annoyance, to spend who knows how much time – perhaps the whole night – there. Steam rising here and there from bonnets, men and children with rags and dipsticks in their hands, the faces of resigned women collapsed in their seats, and also two very pretty girls in miniskirts with spangles in their hair, in a vague state of terror, looking fixedly at their broken-down car perhaps to avoid the diabolical looks of the men, who – as if it were necessary – slow down almost touching them. 'Those two won't get to the party. They're more likely to be made to have it here,' says Guendalina, without compassion. The cars in front of us seem to make more noise than progress, and from the exhausts precise plumes of a frothy black stand out poisonously among the dirty red tail-lights. It is really difficult to breathe but the secret finger-crossing hope that the pier underneath won't collapse this minute gives a kind of scent of lime to the exhaust gases. And now it is pitch-dark and from every direction natural Christmas cribs take shape without any sign of human presence: they are the little lights of the *ranchos* or *ranchitos* packed together on the slopes of the hills which press in all round – press down on the city with their charge of furious poverty and fetid life.

'They seem to be uninhabited,' I say. 'There's not a soul to be seen.'

Guendalina says drily: 'They're all out robbing and cutting people open,' and she gives me a sidelong smile and I feel a kind of shudder.

'Have you ever been in a *rancho*?' and she bursts out laughing: 'What for? to be murdered and then raped? Not even the police go there, or if they go they go in battalions and with their automatic weapons cocked.'

'But polio, smallpox, I mean vaccinating children – someone must go and do it?'

'Yes, at dawn, when the men and women are still drugged or drunk, the social services go there but escorted by police with cocked pistols, the syringe in one hand and the P38 in the other.'

'And during the day what do they all do, I mean, when they're not going about trying to get some food?'

'What food? You mean to get the latest model TV set and hi-fi with three thousand little lights going on and off! But during the day they kill each other for fun, just a trifle and their eyes get bloodshot, they rush home to get a weapon, provided they don't have it ready in their underpants, and it's over, their little domestic show with blood spilt and the neighbours standing round looking on or taking one side or another. It's like a fiesta, human blood – not all of them have fighting cocks or bulls, but a wife suspected of adultery, she is within the reach of even the poorest.'

'A crazy criminal culture just like in the south of Italy, where if they let you live they still cut off an ear.'

'You've said it. A bestial criminal culture even if the poor animals don't come into it. A terrible way of saying they're inadequate, don't you think? A subhuman criminal culture, that's what it is.'

Those American Indians who constitute only a small part of the vice-steeped population of the Venezuelan *ranchos* and those mixed races drifting about on the hillsides (how often will I see a blond boy with light skin squatting on a pavement trying to sell trinkets and will take him, rightly, to be the involuntary legacy of a German or Dutch father), raped by a thousand political promises never kept, bled by drugs and prostitution and by the traffic in babies and children, abandoned to themselves and to the pornography of poverty which so pleases journalism intent on creating nothing but a state of inurement and fatalism in the privileged masses of their Western readers, remind me of certain parts of Europe: the Barrio Chino in Barcelona, Brixton in London, Naples, Reggio Calabria, Palermo, the dormitory suburbs of Rome and Milan and the whole of Turin.

'As for personal safety, Caracas is no worse than Catania, or Bogotá than Milan, or Medellín than Catanzaro and Rio de Janeiro than Mazara del Vallo,' Guendolina goes on. 'There's no point in demonizing Venezuela and Colombia. I have just met an elderly Argentinian woman – she was still in a state of shock. Because of the strikes she had to go halfway round the world to get back to Buenos Aires. They snatched her bag, took everything, and she knelt down deeply hurt, weeping and entreating, with nothing left, ticket and money and passport, there in the street, in full daylight, among dozens of passers-by and shoppers, amid general indifference. It was in the Campo dei Fiori in Rome. Drug-addicts should be put up against a wall and ta-ta-ta – exterminate them all on sight. You . . .' and I interrupt her in alarm because I am afraid that she is asking me if I do not agree with her, what I think about it, I who think that they should be recycled by my neighbour back home – Valsella & Co, arms manufacturers – and then put in the Persian Gulf as floating mines: it would be the only way to try to get them off it. 'Do you think you could get someone to go up there with me to a *rancho*?' and I light a cigarette to allow her to change the subject.

She moves up another gear, slows down defiantly (we are doing twenty kilometres every two hours) and turns her face towards me, stares at me without any particular expression. 'If I were you' (and I notice the peremptory protective tone in her change to the familiar mode of address) 'I wouldn't even try. At the agency we're not so good at providing coffins,' and she laughs full-throatedly. I understand. Since the butterfly clasp was slipping down again she has taken it and thrown it behind her where it has beaten its wings against the glass.

The engine starts to knock, Guendalina spits out a short curse in old-fashioned Sicilian, for a few moments I think we shall have to spend a night of terror on the side of the road. For some minutes I have been making out, beyond the carriageway among the thick bushes lit by the headlights, the outlines of men wandering about – an ambush? I feel hanging over us from the landslides with the hovels of tin and wood and mudguards an uncontainable, obscure, disorientated desire to attack, kill and despoil.

I come out with: 'Here life isn't worth a bean.' It isn't much more than a commonplace reclaimed by *sound values* from a social marsh which has gone bankrupt and she, rightly, bursts out with: 'It's worth so much in Nicaragua then! And why should it be worth anything, life? There is so much in South America – almost all of it out of work, hungry and numb. To give it value you would have to give it something to do, wouldn't you?'

'Life in a slaughterhouse, food for torture. The secret police . . .'

'Those damned armaments! What are they going to do with all these weapons? Who is going to attack us? Like in Bolivia, Colombia, Brazil – drugs and oil and emeralds for export and arms as imports. Why do you think they grant them so many billions of dollars as loans? It is the Western governments who finance themselves by passing through here and giving all the time in the world for repayment to the industrialists. If it were really to improve the lot of the Third World you can bet your boots they would want their money back as soon as possible.

'They have no imagination and are starved of international finance. Take away their weakness for arms and the refining of poppies and coca and all they have left is football. Then some bloodthirsty imbecile like Fidel Castro comes along and they have a revolution. Financed with sugar cane? Not at all. In the usual anti-revolutionary way.

'And there would be so much to do – nature is so rich here – so much to extract, to provide with technology, to construct. We lack nothing. Instead it's weapons and more weapons. Can you see Venezuela attacking Colombia? Because of some frontier landowner kidnapped because he doesn't provide his Indian serfs with old age pensioner whores. Come on!'

I like this girl with her white skirt with a spot of oil on its front, a balanced and violent girl, one who doesn't give in and will deliver the same alarming speeches, I hope, to all the tourists who come within range. Her reactionary views are just right, she is neither sentimental nor populist: an exemplary Italian born abroad and who in place of the St Valentine parades has had the training of a military camp. And then I hazard:

'Do you go about with a gun in your glove compartment?'

'I was taken to a firing range by a friend of mine – years ago, because of the regulations about having a gun . . . Everything was fine. I was with all the ladies and beginners, all firing, an hour a day for six months. At the very least I hit the spleen to being with, then I got closer and closer to the mouth, to the head. You don't realize that they are cardboard cut-outs, after a bit – when you go out you continue to see cardboard cut-outs and instead they are human beings like yourself. You are the first to turn into cardboard. It's odd how after a little it all seems natural, it becomes a sixth sense in your fingers, you feel the need of a blank pistol, even in sleep your right hand goes on gripping it, your arm stretches out perfectly parallel to the shoulder, your feet slightly apart under the blankets . . . I mean, the human face becomes blank, as anonymous as one of these cut-outs, almost to get you used to deprive the people who have to be killed of identity. You get an urge to make a hole in someone's cheek and then you think, how silly, *pardon*, I wasn't thinking, I won't do it any more – I' and here Guendalina swallows and scrapes the car alongside, from which a menacing hooting rises, 'I had been attacked in a lift, they attack women in lifts, because outside, in the streets, in the underground, there are patrols everywhere. And then after that nasty business, very very nasty, I decided to get a licence to carry a gun.'

I resist the banal curiosity of asking her what happened to her in the lift and how many they were and whether they dragged her on to a landing by the hair and ask: 'And now do you have it with you?' because if the car should suddenly give up the ghost I would be the first to be dying to pull a trigger. Because I know that I am a murderer *manqué* and that at least four times over, and the more the years pass the sorrier I am.

'My gun licence yes, the pistol no. I realized that the chances to use it were really too many, you know, it's like shaking hands, like going shopping, you do it even if there are a week's supplies in the fridge. You get to the point where you invent opportunities, the safety a pistol in your pocket gives you leads you to continually risk situations and nasty people, something that doesn't happen if you have only a handkerchief and lipstick in your purse. I sold it almost at once, I got rid of it. I would have liquidated about ten people in these last years, not counting my possible homicidal whims.'

'And the other women on the course?'

'How should I know – they don't do the sort of job I do, going to and fro with tourists in tow with their jewellery much in evidence on their wrists and necks. They will go to the Teatro Teresa Carreño to concerts under escort – for anything else they send men or women servants. Here life is all behind the high walls and nothing but strongarm men back and front.'

'This thing with escorts is a real business, isn't it, like in Italy?'

'For every government soldier in the country there are three private guards and in Colombia more than in Venezuela. If you ask a little boy what he will be when he's big it's rare for him to answer an engineer or a pilot here.'

'Well, in Colombia the Ochoa Coca Co. have a private army, helicopters, runways.'

'A splendid organization. It would be terrible if they went into melons or commercialized the little red votive candles.'

'Is it easy to get a pistol here without a licence?'

'Listen – if in Italy they hire them by the hour for bank raids and assaults and murders on commission, you can imagine what it's like here! They are very expensive, the prices are prohibitive, but since they are more necessary than bread according to the macho mentality in South America and the USA, they all have them, it's like in Miami or New York, a pistol as present when you're confirmed if you're a Catholic and well off, and a sheath-knife in your pants if you're a kid without means making your first communion. It's dangerous enough to have to walk in the street, so you can imagine what it's like to go on purpose into a *rancho*. I hope you'll get over this desire of yours quickly. But now I'm exaggerating – we're not in the Vucciria in Palermo after all!' and she burst out laughing with all her heart – or what is left of it. A chilling and warning laugh with which she says goodbye to me in front of the Caracas Hilton, my umpteenth stopping-place – all luxury and security like an armoured coffin lined with chintz.

In the hotel itself – and almost every evening for six days on end – there is a festive dance of diamonds and topaz necklaces and a jubilation of Buicks, Mercedes, Fords, Chryslers (brand-new these) which come one after the other to the entrance and deposit with pomp and circumstance a couple and a strongarm man, two strongarm men and a single man, three strongarm men and an unaccompanied lady, some high society strongarm men escorting each other. It is Jewish high finance celebrating engagements, birthdays, farewells to bachelorhood, weddings of which tomorrow's papers will report the splendour and the effort. No, I tell myself, you aren't in Brussels any longer, you are in another hotel. Rumour has it that the most desired and most regularly invited guest of anyone who counts has been and is – even in an apparently democratic legislature – an officer famous for his impersonal methods of torture worked out by a computerized programme and for his murderous handshake and big cheery young man's smile with very white and well spaced teeth. The haute bourgeoisie, it seems, is keeping him in retirement with all possible honours while waiting for better times. And here in this morgue which is constantly scanned – with any number of lumps under people's jackets – I suddenly begin to feel more at risk and vulnerable than I would be with one foot in an open sewer up there in a *rancho*. Because I would still be able to speak to a rootless alcoholic drug addict following me with a machete, and not to these people here.

I settle into my room – a rather nasty one – with a kind of feeling of inverted humiliation – a new one. I experienced the same feelings of impotence, of an animal that is being daintily hunted, as at Mondello, in the hotel where they gave the literary prize of that name and I, after half a day on that island of elegant meetings with poets and jury members, went out and saw what was *outside* and went back in and from my mouth came nothing but shit and rage against all the elegant speakers who had never uttered a word that was not about narratology and *nouvelle cuisine*. Obviously I pocketed the prize cheque with all the more determination. I really felt that it was an eight-year-old drug courier who pulled it out of the cash-box of the bald and stammering accountant, greasy, with patches of sweat under the armpits of his shirt, with thick spectacles, hands transparent from the continual worried rubbing together of his fingers, which weren't sure whether really to let it go or to make it disappear into one of his own pockets. Since then literary prizes disgust me, the people who give them disgust me, the people who take them disgust me, above all those who dare not to give me one – after which, in fact, either a gay spa prize comes out or I shall never again be able to have my ill-gotten gains refunded.

And here, looking at the window at the festooned city which is traversed by various sirens, totally cut off from the undergrowth which palpitates with wearied and infected blood, I am assailed by a worry about claustrophobia because there is something completely wrong and false about going out tomorrow into the open sure of being able to come back at any time to the comfort of this funereal safety *from*. But this is the life of typical journalists – to go about in the insanity of *other people's* systems without looking at them too closely if they want to come back home, having saved their skins, to write the article for which they were *sent out;* to go with a photographer dressed in a khaki blouse with matching shorts to the war fronts and the Press Tent furnished with hot/cold/drinking water to delight someone who will demand the shiver of *participation* for two thousand lire. And I am talking here about the good ones – because the overwhelming majority will produce dialogues and documented lies in the first person while sitting by a swimming-pool and saying to themselves 'I was there' when they could very well have stayed at home using the archive. I am not even a journalist and do not know the rules of survival or prudence very well, do not know the demands of the editorial deadline, and find myself here frightened and suffering in front of a minibar full of quarter bottles of champagne. How can one escape from this multiple trap in which the bourgeoisie of printed paper give carte blanche to denounce the corruption of the bourgeoisie in general but only after having got you radically used to being unable to do without its sublime existential delicacies? How will I be able to report on social conditions about which I feel strongly without giving too much importance to the privilege of being in material terms outside? Shall I manage to remain sensitive and emotionally uncontaminated after the rite of initiation into journalism without becoming *good* to the point where I forget that a journalist has a soul that passes the buck while literature like art does not allow this, does not permit you just to be good but demands that you should be alive, linguistically alive, in every fibre of your body? In one way only: by punishing myself for the critical vastness of my aesthetic emotions which are unable to come to terms even with a trip, hotel and expenses paid, in order to produce a fraudulent reportage. And the punishment is always the same – *to think about it*. From the earliest hours of this sleepless night I have been on this bed as if on a sacrificial altar elaborating on a pain which I know very well. It is the one that wrinkles faces up there in the *ranchos* – the pain of the least offensive of animals reduced by the ridiculous calculations the commercial and military capitalist class makes on their scrofulous skin till they brood over hatred upon hatred for everything and everybody, for the animal next door as well as for the little animals they bring into the world, like you in every possible way and yet as much enemies of themselves as you. I do not need much: when I open the door of the minibar once more to take out a bottle of mineral water I have a feeling of revulsion at myself and this place, this hotel, city, villas and *ranchos*. I pour it down my throat rather pleased with my feats of psychosocial alchemy. I mock myself for my impulsive pusillanimity, and have decided to get paid for having not only accepted but provoked this life as a *journalist*, another person who will end up making money out of the miseries that move him – at least he will have had some *experiences* out of them.

'Columbus sailed the ocean blue,' says an old song, and the rest became history. A pity that to discover something only means to have it moved from the old site with the same mad desire to exploit it. It will be the same story this time too: instead of twenty ex-convicts I have a photographer in tow, if possible even more dementedly Catholic than the first, neither thin nor grossly fat, called Capotto (overcoat), whom I find and hang up on the coathanger of arrogance once and for all – it is summer too, I am bound to ignore him. I was forgetting – it will be another story about the colón – the local currency – because that is the Spanish for Columbus.

In the morning, hardened by the long intermittent waking hours broken by those sinister and varied whistling noises which I have never heard elsewhere, the obligatory stop on the Monte d'Avila. I take the funicular immersed in jolly school-girls and any number of extra-young couples, madly in love with each other, whom the sun right overhead makes particularly tender and creamy – when they kiss *à la negro* they must also suck in a little sweat from the nostrils of the other. I would say that they love each other more every moment that passes out of fear of getting bored and because they lack good conversation. The funicular covers a distance of three kilometres and four hundred metres, it reaches a height of 2,180 metres and was built in 1958 immediately after the end of the dictatorship; since when nothing else has happened. The splendid results in terms of the politics of incomes and of the rights of man seem to follow the fall of the bolivar, which follows the fall of the price per barrel of oil which accompanies the fall in the image of President Jaime Lusinchi for reasons no less trivially vaginal than those of Gary Hart in that other continent up there. Lusinchi, like the Columbian president Virgilio Barco, has adopted a non-rhetorical style, a low-profile one that pleased people greatly at first – and much less in the course of their respective legislatures because not only did their technocratic promise to clean up industry and basic services with few words and many deeds fail but they were entirely lacking in that art of oratory which is particularly precious for any politician who is in any case about to be swept away. The people can put up with the lack of deeds – it is used to that – but never, absolutely never, with that of solemn rhetoric that gives it an excuse to make the soup of hope last longer and to keep its mouth shut and be the underdog once again. And so what pretext did it find to ruin Lusinchi and any chance of standing again as a candidate with the elections at the door? The breakdown of his marriage, the rows his neglected wife made in the courtroom. Because Lusinchi fell madly in love and in broad daylight with his secretary (who seems to be not only a lover but also a far-sighted politician – to be precise like Evita Perón) and asked for a divorce from his present doll-wife, who had been living on her own in Florida for years and then was called to his side to form the perfect couple with an eye to the last elections only to be consigned immediately afterwards to oblivion. Except that this time she did not go along with it and began to level accusations and counter-accusations against the unfaithful husband and to ask for an examination of his assets from the four judges. The hypocritical and malevolent base of influential Venezuelan society ended up by attacking this man who has been naïve enough to comply with the law to ask for divorce from the woman he no longer loves so as to marry legally the one he does love. This courageous solution in accordance with what is laid down by law is not in accordance with the mentality of a tribal-rural country and disgusted a society whose wives prefer and accept the primitive formula according to which a male has the tacit and, if not the legal, then the social right to have wife *and* lover, dividing his time and possessions between them. And what in times when there was no political pressure would have been a marginal incident, turned out for Lusinchi to be total political death without any possibility of resurrection. And Lusinchi, who had admittedly the most difficult presidency of the century (perhaps because he is the first who could not legally have recourse to the physical torture of his opponents?), is certainly a man of peace and and now all this story about sweethearts is used by everyone – including those of his own party – to say that he really is useless . . .

The funicular is – along with the splendid ten-kilometre-long underground – very closely guarded and more secure than a safe on the ocean bed, the pride of Caracas. Having set foot on Monte d'Avila I take a quick look fifty metres further up, then I do an about-turn and take the first cabin going down: too much pure air at one time might be fatal. And then all these lovers with bleeding lips . . . In the cabin I am alone with the employee in the beige smock with the zip pulled down – or else it has descended absentmindedly – as far as the groin in which there is a flash of ochre-blonde hair. Sometimes I wonder whether they do it on purpose, I never know whether they are feeling the heat or feeling randy. Besides in the streets there is a constant adjustment of cocks as if they want to be sure they still have one, a constant touching of it and mechanically taking money from their pockets to count it, a feverish checking common to both passers-by and waiters, who hold the banknotes tightly in one hand and go about among the tables like that. Every other minute, having put down the tray, they touch their scrotums and begin to count their hoard as if it might have increased through some magical germination of watermarked paper and if the sum is still the same as before, they can always count on their cocks to comfort the other hand, which will certainly find it a little more swollen than before. I remember that in Italy too they used to do this all through the Fifties and Sixties. Even my father – and one of my elementary school teachers – displayed the big reddish 10,000-lire notes under the eyes of those with nothing as if to say, Come and take them if you can – and he too kept on counting them and spreading them out on the table with the back of his right hand as if his daring were sufficient to make them multiply. But my father was already characterized by a refined neo-realism: he only felt his cock from the inside of his pockets – probably he had copied this distinguishing mark from my elementary school teacher who, standing at attention, performed real trapeze acts on his pelvis with his hand in his pocket – and did not wipe the sweat from his brow with a dirty banknote as I saw happen here in a snackbar.

Suddenly the funicular stops and begins to sway in the wind, buried in the clouds. You can see nothing, as if we had been dipped in a bowl of whipped cream. Here you either get over your vertigo or you throw yourself down at once. Tremendous emotions.

'It's a drop of about two hundred metres,' says the attendant, a student of economics who earns a bit extra on his free mornings, 'but it isn't the deepest bit – that's still to come.'

The cabin resumes a very slow jerky progress. We come out of the clouds: the spread of Caracas is impressive – it disappears at the horizon with its maybe three, maybe four, maybe even nine million inhabitants out of the twenty-two million in the country. Once more the immense forest park appears below us and, my God, the cabin swoops up and down again. I get the feeling that here, *everywhere*, there is something that had been crumbling for decades and was simply waiting for me to bring to an end my precarious existence (which had perhaps been too prolonged) along with its own. And it is swaying a little more than before, the wind has got stronger. On a swing in the sky. The youth comes close to my ear and I turn my back to him so as not to look at him and let him see me.

'Get up, come over here, put your head out, you won't fall, listen to the noise of the streams,' and I obey and get up, a little intoxicated by the fact of touching his belly with my thigh because he presses against me and puts his head out of the window along with mine. 'This is the highest point, two hundred and eighty metres. The snakes in this park are very beautiful – sometimes you can see them as if, because of an optical effect of the air, they were a few centimetres away, wrapped round the dry branches. They are a very special green, like neon. There are yellow ones too.'

The cabin shivers and is imperceptibly troubled, then there is a blast from the radio, they are calling us from down below. I turn away so as not to risk deciphering the exchange of messages. Have we perhaps had a breakdown? Will they lower ladders from helicopters? I hear the youth's voice saying after an interminable moment '*Bien-bien . . . bien*' and I seem to feel the specially green snake slipping down inside my spine. Then from the radio comes a jolly little tune like the ones they put out on a plane when it is entering a storm. 'Darling, I'll teach you how to love, how to kiss, how to smile, darling O my darling!' and, cables permitting, we get down to a background of the rumba. The cabin attendant, following my question whether he could accompany me to some *ranchos* in Boyacá or Valle Arriba, as he opens the door for me says: 'I'm not free either tomorrow or the day after. Why do you want to go there? There are so many beautiful things to see in Caracas! There is a war going on between the Families over coke. Aren't you worried about your neck? And don't try to go alone – I advise you not to – you wouldn't get further than the first nine steps. Anyone not born there – zac!' and he makes a cut-throat gesture. But the young man, a fervent patriot, doesn't wish to be too dramatic and ends up by suggesting that he was only trying to scratch his Adam's apple, shifts the elastic of his underpants a little and adjusts the zip and wishes me good day and a nice meal of *hallaca* (the national dish based on meat and beans) and a pleasant visit to the Botanical Gardens or the East Park designed by Burle-Marx or the recently opened Calvary, and then disappears overwhelmed by the new load of embracing adolescents behind a woman teacher who dispenses tickets and warning glances.

I take a taxi and find myself immersed in a wonderful chaos like Cairo at rush hour – any one of them from six in the morning on. From the open windows of the other cars, given the slow pace, I catch whole refrains of satirical songs, one dedicated to Lusinchi himself and his new flame. Probably improvised by a minstrel paid by the opposition, he sings of Lusinchi's old man's amours and the grand refusal of Juan Carlos of Spain to receive him at court with his concubine, because Lusinchi at his age even makes State visits with his lover and breaches the etiquette of whole royal families with consorts who are faithful according to protocol, and the ballad ends like this: 'A new Evita is his companion for life!' Behind the cruel drawl there is evidence of the popular need for a new ex-dancer who will start off by playing Mamma to the Fatherland from a balcony, one of those good and magnanimous spirits who are presumed to know how the world works only because they have mapped its perimeter in their youth inside a brothel and then stay there with their compasses for the rest of their days which are full of popular (embalmed) wisdom.

In Plaza Bolívar eight little soldiers in blue and gold uniforms mount the guard of honour on the equestrian statue of the Libertador. Down there there is a municipal library, an unusual sight. I go in and the faces of the few employees and visitors have about them something lost, defenceless, sky-blue, citizens like fish out of water, looking terrified, as if they had first of all put a ticket on themselves: 'Beware! Martians!' No trace of aggressivity in them, boys and girls seem to be there ready to rise up for a beatification. If you touch them they might break or disappear. What can it mean to know *more* in a South American country?

At the bus station there is a boy with a trained black mastiff which he makes do extremely funny tricks and then a real attack on a man. The dog performs miracles of blood-thirsty feints on behalf of its master and the surrounding crowd is admiring and generous – the dog continues to throw itself at this person and then another, stopping two centimetres from their noses, its jaws gaping wide, the claws in its front paws bare.

I have an appointment with Diego Risquez, a young film-maker financed by the government, for his second full-length film *America, terra incognita*, which I see on an editing table without sound: it is the story of an Indian taken to the court in Madrid in a cage and kept prisoner there until a princess falls in love with him and gives birth to the first bastard hereditary prince who will go on to conquer Europe . . . a fable turned upside-down, full of boring allegories and legends which mix together the witchcraft of Malinche, Montezuma's woman and later his sinister betrayer to Cortés, with the Greek myth about the Amazons. Risquez has two huge parrots in his garden and at least four men servants; the film is obviously dedicated to the liberation of his suppressed people. Before this Risquez shot a film, also made up of pure images and without a plot (so as not to risk saying anything too clearly that could be placed on one side or the other, which is very risky, for the government changes very often here), called *Orinoco New World*. It follows the course of the river of that name which is studded with Indian tribes: at a certain point a mermaid suddenly leaps out and a turtle-man rises up, projections of the oneiric delirium of the Indians in the grip of *popo*, the strongest and most devastating hallucinogenic root on this earth. When a film or novel or painting has no political message you can be sure that that is what it is about.

An evening party with Caracas' *jeunesse dorée* from the fine arts and crafts (photographers, models, painters, set-designers, designers) is enough to give me my fill of all the parties to which I am to be invited: the slightest sign of *direct* political interest sows panic and distrust among these privileged artisans who call themselves artists. Some of the things I say, which are full of the usual common sense, are confused with Communist anathema and those present at them swarm off to pour themselves a drink and distance themselves. Because here, as in Bolivia, serious Communists have never had on average more than eighteen months of life – and it is clear that here the *cultured* classes, the representatives of art for art's sake, intend to live longer than that. But they are also very uninformed. It is impossible to have a discussion with them (besides the music is at full volume) and I shall never be able to explain to them that I was *never* a Communist ten years before Gorbachev. The custodians of art, ah! tomorrow, just to give an international example, at the Teresa C. Theatre, Maurizio Pollini, who will refuse me an interview after I pursue him through curtains and dressing-rooms and stages, out of fear of the photographer (to the press he will issue the usual photograph in the style of Arbas taken thirty years ago, and now the ridiculous differences would really be visible, he is just a little penguin dressed for the part with a stolid face and a belly which throws up the tails of his waistcoat). What else can he perform being sponsored by the Unión Visa Bank if not Chopin Scherzo No. 3 in C sharp major (Opus 39) and Liszt *La gondola lugubre* first version? How I envy those who contrive to be so exalted without in the very slightest impairing their patrimony of stupidity. Great and idiotic – destined always to be amazed at things.

At Sabana Grande I at last track down the Swedish Bath and become drunk on sex with men of at least five races and different mixtures. I take no precautions, without sex I would be lost. If it works it works, if not, patience! Late in the afternoon, on the way out, some shots, not very far off; I get into a taxi and ask this other taxidriver – he too a Sicilian by origin and who for the last twenty minutes has been preaching to me like a reactionary revolutionary:

'What are these sudden explosions?'

'They'll be fireworks. Bangers.'

'In the afternoon? But I can't see anything.'

'All the better. They were stray bullets,' and then as if lost in thought: 'They need to kill five thousand of them, five thousand and this city would be inhabitable again – five thousand rapists who keep on raping, corrupt policemen, mafioso politicians and drug-dealers.'

'But where? What has happened?'

'What difference does it make in any case?' and the conversation is broken off.

You will look in vain in the papers for the page with the crime reports: people kill each other at night and no one will ever know – except, I discover, on Tuesdays when they do a count of all those killed, which is never the same from one paper to the other. The number killed is 'roughly', 'not less than', 'it appears that the number of violent deaths last week end was' – not like in Israel, where there is a perfect, obsessive accounting department which keeps an exact score of the dead. Certainly if even the anarchist taxidrivers are silent on the subject it must be serious. I get out in some street in the centre and he keeps the change, adding: 'They ought to kill them all if you really think about it. Five thousand at a time.'

I am dressed in the most modest manner possible so as not to attract attention. I have been advised to take off my plastic watch and the rings and little chains I have never worn. And with my Peruvian bag over my shoulder I will stroll through the city. I meet two foreign waitresses, one from Bogotá and the other a Peruvian, on their day off. They want me to buy them candyfloss at a booth, then they meet a Brazilian friend, she too an immigrant, and the three of them court me in a bold but languid way, all talking at the same time. They miss their own countries, their families, they want a scarf, they want a huge handpainted fan, they want the moon, they want me, they want to carry me off so that I will carry them off in their turn. They are all three very sad and scatterbrained, they give me their addresses, will I send them a postcard? But why am I going away now? Where do I live, how long am I staying? And tomorrow?

Since I have too often taken a wallet out of my bag, after a while I notice that I am in the full glare of suspicion and that some types are following me looking like lazy, absentminded loafers. But I have never worried much about the warnings to tourists and usually follow those I gave myself fifteen years ago to people going to New York or Naples which, bringing the figures up to date, would be: never be robbed with less than fifty thousand lire in your pocket or there is serious trouble. Now I am quite convinced that my canvas and leather bag with its coloured patches has caught the eye of those disinherited people who are drinking tins of Coca-Cola and leaning against the billboard scaffolding among carcasses of cats and fruit skins and rotten vegetables. Apart from my wallet I might have in it my passport, an item greatly desired here in order to emigrate, or be carrying in it the watch missing from my wrist. I go back to the hotel after having given one of them a look that said either you or me, choosing the most open and busiest road, and deposit my bag. In the street I have noticed that not even the women have a purse any more, or if they do they keep it hanging from their necks or tied round their bellies like donkeys. And yet Caracas is overflowing with North American tourists because of the exchange rate. The Hilton is literally invaded by them, like any other hotel with three or more stars – besides there are whispers that quite a few elegant Europeans and Argentinians come here for safaris, which are exclusive to the point of forming sects, into (*entre nous*) the most impenetrable parts of Guyana, hunting for the last Indians in a savage state whose severed heads are displayed at the end of the day as if they were toy rabbits.

It is not for nothing that the big Nazi war criminals set up *fazendas* here and round about: here along with the air you breathe the smell of human blood, which does not seem to flow because of particular individual ferocity but because of a great natural laziness to search for other methods of persuasion or consensus or sport. After a few days my feeling is firmly embedded in the absolute separation of the social classes and becomes a terrible sense that it is not a question of riches or poverty but of an unbridgeable genetic difference like that between two different species of animal which, because of some vagary of geophysical destiny, occupy the same territories. This fight to the last drop of blood then continues to atomize the human agglomerations even in their most infinitesimal structures, right into the interior of the family itself – to the point where it lacerates the individual who is split, one part being his inexorable enemy. And my gaze is always directed up there to the *ranchos* where not even the umpteenth taxidriver wants to take me and shrugs with a grin while he is very happy to take me to the Museum of Modern Art, which is just beyond the elevated passageway in front of the hotel, but he has taken good care not to tell me so and takes me on a pre-Columbian wild-goose chase before depositing me at the spot where he had picked me up a quarter of an hour before. There are innumerable portraits which Bolívar (1783–1830) had done for him by his contemporaries and very few whole-length or on horseback because he was really a little fellow and obviously feared that his moral and physical stature would clash.

I realize that I want nothing apart from a pinch of justice and that I find it embarrassing that I still haven't got into trouble. I see nothing and nothing interests me in these ethnological beauties. I run my eye over metre after square metre of murals, take my fill of taciturn or frenzied men with the same indifference. It must be the price of surviving – to die internally. The funereal vitalism which I breathe in the people's breath, especially that of the middle class which one perforce brushes up against in the Hilton, petrifies me. I take refuge in the lair of my room, resolved to leave it only as much as is strictly necessary until the moment of take-off; to buy cigarettes and go and get well laid in the saunas which swarm with unimaginable *machos* whom I run through like whores to see if I manage to pick up AIDS and then announce it to this bloody masked ball on the Martini Terrace with rich presents and favours for all. But then after an hour my distress wanes and midway between depression and the desire to break off this trip at once and never undertake another in all my life, I go out into the city again and find myself in Plaza Venezuela in a cinema where they are showing *The City and the Dogs*, taken from the novel by Mario Vargas Llosa. The poster shows two faces about to bite each other as if instead of talking they were baying and instead of teeth had fangs. The slogan for the launch of the film: '*Para sobrevivir en esta vida de perros, es necessario morder más fuerte que los demás*' (To survive in this dog's life, you have to bite harder than the others.) Even if the action takes place in a barracks in Lima and not in Caracas it is all the same, and after ten minutes in the deserted cinema I miss Lubitsch and beat it.

Of the receptacles a man had at his disposal into which to pour his violence I have already filled all to the last drop and, starting with each extra drop, run the risk of death by suffocation. I no longer pour anything out, I take it in. There should be an antidote to stop water from turning into ice: a little love. There is no difference – I delude myself – between my resistance and that of someone tortured by months in prison in a stadium, because here the institutionalized torture continues more or less everywhere these days, including Italy.

I already wish I were somewhere else with a brain less exposed to this populace which exhibits on the streets everything it can sell. A little girl sells pine-cones emptied of their kernels for hanging on a possible Christmas tree for people as poor as herself. The stalk of the cones is threaded not with a little ribbon but with a piece of soft green wool to take the place of a tassel. There is one man who sells paper glasses painted with a little spraygun and then expanses of knick-knacks and tiny terracotta objects among waxed paper covered with pieces of papaya or slices of watermelon laid out on sacking. I buy a little coloured balloon from a child of three or four and he stares at me in astonishment. I wander about like this for a while as evening falls, with the balloon dragging on the ground, as if I were numbed, trying not to think of anything.

This country has been abundantly blessed with oil deposits and agricultural potential and is on its knees as far as seven-tenths of its population is concerned. And to think that Venezuela is, as of today, the most advanced example of South American democracy. The whole country is an entrepreneurial hell for petrochemical and energy schemes liable to have a dynamic effect in the future, in the hope of breaking away from the United States or of becoming one of them in a very near future, the fifty-first state. According to Alex Ferguson, lecturer and researcher at the institute for tropical zoology in the Science Faculty of the Central University of Venezuela, seven Venezuelans out of ten and almost the whole of the rural population (the *campesinos*) live in a state of undernourishment. More than half the babies show degrees of malnutrition. Gastro-intestinal illnesses continue to be the principal cause of infantile mortality while traffic accidents are the principal cause for the population under thirty, so much so that at this rate a real generation of disabled is coming into existence (5,000 dead in 1986, but a figure of 8,000 was reached in previous years). The seriously injured in 1987 numbered 65,000. I am running these figures over in my mind while keeping up my courage in a taxi because this one overtakes indifferently on left or right, blocking the road each time for someone who thought he was craftier than him. Nor do the bends help much to prevent accidents: the raised highway which cuts through the city was built with a lefthand camber when you want to turn right and vice versa, and it wouldn't take much to fly right off the road. All the taxidrivers are in a hurry to get there, in any case there is no meter and the tariff is left to the ciribiricocacola stoked by the heat of the driver.

Professor Ferguson again: 'Two million Venezuelans of working age are unemployed or under-employed. Two out of three families and almost all the agricultural workers earn a salary below the subsistence minimum. More than half the population live in the *ranchos* or in dwellings without running water or sanitation. One family in four in the national territory lives in areas where water and light are intermittent or permanently rationed. More than a million fellow-citizens are in nuclear families whose income is less than two thousand bolívars a month.' (An average taxi ride costs 400 bolívars.) 'As you can clearly see, the reality is very different from that presented by official speeches and the State publicists. The reality is that – in spite of multi-million investments (in dollars) – the production of food for direct human consumption has constantly fallen from 1950 to today. The same can be said of the availability of drinking water, the quality of the air we breathe, the physical, mental and spiritual health of the Venezuelans, the ability to produce employees who are not bureaucrats' – the professor uses for 'bureaucracy' the illuminating expression 'craze for passing things on' – 'and then one could hold forth on the personal safety of the inhabitants of Caracas.'

In the Caracas Hilton every ten floor tiles there is a policeman with belt and pistol which draw the eye to their paunches and other very visible goods. I go to the pool to set up a seduction.

Here the slaves remain passive, they are a dangerous burden, and are all the more dangerous because no one makes it his business to give them false goals linked to false wellbeing such as we have. I explain all this to the beautiful Creole pool attendant, who is also an intellectual, later on when it is the moment for a cigarette – he had two hours off duty. He does not understand my question, 'Is there an enlightened bourgeoisie here?' – a concept which totally escapes him, and not by chance, because here in South America there are castes as in India and no caste is familiar with a conceptual framework which is not its own. 'An example of active slaves?' I ask him, since he is looking at me in a childish way. 'Metalworkers, journalists, railwaymen, insurance agents, building workers, mafiosi, people that is to say who in their own ways work for society, often making useless pyramids, but at least they don't sit idle, and I can forgive the desire to throttle the first person who turns up and has forgotten the keys to his house. A real capitalist system has nowadays the responsibility for giving work of some kind to almost everyone. In Italy, if it were otherwise a real revolution would break out. People want to feel *useful*, specially if they are keeping a seat warm or teaching things no one believes in any more. The true, great enlightened capitalists think of this alongside their profits because *all that* is their profit and peace of mind. The enlightened bourgeoisie considers the poor to be an inexhaustible mine of wealth and exploits them in a way which people then say is an intelligent way . . . But here the rich, if they could, would put a barbed-wire fence round two-thirds of the population and set fire to them.' My young pool attendant puts on his clothes and I begin to pack. If I could I would leave this very evening. I think that Italian servitude is decidedly the enlightened kind – at least in the north: the reality of the south escapes me completely, it seems to me to be a muddle of so many little South Americas inhabited by great heroes with a tear on their handkerchiefs and the best lawyer and a couple of magistrates with a weakness for the cream pastries at the bridge club.

I left with the image in my head of that girl whose brains were blown out on a balcony of a house in Southern Italy and who still has not abandoned me. I carry her with me like a suicide which infects every attempt to stay alive in spite of everything, and for a month now – two in fact – I have been trying not to shake off the delirium in my limbs which are hers at the moment when, caught in the sights, she opens her eyes wide and her little body is struck down and falls against the railing . . . Because soon I shall forget that half Italy is reduced to savagery and the other half is heading in the same direction . . . On a plane to Bogotá I leaf through the Bolivian daily with the sarcastic name *El Espectador*: 'Some 130 million of the inhabitants of Latin America and the Caribbean live in poverty. More than a quarter of them are concentrated in the sub-region of the Andes. For more than 13 million children and adolescents between 0 and 15 years life is spent in conditions of absolute poverty and neglect.' The panorama is described by Teresa Albánez, director-general of UNICEF. But here in *El Diario de Caracas* is an advertisement conceived with a verve worthy of Hollywood entrepreneurs: '*Lo sentimos muy de veras pero . . . Hay veces que nuestros servicios son necessarios – FUNERARIA MEMORIAL C.C. – Calidad en servicios imprescindibles.*' (We are really sorry but . . . sometimes our services are necessary – FUNERARIA MEMORIAL C.C. – Unbeatable quality of service.)

But I have so little time to stay among the clouds, I am already back on earth. At the Customs – what with masses of forms and visas and declarations a person has any amount of time to take X-ray photographs of twenty policemen and as many sniffer dogs (they sniff anyone coming in, you understand?) – there is an immensely old American woman who reduced the whole crew to despair because, being in a wheelchair, she wanted to take a stroll in the cabin and kept on pressing the service button and was never satisfied and if they brought her coffee said she had asked for tea and vice versa. And now, over seventy and freshly wigged à la Zsa Zsa Gabor, she wants to go ahead of everyone and is trying to persuade the steward with watery eyes that belong to the kind of perfidious people who are to be pitied even when on the point of drawing their last breath or have it drawn for them. The old crone roars that she is unwell and I, finding myself near her, say; 'Signora, please, stop shouting in my ears, it will soon be our turn,' but I don't think she has understood and says, just as if I had paid her a compliment for how well she looks: 'Young man, the best of the bread is the crumbs and I don't want to feed them to these people here,' and I willingly let her jump the queue.

If the best of the bread is the crumbs, the best of a fuck is the cigarette. And if someone doesn't smoke? All the worse for him.

And when I took out my money I had a fit of dizziness and

realized where the mad stench came from that has been accompanying me all these days – the smell of money. Colombian pesos run through your fingers like flat insects alive with a kind of permanent decay. It is a smell of boiled carrion which insinuates itself everywhere the moment you take them out of your wallet – a heavy smell in the air like when they kill the pig and then throw boiling water over it and then begin to scrape off the bristles. It is an olfactory phantom which dogs your breathing day and night in and even when you are sitting inside somewhere and least expect it, a whiff of rotten watermarked paper allowed to escape from a pocket comes and brings you together with the putrid destiny of paying for your life with the gangrenous stuff of those who have died a violent death.

Bogotá exists, divided substantially into the north (rich) and the south (poor), but it exists. On my arrival at the Tequendama Hotel I forearm myself against the welcome and the alarmist talk ('Mind you take that watch off your wrist and put it in your pocket,' and you say to the porter: 'But it's worth maybe twenty dollars,' and he says: 'The violence you suffer for a plastic watch is the same as for a Rolex') with eighteen hours of unbroken sleep; what a headache, it must be the altitude (2,600 metres). On the bedside table I am obliged to re-read a little card in the shape of a pyramid which at paragraph 3 says: 'If you are approached by individuals who say they are police or guards, before replying to their questions contact reception in the hotel.' The problem is – would they give you time? At eight twenty the first explosion or shot. I admit that I am not very enthusiastic about going out and it is also raining. I go to the Museum of Gold – probably the most astounding museum in all South America; founded in 1939, it contains thirty thousand pieces from the different cultures which occupied Colombian territory before the arrival of Columbus. After the first five thousand pieces I can't take any more of so much 'sweat of the sun', which is what gold was held to be by the tribes of the Quimbayas and the Tumacos and Calima and the Tierradentro, and arrive exhausted on the third floor with the splendid Room of the Sun. Thousands of necklaces and *poporos* (to mix the powder of marine fossils and chewed coca leaves) to represent the Spanish dream of Eldorado which never existed nor has been discovered. My head is simply elsewhere: two children there in a ditch and why did their eyes seem to be coming out of their heads? And the one that had a grown-up's jacket which came down to his feet and under it he was naked and filthy, why did he show me his teeth? Were they five, six or seven years old?

At four in the morning on Christmas Day from the eighth floor of a spacious double room, big enough for three, I see through the rain a figure lying over the low railing of the garden with its fountain and statue. The figure, which is bent double, is hardly more than a tiny bit bigger than the pile of indistinct clothes at his feet. To stand at a window and look out is not a real destiny. Mysterious appearance of outside from here – a man in a city sleeping broken in two who then straightens up a little, goes and lies down on the wet grass and curls up like a foetus and puts rags and cardboard over and under himself and does not move any more. Then Montserrat began to send the first gleams from behind the crests of the mountains. My man is still there, standing out more and more under the black of the trees, dawn is approaching. On the radio the love songs about men/women are more serious still: always the same rhymes, always a don't leave me/I won't leave you/you have left me/my life is yours/you make me die. And then in Spanish they have something particularly funereal and stupid about them: couldn't they threaten a little less in love and give shelter to the hundred thousand madmen and tramps under forty who are scattered over the wet lawns of the city at night? Then they do their sums on the radio: there are no fewer than a hundred hostages in the hands of guerrillas in their various factions The figures are approximate here too, just as when they announce the death from the nth attack in the parishes of Medellín or Cali or Barranquilla. They arrived in a few units armed with submachine guns and they killed ten people including priests, children and the faithful, perhaps twelve of them, maybe twenty, and they took away the money-box with the Christmas alms – twenty dollars in all. It feels as if only part of the population has ever been counted. But guerrilla warfare has not yet reached Bogotá, and the CIA (Centre for Immediate Aid, thought up by General Fajardo a year ago and composed of young soldiers quartered in nice wooden huts here and there in the various *barrios*) is having an unexpected success in aiding – and in the long run warning – the citizen under attack. The young men look more like nice boy-scouts than soldiers and in their free time – to add to their image of collective trust – tend makeshift gardens round the huts. In other words they are the exact opposite of the macho-repressive figure of the South American policeman.

Much has been written about presidential power in Colombian institutions and very little about the power of the military which – the bad habit of slaves – is at its service but on certain occasions determines it. The higher levels of the army in Colombia are not associated with economic power, they do not constitute either an aristocracy or a haute bourgeoisie but a middle class, unlike in Argentina and Brazil, for example, where the military are owners and administrators of great enterprises. In Colombia they don't manage big mining or metallurgical companies and are only directors of State enterprises connected in some way with the armed forces. But the Colombian military's lack of real economic power does not stop them from feeling totally identified with the interests of the bourgeoisie, particularly in its defence against the guerrillas who apply pressure for a change in the oligarchical system, or against mass institutional claims such as strikes or the people's marches against unemployment.

The army defends the patrimony of the bourgeoisie and the institutions which preserve it and protect the status quo more because it corresponds to the ideological fetish of the anti-popular subculture than for real profit – that is why it is seen by the people as the main enemy: because the people are right.

I take a *buseta* and am driven about aimlessly – but I know what I want to see: the groups of children who in order to survive have joined up with the madmen and formed bands of thieves. There are also young girls, all the foetuses which in some way have survived from the filth in which the child-mothers threw them, prostitutes for the most part between twelve and fifteen, children from the countryside or from the *ranchos* abandoned here when two or three years old, to live on sewer animals, mice and dogs bashed to death in their sleep with a stone, or fed by some madman or tramps, in the hands of pederasts. Liliana, an agent of the CIA, tells me on the telephone that 80 per cent are syphilitic and provides me with a figure I am supposed to believe: that there are probably not more than 300. So there will be not less than 3,000.

Is it possible to arrange an appointment with General Fajardo?

Bits of paper in the wind and groups of begging youths, black as chimneysweeps, dragging behind them pieces of polystyrene in a gully thick with liquids from outfalls. Their little carts and supermarket trolleys jump out and in, overflowing with little plastic bags. I get out of the *buseta,* I stand watching them, I make a move to get closer but four of them advance on me threateningly. I throw them a handful of change and make my getaway. The stone says 'Calle de la Alegría' (Street of Happiness): it is invaded by people queuing to go and see *Jaws 3;* a little further on there is a cinema where they are showing *Hablame sucio,* that is 'Talk dirty to me', an imported Italian porn film which I must have missed. A girl with a naked belly and the bundle of a new baby is the very last person in the queue, which is at least two hundred metres long. She holds it in her arms as if it were a tabby cat, now she is holding it between her shoulder and her neck. She throws away a piece of chewing gum. The population is very young. On a shutter they have painted: 'Indiferencia = Complicidad'. The main street is lined with little stoves and grills and barrows belonging to itinerant vendors selling boiled maize, spits of meat with a paprika crust and huge wafers filled with mango jam. Hare Krishna is here too: among these citizens of Bogotá there is a European idiot with his little bells, one of those people you would pick out from among the thousands whom he even tries to imitate in the colour of his skin. They are making the usual movements back and forwards with little hops and singing a monotonous tune with a touch of the rumba, then they distribute leaflets and one of them begins to speak: about incarnation, also a profession of anticommunism which goes very well with propaganda for metempsychosis in general.

I come up against the proud figure of a stray dog standing motionless on the pavement. It stares at me: the dogs look like hyenas here, they have something disturbing – something human about them. Mangy and inquisitive, they do not go about in packs but each one on its own. Their eyes are not normal, they scan you with a quick cunning glance, and the question they dart at you is so incommensurate that you feel lost as if faced by the Sphinx. They ask you: Are you still alive? And for how long? There are some parts of you that interest me – tell me where to find you when you aren't on your guard. At this moment down there are four sleeping figures: two on the softness of vegetable rubbish, one in a basket (a girl who continually scratches herself and keeps pulling a blanket over her head), one on the ground who has nothing either under or over him and who you might say from his helicoidal position has been trying to cover himself with himself. It is difficult to believe that we all are subject to the same biology. I am standing here by the parapet of a bridge and look down and ask myself where I went wrong. Yesterday, Christmas Eve, the number of violent deaths was forty-five – fifteen killed by the guerrillas alone. On the other hand 1987 was the year of industrial recovery: there was a growth rate of 5 per cent and inflation barely reached 29 per cent. If there were only three hundred of them what would be the problem? If we count the foreign embassies, all run by sensible, child-loving people, several young couples still without heirs, a hundred of them could easily be adopted by the newly married, newly appointed embassy staff, the other two hundred by local industrialists, who could at least count on offspring who will never be lacking in grit and jungle sense.

If I could take a couple to Italy I would do it with my eyes shut. They are ill and who cares? They are infested and what with? Some are HIV-positive and so? The whim to do oneself a good turn through children knows no limits. People who love no one love children madly. I may be a mother manquée or an egoist but I start from the principle that the further an adult keeps away from infants the better it is for the infants: I don't just love them because they are weak and vulnerable, but because they exist and that's that. And if they already exist one might as well give them a hand to live and withdraw it when they become invaders. That is how I see it – but perhaps it is too easy: I have no children of my own and perhaps this attachment of mine to the dispossessed is too abstract. The fact is that I go back to the hotel and have another unpleasant sleep to put out of my head that other old and true and new story: a car stops in some village or other, they take one or two on board, they put them in private clinics and bring them back in a couple of weeks – lacking an eye or a kidney or a lung.

The waiter brings me up a succulent tray with all the strange things on the menu: I did it on purpose to try with my hand and palate all the injustice for which I too have perhaps long been the executioner without knowing it and the waiter says to me: 'Don't you feel well?' and I say brazenly: 'No – I have only filled two pillow slips with tears,' and he says: 'Eh, far from home – ' and I say 'No – here in Bogotá,' and I accompany him to the door. Then weeping I spread the first slice of bread with scrambled egg and caviare. Down in the hall I meet a lady from Tuscany talking to a woman-friend and I interrupt her to say: 'How nice to hear Italian. On holiday?' and the lady says: 'Yes, we are doing here, then San Augustín, Cali, Medellín, Villa Leyva, to get an idea of Colombia and then get it over with.' I am left speechless.

The city is papered with enormous hoardings with the faces of politicians competing for the *alcaldia* (the mayorship) of Bogotá. That of María Eugenia Rojas, who seems to be haranguing at the top of her voice, is red with a white face and pink lips. It looks the prettiest to me. In Colombia – apart from a weak opposition party, the Unión Patriotica – there is only one slight difference to mark the ideological watershed between the two existing parties, the conservative and the liberal: the first maintains a counter-reformation relationship with the Church, with which it forms a single political body, and the other is a tiny bit more progressive and instead of going to Mass every day goes only on the days of obligation. Here it is not parties that confront each other (exactly as in the USA and in England not so many decades ago) but men, charismas of concentrated individualism to whom belonging to a party is almost like an obligatory fig-leaf, not a whole costume. In a few months the election of the Mayor of Bogotá will be upon them (an office which in terms of prestige and economic power of decision is scarcely second to the presidency of the republic), which will see at the very most a confrontation between two children of the inner circle: Andrés Pastana (son of the ex-president) and María Eugenia Rojas (daughter of the general who held the post of dictator from 1953 to 1957 at the wish of the government parties themselves). The first is conservative and the second liberal and both are admired by the side which is formally opposed to them. María Eugenia, as she is familiarly called, even by her detractors who find the only thing wrong with her is having a cunt instead of what would be right in politics, although not favourite in the opinion polls, enjoys the feminist magnetic power over women and could at the last moment upset the dumbheads in her favour.

And the central theme of the clash turns on this question: to renegotiate or not renegotiate the foreign debt? The *foreign* debt of Bogotá amounts to 290,000 million pesos (1 dollar = 260 pesos) which costs 75,000 million pesos in interest a year, while Colombia's *external* debt (so not between industry and private commerce but between governments, not least the United States and the Japanese ones, who are particularly involved on the Brazilian front too) in global terms is 15,000 milliard dollars, interest on which now equals 43 per cent of the exports – that is to say at the danger mark. Another recurrent topic in the electoral campaign is the personal safety of the inhabitants of Bogotá, the fight against the drugs traffic (which will suffer a severe blow to its credibility following the freeing from prison – on the sly – of one of the Ochoas), and health services which are almost as nonexistent as public security.

A lexical curiosity: in view of the speed at which these loans are requested and obtained they are called Jumbo and Concorde Loans, while for the current year they will work on a loan already forecast for December (and which seems to be a loan camouflaged so as to honour the interest already owed) which will be called Challenger.

It is no fairytale that the Colombian drug traffickers proposed to the government to clear the foreign debt *on the nail* provided they outlawed the extradition of arrested traffickers from Colombia to the American courts and allowed them to act with the utmost freedom of movement in their internal trade. It seems that the government hesitated a little before the big summit in

Miami with these big bosses of whom it is whispered that they are so very professional that they have never in their lives sniffed a grain of cocaine. If it is really true that the demand for cocaine in the States alone amounts to more than 1,000 kilos per day, one can understand that these indefatigable workers commuting in helicopters from the Andes plantations to the Bolivian refineries (while the coastal trade in Brazil has been taken over by the Lebanese) not only have no time to sniff it up their noses but not even to inhale it.

I go up to the house of the Libertador, where in fact Bolívar very seldom set foot and which was lived in by his lover. Bolívar came here to hide secret documents in the secretaires and the sofa-legs, and to hang more gigantic portraits of himself; since he was 1 metre 58 cm tall, he had pinched from France – along with colonial baroque – Napoleonic *grandeur.* Whereas at the beginning of the nineteenth century any amount of marble was imported from Carrara, not a single scrap is imported any more and Italy is allowed to export only low-tech machinery. The guide is called Consuelo and looks like a Swiss nun. Since she likes me and asks if I don't want go to the salt cathedral in Zipaquirà, she also goes so far as to tell me: 'Ask for a witness if the police want to search your room for drugs, because if they insist and there is none they make sure they put some there – if you knew how high the demand is for careless unprotected scapegoats – they have to show that they're doing something!'

I go to the Italian embassy to see if there are any Italians in the Colombian prisons apart from the Italian attachés themselves shut away behind doors and windows with guards and gratings. It feels as if they are about to move house. The Italian ambassador with the foreign name is packing his suitcases and is very taken up with refusing the latest cocktail party invitations. His assistant receives me – I shall call him Dr Mazarino – who has just about a half-idea about who I am and yet opens up with political confidences of a certain seriousness and personal risk even if he had learned them by heart – and which, since they arouse my respect, prevents me from putting them in his mouth at the same pace. The consul or ambassador arrives, sweating, corpulent, in his shirt-sleeves, half on the point of departure, half on the point of declaring war: they have given him a very quiet post in Europe and, being used to hot climates, he is not at all happy. He reels off a few excuses because not even he has the least idea of my reputation as a writer and they will never believe my real embarrassment when I try to make them understand that it is a relief to me that they don't realize it. Otherwise I perhaps wouldn't even be there pretending to share their interests, which are tied up with the preservation of the Italian ministerial oligarchy – it is the first association that springs to politicians' minds when they think: 'So he's one of us!' as they address the first intellectual who happens to pass through and who is 'in the swim.'

Doctor Mazarino says of the little fish in the net whom every so often the local police has to pretend to arrest for a while: 'There are three of them – two men and a woman. I am convinced that the two men are inside because the amount they had was too modest – do you mean to say that people come here to be so stingy? The fate of the woman is more interesting: it is the second time she has been arrested, the sly one, the first time they gave her thirty-nine months so that they could expel her at once, because if they are given forty they have to serve the whole time. She waits two years, in the meantime she becomes an addict and then she has a nasty new nose made, then they catch her once more at the Customs with a kilo of cocaine in her suitcase and there was the aggravating circumstance that she had entered with a false passport. If instead of making her a new nose they had remade her fingerprints it would have been better, and now she has to serve thirty-nine plus thirty-nine and Italy has washed its hands of her.'

'Does no one ever go to visit her – a relative I mean?'

'Yes, we go sometimes but you know – we take her food and other things – stuff for personal hygiene – it would be worse with money. In the meantime it comes out that she has – she was getting thinner, was vomiting the whole time . . . Not just some crisis over not eating. They have isolated her . . . in short she's finished. She is thirty-two.'

'She has got AIDS?'

'Yes, she's a skeleton now and can't even stand up. The classical love-story. She told one of our women employees how it began – because of love, as usual.'

'Like all our women terrorists. Goodness knows why the most aberrant ideologies are born from a particularly good fuck which after a while – the idiots – becomes "motivated". And he obviously hasn't been seen or heard of since.'

'As I have told you – as solitary as a dog. She keeps on shouting "Mamma! Mamma!" She doesn't even mention the name of the man. Out of fear.'

'Of what?'

'That they may come to know who he is. It's as if she were defending him to the end, you understand? And now all she wants is a little morphine or to die as quickly as possible. From her photos you'd say she was once very beautiful and even happy. We sometimes go and protest because they don't even change her any more and she doesn't have the energy to go alone to the toilet. But there's not much one can do. A strange fate, don't you think?'

I have two little sleeps on it – each of six hours.

In his study which is overflowing with brass knobs and flags, the forty-year-old General Fajardo, a real eyeful even for the least concupiscent eye, after a talk of about an hour, he in shirt-sleeves, brown hair on his knuckles and so close that I have to resist spasmodically the desire to touch him, tells me, squandering that dizzying smile of his after which I have to limit myself to being overcome by a monumental state of trepidation (that is why I am not reporting any of the conversation – don't remember a single word of it): 'If these children interest you so much there is a way of seeing them at close quarters.'

And I swallow and very nearly come out with: 'And what about you?'

Liliana, Adriana and Angela are the three policewomen who have the job of taking some real food to these zombie children. Since it is impossible to get near them one by one during the day they collect them, let's say, in their sleep in hovels or cellars in the suburbs or districts under construction. We arrange for me to accompany them tonight. While waiting for this and for my crush to wear off I watch TV. Cartagena, the Heroic City, today has become the Rimini of Colombia and now is regurgitating with beauty contests. There is even one at Cali. Miss Coffee and then Miss Something Else at Medellín. But here are the beauties of Miss Colombia parading in bathing costumes so cut away that, bob's your uncle, they get sucked up in between the buttocks, and there's much embarassed fumbling of little hands with lacquered nails round their buttocks to get them out. It would be easier if the candidate who is behind did the favour to the one in front of her and so on. Soap-opera beauties, bubbly hair, never a tiny wrinkle – sometimes they are accompanied not only by their mothers but by the mayor of their district. It is postwar Italy. Interviewed, all of them have dreams: a white dress and to work in television – shrewd and up to date – they know that no one works in films any more. Several become television announcers, and in fact here is one ex-Miss Colombia coming to tell us how many died today and remind us that the famous painter Belancourt has been in the hands of kidnappers for three months and they know neither why they snatched him nor whether he is dead or alive nor what they intend to do with him, since the family has not even had a request for a ransom. Then football: here, as in Caracas, they follow the fortunes of Italian football with trepidation and on Mondays have all the matches recorded. The players have been saying the same two or three things since the Middle Ages, I think. There is no evidence that there was ever a player who had a fourth thing to say. Pop-corn and *circenses* and the same thing over and over again.

At half-past ten I get on to the truck with a male driver and the three very pretty policewomen. There isn't a lot of food: in reply to my question about contributions in hard cash to this public assistance service I suspect that it amounts to a whip-round between them and that is all. They are very vague and shrug. Then there was the most horrible scene I have ever had to take on board: by the light of electric torches we have penetrated into an abandoned building and they were all sleeping and were bundled one on top of the other, little animals taken by surprise, black or naked, little creatures who were suddenly happy because the girls had come to visit them and all with their *boxa* in the hands – a tin full of vinyl glue (exactly like the kind carpenters use) which they all inhale from morning to evening, the drug of poor children, the dummy that deadens the bite of hunger and cold – and of fear. When they are having a very hard time and are particularly hungry or cold they swallow a piece after chewing it well. The first things to burst are their little lungs. That is why those two in the ditch had staring eyes. This evening there is only one little girl but it is not possible to pick her out, it is all dark and they are all munching away and shouting exultantly out of their rags and one for a moment abandons his head on the breast of a girl or another comes and touches her hair and then flees because all you can see on the wall are dark shadows of little outstretched arms or clusters of heads indifferent and unmoving. Let's get away from here, I say to myself, let's pretend not to have been here, all that I lacked was to see this, and yet I only pointed my torch upwards. I felt the whole rhythm of my inner organs become faster, shall I never manage to develop the emotional detachment of the perfect observer? Why must it be a question every time of *your* life, *your* death? Why did you come here? I had to. And I knew it all already. I had to see what a large part of Italy is turning into.

In his log Christopher Columbus wrote of the Indians: '*Son la meyor gente del mundo y mas sana, aman a sus projimos como a si miimos . . . son fieles y sin codicia de lo ajen.*' (They are the best and most healthy people in the world, they love their neighbours as themselves . . . they are faithful and without coveting what belongs to others.) That is to say they did not even have a linguistic or moral code to express the concept of alien, of foreign. Another person who, confining himself to thinking he was only an artist of the ocean, made a wonderful discovery and in words (above all *sincere* ones) expressed all his respect for the peoples while his shipmates were beginning to profane their tombs and create ad hoc new, flaming Christian cemeteries. To my constant preoccupation with the connection between the intellectual and society (between *the aesthetic navigator* and the *ethical* stagnant water) María Eugenia Rojas gives a direct reply in an interview with a daily paper. Question: 'Have you any plans for cultural development?' Answer: 'It is odd how personal insecurity and all the other symptoms of social malaise are a cultural problem in the widest sense of the word. If we foster a participatory community culture we have made a big advance toward the solution of this problem. Because culture is not only the consumption of aesthetic objects but nothing less than the global existence itself of a community.'

At Zipaquirá the cathedral is an immense mountain of salt excavated to a depth of twenty metres, and the only church in the world in which there is no water in the baptismal font – it would evaporate. Passing in front of one of the many altars I do this with my finger and put it to my lips: the shrine tastes of beef cubes. A church of cubes.

Then I go down to the market – I hate little markets, obligatory goals and the same everywhere even in Addis Ababa – and at once I come across an unexpected festival atmosphere, the women call to me from all sides to their roasted tripe and blood puddings and boiled corn and black bean soups and the anxiety of this stay of mine is dissipated a little. What comes towards me in a determined way is a black woman – neither old nor young – as thin as a rake, with a white turban knotted in the centre. She is carrying a tray bigger than herself with sweetmeats filled with honey and cries out to me: 'Ah, the Bogotan men, all dandies,' thinking I am from the city, and then in a lower voice but still too loud because a dozen or so of the pedlars sitting crosslegged on the ground begin to laugh before she has finished: *'Tengo la cuca negra, tengo la cuca negra, comprame la cuca, comprame la cuca negra!'* (I have a black sweet, I have a black sweet, buy my sweet, buy my black sweet!) And it is only when I get back home that I understand that this sly woman with her tiger's canine teeth maybe meant by *cuca* her browned sweetmeat.

In the papers, sketches of the faces of young women who have disappeared: a group of three for example, Diana Marcela Mendoza, eight years old, and her mother and aunt. *'Desaparecidas – Ayúdame a encontrarlas*!' (Lost – help me to find them.) They had taken a *buseta*, they were supposed to go on a journey to the north, they had little money with them and never arrived at their destination, they have disappeared, lost for two weeks – for ever. It is from this sense of existential precariousness that the emotional fury I read on people's faces comes: to live everything here and quickly, love, hatred, jealousy, the lust for power and wealth, not to wait till tomorrow for anything, because in a moment a stray bullet in the air, a round-up, a paramilitary attack, a thief quicker to pull his knife than you, a banal squabble in the street, a coup d'état and you're dead. In the last two years five hundred Communists of the Patriotic Union were killed by drug-traffickers and the extreme Right. (Communists of the *extreme left, decent* people here say disgustedly, but they are simply simple Communists who are seriously trying to restart the agrarian reform and support the mayor, fight the drug traffic and snatch the peasants from the hands of the guerrilla formations.) A few months ago the head of the party, Pardo Leal, was murdered. Aria Carrizosa, the ex-minister of justice, has gone so far as to give a certain political legitimation to these indiscriminate murders and hence to the more than two hundred armed committees for self-defence with picturesque names, with a great deal of reactionary chic on the lines of Saviours of the Fatherland, and of anticommunist fanaticism that in Italy would be bad taste even at a Rotary dinner. An odd fact: Carrizosa threw away his career *at home* because of a banal scandal (the illegal importing of a Rolls-Royce from the country where he had previously been ambassador) and his place having been taken by Murtra, he went back to being an ambassador until the waters subsided – that is to say have been muddied again in his favour. It is really amusing how Colombian ministers in disgrace recycle themselves (on their own and thanks to the power of the Families more than to that of the individual) into ambassadors and ambassadors into ministers. In this sense one has to recognize that they enjoy greater elasticity than the Italian ones who go to and fro between a few ministries along with the whole cabinet.

When a man is neither afraid of nor desires death the world ought to want to know more about it: the world should love only what it no longer feels itself to be represented in and, in the bitter struggle to make its own something it finds repugnant because it does not mirror it, allows it to shatter the stratified illusion of its identity and . . . at least brings it up to date if it does not enrich it. When one talks of history one should specify that we are dealing with a phantasmal grafting of the history of animals, which are no longer truly *such*, and that of men, who have failed when faced with being the sons of God. History is that of a hybrid which has falsified its genealogical tree to such a point that it can no longer climb it. Man will remain an imperfect animal and therefore in grave danger, because he does not know how to defend himself from his own psyche which, after centuries of training, is still no great shakes and gives itself airs the more it is suffocated in itself, in its petty nature which is so fragile and weak that he actually has to hold out the prospect of somewhere in the beyond which can erect an immortal altar to his ridiculous blunders down here. What one lives remains a mystery. Values are a pearling of morning frosts to trace the course of which raises more and more smoke. *For ever* is a concept which does not apply to us just now, individually; it is a signpost set up beyond the range of our possibilities only to tell us to listen and understand *in the present*. Even a reflection is enough to make me vibrate with eternity, a gleam of light on a pool of water. If I had been hidden underwater in a whale I would have crossed all the frontiers of my existence; just as I find myself keeping awake an unknown humanity when I am asleep, so certain sleeps are constantly dedicated to me in various parts of the world. They think of me when the water closes after the dive over the blond head and the white heels. The head re-emerges and smiles elsewhere. But I am happy just the same – it will smile to someone else but it will smile to someone. End of the dialectical dream, typical of every time I have to take off and fly.

Manaus, jungle of Indians and Italians! Of electrical household appliances without VAT, ex-mayors, traders, businessmen and dentists – all Italians in general. But before embarking on the crossing to this traditional binominal Amazonia/good old Italy I want to relive once again one of the most beautiful love stories I have ever witnessed. I am about to board the 22.30 plane from Bogotá to Manaus coming from Mexico and am getting ready to celebrate New Year's Eve on the plane. The plane is already ready for takeoff, and given the circumstances there are very few of us at Gate 7, and when she appeared from the back of the semidark corridor we all held our breath and not only I but all those present fell silent as amid the muted propellers we heard her steps one by one re-echo, beating time with her slim heels. With a loose-limbed and refined gait she appeared to us at first like a vertical black thundercloud and then when her tall figure, swaying its hips slightly, had detached itself from the cloud and was already smiling ahead as if to the whole world, *she* appeared in all her glory. Her hair, chestnut and loose, with a not too symmetrical fringe, a beautiful oval slightly smoothed from the cheekbones to the chin, thick lashes and a nose with a slight and extremely delicate curve. We waited motionless and embarrassed and someone took out his handkerchief, passed it over his neck and spat into it a flood of excess saliva, we waited, as I was saying, and counted five, four, three, and followed impatiently the imperceptible flutter of the blouse with the half-length sleeves, black over tight black trousers that came to just above the naked ankles . . . but she passed through the entrance and her smile became more specific, more focused in a precise direction, and there he was, a pilot from our plane. Then they were already side by side and without even embracing her, without even kissing her on the lips or mouth, he took her by the waist and whisked her into the plane. He – shit! – has a fleshy mouth, a square jaw, is fair-haired and of course has blue eyes, suddenly excited so that they have a tinge of yellow like pumas as he made way for her through the stewardesses on the ground and on board.

And now we are in flight and she (without a single jewel and in all not more than a few hundred lire of makeup) is nibbling in the non-smoking area at the largesse which the company unceasingly provides for us in the business class. I never eat or drink in a plane, apart from water – I let her eat for me, perhaps one day she will tell me if the food was good. As a pledge of love she will spend this midnight as best she can in the only possible way – flying with him a few steps away, since he could not get out of flying. He has a goal out of duty, she out of love has the same as he – Brazil, Rio de Janeiro, then a half-day stop, and then Montevideo, Buenos Aires, who knows. She is not only a woman, she is one of these people who, when the papers make you feel the unworthiness of the world that has given birth to them, and that nothing that exists around us is worthy of this emanation, has the confident beauty of truly beautiful women of any age (whether twenty-five or forty years of age of which she can give another woman fifteen), beautiful by nature. There is not a shadow of affectation or phoney sexiness in her gestures, in the affection with which she caresses a child who is going to and fro, in how she thanks the hostess who hands her a blanket, in how she manages to be at the same time detached and thankful for everything. And he has already come out of the cabin two or three times to drink a toast with her while she raises her *flûte* and swallows perhaps four bubbles and then, gazing at him intensely, a long and decided sip which could give unforgettable shivers to the most hardened of voyeurs. Clearly he is a gentleman who does not suffer from premature ejaculation because they look at each other burning up fire to stoke it the more, they have sex with their eyes and resist, they do not kiss – out of discretion and a sense of public spirit with regard to us passengers, who are alone, lacking appetite, a depressed couple with the woman constantly tossing and turning among emerald-green fingertips all lumps and bumps, one man reading a thriller, my new photographer who doesn't even talk about women, an uneasy Korean woman with a peaceful and contented baby in her arms, apart from me who am cheek to cheek with the Rio Negro down there in the dark and the fringes of luminescent foam on its shores – I presume.

And when we landed in Manaus she kept her face turned away and I pretended to fumble with my bag to see her lips without lipstick and her nostrils. She kept her face leaning on the arm-rest and her hair completely screened her and then through a lock of it (because she was pretending to herself that she was sleeping, as often happens in a plane) I saw an eye open and look at me and immediately shut again and she did like this with her hand and put all her hair to one side and made me the gift of her profile of an Indian goddess sharing the vainly sighing destinies of those like me who have no intensity to share. Perhaps at table she is a specialist in small-talk but there is no doubt that she is a generous and active lover or wife – because tonight in this flight of hours which, after all, has nothing to do with her, she is there, was there, has been there, and he will never forget it. They may even become separated but in his life this journey of hers has been one of the most important stages in the existence of fair-haired men with blue eyes. As with me – once, years ago, I asked someone if he would come and pick me up at an airport and he came and I have never forgotten it – and now that I think back to it, if I hadn't told him he wouldn't even have got there by himself.

In the night the taxi runs along under a cloak of humidity and occasional fireworks towards the Da Vinci Hotel. The revelry of New Year's Eve has already died away everywhere, I have forgotten this parenthesis in real rose-pink and the graffito read in the toilet in the airport at Bogotá: 'Do something for your country – kill a policeman.' The Da Vinci is sinister – dusty plastic palms – a porter stupefied by sleep and a life of resigned noises through clenched teeth; everything smells like liquid cat-shit. After an eternity with some Italian tourists trying in vain to phone Italy (there is no switchboard here and the operator is none other than the same exhausted porter when he decides to disappear into the back office), I arrive at my room, and when I open it I am assailed by a stench of vomit and dry-frozen shit, as if it had been imprisoned there for decades in that mud-coloured moquette. I open the window, holding my breath, from outside the stench of the kitchen comes to mingle with the first, the ventilator is out of order, I rush down and protest at the top of my voice. The porter, who is young, a member of the tribe of tired whites, jerks his chin to say No, there is no other room free – he doesn't even say 'Sorry', there isn't one and that is that. I insist, I say for goodness' sake, I can sleep anywhere, even on the floor, but the air has to be breathable, please find me, you must find me a corner away from this dunghill. A room turns up – I open the door: underpants, empty tins, little bags of food scattered on the moquette, toilet articles: 'You see it is already taken,' and he is quite unperturbed. He lets me brood on my rage for another half-hour, I don't give in, and in the end I have a decent room with a tolerable smell of feet and ammonia. In the morning I find they have no lockers: I phone the agency and book a room at the Tropical Hotel outside the city on the river.

While I am waiting outside the hotel for a taxi to deign to turn up I chat with an elderly couple from Catania. I say: 'What a disgusting hotel!' and she says: 'Fortunately we are stopping only for the night' and I say: 'What nice places are you going to?' and he says: 'We are going to Rio partly by jeep partly by canoe' and I say: 'What an undertaking!' and she who, if she were to go out in Catania after six in the evening, would disguise herself as a Capuchin friar and would slip her money into her brassiere says: 'We'll do about four hundred kilometres a day, we'll stop and be put up well in villages' and he says: 'At least that's what they told us in Italy' and she says: 'Adventure is an adventure' and I say: 'There was an inquiry last year into the hundreds of rash tourists whom certain agencies send first into certain places as guinea-pigs, I don't know exactly how many died' and he says: 'They say the spiders are the most dangerous' and she says 'And the mosquitoes' and I say: 'Are there many of you?' and he says: 'Yes, all from Catania, at least here we become friends' and she says: 'I'll suffer from the heat' and he says 'We'll go hunting butterflies.' Who knows if they were ever heard of again?

The Tropical Hotel is a city constructed round a circular swimming-pool, and I hate circular swimming-pools. Between yesterday and today two hundred and fifty, I repeat two hundred and fifty Italians arrived here, over forty, all respectable. An Italian whom I shall call the Monster from Florence is saying to a couple of Italians from Sardinia: ' . . . I have a pistol, loaded, but in the office not at home. At home a rifle does me,' and the Sardinian lady says: 'These days what one would need are nice little guns on the gateposts. We . . .' But I am distracted by a couple of faces which I seem to have seen already in the splendour of youth and who now – above adipose tissue and drooping tits, protected by mirror sunglasses – have sucked in their lips and show off like successful scoundrels: they will be the usual heads of public works departments from the provinces and authorized salesmen of reconditioned cars. Everyone who had told me astonishing things about Manaus – a city on the river with a million inhabitants which is more and more adrift and flanked by oil refineries – now that I think of it all had something wrong with them: a jeweller with the mentality of a disc-jockey, male oculists with a smell of incest, a mixed-up girl who had overcome the curse of heroin thanks to a course of white wine and soda water and had seen that pretty film shot in these parts, *Fitzcarraldo*, ten times. And here there is a fine selection of those shameless types who are over the top in everything including good manners. It is incredible the number of people in Italy who manage to get a position without ever staying in their job.

In two days I have not seen a single tourist of *my people* with a book in their hand.

The Female Monster, wife of the Monster of Florence, with a Botticelli face portrayed among the bookies of the Cascine in moments of panic, has with her a book with a blue cover entitled *Romanza*, which will be, I imagine, about the tearful life of the crocodiles raised in tanks by Gucci. The old and worn couple who arrived in *pareo* and Bermuda shorts are from the province of Avellino, she wearing her heart-shaped emeralds mounted in brilliants and emerald rings, a little younger than him, the same in every respect as Maria Pia Fanfani but twenty years younger, which she wears well, but straw-blonde, with the contrite air of the post-earthquake millionaires, a jewel of reconstruction, ready for anything, even to being the faithful wife for life. They stretch on their lilos as if on a bed of thorns, order two coconuts. He is squat, his face hewn with an axe, a frown on his brow his basic attitude towards society and the wickedness of this world, a belly that spills out three times above his too tight Bermuda shorts, a man of few words; she eternally worried about how to find a subject to shake him out of his accidie. She strokes his belly a little and his patent-leather belt a little, she takes his hand and talks and talks to him, who is arrogant, indifference as a defence to the bitter end, she with a tear here and another there, one of those women whose only topic must be what she is experiencing, what she is feeling and whether her only son is screwing enough women in Rome, where he will be studying public administration in a modest *garçonnière* in Parioli – and then she will modulate her voice to elaborate over and over again on people's envy, the greed of poor relations and a secure old age.

He lies looking round him like a bullock: without moving his neck, with the hateful air of someone who has too many skeletons in the cupboard and not enough new ones being delivered. He seems not to listen to her and enjoys making her feel that she is on loan for twenty years. He responds to her usual overexcited speeches, heart in hand, with the haughty superiority of someone who has already replied to them once and for all. Then she looks into the void before her, worn out by her mechanical jumping up and down, tired of conquering him, she concentrates fearfully on the void of worry in order to find as soon as possible a new way of repeating the same things – exactly as in the plane she let go his hand and turned her head towards the window and raised a triangle of her handkerchief to the corner of one eye. When dinner came – the immense dinner – he made a gesture of refusal to the hostess (oh, the untidy fifty-year-old hostesses of Varig! a fine example of the creole with a wobbly tooth who, having been there since 1963, you feel could lose her patience in the twinkling of an eye and give you a tremendous slap in the face at the second glass of water – but then you forgive them everything, good, kind, old ladies on their twin-motored broom-sticks). While the ex-beauty who has learned to be in the world timidly asks and asks again – four *flûtes* of champagne, eight cakes – he skips the lobster in disgust (and feels a touch of bad luck about flying) but she dives into it ('with another spoonful of Dutch sauce,' she said because she had a moment's failure of memory on the tip of her tongue and, being unable to say *béarnaise*, placed Berne, which has nothing to do with it, in Holland). Then she finishes off the mixed grill, the Russian salad, the cucumber salad in yoghurt, the sweet (he will consent to *crème caramel* with coconut milk) and then, refuelled, she starts up again with her boring account of her bejewelled suffferings.

But the most significant couple of tourists at the Tropical Hotel and probably in the whole of Amazonia is a seventy-year-old father, in the Yankee style of an Italian provincial town, tennis shoes and socks up to the knees white like everything else, with his son of between thirty and forty, dressed exactly the same as he but in light grey. In fact they are not a couple but a trio but she, the mother, the wife, the accused, overdressed and looking covered up in her purple frock, keeps her distance and never intervenes in the unending talk between the two men who walk hand in hand up and down the length of the hotel for two kilometres – to get to my room I have to travel eight hundred metres.

The son is feeble-minded, walks in a monkeylike way, and from his mouth downwards there extends a glandular malformation on the lines of the elephant man. They walk indefatigably between the lobby the bank the boutique the pool and the garden and every so often the idiot stops and seems to rebel weakly at some prohibition. He would like to go into the water (unaware that the shafts of hatred from the Woman from Avellino have turned it into chloric acid) or to clamber up the mangrove in the hot house to catch the captive toucan, and his father takes his hand again, squeezes it a second and with a voice of atavistic matter-of-factness warns him: 'No, no, Luigino junior, you'll wet your clothes, no, no, Luigino junior, you'll dirty your hands.' The carpet of diminutives is unrolled as an antidote to the guilt, never recognized, of having begotten him too late in life. I can see that she, some twenty years younger than her husband, would let things slide, perhaps would even let them slide for ever. And the three resume their infernal circular walk, appearing and disappearing at all hours in the corridors and on the stairs, the idiot junior who always wants to go somewhere else to make his disgrace complete, and the good senior – certainly from the textile trade – who always takes him where *he* wants to go and who doesn't want to go anywhere but to kill time in front of and behind a glass coffin. And she this afternoon is all in crumpled beige linen, modest, as if she wanted to make herself a little less visible than this morning and follows the couple's trips, a one-time great beauty with average education and solid principles, who wonders if it was worth while marrying for love someone so much older than herself with whom, for her own reasons, she has finally agreed that she is congenitally to blame, she who scatters her existence between a fashion show and a holiday among the American Indians (kept in a vacuum somewhere till they have to dance or sell arrows and feather head-dresses), of whom she has become, day after day, the guardian shadow, the schizophrenic shadow of the hearth that excludes her.

A highly coloured delta-winged plane cuts through the sky, circles over the round pool, comes lower heedlessly crushing us under its boastful noise; a black woman shouts to her friend who is at a table with three good-for-nothings who are somewhat snobbish where experience of sex is concerned (you know – AIDS – as if it could even come to such unworthy and inexpert people who for three years have been screwing away from home, confining themselves to rubbing it between clitoris and navel, reckless characters who have taken out insurance cover). The three men, who are very, very, very vulgar, will be: one of them an upper-class Socialist who has not renounced the gold chain and crucifix, one a petty bourgeois right-wing dentist from Sassuolo, and the third a designer from Rezzoaglio, boon companion of the second who is trying to involve the first seeing that, the way things are these days, there won't be more than half the pleasure. The friend called by the others does not answer and the three feel and touch her in a friendly way as if sipping the amber skin before the final drink (we are talking of two does with swimsuits so transparent that you can see the stitches of their appendicitises and one is shaved as smooth as the back of my hand and the other hairy enough for two). 'Liquor, Liquor,' the first keeps on shouting, because, whether it is her first or second name, that is what the girl with the three men is called and since this morning has done nothing but ask for a finger of Coca-Cola and three of rum. It is obvious that Liquor is no longer in a state to reply or to keep at bay the six paternal hands which are more exhibitionist than desirous – this isn't just a literary sketch! This is humanity and there is nothing to add if not other sketches. (And at last I managed to say what the Indian goddess in the plane was like, I have called her Lilith because I was not satisfied and all these days have been searching about for an adjective or an expression to define her being: Lilith is a *concrete* woman, that is it, enriched by the autonomous thrill of a clay which has dug down to the origin of its own femininity which cannot be renounced.) Ah what a mess humanity's career has been from the Neanderthal to today, that is to tomorrow. What has been the use of distancing ourselves so much from the psycho-motor articulation of the ape? Besides, chimpanzees have so much more really free time.

Next day we take the boat and go to see some of the confluences of black-watered rivers – the Rio Negro which flows into the Solimoes from which the Amazon is born – as well as a hectare of jungle, made ready and raked over for the purpose, of which the only sensation (amid descriptions of incense for *macumba* extracted from the trees whose bark is burnt a little every morning by the multilingual guide for the tourists to smell and lianas thanks to which one can take souvenir photos) are the high-heeled shoes of a midwife from Caravaggio who walks in front of me. And then Frances Brennet, an American lady over eighty, who tells me she travels alone. It is not true, I come to learn from her four fellow travellers, who say they are wretched after a couple of weeks transporting her, supporting her and brushing up her memory: the spokesman for the little group, an American who is working with the University of Aquila on a scheme for recycling premature pensioners from Italian State organizations, says that the moment they get home they'll each take a month's rest. Frances with her incredibly green eyes would like so much to go in a canoe on the lagoon but she has put her knee out and 'Wouldn't you like to lift me, young man?' and I pick her up – she must weigh twenty kilos with her purse – and lower her into the canoe to general applause. Her name, she confides in me, the real one, is Vincenza Sottile, of Palermitan parents, married to an Irish officer who died three years ago. They were great travellers, but he never came to Brazil, always China and Sicily, because of his blood pressure, the doctor advised him against Brazil year after year and now, with him dead, she has come because it's almost as if she was bringing him at last. And she flirts and twitters at my compliment on the uncontaminated colour of her eyes, and hides her laughing mouth with a little hand, and says that now she wants to go to Tibet, to Nepal, where there are sherpas who carry one . . .

And on our way back from a supermarket for Indian craftworkers (with the deprived look, with the sad smile of people who have lost everything, of people who, having left their bodies in the first rubber plantations on which Manaus was born a century ago, have also seen their spirits carried away imprinted on all those still and film cameras which *immortalize* the little mortality that remains) a boat overloaded with Indians came alongside; it goes to and fro between the villages on stilts for miles along the banks. I did not see a single smile, they looked at us, towards the big blue and white boat, without expression, with their hands in their laps, the children too placid. I should like to quote the famous raft of the damned which hangs in the Louvre but it feels to me like a kind of affront, as it would be to say that 'Sarah Bernhardt was a guest at the famous Teatro Amazonas (1896) in neoclassical style' or that the 'glass windows in the market were designed by Eiffel of the Eiffel Tower.' And what did I do? I went round asking for money from those who took their photographs or had their photographs taken, starting with myself so as to set an example and pull them all in. Violence for violence, which began exactly when, after the first forest clearances, a haggard congregation of Jesuits arrived, determined to oppose the principle applied by the landowners of São Paolo, Bahia and Recife, according to whom the Indians were to be considered only to be slaves and unpaid labour and, promptly, a papal bull arrived supporting the landowners who on their own would not have managed to chase away the Jesuits. This time, too, I did something to deceive myself that I did not leave too nasty a memory in the wake of our boat on which I too then turn my back.

An elderly chimpanzee, squatting in the fork of an India-rubber-tree, a blade of grass between its teeth, is having a rest after a meal. It looks at us ironically as if we were a pack of fellow countrymen down on our luck and then narrows its eyes and seems to ask: 'What does the world cost?'

This morning too I called Aldo asking him to take me to kindergarten. My mother, who is the sister of my uncle Aldo (who doesn't want to be called uncle), dialled for me and I said to him: 'Here is Adele and she wants you to take her to kindergarten here. Here she is.'

'Ciao, my love,' says Aldo as usual, 'did you dream about gold or silver? Did you dream about Mother Asdrubala who came to peck at you?'

Sometimes I don't understand right away what he means, but I like him just the same, I wait for a moment thinking about it because he uses words I don't know and have never heard before. Mother Asdrubala is a nun with a yellow beak, a hunch-backed dwarf whom he wants desperately to bring into my life. Every morning he invents another instalment, yesterday he had got to the point where she was opening up a child's tummy with her beak and was beginning to pull out its insides. Disgusting.

'I dreamt about poo,' I blurted out, but I don't know what dreams about poo are like. When I try a third possibility other than gold or silver he is happy, grins; if I am there he lifts me into the air and I end up in his arms which hug me like light wings and he kisses my hair and behind my ears. Sometimes I tell him that I dreamt about daisies, mud, a pencil, to please him. He thinks that to have more words is to have more life – still in this one.

He adds: 'But you don't just want me to take you to the kindergarten, do you?'

'No – yes!' And then in a low voice: 'I want to go to Pipa's but don't tell Mario and Mummy.'

Pipa is a tobacconist where the owner makes little bags of all sorts of sweets. Since I have caries, my mother doesn't want me to eat them, but Aldo doesn't care.

'If an uncle doesn't spoil his nieces what use is he, isn't that right?'

'Right,' I always reply. 'And then you are Uncle Thingummy – '

'Uncle Wallet!'

He taught me that himself. One day he said to me: 'I shall buy you – that way you won't ever escape.' He succeeded. When he goes away I frown because if he doesn't buy me sweets no one will.

He says he is going to Africa, to Milan, he always says where. My ear has got used to it now, by dint of hearing names of countries and cities I have formed an idea of the world and that Montichiari is not the only place there is. He has a big map above his bed and with a broom handle he points out all the places he goes to. Aldo doesn't seem able to do without the world, without that world there, and I, who cannot do without Aldo, cannot do without all his crazy blackmailing attempts to force me not to do without him. He is the only one to say to me for example: 'Watch out – if you are good I won't buy you anything' or even: 'If you make a fuss I'll buy you something.' I begin to pretend to be good or pretend to make a fuss and then when it turns out that

I have to be like that really, it is no longer the same thing – it is more amusing, I feel that it wouldn't take anything to make my play-acting true and the truth play-acting. Aldo wants me to be alert and a rebel and very well brought up, but let's be clear: he loves me for my beauty, because I have straight and not identical legs, because he says I look like his sister, my mother as a child, and because I am a little girl as old as a hand without the thumb, which I have difficulty in holding down, so that everyone says I am five.

And then as always, Aldo ran to my house, I was at the door waiting for him, blue jeans and a blouse, because I hate little skirts and everything that has buttons and makes me feel I'm suffocating. The kindergarten is just two steps away at the top of the hill, I could even go there alone. But Pipa is further off, I can't go there alone, and he, as if my family weren't enough, keeps repeating to me the difference between right and left, because you have to turn your neck to one side and then from that other side to the other again, if not the cars run over you and make jam of Adele – which would be me – with a topping of candied fruit, he says.

'Let's wait a little,' I say to him. Meantime he looks at me as if he had to recover from his astonishment every time, 'because Mamma and Maria are leaving in the car. Don't let them see us.' We begin to hang about at the gate because we don't want to be seen setting out for Pipa's and not the kindergarten. From behind the window my mother begins to shake her head because she has smelt a rat, but I pretend not to notice. Aldo laughs and says: 'I am your little slave, your servant, one day I'll manage to say No to you, you'll see.' 'Just you try!' A reply like that guarantees me an extra ration of sweets. Because of being greedy I am forced to invent replies that aren't natural.

'You'll end up intelligent too,' says Aldo, sighing disconsolately. 'Intelligent and arid. Instead you must become generous.'

'How?'

'With yourself – to have so much Adele that you can give her away in handfuls.'

A mystery. Meantime I shall think about it. Then we have already turned off towards Pipa's. No sooner have we left the tobacconist's with the cocker spaniel that barks and hates my uncle, with my little bag in my hand, than he says: 'And when I'm not there any longer?'

'Someone else will buy them for me.'

'Who?'

'Another uncle.'

'Who is your favourite uncle who lives at number eight, Via Antiche Mura?'

'You,' I reply promptly: he's the only uncle who lives there.

'This afternoon I am going away,' he says. I'm used to it.

'Are you going to Africa? You see – and what will I do? I'm bound to like someone else better. You are never there.'

'Of course you must like someone else better, anyone at all. I'm going to buy two black babies.'

It is his fixation – every time he threatens to bring back black rivals. But I don't believe him any more. Once he brought home Jennifer, a little black girl, but I saw right away that it was a doll.

'And when are you coming back?' By now we were at the kindergarten door.

'I'm not coming back ever,' he said drily, cruelly. I began to cry and my sweet went down the wrong way. But I suddenly realized that I was pretending to cry even if I had real tears. I seemed to see my father nodding his head as if to say: Good girl, go on pretending to cry because your uncle likes it. Uncle Aldo has already made his will, oh he makes one every month, like all madmen, but in the end, after changing some details about lesser beneficiaries, he always leaves everything to me. No one has ever asked him for anything but seeing that I am there – but my mother says it will be something if he doesn't leave us with debts. I quickly realized on the first step of the stairs that I didn't want my uncle to die and leave us everything, that that aeroplane could wait a little longer. Then he says to me: 'I'm joking, I'll be back soon.'

'What will you bring me?'

'A necklace? One for you and one for Maria?'

'But little chocolate eggs. I am too small to wear necklaces, and then there are the drug addicts who snatch them from your neck and cut your throat. My sister wet the bed last night – I didn't.'

'I won't tell Mother Asdrubala, you know she insists that children must wet the bed at least twice a night.'

Consoled, laughing with a remnant of tears which have made him the most loved man in the world, I left him behind me. I already have a sweetheart at the kindergarten and he doesn't even know. He is one of the big boys, the highest class of children. When I tell my sweetheart Flingio the things my uncle says such as 'Life of my life!' 'Who loves you more than me?' 'Come on, become a little girl!' he tells me I won't become little because I'm already medium-sized. My sweetheart, being a normal man, doesn't understand anything and that is why I like him, because there is no danger that he'll make my head giddy like my uncle. Drunkenness is not good in children, they have to think about marriage and having children.

At night Aldo shouts in his sleep. I heard him the first time I stayed and slept at my grandmother's, who is the mother of Aldo and my mother. If he shouts in his sleep it is because he doesn't know he is shouting, he doesn't do it on purpose to, let's say, frighten us. Now I am used to it but at first I was afraid and started up out of my sleep. My grandmother says, tucking the blankets in well:

'Sleep. It's not quite right. But then he gets over it.'

But I lie there for endless minutes waiting for the next shout and wonder why, why does he shout like that? What is happening to him? Who is hurting him if he is alone? Sometimes however after shouting he laughs with certain icy little laughs that give me goose-flesh. He seems to have a lot of fun when he's sleeping. In the morning however he is cheery and jaunty. The moment he sees that I have been sleeping in his house he comes and lies down beside me and looks at me sleeping while my grandmother is preparing our coffee in the kitchen and tells him not to wake me. When I notice that he is there I push him away because I am ashamed and I don't like to have anyone about when I wake up – certainly not a grown man. When I wake up I am always sorry not to have slept at home because the first person I see is not my mother. There is a mystery in Aldo's life and I cannot discover it because I am a little girl, and then it is best not to discover the secrets of people who want to buy us: it is enough to exploit them without selling yourself and amen. Since he once said on television that he would give his life for me (but I'd first want to know what life) I find it difficult to believe that he would resist if I took his, so we could inherit right away – he doesn't own much but I would have sweets for the rest of my life even if he wasn't there any more. He told me this too because he has taught me all about the sixty years of royalties which every writer's heir enjoys. But grandmother – you musn't wish she was dead because she spends only a fifth of what she gets as a pension and all the rest is in her savings book and what is left is all extra and it's like having it in the bank with interest, says grandmother. Aldo phones me every day, he is worse than Flingio, who is better, because even if he's in the top class, he is smaller than me and I can even kick him. My uncle is always alone, he spends almost all day in his hotel in Brazil . . .

'Hello Adele!' I shout on the phone.

'Adele, go on, it's Aldo, come here!' my sister encourages her. 'She doesn't want to come, she says she had a terrible head with planes crashing in clusters and for two weeks now she has been waiting in front of the television set and you'd promised her that you would crash and instead you "are talking". Come on – he's still alive, he's not a ghost.'

Well –

For twenty-four hours I have been trying in vain from the Carlton Hotel in Brasilia to get in touch with Oscar Niemeyer, who had the idea of a *dépendance* of Brasilia at Segrate. I am stuck on the telephone arguing with the operator because, forget about abroad, it's a question of a telephone call in town or to Rio de Janeiro, but nothing is to be heard, only noises, and I shout, present my particulars and explain and plead and begin from the beginning again and drop the broken receiver. 'Let's try again,' I say, and the *operadora* screams an unwearied '*Un minutin*' and the little minutes are long and worrying like my sore stomach and kidneys. Because since traditionally one gets dysentery in Brazil, I, who could not come across such an ordinary place as a loo, have been a martyr to constipation for four days. When the line gets through you hear absolutely nothing, and once again I don't know whether this very famous architect who has his eightieth birthday one of these days is with friends in Brasilia, in his office or at home in Rio, if he isn't there at all (having maybe been summoned by some new big Communist chief in the East) or maybe doesn't exist any more. And to think that I was so pleased that finally that windbag Yourcenar has kicked the bucket, she who with her *Memoirs of Hadrian* did more damage than HIV – she covered up other people's anuses with bogus classicism in order to cut short their enjoyment.

The impassive and sing-song voice of the operator when I begin over again to complain about Brazilian telephones strikes the usual note, '*Un minutin*'. and then the whole refrain, '*Un minutin por favor*', and we are back where we started from. Meantime I decide to call a doctor because I feel that my legs are trembling, I am cold and the ghostly surge of the water-bed is wearing to my nerves – I feel as if I were pushing my head down into my insides and naturally it will never get through them. The doctor says he can't come just now but at twelve forty yes: I decide nevertheless to try a modest sightseeing trip through the city to get an idea at least of what miracles reinforced concrete can perform. I leave with a little group of four Brazilians. Brasilia is a staging point for tourists, people prefer to go on to Bahia; for that reason, because no one goes there, I preferred Brasilia to other more crowded destinations. Thought up by Lucio Costa and embellished as much as 80 per cent by the genius of Niemeyer, Brasilia presents an urbanistic structure in the form of a bird – of a plane, said the Creole guide (she is speaking Portuguese), thus bringing it up to date. Starting from the rationalistic principle inherited from Le Corbusier, that is to say the separation of functions, this city, at least on paper, has everything I dislike: the ministries are at the head ('On the flight deck' says our pretty guide, who is mild and out of her depth like a child who is doing the same trip round the sanctuary at Lourdes for the thousandth time), the buildings for local government in the tail, the residential zones and the commercial centres are in the wings, while the *high-class* residential areas are beside the artificial lake. According to this principle we will have every kind of school together, all the hotels alongside each other, the sports centres with their various specialities all brought together in the same centre, and so with all the banks, all the airlines etc. Since at the base of this structure there are the arterial roads and six lanes in every direction and the principle that if you don't have a car you must use public transport, you are done for. You'd do a couple of different pieces of business more quickly by canoe on the Rio Negro than here because the two places in question at the moment are some tens of kilometres apart and in Brasilia one is not allowed to come across something *by chance* – a little restaurant, a chemist's, a newsagent's, a jeweller's. It became immediately obvious to my eye that this determination to group together all the hotels in the same area is immensely stupid, since the visitor is excluded from any possibility of local encounters – he will only ever encounter other visitors like himself, and the streets round about are merely a prolongation of the hotel foyer itelf. On the other hand it is equally comprehensible that, having had to start from scratch without pre-existing infrastructures whether urban or historical, there was not the problem of moving out of the centre the typical little establishments with rooms to let in Montmartre or the neo-classical façade in a picturesque district of Madrid on which to construct an ultramodern hotel apart from – or indeed thanks to – the dozens of booths of native cork in the surrounding neighbourhood. Result: the hotels are all the same and all there and what little night life there is will be round about and all the most desired restaurants in the same skyscraper floor upon floor. When the container is the same, the entrance the same and anonymous whether it is to the Italian pizzeria or the Argentinian *Churrasco* you feel a need to give them a special atmosphere *inside*. A city like this in Italy or anywhere in Europe would close down the day after its inauguration – but in Europe there wouldn't be the need either to create a city from the ground up as there was for Brazil, which for more than a century had been planning to move the capital from the Atlantic coasts.

Brasilia, after its first years spent floating aimlessly, has taken root and is very well provided with living quarters and services to which the presence of power imparts a halo. New middle-class inhabitants continue to arrive while the workmen who built it have remained in the huts on the outskirts, the same ones as were put up to provide fleeting lodging for the Indians and other construction workers and which are now real centres of poverty and rubbish bags for the refuse of human exploitation here as everywhere in Brazil. Brasilia remains Brasilia because it is here, if it were elsewhere it would be a banal Peoria. And just recently the UN declared it a Monument to Humanity – one feels like asking which – and meantime even these Pharaonic streets have come to the brink of collapse. However Brasilia is truly a garden city, since the green spaces are, at a quick glance, at least 500 per cent more than the built-up area: by European standards one could build at least two other Brasilias and various Rio Bo's inside Brasilia. It is not a luxurious kind of vegetation and there are few flowerbeds; it reminds one more of the pretty German Neustadts built after the war with a little lake, conifers rather than mangroves, the little alley of red gravel, but kilometre after kilometre of it in all directions. It is undoubtedly the cleanest city in Brazil – the politicians' love for the ecology of the place where they are going to live is well known . . .

The little bus takes us to the television tower to enjoy the panorama of the city, but once I am faced by the lift my insides do a double somersault and I rush back to the hotel on foot, experiencing the panic of having to cross streets that never end and do not even have a set of traffic lights. In the hotel I suffer a little, victim of yet another atrocious false alarm. But I am pleased because I am mathematically certain that sooner or later I shall have before me a *minutin* of guaranteed happiness. Meantime there is no choice – either be happy or burst. And I resume my telephonic search for Oscar, aided by the operator who now spits out her remarks about *minutin* with clenched teeth.

Someone knocks at the door, I go and open it – it is the doctor. He inspects me in front, from behind and from the side. To be brief: he orders a purgative called Prompt (pray heaven it is) in exchange for a fee of six thousand cruzados (more or less a hundred thousand lire), which has the power to make me lose my voice as well. I unhook the receiver, making a rough calculation of what relationship I shall be able to work out between each hectogramme and the cost in lire of my happiness which is now under fire and . . . '*Un minutin un minutin un minutin*!' the little voice exults and yes, it really is the office of Oscar Niemeyer and you can hear everything and hear clearly! Having confirmed the appointment – in Rio de Janeiro unfortunately and not here, and in two days' time and not tomorrow – I ask the female voice with a feeling of having been miraculously healed: 'To whom have I been talking?' and the voice says: 'To Maria de Lourdes' and I say: 'What a nice name! So apt!' and she says: 'I'm sorry?' and I say: 'I said you have a lovely name, signora' and she says: 'Thank you – we'll talk again soon' and the exclamation has about it something seraphic and insincere that enchants me. The page arrives with the Prompt and I shall be constantly unfastening and fastening my trouser-belt. I say to him: 'Do you happen to know – do they serve frozen piranha in Manaus?' And he says: 'What was the vegetable?' and I say: 'Purée of peas on one side and puréed spinach on the other' and he says: 'Alla milanese' and I say: 'Yes, the fish was done in breadcrumbs' and he says: 'Then it really was deep-frozen piranha.'

And next day, having taken my purgative, I am worse than before, I wander about my room and don't know whether I shall be fit to take the plane to go to Niemeyer. I look at Brasilia from the window – a garage being built but where construction has stopped, a building that seems to have been destroyed by fire – and then I double the recommended dose. My kidneys feel like two mines on the point of exploding, up and down my backbone, and the pain is unbearable and I am shitting blood. But my documentary instinct impels me to get on to the same bus as yesterday evening, hoping to have time to see some more of Brasilia, in which I should like to leave something of myself. At the entrance to the cathedral are placed the somewhat surly statues of the evangelists St Luke, St Mark, St John and St Matthew, and inside it feels as if you were in one of Bayer's conference halls. However prayer here must enjoy greater essential qualities, the God/man relationship be more wearing than elsewhere because it is more difficult. The power of attraction must be already there in the man who cannot put his hope on any external magnet with traditional powers of influence. No charisma of shadows and half-shadows – ancient or merely old – in which to pray is also an immensely pleasurable state of the body which meantime is resting. I mean that in our churches (big and small) the person praying from the very first moment attains an intimacy with God – or at least a state of *natural* predisposition – can find a corner, a little altar, a grating, a shadowed area, can take advantage of his desire to hide from any kind of eye and therefore to give more depth and substance to the sweet cowardice of animals that have a need for incense, silence, secrecy, and mafia-like deals between himself and the Lord. Here all is light, blinding, dancing, cutting, raining down, and as for noise trucks seem to run behind the chairs – the kneeling cushions have been done away with, although they are so good for sciatica. From the ceiling hang aluminium angels, and they too give off gleams to wound the eyes, to remind us that it is time to waken our consciences. What I want to say is that to withdraw into oneself in prayer here presupposes first of all total sincerity with oneself, which is not so automatic for everyone: you have to put everything into it to the point where, if you succeed, you find that prayer is now superfluous. There will no longer be time enough for the believer to be capable of establishing new ways of dealing with God, who is either the same (and so always dwells in the same Romanesque-Renaissance-Baroque-Romantic atmospheres) or moves house and is no longer there. Indeed in the first as in the second church, the Chapel of Fatima, there is no one at prayer – but there is a great deal of informal business going on on the steps: semi-precious stones, chips, plans of the city, beggars with legs, with one leg, with none at all, creole women selling lottery tickets, boys selling roses like the old-fashioned ones with a perfume and thorns.

The Esplanade of the Ministries lines all the various ministries along the Eixo Monumental – contrary to the pilot scheme according to which they should all have been the same. The Palacio de Itamaraty (the Foreign Ministry) is the most interesting of the few which represent architecture as such: it is surrounded by a sheet of water which in turn reflects, reflecting itself, the pillars of reinforced concrete and the walls of glass. You will notice that the patina of time on the reinforced concrete – a patina to which no eye is yet accustomed – is particularly sad because the buildings do not seem so much ugly as incurably old and will certainly never become *ancient*. The work of the agents in the atmosphere attacks the cement with a kind of dry paste or thin sooty skin like so many streaks from open drains or drains constantly discharging piss from a weak-bladdered spirit, more incontinent than destructive.

And then on through the university city, which is long and serpentine, we continue through the Square of the Three Powers, the most famous in Brasilia, situated behind the Congress and between the Palace of Justice and that of the Plateau, where no one goes to see the changing of the guard – neither at 7.30 nor at 17.40. The two famous warriors by Bruno Giorgi standing out obliquely in an improbable martial ballet and the persistence of the sun on the pavement does the rest – it is truly a De Chirico square, almost deserted. The face in bronze of President Juscelino Kubitschek (great friend and supporter of Niemeyer and endowed with absolute determination to will Brasilia into existence: it was born in four years between 1954 to 1958 and in 1960 had the present final look) stands in the centre of a wall of marble (all the marble here comes from Carrara) above a muddy pond in which at the moment float three paper cups, a pink condom and four tickets for the nearby history museum: what can be more metaphysical than this!

In Kubitschek's mausoleum I suffer a moment of confusion: motionless in front of the fine black catafalque my guts begin a private run of their own, perhaps excited by the light which spreads from the top of a fiery-red window, and I do not know where one turns to deal with things quickly in cases like this. I run down the exit tunnel, back and forth, they point out a toilet to me, this too a mortuary. I take down my shorts with deference and nothing once more. In complete peace of mind I continue the visit to the library (very fine bound volumes, all uncut: Joyce, Flaubert, Gide, George Sand, evidently politicians, often having mahogany shelving at their disposal, do not resist the whim of having them furnished!). As I am taking the books down and turning the pages a soldier in white arrives – a cross between an Alpino and a sailor with a very tight crotch – and tells me very nicely that one can't touch them and I stupidly say to him (as if he gave a damn) 'Good titles' without taking my eyes off his two batons, both of them impressive even though both are in repose. But Juscelino, even if he was not subject to the unfortunate prejudice that one has books in order to read them, is someone I like because, before embarking on his political career, he had learned to do something else – in fact he was a surgeon of recognized quality and had put right not a few war-wounded with his pianist's hands in the wake of the Brazilian battalion. In Italy the majority of politicians are born *politicians*, and if they learn anything it is at most that specialism which is a stage higher than that of innkeepers – *economics*, which is the antechamber for those who cannot learn anything else but who demand a kind of ermine at all costs in order to dress up the vacuum in their own pockets at the cost of other people's.

Another church, this time of St Giovanni Bosco, considered with reason to be the most beautiful in Brasilia even if it is not by Niemeyer. Alongside the institute of the Salesian brothers who throughout Brazil surpass the Jesuits in terms of fame, coming just second to Cicciolina. The church is a lagoon of dark and light blue glass in high thin arches like lances made from splintered skies. Two young men, very withdrawn, are praying, one standing the other sitting – suffice it to say that their blue jeans have buttons and not a zip and are very tight behind with the seams running across the buttocks and not down the middle. How exciting the ultra-goody half-breeds at prayer are, the seriousness of their faces, usually so merry, the concentration of their minds on mystical fervour instead of on a football player brings everything else into particular prominence. Who knows whether the Salesian fathers wiil ever read the highly documented article by Virginio Mazzelli in the December number of *Babilonia* which begins like this: 'The secret about the homosexuality of Giovanni Bosco is one of those secrets which are really no secrets at all . . . People have been talking (and writing) about it for years.' Some chapter headings? *Si ego non scandalizor, quia vos scandalizamini?* and *Domine, non sum dignus* and *Spiritus carnis, me colphissat* and, it was to be expected, *Sinite parvulos venire ad me*. I take a quick look at the statue of Don Bosco. It seems to me that the folds of his habit are a little dashing and I am out and go back to the hotel. Brasilia is not a city, it is an invention taken from a dream which is much less collective than we might like to think, yet the millions upon millions of dollars it cost could not have been better spent (and certainly the military who took power in 1961 not only must have had a good many regular weapons but also a quiverful of arrows for their bow) in view of the fact that here, as in all the other countries in the north of South America, the money (often other people's and even more willingly not repaid) is eaten up without causing any chimera of individual greatness (a class, a man, a single fresh direction to the system) to be followed by a scrap of terra firma – or at least fairly firm.

Brasilia to Rio is 1,200 kilometres of suspense in a plane, but here I am already in the Avenida Atlantica at Copacabana, where woman is queen, woman is sovereign and it is raining, making for the studio of Oscar Niemeyer, which I presume must be some kind of stadium; but I am mistaken: Signora de Lourdes with the slight squint which gives to her glance and her maternally blessing hands a certain friendliness, introduces me into the spacious but unostentatious office where a pair of colleagues do not even raise their heads and the healthy disorder of the tables and chairs and planimeters on the walls says in a peremptory way: 'Here we work like mad.' There is not a knick-knack, not a plant, and I like that – then the secretary signs to me to go in, that the architect is ready to receive me. So as to keep things simple I right away address Niemeyer as *maestro*; since he replies using the familiar form of address and is smoking a *toscanello* I say to him; 'Can I have one?' and we haven't time to sit down in this small but comfortable and rather badly lit office before we are *comrades* – he sets great store by his international Communism, that one knows, his age, the nostalgia, the Leninist observance (as if in a private chapel) from his most tender years. I realize that this is a case of officiating at Communism as the Façade of the Great Men of the Fatherland who are still convinced that the façade is part of the foundations.

Oscar is tiny and elegant, a questioning look but an accepting one, with a curiosity that is vigilant and closely guarded. I: 'Let's talk about the Mondadori building which you did at Sagrate and about Arnoldo, do you remember that period in your life?' He: 'Arnoldo was very nice but I didn't deal with him, I dealt with his son Giorgio. Giorgio Mondadori didn't just want a head-office, he wanted an architectonic work of art. Oh, he was enthusiastic about the project, he was so alive in all respects, he exuded energy from every pore. I suppose I had a chat with Arnoldo a couple of times, he told me how he began, how he printed his first book and didn't even have the money to pay for the paper.' I: 'And you believe that?' He: 'Shouldn't I? Perhaps, now that I think of it, he liked to make things up. Certainly he and Giorgio were sparing with their time. In 1966 I arrived from France, Malraux had discovered a little law about exiles according to which they automatically became French architects and I could work and then, thanks to to my friendship with de Gaulle, I began to work all over the place. I knew everyone – I was a great friend of Sartre, who was not only an intellectual but a man who wanted to act, who underlined the need to be *on the spot*. I drew up the plans for two universities in Algeria, Boumédienne was a great friend of mine, I did the UN headquarters in New York, in short, I began to work all over the place in 1964, I did the headquarters of the Communist Party in Paris – that was in '67. But who are you? A writer you say? I read a lot . . . what's his name . . . he's an Italian . . . he wrote *The Woman of Rome*?' I pretend to have no idea: 'I wouldn't know' but he insists: 'He is more or less my age . . . I read an interview recently . . . what a character, all that sex at his age . . . in great form, eh?' I come out with: 'Actually he's lame.' He: 'What's that?' I: 'Now I remember, Moravia' and he says: 'That's him. And who is your publisher?' and I say: 'Mondadori' and he says: 'Giorgio?' and I say: 'No, Leonardo.' And he says: 'Is that his brother?' and I say: 'No. Giorgio is the brother of Mimma Mondadori and of the wife of Formenton who is now dead' and he says: 'Formenton – I remember well – he went straight to the point with a smile. But, I'm sorry, isn't Giorgio a publisher too?' and I say: 'Yes, but he publishes specialist magazines, I write novels, I am with Leonardo' and he says: 'Ah Leonardo, and who is he?' and I say: 'Mimma's son and Giorgio's nephew' and he says, more and more lost: 'And who is his father?' and knits his brows thoughtfully and I say: 'Ah, that's something a lot of us would like to know' and he says: 'Did I know him?' and I say: 'Listen, if you don't know . . .' and he says: 'Yes, now I remember! Small, thin, without a hair on his face, crazy about golf' and I say: 'Leonardo is very tall and strongly built and as far as hair goes is about average, I imagine, I don't know about golf' and I cough: the conversation about his rival was better. 'The building at Sagrate . . .' I remind him. And he says: 'Well, in Milan they wanted to build something . . .' And I say: 'Open space?' and he says: 'Yes, that's right, open space, because buildings have to be made for intellectuals not for princes' and I say: 'Remember that before being intellectuals, at Sagrate – as everywhere else – they are workers in subordinate positions and they all complain about this open space because it is difficult to get used to the thought that the person at the next desk or behind the bookshelves is listening' and he says: 'They could speak more quietly, couldn't they?' and I have the feeling that here the Façade collapses in a big way. He stares at me, perhaps annoyed by my kind of sniping observation. I say: 'It seems to me that the head office of Mondadori, which is indisputably a work of art and remains so, like everything else has another side to the coin: it functions so well for the bosses because they can move about, increase, diminish or eliminate sections according to the need of the moment but, I'm sorry, to anyone that works there it looks to me like a poultry shed. Suppose two people in the open space can't stand each other – what do you do about it, seeing that they have to be face to face for eight hours? And then the way you have to use to get there and slip in between the cars that arrive at your backside from three different directions and you have only a few metres to reach safety! It's more dangerous than the Paris–Dakar Race!' and he says: 'But I didn't do that, they could change the entrance, couldn't they?' and I say: 'That's great. Apart from that it all seems great to me – from the canteen to the ducks to the big fish to the fire-escapes, so theatrical. But these unending floors?'

Niemeyer summons help from Maria de Lourdes and asks her for a glass of water and for a very long minute sits and looks at me formulating questions about me which I shall never know. I console him: 'I'm not saying this – I don't work in it permanently – but they all complain. Maybe it's because you didn't think of a democratic unity when you formed an idea of the Latin intellectual employee, but the Italians still want their little office with the spiders' webs up there and the privacy of the little fern on the window-ledge for when it rains. There if you have a stomach-ache and don't want to share it you are forced to train your arse in ventriloquy in order to blame someone else. Just imagine if a wretched woman proof-reader lets out a fart – it re-echoes through the whole floor, and if it doesn't re-echo it is worse still and the sense of guilt reaches stratospheric dimensions.' He swallows all the water in the glass without taking his eyes off me, opening them a little wider. And I continue trying to soft-pedal but unfortunately sincerely: 'I am telling you this because I really would like to work in a space like that and I don't mind my own farts or other people's but you see I am an odd man out – not only have I nothing to hide but it would never enter my head to hide it. I enjoy things too much this way,' and he says: 'I hadn't thought of that – I always had in mind the well-being of the workers' and I say: 'And you were wrong – if I can feel wonderful there it means that for anyone else it is death by Chinese water-torture, believe me. And when you planned Brasilia did you foresee that the *candangos* (workers) once they had finished would be shoved to the outskirts and that what were temporary huts would become real shanty towns?' and he, getting more and more interested, says: 'Just as it was finished, the military came to power – it was the military who drove out the workers – I had built residential zones for them too.' And I, the moralist, knowing and clear-sighted, say: 'Ah, the gap between intentions and results! It is always like this – I don't really blame you – the fact is that if the ideals don't incorporate the cost of the maid they become something else and one always has to wait till *later* – I understand you' and he says: 'Of course you may or may not like Brasilia but it is undeniable that it is a concrete, efficient, living city' and I say: 'There's no question – it is a splendid base on which to construct a city' and he looks at me more and more shaken and fascinated. I only ever carry out the same interview – the one I would like to be the subject of.

And we chat a little more (about his monument against torture, which no Brazilian administration wishes to have on its own soil) and then Oscar takes off: he shows me the typescript of his memoirs, which are unpublished, and I ask him for a photocopy of some pages, even if I have big difficulties with the Portuguese.

'They are inviting me everywhere for this eightieth birthday of mine – even my friend Fidel – have you ever been in Cuba?' he asks with a smile, imagining that Castro at least is untouchable, something solid shared by two Communists *like us*. And I say: 'I wouldn't dream of it! A handjob and twenty years in prison! The same treatment as under Perón and Videla, who fed us to the sharks! There are anti-homosexual laws in the land of sugarcane and they'll have to stick it all right up them before I set foot there. They invited some of my Spanish friends – there is an *opening up*. Nothing of the kind. People with any sense – homosexuals or not – don't go anywhere where there is apartheid' and he, taken aback: 'I never knew that' and I say: 'That's bad – it's the truth – and where there are these laws, believe me, things are also very bad for the female condition and Communism is a ring-a-ring-a-roses with me, you and him, but the people don't come into it, they never do. Even the comrades with study bursaries have problems about going to Cuba, so you can imagine if I'll go there from my own pocket.'

Then Oscar shows me some very delicate drawings of girls on the beach – he is having an exhibition of watercolours in his daughter's art gallery. And so we get on to the subject of *women* and his eyes light up by magic. You can feel that he is still mad about them: 'Until six months ago I did not think I was eighty, then six months ago I saw some boys playing football and I jumped up, I wanted to play too, and I understood something – my mind is all there but my body's not there any more . . . Like with women – beautiful, delicate, passionate women – sex – ah! women are the only *thing* more important than architecture . . .' and I say: 'Have you had a lot of them?' and he looks at me as if to say you can't ask certain things but one feels that he has had them by the bagful, the basketful and – in view of the delicacy of his *no comment* – a picnic-basket full. I ask him: 'And now you are eighty – what will you do?' 'Ah my dear, I haven't any time to lose now – I have to roll up my sleeves what with everything I am doing – the museum for the Indians, the conservatory in Brasilia, the memorial to Latin America at São Paolo . . . Have you seen the *sambodromo* at Rio?' and I say: 'Yes, I went to see it before coming to see you – I like it a lot,' I lie, and he says: 'Before they were always structures that were put up and taken down, now it is there and it is not carnival and the samba schools are on holiday. It has all sorts of other uses – do you know that we have made schools inside it' but obviously he is worried and would like to talk about other things, because he takes up the drawings with the girls in bathing costumes: 'This Moravia is – how does he live?' 'Oh, he's just got married' and to turn the knife in the wound I blurt out: 'To a Spanish woman – oh, very pretty, almost young.' And Niemeyer suddenly is short of breath and then swallowing hard he asks: 'But does he possess her?' and I allow a very long pause to intervene and he stretches his neck and his eyes look sharply at me as if to invoke pity and I say: 'I don't really think so, she will give him some little kisses and then she leaves it alone, you know how it is – I don't know' and, accompanying me to the door he looks at me with complete gratitude, asks me if I am accepting an invitation this evening to the Italian embassy where a prize will be given, and then he comes out exultantly with: 'Without carnal possession it is no use – they can all do it!'

I take wings down the Avenida Atlantica, searching desperately for a taxi. There isn't one, my guts – oh my God, this is it this time! In my room the telephone is ringing and I don't even wait to know who it is and shout '*Un minutin*', drop the receiver and ah! sit on the loo and savour the pleasure, striven for so hard, of eternity *in fieri*. This too has been accomplished.

In Rio and it is raining. For a week I have been hidden away in my hotel room with the blind drawn, the television off, the lights out, except for the side one in the bathroom. I am ill. I feel like death and go out only to bargain for topazes and gems in the foyer. Every so often I draw aside the curtain and see the usual scene on the beach at Copacabana: small teams playing at football the moment a little sun comes out and the faces of tourists at the window looking at the same scene from other hotels. I have walked about a bit but remember nothing of what I saw – never more than an hour a day, then I have convulsions. The statue of Christ on the Corcovado is invisible because of the clouds – not that I look particularly in that direction while waiting for the results of the latest lab examinations – of blood and stools – so that I can take the right medicine. Having established that it is not a case of a rectal discharge as I had hoped, I am convinced that this colitis and gastritis and kidney-pain goes back to my swim in the lagoon in the Rio Negro up at Manaus. I know it was dangerous, but after so much care with the bottled mineral water how could I resist on an oppressively hot day jumping into water where a cayman has been sighted on the left and the guide has thrown bags of scraps of bread and meat to concentrate all the piranhas on the right? I went to the Italian embassy too to please Oscar Niemeyer, who got at least thirty kilos of sculpture and the prize of 50 million. He wanted at all costs a copy of the Portuguese edition of *Seminar on Youth* and I brought him one, but then I didn't go to the dinner. The pretty and still young consul from Puglia made a speech that was so long and unlistened to that I feared the worst even at table. Apart from this outing and a dinner with my publisher I have done nothing else – and – yes, three interviews on television and four or five for weeklies and dailies: a struggle – but a necessary one – not to include in what I said that the nice thing about South America is not to go there but to have been there and that I am viscerally, inwardly ill.

I also met some Italians who are typical of Rio – fifty years old, from Rome or Pavia, with grizzled hair very well combed, impeccable shirts, sportsmanlike bearing, alone or in little groups of three. Some were buying flats at Ipanema and Copacabana, they already knew that you can get a maid for a maximum of a hundred thousand lire a month, some have been coming here for five or six years already, and oddly enough their professions are ambiguous, perhaps unspeakable, and they all say they are bachelors – they never wear wedding rings and it isn't possible that a bachelor should want at a certain point to *start a new life* if it is already so perfect as things are. In general they are businessmen, rich accountants, people who have closed down by a fraudulent bankruptcy small but profitable businesses and probably have made a secret but unalterable agreement with their respective wives from the past.

Round the hotel, the ugly and really too dear Meridien, on the pavements and between one car and the next, little family groups composed of women and naked children sleep on cardboard. I have got to know several of them because if I go out I go out at first light on an alms-round even if they don't give a receipt and I run the risk of being pathetic, as those idiots say who are afraid to give charity because it wouldn't be elegant, or else give but get third parties to say so because to say it personally would be in bad taste and not to say so unthinkable. Here it is a fashionable activity like any other – it's part of the trip – if you go to India and are not armed with hundreds of rupees, what sense would there be in running away from the agonizing sadness of golden oldies? I make my daily race in stages with my verbose bounty and stay a while with each of the beneficiaries for a little chat. They are almost all called Maria, only the old ones who give themselves some airs have added to Maria an Asuncion, a Carmen, a Dolores etc. The most down-to-earth is called Maria and that's all. Maria is an illegitimate grandmother of sixty-four and is here at the corner by the chemist's with an illegitimate granddaughter, Maria, who is sixteen, and two little Marias, daughters of two bastard sons, then a Mario, in swaddling clothes, belonging to the granddaughter, then a Marietto who is two years old given birth to by a sewer and taken up by her – in any case when there isn't enough for five there isn't enough for six either. Two of the little ones are trying to skip with a piece of wire. Both are naked and covered with snot up to the neck. Maria, the grandmother, hasn't had a house for ten years – she wanders here and there barefoot with her screaming caravan and every so often she stops and they all arrange themselves *there*, measuring out down to the last centimetre the perimeter of their space which no one ever leaves, never, not even the children – for they neither move a metre away nor cross the street, because perhaps it has already happened to them to turn round and not find anyone any more or not the same Marias anyway. On another piece of cardboard, with an iron barrow alongside overflowing with little plastic bags stuffed with discarded prime necessities, stands a youth in blue jeans, looking as if he were half-dead, his skin swollen and fat – the skin of someone who is ill and is getting over a poisonous dose.

On the other side of the street is the first transvestite beggar I have met. There are a great many here who have had the operation and who, given the fall in demand for sexual manpower, gang up with the tramps among whom are many negroes of about thirty and a lot of youths of about fifteen, dark and fair-haired with a two-day beard and the monstrous face of someone who was convinced that one sex was preferable to the other and had himself castrated or had something added that sticks out, not knowing that in any case males give the most precious essence of their virility (which is the quintessence of femininity) not to another man, far less to a transvestite, however equipped, but to another real woman like themselves. Ever since I noticed that *real* men can only be technically homosexual and that they enjoy it too much to use their heads about it as they do with women, who have the advantage of making them enjoy sex infinitely less but are the subject of posters on trucks, I have become very sceptical about the fatigue of every seduction. Well, I cross the street and the tranvestite who has a real rake in his piled-up hair and a crescent-shaped chopper (yes, for chopping vegetables) looks at me as if I were a Martian and I say to him: 'I am called Aldo, I am Italian, what about you?' 'I don't know,' and he looks away. 'Do you want five hundred cruzados?' (six dollars) and he perks up. 'Even more' and then, whispering: 'It is dangerous to talk here. Everyone can hear.' 'Who?' 'They are envious, women are envious of me.' 'Oh yes?' 'Because I see and talk to Our Blessed Lady.' 'The Madonna?' 'Yes, yes,' and he puts the bank-note in the pocket of his torn trousers. With the other hand he chops at his head a little and grants me a formal and horrific smile so as to get rid of me as quickly as possible.

I reach the gardens on the outskirts, all the benches are occupied by people with naked bellies and gaping mouths. An early riser is washing his clothes at the tap. A bench with Maria and two little Marios, motionless, silent with their eyes fixed on the milk bottle the woman is opening. The woman is creole, with a few rotten teeth. She must have been a tasty mouthful in her day and now she is a piece of shit. She doesn't know the fathers of the two children, she is waiting here because at midday she has a friend who brings out to her the leftovers of the staff of the Copacabana Palace – I presume that the staff keep the clients' leftovers for themselves.

Then I go back to the hotel, telephone Dr Cisney – nothing – neither in the blood nor in the stools – he advises an anal examination. I go for one – a thorough inspection with a bill that is also accurate – unspecific intestinal infection. Antibiotics and fermented milk products. And rest. It rains for two more days. The moment it clears up I feel I have a duty to climb up (have myself taken up) to the Corcovado whose Christ is still hiding. I leave the hotel only to go to a sauna famous for its tarts: I pretend I don't know, pay, allow myself to have a towel wrapped round my hips by an attractive naked milk-white lady on stiletto heels, give her to understand that I only intend to stay for a little, turn round – desert the place. The sauna is called Oasis 123 and the pamphlet given me by a taxidriver says *'Luxo e conforto aliados, para lhe dar mais prazer'* (Luxury and comfort combined to give you more pleasure). The text is multilingual and continues: 'The paradise for the modern executive. Come to the Thermas Oasis and forget your everyday problems – show, complete relaxation, American bar and much more. Permanent medical supervision.' I pay and leave to the great scandal of the cashier. So paradise is over and the modern executive now tosses himself off with his attractive nude in slippers with pension rights.

Since last night I saw lights at the edge of the sea like candles, this morning, as it isn't raining, I went for the first time on to the beach. It was about six and apart from a German fisherman with a net and melted candle-ends on little sacred images there was no one. I put a foot in the water and the first thing that comes at me is a little wave of shit and twigs and stalks of white roses. My God, I thought, what a sublime combination. But I wasn't able to connect the two strains of relics, to see a connection between them. Until from the other end of the beach there appears an immense woman dressed in white gauze who held by the hand a young woman with a bunch of white gladioli in her hand. They stopped and the enormous woman with the fluttering white tunic talked as if giving instructions or repeating formulas and gestures which the girl had to repeat bit by bit. Then the girl turned her back to the ocean, lowered her knickers and with her right hand began to throw the gladioli behind her. Surely a nice *macumba* accompanied by defecation to make her lover come back.

The white of the gladioli is love melting away, the dark brown of the little bits of shit the corporeal being of the lover fragmented by distance. Then another girl arrived while the first went off and left her place to the other with a bundle, this time of white orchids. The same sign of the cross, same grimaces, same squatting posture. Then I learned that if it really doesn't come, pee is enough to have the desired effect on the waves that are the bearers of hope. However that may be, at eleven finally full sunlight in a clear sky beside Christ with his arms spread out and symmetrical under his Liberty dress (it was put up in 1930) and those thousands upon thousands of bathers have descended on to the beach which, lacking throughout its whole length a single public amenity that is usable, is also the place for a collective *macumba* of pee and poo.

From yesterday to today the dollar has gone from 78 to 85 cruzados and a coconut from 50 to 60; this morning's charity had already undergone an inflation of 8 per cent in 132 hours. It is normal that it should be so if it has to reach at least 400 per cent per annum. At the museum of modern art the Beggar with the Dogs has taken up position in the centre of a traffic aisle – he is the most protected and unapproachable man in Rio. Now he is dozing but he is ringed by four puppies, all white with pointed paws and necks thrust forward in a challenging attitude. Anyone who dares to approach is instantly attacked and in five minutes there are at least forty stray dogs which as if at the bark of a trumpet-call, come running from every side and every district. The Beggar and the Dogs together inspire terror in all the restaurant owners, so much so that no one would dare to deny them the leftovers, so they all eat, man and beast. It cannot be said that they behave in the same way to the children – I was eating in a popular place waiting to go to the theatre to see *The Woman from the Brothel* (the fantasies of a frustrated housewife who in the solitude of her fully equipped home, plays at being the *maîtresse* with four doll-whores in the time before she removes her sequins and slips on her dressing-gown and apron at her husband's arrival) when they arrived in a gang of eight – among them a plumpish kid who couldn't push his way through – to seize things left over on the tables, which had not yet been cleared, and empty them into a sack. One had a pot and another actually a plate. The waiter arrived and from a corner took a wire whip with a grip made from a paper napkin and began to wave it in the air without hitting them naturally (or maybe not naturally) but making them retire enough for reinforcements to arrive from the kitchen. The children were determined, they really attacked, they drew back and then threw themselves headlong on the tables and I was already on my feet, shutting my eyes tight and feeling ill and repeating aloud 'No no no', and offered them my still smoking plate but they had already all been chased away and I left everything where it was and went in search of them but there was no one any longer to the right, which was the way they had turned. To heal this wound I punished myself by staying in my room another two days. Drum-rolls arrived, the carnival is upon us and I don't want to find myself here and I feel worse and worse, much worse than if they had discovered I have a cancer or am HIV positive – it is an incurable and mortal illness mine – whereas for anyone else it is possible to feel 'alive' from the fact of living, I live only because I am alive. Rhetoric or presumptuousness – but there are not so many of us left! And tomorrow, my intestines and their sodomized as well as somatized catarrh permitting, I am leaving, I return to my South America that is coming into being. But first, rain or no rain, I want to take the little train to the big Christ.

And this morning at seven-thirty it is already 27° and the air is really burning. I get myself taken to the cable railway by taxi but on the slopes of the mountain the queue is really too long and I can't risk standing two hours and then perhaps losing my place because of a sudden intestinal attack. And suppose I got to the summit on foot? I laugh to myself – it will be at least four hours' climb. But let's try. Villas, hand-wrought gates, favelas, not too surely loaded on top of each other, I make my way on quickly and decisively. Should I pretend to fall and then get up again? Ah, how I like the Imitation of Christ when I know that I can at any moment call a Cyrenian in the shape of a taxidriver! A truck with high sides of plywood caught sight of at station x (not X because there are still a lot to come); two guys with two children, a little boy and a little girl as like as two drops of dirty water.

They hold out their little hands; I give the due amount. One of the two men turns his back to me and continues to scratch his scalp obsessively and to shake his head and utter confused words; the other, who is also squatting, pretends not to see me. I say something to him but he makes a sign with a finger on his lips and ears: deaf-mute. I notice at my feet a box which is raised at one side, covered by a worn piece of old red velvet. The eyes of the man in front of and below me are bloodshot, his face gaunt, and his expression one of a madness which is not true but which he has acquired as the last defence against the drumbeat of despair. The companion at his side continues to scratch himself and now lifts a rag of a jersey to hide from my glance his face in profile: he has very short hair, flapping ears; the two children have the most delicate lineaments, they could be the children of one of El Greco's angels. I take out more money and offer it to the deaf-mute who suddenly says: 'This person next to me here, this filthy woman, is not my wife but my concubine, and these are our children. She is mad now but I am not' and I give a start and turn round to see in the male comrade of earlier the present ruin of a woman. Monkeylike, insane, hieratic, full of lice, this wreck who rages in a whisper and kicks at the wind is a mother. The drawer moves, you would imagine that under the moth-eaten piece of velvet something was kicking – the family's puppy. The father follows my glance and raises that sort of tent and – a little boy with a broad smile which becomes a silent laugh like a bomb of happiness that bursts out of a pink kite. And the father says, whining and surely affected by coca-leaves 'I'll come to Italy too one day, one day I'll fly in a plane and see the sea underneath but without her, she isn't my wife only a concubine' and I would like to say to him – You know we have so many people already, stay where you are, or even Give me this little Mariolino, sell him to me, he's mine already. The woman raises an arm to strike him, he parries the blow, gives her a slap but a light one not nastily.

I and the child are there laughing, forgetful, each mad about the other. I tickle him, I sit beside him while his little brothers hold out their hands again and the father mumbles and she begins to complain through her teeth and to shake herself, and the father pulls up his little vest to show me that he is a little boy, and he was all sweating and had a scab on his navel, and since I couldn't steal him (even if I later kept thinking for days on end that if I had asked him he would certainly have relinquished him and I too would have blotted myself with the injustice of adopting him, out of need or out of need for love, from parents who, whatever they are like, do exist) and I cry easily, I stroke his little feet underneath, a slight tickling, and he laughs and laughs and waves his arms and legs and I let go of the little curtain and begin to run without turning round. An auricaria with a blue butterfly is the ideal thing to have a piss against while getting one's breath back – it is as if this Mariolino had abandoned me to my fate, not I him to his. The sun strikes down and causes all my determined sentimental languor to ferment in me, and for days and days the emotional disturbance awakened in me by that marvellous and unexpected creature has had no end (a man new-born who doesn't care and smiles at you, yes at you) – a creature who will no sooner have managed to sit up than he will already be a little less marvellous and like his brothers will learn the mechanical refrain of survival, 'ten cruzados, twenty cruzados, sir', forgetting about them the moment he has got them to return to the attack, raising the price.

At another station there is a young engaged couple. They are making trays of butterflies arranged under glass or Plexiglas and they go and sell them to the tourists at Ipanema – they aren't dear. It is a bit awkward to carry but I buy one and start climbing again. The big stone statue seems always further off – and every so often, according to the bend in the path, disappears. There is a woman climbing up with me, she has a basket of red candles: 'With one of these candles even the most absurd requests for grace can be fulfilled.' I buy a candle and throw it into a gully the moment she is out of sight. I am sweating well, I take off my shirt and vest – a blister is hurting me because of the leather strap which is cutting into my left heel. I see a man huddled up, his face covered with a page of a newspaper and his jacket all over the place. He has one hand on his crotch and a few numbed dark brown fingers make me think he is losing his balls. I can't waken him as I had at first thought to tell him: 'Look I found them for you – you had lost them on the way.' Then a little family group of elderly parents with a daughter older than themselves was coming down, riding on three even-paced donkeys, obedient as puppies. Two bends later there is someone crouching on the ground all faded black – he looks like the chimney-sweep of the fairytales – he must be thirty or forty years old, like a little ravenous beast he raises his ferret's eyes to me and waves his hand and a shoebrush. I take the risk of having my shoes cleaned for the first time in my life. He makes me sit on a litle wall on his rectangle of foam rubber and the little heap of mobile rags raises his head, winks at me, rubs his eyes as if he didn't believe in so much manna so early in the morning. I put the first shoe on the foot-rest. '*Que calor!*' he says, taking off his colourless coat, and he begins to squeeze cream from the tube and then to polish. At his feet are at least five boxes of polish of different colours, four brushes of different shapes, two little plastic bottles with a wax-based liquid, two strips of cloth on his left knee. What strikes me is that this slightly simple man has no trace of beard on his dirty face. Suddenly he raises his head, gives a tenderly frightened smile and says loudly: 'Good morning to you, sir!' and I say: 'Good morning!' We are silent for some interminable seconds. 'What are you called?' I ask him. 'Victor Hugo,' says the miserable creature. I can't stop a gendarme's smile – a stupid one. 'Do you have a family in the mountain?' 'No,' and he looks round as if to say I have everything here, the brushes and the polishes. He continues to brush. A slightly distinguished-looking passer-by stops a couple of metres away, takes out his cock and pisses on the agaves, he shakes the drips off thoroughly and bows to me with his chin and I return his gesture. 'Where are you from?' I ask Victor Hugo and he says: 'From behind the mountains – it's all one landslide. I am afraid,' and he goes on to the other shoe, not before making the second sign of the cross. Every so often he shrugs to himself and laughs – but his eye remains wary as if he were ready to flee at full pelt. 'How old are you, Victor Hugo?' I hazard and he says: 'Eleven' and I cry out like a madman: 'How old?' and my heart begins to beat hard. 'Eleven,' he repeats and I jump to my feet. 'How old?' I give him a whole lot of money and compel him to endure a caress which perhaps was a punch, pick up my tray of fossil wings and somehow I too arrive up there at the Big Stone, laughing at myself and at my feet which are no less polished than my shoes, which were of course not shoes but sandals. Busi – sandals!

Paris occupied, Paris invaded, Paris which, offering the last vertebra of its undoubtedly dinosauric backbone to support the new immigration waves from Asia, the Antilles and the provinces of the interior, welcomes after the thousands of visitors to the Agricultural Fair at Porte de Vincennes, the horde of gloomy barbarians of Ante-Post Fashion: smoke-grey buyers, dark accredited women journalists and obscure swaggering American mannequins and Scandinavians trying to be dark-skinned, doleful photographers and sightless cameramen, funereal waves of inquisitive people in black who push in the Métro, in the taxi queue. The traffic blocked everywhere and at what are usually the quietest times by undertakers, sacristans and birds of ill omen in general. And welcomes me, the neophyte, who for three days have not been able to have a further night in the disproportionately dear hotel in which, every so often I go to sleep as much as is strictly necessary and wash my private parts. Something has gone wrong with the bookings and the only employee by day (because everywhere in Paris the personnel has been cut back to the bone and nowadays there are Russian queues at the tobacconists' at the corner) keeps on smiling at me mockingly while telling me that there is not a room to be found – not for three hundred nor for six hundred nor for a thousand francs without breakfast. I ask if there is any news even when I come back early in the morning but I never come across the same black night-porter: they must be an entire Franco-Abyssinian saga so many are the black night-porters who take over from each other, yawning and so crazy in their sleepy superiority that I don't even try. No one ever knows anything. Tomorrow morning they will know whether I can stay here to sleep or not and there are five clients in the same position as me – so that this little three-star hotel, all long and narrow, ends up by becoming His Majesty Versailles *garni* in person.

The first appointment I fix haphazardly is with Elisabeth de Senneville at the Hotel St James et d'Albany, Rue de Rivoli, at

11.30, where I have to climb over the catwalk to get in to the second row. Since I am punctual I am usually almost alone. Then little groups of plump Japanese women begin to take up position already very different from the cliché in vogue some seasons ago. Definitely taken over by the most Mediterranean of *looks* (which is anyway the invention of their fellow countrymen who are so clamorously innovative in terms of a setting sun dawning once more in yen), they display flamencoed hair-styles with metal combs in the chignon, eyebrows dust-red to form indigo elytra which magnify the eyes less than once upon a time, circular earrings or highly coloured Plexiglas pendants, fleshy mouths à la Jayne Mansfield, a gypsylike way of suddenly turning their necks and eyes in an unexpected olé! before composing themselves again in a state of contemplation which is all mourning and semi-absence. They have, one might say, a new way of inserting their bodies into the social space and their décolletés are knowing about their unusual generosity. It seems to me that these women, traditionally considered discreet and timid, have become shamelessly taller in the last months and less falsely thin, with their tits showing in the Western manner: they exist, carried high, no longer small, indeed conscious of moving, pretty and round, of breathing at ease. With the Japanese buyers arrive the Koreans and the Hong Kong Chinese. Asian women have once and for all acquired a cocktail beauty which is almost unattainable for the European Community women who are still too attached to the idea of themselves-in-the-year-2000, which they force themselves to keep up for fear of losing the positions they had reached. The extreme Orientals, with iron determination, have tapered themselves to a pure metasexual whim which perhaps concerns no male other than themselves. It is for this reason that they are so feminine and at ease and glamorous even if they lengthen their stride like the Swedes or cross their legs like the Texans or laugh like women from the Abruzzi. If they have abjured the kimono and the geisha melancholy it was certainly not to immolate themselves in another hairshirt however fashionable – and they are all comfortable and radiant, bursting with wealth and health, their skin is pale and stretched, and the wellbeing they inspire by breathing renders them nippled and forgetful of millennia of backbreaking slavery.

The salon, which is all Bohemian glass and sofas in pink velvet, has filled up incredibly and I have had time to look at all those present one by one as, accompanied by magnificent twenty-year-old men, they took their places. Not much sign of Italians. Waiting makes the air a little tired already, my sense of smell reaches where my eyes could not – with my nostrils I have acquired eyes in the back of my neck. The seats at either side of me say – the one 'Madame Beauté' and the other 'Madame Truffe', both of them absent at the moment, one of them will no doubt be making herself beautiful and the other sniffing herself in order to wed the Chanel to her Venus triangle after quarter of an hour of uncertainty whether she should wash herself first or not. The perspiration round about becomes a little strong, and the bright lights warm up the horrifying deodorants of armpits being fumigated – there is one woman behind me who gives off curdled camellia in a bain marie of emmenthal and washing-up liquid. I fan myself with my programme, let's see: *'années 1990 floqué flanelle grise su polo molleton chiné gris'* and at last the bright lights are lowered to flare again suddenly in a new burst of light, sharp, acrylic, with a canary-yellow flare over the first head to appear. Breathless, my two young ladies have gone past each other while treading on my shoes; they apologized to each other and plumped into their seats beside me, one ugly and the other stupid. A powerful soundtrack – you would expect austere models, not very witty or pretty and never under thirty, the ideal age for playing the little girl; instead comes a succession of tall, thin eighteen-year-olds in *'mini robe trompe-l'oeil imprimé tableau femme au serpent'*, hooked noses, hair dishevelled or like a drowned woman's. Youth is the agony of fashion. A face arrives that says 'hygienic services', *'chemise popeline col cassé rayé et gilet dessin cachemire rouge,'* another who to judge by her face should be carrying a blood-drip, skirt halfway up her thighs, in pleated elastic, with 'I am a star' printed on the back as if one didn't know that her little bottom is the star of stars. The parade is closed by a group of little girls with a few little boys covered in coats like teddy-bears, a little jewel irresistible to mothers who, since they dress up their dogs like little children, will not resist for once dressing their children like dogs. Then the creator appears, Elisabeth de Senneville, a modest and impossible woman with a shabby air of suffering, the drawn smile of someone who has sent her soul to the wrong address and, since it has been returned to sender, has not found anyone to take it in.

A great rush – no snacks – not a cracker – not a little glass of champagne – none of the liturgical post-baptismal rites which give so much pleasure to the professional pagans who adore to stuff themselves and complain about the reception. But coming out of the Albany under a kind of pre-Hiroshima sky I am pervaded by a modest happiness: as a youth I was so extremist and did not accept that, faced by even a single man in difficulty (who usually, if it was not one man multiplied by the people of a whole nation at war, was me), the whole world did not stop right away to question itself about the obvious injustice of excluding from the general motion this particular rusted life and at once run to find a remedy. Today I at most manage a somewhat forced craftiness. The days are more and more rare in which I do not succeed in reconciling cannon-fodder with *'des flanelles, des chevrons, des carreaux-Shetland, des Donegal tweeds, de l'alpaga, des moleskines'*, and taking the Métro at Les Halles, at the sight of a dozen boys and girls, complete tramps or alcoholics, while a Jamaican is trying at the top of the unmoving stairs to get it into the mouth of a terrified foreign woman who cannot manage to raise her eyelids, I think that in Daniel Hechter's collection there will be *'une note claire avec des tenues monochromes à base d'écru'*.

In my hotel I read one by one – almost as if to confuse myself and so to be in form – all the dress shows there have been and will be in Paris over these days. There are exactly one hundred and twenty and the trade names whispered out loud in the bedroom become a stupid recital of absurd examples of smart clothing going to and fro, racing from a salon to a princely loft to a garage to a Porte de Pantin ('puppet' in Italian, where Gaultier will be on parade), a kind of counter-chorus of obsolete noises, of too many seasons ago, good for sending to the Red Cross in gift parcels stamped with those blurred burnt brands that read *Lebanon, Israel, Iran, Iraq, Guatemala, Tibet, Belfast, Afghanistan,*

Sicily, Calabria, Chicago, New York, Armenia . . . It is right that fashion doesn't stop its merry-go-round, its well-known short/long, symmetrical/asymmetrical cycles: those people who can still walk about the streets without noticing the general curfew worry more about how they will be dressed than about knowing how to get back home. But it is already time to make for the *Cour Carrée* at the Louvre for the collection of a certain Christian Lacroix.

At the Porte Marengo I catch with what remains of my only tympanum some immortal reflections of the fashion addicts, those addicts with their emery-papered black 'look', black rendered opaque, damascened black: they think that fashion as a mass phenomenon cannot do other than perpetuate itself, being the only essence that cannot go out of fashion. But they are mistaken – after the Ego and God, Fashion too is dead. The rite is funereal even if no less triumphant for this, but it is the Indian summer even for those who go on playing at Indians. Fashion becomes a graveyard squabble between little women of both genders falsely warring with each other and too little inclined to take off their clothes and little men all busy overdressing in order to set their signature on their substantial lack of confidence. Fortunately the only fashion that will never set is not fashion but the stupidity with which it too (like so many other branches of contemporary industry) draws on bucketfuls of computers in order to conceal the final installation (at least where our epoch is concerned) of an emotional and therefore political inner void.

From the entrance of the courtyard one has to pass through three filters waving very visibly our strictly personal invitations. The last examination for admission ends with a search of bags and bodies. I get a heavy-jawed character with pink freckles out of *Gone with the Wind* who leaves me stunned – and it is only at the end of the day that I will realize that with one excuse or another I went out no fewer than six times in order to get felt. I go into the big tent and sit down and am suddenly assailed by a smell of stupidity. I turn round: they are all there I imagine. The correspondents of *Vogue*, of *Annabella*, of *Marie Claire*, of *Donna*, of *Moda*, of *Grazia*. A smell, in a special way, in spite of everything, of *Amica*. They are the doyens of the page 2s, with quotations from Tex Willer/Rasputin/Justine all included, refunds at the bottom of the list. They are mad about prose 'in colours, the oiled fabrics and the synthetic silks which shade off into apple green, aniseed, emerald, flame red, fuchsia, orange, silver gilt' and this when they are having a good day. They have kept a mentality worthy of a parish schoolmistress, are enemies of women who persuade people to buy, and that is why they send them to Paris or anywhere else (where even incautious writers whether *engagé* or minimalist, supplied not with bombs but with bonbonnières, have never set foot), and they all declare themselves tired of there being nothing new, they complain about the weather, the exertions, the excessive number of shows, the lack of a real idol. People who ten years ago would have had a certain chance in part-time employment by the hour and now, blackmailed, ransomed, well suited to their new status as Valuable Idiots, they abandon themselves to looking eternally jinxed, having confused emancipation from the domestic hearth with progress. You need something very different from dealing with *costume* in order to change one's face or at least one's mask! But I feel a certain tenderness for them – I know how difficult it is to sacrifice to Fashion all the talent and gifts one has never had. They are more or less the same people who when they are sent to interview a writer of whom they have not read a line (unless it be a previous interview) ask, scarcely five minutes in, 'What sign are you?' in order to begin from there and draw a portrait of the interviewee, passing meantime to the familiar form of address. I have sent off a few of them with a flea in their ear – and the word must have got around, since for more than a year no fashion journal has dared to contact me.

Benedetto Lacroix, it may even be true that, as the rumours go, he is married and moreover heterosexual and that therefore he is forgiven everything, but an hour late is too much! This sexual rarity (which Lacroix shares with Cerruti, who is also on my programme and who at the end of the show will turn up on the stage in a little yellow jumper thrown over a jumper of sugar paper in the V of which are inserted glasses with rectangular lenses, an exhibition of himself at the limits of the author's arrogance and goodness of heart) must have contributed not a little to the creation of the Exotic Myth. Something like this had not been seen since the Phoenician murex dyers, strenuous womanizers had they not been monogamous. The most fascinating point about this shithouse is the stage just inside the entrance to the big tent where black telephoto lenses go up and down like waves as if emerging from muddy waters. They are fighting each other for a centimetre, a millimetre, and if one of them changes his place he carries with him in the course of his imperceptible conquest a whole row of zooms, thus imparting to the row above and below a contrary movement to reappropriate the infinitesimal loss.

And now the music floods the feigned suspense of a wait that is more bored than trembling with excitement, in which I happened to cast my eyes at least twice on a certain Moschino, an Italian designer, who too is black, small, squat and bronzed, with the unhappy expression of someone who is going to be faced by an IOU bigger than himself. And unexpectedly Natalia Aspesi comes and sits beside me, already in a coma, along with someone she introduces as her cousin, Anna Piaggi by name, who I presume deals in the mopeds with almost the same name from which she removes the mudguards to make hats for herself. But the parade has begun and we haven't too much time either to observe each other or to observe the process of observing. The whorish female cupids with a stride that takes one's breath away parade, but from the air they take on at their second passage you would think they have become models because no one had ever thought enough of them to make them good housewives – apart from that, they would have all the muscles necessary even for digging the earth and harvesting with a sickle. The winter advances 'at once bare and variegated' in which the tunics and coats are trapezes, the skirts naturally bell-shaped, and the trousers have two legs etc. An equestrian parade, circus motifs, cockades on the sleeves, sleeves of white organza shaped like arum lilies for *le petit soir,* all very wearable, sensible, even the embroidery which will be oriental or at least ethnic like those of a little shepherdess from Herzegovina ready to make a fuss; *le grand soir* georgette and printed silks; the colours – as you like. I say to Aspesi who will look startled out of pure good manners: 'Great God, did you see what Dixan-like faces they have? Where did they get them? There isn't one beautiful woman even if you paid for her weight in gold!' and she says: 'But you'd take good care not to weigh her' and I think to myself that at the right moment I shall make her pay for this. Indeed since we are both taking notes (which I shall be careful not to throw away immediately) I catch her crouching there with her eyes on my notepad and she quickly turns away her needle-sharp eyes. 'What are you doing – are you copying from me?' and she says: 'A word or two' and I say. 'I feel honoured' and she says: 'Don't mention it – in fact if you give me another . . .' and we go on cooing to each other, leaving – but not for too long – the models to their '*look pêche pour partie romantique le long des lacs et des rivières*'. I say to Aspesi, waking her up. 'A coat like that will cost as a minimum two hundred and twenty or two hundred and fifty thousand lire' and she stares at me and shrugs and I come back at her: 'But even if someone is dressed like that where can she go, what can ever be grand enough for her and for her Norwegian pastel-coloured plaid which she would in any case have to take to the dry cleaners after two hours of these filthy pavements, of this toxic drizzle? In short – a woman dressed like this, who are you going to give her away to?' and she says: 'But no one wears them – the question is superfluous!' and I say: 'There's no one left to give her away to' and she says 'You're getting warmer!'

And the moment Lacroix appears, as pink as a little guineapig and not at all bad, all are off to Mugler's, where in an hour's time the self-same spectacle is repeated of the impossible wait and where a young English woman is saying to her German neighbour, summing things up: 'Gaultier, Armani, Versace, Gigli . . . not one of them gets away with it' and one says to the other: 'God makes them and doesn't put them together, they come up too much from nothing and Nothing is their destiny' and the other to the one who is still there: 'Do you mean that apart from Rei Kawakubo they are not human?' and she says: 'Not at all – much better than human – they are *designers*. You have to use your arse to skin the imaginary big cat. They are ideal – a really masculine prick would never manage to design the sleeve of a kimono – it has other things in its *head*.' 'So?' and the real narrating voice says: 'A subterranean autostrada with a river on top of it. Have you ever been to Antwerp? Ah, what really masculine pricks!' Certainly you always need to have a special ear to catch such dialogues. And when even Mugler with his bat-women, vampire-women, diabolical women, witch-women, mutating and sulphurous, has also closed the lid of his coffin, I at last go out at dusk into the splish-splash of the thin Parisian mud. Who knows if they'll keep me on at the hotel or will make me move out. All those multi-coloured tights were the only things one really had never seen, and also the underpants up to the waist in one piece with stockings. The flocks of black coats and rainbow-coloured long hair are going here and there, searching desperately for a taxi, it is raining, not even any budding talent around. This evening people will meet again at the Bains-Douches or at the Palace, they will change into a new black *mise*, will come to conclusions about taste and about those newly suspected to be dead, and in Anna Piaggi, whom I see appearing to levitate among little veils and old lace, and inlaid on her back in a dimension that is all skin and balls (the old lady has guts) at cockcrow will try to remember where she left her rabbit-fur scooter because she must be quick, because she has to be back in her place at Madame Chandelle's, in the famous museum, because I was there too, but so was she.

Paris is a doll in bits, Paris is a naked doll, Paris is a doll . . . Under and in the muddy skies, skirting at a walking pace a mush of passers-by chilled by the sudden downpours of rain, I go in search of something of Paris which has remained stuck in my head like a peal of bells that neither goes on nor stops. A little majolica dancer who, stupefied by the rhythm of a stasis, spins round and leaps – in the classic posture of arms in an incomplete arch – on her points in little red shoes and an emerald-green tutu. They might be golden feathers that flutter on her sides and her get-up would be that of a little boyish girl of the Thirties with a fringe and kiss-curls on her forehead like Josephine Baker. To jump – so to say – from pillar to post, the day before yesterday at the Agricultural Fair, at Porte de Versailles to be exact, I was looking at a computerized machine for harvesting olives and grapes and had the impression in the crush of a sudden warmth on my back which was running down and spreading over my buttocks. A strange pressure, which was not simply due to two groping hands but like the laying on from a distance of several hands. A spiritualist session standing up, that was it, and in the most unexpected place. I turned round and four eyes stared at me as if in me they perceived the sign of recognition and one of the two corpulent and surly cowherds flashed at me the scythe of an obscene grin. When I began to move away both pressed against me, I felt the hard sex of the other one, whose face was blank with an expression of stolid apathy, stand out against my thigh. There is an atmosphere of digested putrescence. But let us jump back to where we were.

Jeanne and her photographic gear are sharing the back seat of the taxi which had been called by radio – a woman who has not yet turned round is driving: her brown hair which is caught up in front of me by a maroon ribbon together with her big black eyes framed in the rear mirror, offer to my glance which rests on the ring finger of the hand on the steering wheel a very beautiful married woman who is also vaguely exotic. Jeanne watched me look out and perhaps also look in. I have never worked with her, I don't know her at all apart from the not unimportant information which she gave me about her mother: 'But Mamma, I said to her, you should be pleased with my situation – we women don't get AIDS!' Jeanne is got up like a Sandinista guerilla on a mission among the banana trees with a couple of pineapples in her cartridge pouches and says nothing. I told the driver to take us to the Père Lachaise cemetery and she said: 'Ah, I go there every Sunday when the weather is fine – I take the children there – it's a pity about that gang of old men who play war games with peashooters and play tricks from behind the walls.' Jeanne has only one complex: about her breasts, which overflow from a sea-green jumper and from under a furious pony-tail of curly hair of strange disturbing colour. Apart from that she was very happy to tell me as we ran down to the porter's desk: 'I am still half-asleep, my friend is such an ordinary little woman – if every so often I don't slap her face and don't let her see me throw a plate at the walls out of jealousy which I don't feel, she doesn't think I love her any more. I broke crockery until dawn to please her. But why do women not see anything without a scene? Why do they not understand that one can love and be at peace with oneself and the world? No – instead if you don't put on a tragedy on demand, if you don't shout and knock them about at regular intervals, they feel abandoned, useless, rags. By nature I am submissive but practical, I don't have extravagant roles for a woman, and instead she is always there wanting me to have balls, which, thank God, I don't have . . . they have all got in their heads this cliché of the male and the female of whom, lesbians or not, above all they all have a mythomanic idea which is far from reality. Drama first of all, that's it, then afterwards they enjoy their magazine. And when she is really warmed up I would just like to collapse with sleep, I'm so worn out . . .'

From the Odeon up and down narrow, clogged and slippery streets the taxi, snail-like, seeks out an uncertain, unusual route among crowds of black raincoats, transparent plastic overalls, heads sheltered by newspapers, coming out of the Métro stations. It is as if one were penetrating slily into the physiology of a body which recomposes itself at the very moment of its decomposition and the juncture between those two synchronous states would be provided by the legend of life: that life prevails over death and for this reason invents for itself various legendary lives. Old popular myths set to music by an excruciating voice which has acquired in the street the sense of timbre and of the distance to be filled, a way of raising the arms to heaven and letting the little prematurely bald head fall forward at the end of the song while the applause roars at, let's say, the Olympia. When a star dies the star takes with her all the applause received in life and after being compressed underground for a little they begin to emerge in the form of astral echoes. The star recalls to herself her prodigious feats for the silent celebration of nostalgia for the minor and infinitely more harrowing myths. It must be this spell of memories, often invented or grafted on to someone else's memory, that impels some individuals to bring fresh flowers – all the better if white – each day to the bright tomb of Alphonsine Plessis, the Lady with the Camelias. *La Traviata* par excellence, deprived perhaps in her life of any real access by others to her true life, she lives again today, as then, in the sentimentalistic game of obscure devoted fans. It would perhaps be unimportant to any of them to know that Alphonsine was a cold and frigid peasant woman who landed in Paris to escape from a rapist father, a girl as beautiful as impossible and to whom to mock men (their utmost sexual aspiration) cost nothing, not even the effort of a calculation: the traumas experienced in infancy had made her into a pure animal innocent of any desire for an identity of its own. With me I have a book which every so often I alternate with my newspaper. The impossible title – *My Life* – the improbable author, Isadora Duncan, of an iron generation, Hellenic, 1877.

. . . They were funerary monuments while still alive, dolls with public splendours and private miseries prone to the sickest need of ordinary people with little life of their own – the need to adore someone with even less life of their own as Piaf, the Pygmalion-like creature, had understood, advising her stage lovers to sing 'love songs for the unhappy and those with complexes' and who once, when the curtain fell, with tears in her eyes because of her old war-horse 'Mon Dieu', confided to Eddie Constantine that while she sang she was wondering whether if she sold her car and her house in the country she might be able to buy herself a Rolls. Psychic dolls, knowing or ignorant, who often, caught in the mesh of the projections subtended by their admirers, brought on – with alcoholism or drugs – passions which, when they were awake, did not wish to come but whose unconscious choreography they contrive to mount on a stage that was dazzling also because of its exciting squalor. The rise and ruin of well-acted passions was acted out under eyes which were *indiscreet* but indispensable, the chimera travestied by real thrills for their beloved public, the impetuosities, betrayals, adulteries, acts of prostitution, in time with the frenetic slow motion of the *artistic* existence until *physical and moral* ruin was followed and relived comfortably in the stalls, second by second, and the last trill or movement of the thighs left behind it a collective secondhand purification, the individual certainty that hope is the last thing to die or even that love knows no age. Ancient dolls (the Contessa di Castiglione, who lived across the road form Proust, according to the map), articulated dolls, talking dolls, *savantes*, dancing dolls, with batteries or keys, dolls lost or scattered by the wind (Maria Callas behind whose tombstone there must be a ghost of a corpse, seeing that her ashes were scattered in the Greek seas), dolls reassembled in the laboratory of the late Monsignor Renard, in Rue de l'Échaudé, or in encyclopedias, in a fans' club. In a block of silky marble with the sun behind it which scatters golden rays, a dawn, which has certainly had a face-lift – Dalida, the photograph of whose tomb I have with me. Dolls hollowed out by success or the loss of success – lone dolls, who one evening with their little hands release their imaginary grasp on the world and commit suicide to avenge themselves and to repay their adorers, who are guilty of so much mummification, using the coin current among guineapigs who are alive only in words. And now their punished admirers are learning to recognize themselves and from being one become two, and then three and then three thousand and bring into being a Broken-hearts Association in which to venerate She who Wears the Sense of Guilt for having no very clear idea of what to do about certain lively and secret shame-inducing pulsations. Dolls who left their mark on an epoch, a decade, a time between two wars, the fall of an empire, the transition to a republic, a democracy or simply the revolution which was more stable in those days: the mocking use of the accordeon as a weapon of national, popular disobedience to the *bourgeoisie* of Gaullist power. Dolls from the slums or the conservatory, a Street-Sparrow, a Casque d'Or, also a Communist in her own way, a Casta Diva with her pretty hats that would suit a respectable housewife, a Female Suicide bearing the marks of affairs with male-suicides (three in the case of Dalida), vampirized vampires, ashes shining in the sub-cortical curtains of people who live encased in armour, who will never tell you the secret reason for their pilgrimage. People who at this moment are buying on Boulevard Saint-Michel or Raspail or perhaps a hundred kilometres from here a little bunch of violets or a vase of cyclamens arranged carefully on the next seat and the guard who by chance glances at them or the passengers in the Métro who do everything in their power not to jostle it, will never imagine the destination of these flowers and why that woman, that man, has in his or her fate a legend of tuberculosis which persists a hundred and fifty years on.

I know from experience that visitors to tombs are not chatty and that when they agree to speak they mistake geese for phoenixes of Araby and that they are visiting a mysterious mystery carefully unburied and reburied before and after every conversation on the subject. Who knows for what arcane pain or frustration they have been able to identify their own life with that of a dead woman seen perhaps only in a film or heard on the radio or put together again in an opera with a salon with beautful big chandeliers to illuminate the progressive and erotic invasion of subliminal catarrh. Two of Piaf's lovers have told me of a hypothesis at which I had arrived by myself merely by listening yesterday to 'Mon légionnaire', 'Mon amant de la Coloniale' and 'Le fanion de la Légion': the 'mon amour amour' offered her mauve bed to almost everyone because she passed her life expecting an unattainable orgasm. The exes go on pitilessly. She subjected them all to a test of disgust, the aim of pleasure: in vain she yearned – male after male – for a man who would be capable of resisting her destructive ardour once she had him in her grasp. She offered herself to the *real men* of *Quai des Brumes* as *the real woman*. She never had an orgasm – a tiny and vicious being, the most irresistible of frigid women and tarts: dirty and ugly sex, the voluptuous twists and turns of an impassioned breast that was all hunger, impulses, morphine and further down still, vaginitis and cysts and syphilis. The solitude of the unmentionable: their tiny humanity, simple, a stalk too weak to bear the poisonous flesh of all the chimeras of other people. Perhaps each visitor is convinced that he or she is the only one to have understood *who* that sacrificial victim was who immolated herself on her own spontaneous stubbornness. Yet the only thing that counts is that Piaf's voice, then as now, sends shivers down one's back – and the texts – by real writers – are still harrowing, since prosody rules there with a rod of iron. How much sweat to make a *musette* waltz – done contrariwise, jokingly against the traffic, against everything, the overturned rule of the existing rules, a rule in its turn.

Edith Piaf was a genius and geniuses *are* the dolls of their time. But among all these conjectures – of which I have not given the slightest hint to Jeanne, who is trying to catch in the rear mirror the almond eyes of the amber-coloured taxidriver with the oriental profile – here is another making way for itself, called up by a pathetic apparition at a traffic light in Barbès: an old woman with a big black plastic bag from whom the wind has snatched her hat and wig. She is pursuing her precious shame amid the wares of the Africans who are roaring with laughter on the pavement which is covered with a big sheet of plastic patted into tiny beehives. Bees, Queen Bee, Praying Mantis, Drone, and in the end after all that can-can, Goya to the disorientated trot of an old woman mocked by black men.

Jeanne was saying, ideally turning her attention back to the slightly wide-opened eyes in the little mirror: 'You either like women or you don't. Then there are the halfway houses. Which most people go to. Not only men but women.' I open, by no means at random, Duncan's book: 'Having arrived in Berlin I got myself taken to the Hotel Bristol where in a magnificent apartment I found Loïe Fuller in the midst of her usual retinue. A dozen beautiful girls were round her, some stroking her hands, others with their arms round her. I remembered in my innocence that my mother, in spite of the deep love she felt for us, rarely gave us a caress and I was amazed by these displays of extreme affection which were entirely new to me. I sat down a little to one side, astonished to hear for the first time unknown words which seemed to me to be the currency of their conversation: "My sweet little dove, my tiny one, my adored one, my love . . ." It was the first time in my life that I felt such a warm and sensual atmosphere materialize . . .' and Jeanne as if reading my thoughts says to me: 'Do you want to see the Realm of the Lesbians first? You might find it interesting. I know a woman who sells parts of old dolls.'

I look at her, look out of the window – there is a fat girl with a stall of giant asparaguses in front of her and, waving one in front of her trouser-fly, she is shouting at the top of her voice: 'Ladies, look what sort of thing the earth makes', then I turn round and look at her questioningly with a sabbatical trace of suspicion and distrust. 'Let's go!' I say and Jeanne says to the driver: 'Porte de Clignanourt – do you know where the Marché Paul Bert is? What is . . .' but I get in first and ask: 'What is your name?' and the woman at the steering-wheel, who is now offering us the face of an austere belly-dancer in a Delacroix painting, says: 'Fatma. Why?' and I, being too absorbed to answer, say: 'Ah, I didn't know!' and Fatma, uncertain whether to smile or not says 'What did you know?' and I say: 'That perhaps you are not of French descent but Italian or Arab' and she says: 'That doesn't take much, nosy. First the cemetery and now that we have arrived, the little flea-market. It will take another half-hour with this traffic. Are you pleased?' and Jeanne says: 'We are very pleased – we're going to find a friend of mine who sells old-fashioned dolls. She is a harmonious dwarf' and Fatma, turning to me in the rear mirror, asks: 'Do you suddenly want to buy a doll?' and I say: 'I don't know yet – I don't think so. I've even managed to survive without the plastic inflatable ones – so you can imagine' and Fatma at last presents us with a dazzling smile devoid of any malice. I look at her beautiful hands lying casually on the steering wheel, which are the typically chapped ones of a woman who has two jobs, and I stare at her in the litle mirror to see if by chance her eyes too, because of this frenzy which consumes me to separate flesh from celluloid, have not also in the meantime become glass ones.

No – I don't think so – this Salammbô transplanted into a limousine of another time does not dance, does not sing, does not drink and does not smoke, this woman is securely alive with the indispensable minimum of transgression. A serene Muslim woman, come from semi-desert zones, had certainly not done so to see on the banks of the Seine the mirages she had fled from in her own country. I like Fatma. And I like Jeanne too. I should like to be the maker of a four-wheel affair together with these young women who will be in full flower for a long time yet – a Tunisian and an American of Russian origin whose paths have crossed thanks to the good (laconic) auspices of an ano-italic narrator. 'I have been a taxidriver for many years – but why are you so curious? And why do you go from one address to another?' and I say: 'I was thinking of all the attempted adventures which a beautiful woman like you must confront in this work – adventures with other men obviously' and she says, laughing a little disconcertedly but full of charm: 'You are mistaken – all my clients behave correctly – I am a karate brown belt and I just have to let them know that for them to keep their hands to themselves. And then they go into the back seats' and Jeanne says: 'Have you been in Paris long? Can I take your photo afterwards?' And she says: 'If you really want to. I came to France in 1973, I already had a little boy of three, when the time comes for military service he will have to decide whether to become a naturalized French subject or remain a Tunisian, but he will have to do his service, I think it is good for a man, they need it: but my little girl was born here – she's French. A French Muslim and first-class private schools for both of them. I and my husband work like blacks but we are insistent on education' she spells out with pride.

Among overpasses and traffic barriers we have arrived and we drive past the booths of what is now called only from tradition the marché aux puces seeing that the prices are as prohibitive as everywhere else and where the goods are no longer 'old', or 'secondhand' but 'folk-craft of the recent past' with labels all over them and any haggling over the price taboo. 'Would you mind waiting, Fatma? Meantime here is the money for the trip.' 'Certainly, with real pleasure' and I say, standing out there in a puddle balancing on my heels ('Being prevented from dancing on his toes he tried to imitate them by dancing on his heels' – remember to put it in my fifth and last novel): 'Come on – you're not trying to tell me that with a driver like this the customers are so rude that every one of them is well-behaved' and Fatima says, blushing but definite: 'I am a happily married woman, and a free woman. Free to do this *dangerous* work because there is the most absolute trust between me and my husband. Certainly I don't make up the way I would like . . .' and we set off through alleyways and the reconstruction of a *bistro d'autrefois*, all brass and gleaming mirrors, on the left towards the Empire of the Lesbians.

Of the unmarried women and divorced ladies standing or sitting among slightly worn *consoles* and divans, *fin de siècle* lamps, bronze statues and opalescent marble busts, there are at a glance about ten, some wild and neglected and others stiff and formal with an opaque look. I admire a little Liberty vase, I ask the price, and the young woman with the straw-coloured hair whispers a figure worthy of Sotheby's. From the corrugated gutters there is a steady drip of little drops down inside the hood of my jacket.

Jeanne lowers her voice and begins to gossip – in fact to tell tales: 'They are famous because since they work as a couple with the lover of the moment with whom they share the business, they all end up cuckolding each other and going the rounds of the various stands. Each one, you may say, has been or will be with another woman. They grow old in a merry-go-round into which no new blood is admitted. When they are definitely old they find themselves back where they were before, I mean, at the stand from which they began to give off their amorous humours. Each period has its own lesbians. These ones here are different from me even in their smell – they smell a little of incense, don't you think?' and she says these incredible things with all the fellow-feeling and sense of sisterhood worthy of an ornithologist for a species that is becoming extinct. 'At a certain age first love, I imagine, is never forgotten and the first antiquarian, the initiator, gets over it with the latest in her turn,' I observe. 'They take each other's places clockwise, thus imparting to the clock an ogival shape. I think that the passions and crushes (there is no difference, according to me) of lesbians are notoriously stormy and peaceful, long and short, almost like any others of any other species that plays snakes and ladders before breaking off with the boring final sight of anatomical parts which have met, clashed, snuggled in, caressed each other, penetrated each other, contemplated each other, been sucked and abandoned in the pompous business of trying to give a lasting framework to the fleeting moment – and the only frame arrives hurling itself discus-like in the wind, like a menhir of the mind which only in itself and in its own eclipse finds that truly fixed mooring on which to hang itself for ever. And perhaps not even in itself, seeing that it isn't there any more. Then there would be the *dolls*. But that's enough!'

The owner of the shop, which is all beams and plywood and lofts, receives me with the manners of a great lady, pulling her nostrils down a little and puffing out her upper lip, enough to give a feeling of professional and worldly expertise. 'Call me Papillon like everyone else,' she tells me with a fluted voice, this lady with her bewitched age, tiny build, dressed in velvety dust, moving about with agility among heads big and little and boxes of buttons and crumbs of tortoiseshell and bone and chipped arms and tiny lace clothes and snuffboxes overflowing with little pearls sold by weight and then little plastic shoes – or velvet ones – of every fairytale size, petticoats of tulle and cretonne patched or mended, worn little aprons of georgette, hairpins, hatboxes which stand on the palm of one's hand, rare whole dolls and a profusion of backs of papier mâché or china, two huge tousled heads. The hair is real and a feeling of unease at the touch shakes me out of the childish frame of mind into which I had fallen. Real hair then, twenty years old – nuns, serving-girls, converts, peasant women, the hair of resigned ladies, dolls of Christ as well as mechanical dolls from madhouses. My glance falls on a row of little vases containing eyes of various sizes, brown and blue, the whole eyeball or only the convex almond or only very narrow pupils. 'How is business?' and Papillon says, fluttering her few eyelashes sadly: 'Not very good with the elections just round the corner . . .' 'Because the elections put a brake on this kind of business too?' and she says, fluttering her eyes to the utmost: 'Elections in France bring everything to a stop, including dolls. People count every centime. But if you're interested in dolls why don't you take a book? There are so many of them, you know.' 'Yes, I know, but they don't tell me what kind of people buy them, collect them because . . .' 'First and foremost they are nearly all disenchanted collectors – don't imagine that they have any sort of inclination . . . a form of investment – certainly collectors on a small scale come here and then there are – and then – ' and she stops, looks me up and down, looks for confirmation that I am not a counter-agent, and says: 'Look there are, as I was saying, whole libraries about dolls, illustrated and priced according to their format and period – ' 'No – I'd like to know something else – apart from the collectors, in short, the kinds of fetishism, particular stories for example' – I was about to say 'paedophilia at one remove' but I apply my brakes in time.

My indifferent, all-forgiving tone cannot have escaped Papillon, or the fact that I now consider fetishism – perhaps out of desperation – to be the last shore of poetry and freedom with oneself and, raising my eyes to heaven, the gentle souls who practise it. The harmonious dwarf contemplates yet another spot of embarrassment and wrinkling her face like parchment allows a little air to whistle in a very caried molar and says, passing her tongue over her yellow teeth: 'Listen, I am usually discreet, and you know Paris is no bigger than a handkerchief . . .' and gives me to understand that first she must play about a little with a reticence that is theatrical and truly Parisian. I let her go on as she pleases and then begin to stare at her and she starts in a low voice as if she were betraying a secret of the confessional. 'Well, just yesterday a buyer came back, he had bought one from me that wasn't of the cheapest – I don't have complete important items I have pieces chiefly – and this gentleman in his fifties who had come here with his wife says: "Your doll isn't well, it has got a lot thinner these last two weeks, what can I do?" and I replied as if there was nothing odd: "You didn't by any chance put it in a room where no one ever goes?" and he says: "Yes – how did you know? It is on the bed where my sister-in-law died, the bedroom is usually shut" and I say: "You see? You must put it every day where people come and go, you will see that it gets better right away." Do you think he's mad? Not in the slightest. Or that I am mad? No – I am the accomplice in a pain. I take part in pain as if in a game. How do I know – maybe the business with the sister-in-law isn't true at all – maybe it is his wife who sends him, maybe it is she who finds it hard to put up with and invents ridiculous fears. Maybe they lost a daughter some time or other and they have had no heirs. But these are rare cases – most people compare prices and pieces, swap them, deal in them, go to auctions. An investment, I repeat. And it has never ever happened to me that anyone has ever bought an old doll to give it to a little girl as a present – perhaps to start her off. No. A month ago the daughter of a well-known collector picked up a museum piece and her father who came into the room unexpectedly caught her in the act and almost beat her to death and now the little girl is in plaster and he is inside. It was a doll with its mouth closed – they are worth much more than ones with their mouth open, which are more recent. Apart from her ribs, he knocked out her teeth – his daughter's teeth – imagine that. A few cases of very rich childless women, children in their forties who buy a doll for a penultimate plunge into infancy. It means that they renounce everything in their lives, their marriage and extra-maternal affections. They are the most defenceless of women.'

I say looking sideways at her, inviting her to a slightly *osé* confidence: 'And do they allow themselves to be consoled?' She pulls in her cheeks and turning her back to me says: 'Certainly not by me. Then there is a husband who collects them because he can't have an erection when making love unless he is surrounded by dolls with wide-open eyes. He needs lots of them and always new ones – there's a constant coming and going to buy them and to sell them back, to bargain. His rich wife – he's as poor as a church mouse – finances this neurosis of his. She couldn't care less. I would be deadly jealous if my friend . . .' but she breaks off and bites her lip. 'Well you know people are very lonely these days. Very unbalanced. Try to speak to someone you don't know in the street, you'll see the way they look you over or the fear that leaps out. Life is very hard – specially for women – cases of vandalism, sexual assaults – they don't even get into the papers – they would have to take a whole page every day for them. I am also a *bouquiniste* by the Seine with prints, old reproductions, old scores. Every so often they set fire to one of our stalls. It doesn't matter whether they are men or women. They destroy – just for something to do. You know anything that sticks out from a stall, from a beam, like a padlock or a bolt, is pulled off, torn away? To me it's a wish for self-castration.' 'What did you do before this?' 'Secretary in a town council. I worked for the public building department.' 'Ah, that's why you are so good at deciphering the phallistic Freudian phenomena of the pavement!' I kiss her hand exaggeratedly since I have to bow down very low and we go off. She waves her hand which looks to me like a little one, cheerful but detached.

Fatma seemed anxious to see us again, she gets into gear and the traffic becomes a little thinner just before midday. In a flash we are at the Père Lachaise cemetery. A photo of Fatma and the end of the affair! We leave her to the next well-behaved client. Jeanne and I study the map and I say: 'Let's go to Simone Signoret, Section 44, and opposite in the Columbarium there is Isadora Duncan; one more – one less.' 'Where does Simone Signoret come in?' says Jeanne and I say: 'I am afraid I was rude to her once.'

'You were?' 'I'm afraid so – I'm not sure. Perhaps not – seeing that I didn't mean it – but who knows what she felt?' Jeanne shrugs at my sudden silence: the less a photographer knows the better. All she has to do is obey, that is all one asks. However Jeanne accepts with good humour to be led – she's not stupid like those other two in Iceland and South America who wanted to do whatever came into their heads without having anything in them. Jeanne has read all of my novels that can be read in French, she is mollycoddled by me. I have told her that when we are received by Zizi Jeanmaire she must not take part in the conversation for any reason. She is to take her photographs and that's all, say hello on entering and goodbye as we leave. Jeanne jumps to attention a second before my command comes, I adore her: she goes along with the feigned game of hierarchies and learns in a second psychological niceties which usually never enter a photographer's head even after Lumière-years. Jeanne enjoys from one moment to another real intellectual autonomy; my little theatre of cruelty didn't last long with her, she was able to cope with it without being obstinate and I trust her entirely. I have learned to tell her afterwards, when it might seem irremediable, what I should have imparted to her before she took her photos. So that she can get used to a private eye's sense of smell and learn to see with the only eyes that count here – mine. She is too good by now to be content with her own and I entrust her definitely with all four.

As we make for the interior of the Columbarium I tell her straight out: 'I remember Simone Signoret in the garden of a villa outside Lille, perhaps at Roubaix, at the end of 1969 or the beginning of 1970 – she was going in and out of the door – inside there were all the technicians and lights and cables and so on – as if unable to be at ease because after goodness knows how long I was still there with Yves Montand, talking about what else but women – his, naturally. La Piaf, Marilyn Monroe, the American scene, everything. Montand wasn't filming that day, I was waiting to be called. I had got to know an assistant to the director, Costa-Gavras, and he had given me a part that lasted three days. The film was called *The Confession*, it was set in Czechoslovakia and I played a plain-clothes policeman. I had a fur-lined coat that came down to my ankles and they had cut off almost all my hair. Well before that I had seen Signoret a couple of times, I think when I was working in my transport agency, in the same *bistro* where I was a friend of the owner, an elderly lady with rows of blister pearls which existed alongside the false pearls of a very distinguished lady friend. They said they were sisters. The few artists in the city went there. Both times it had been early in the morning – it couldn't have been earlier – and she arrived with a devastating thirst and without expression knocked back a couple of cognacs, her face swollen, full of wrinkles, sleepless, her eyes fixed on something – perhaps the label on the bottle. There were only the three of us, there was no one else there. Having recognized her, I had greeted her with all due respect, she made a gesture with her chin and a face which made me desist from any civilities, I turned my back on her at once. The first time. The second time, I say hello to her again and she comes out with a curse, to which out of good manners I do not reply but swallow hard. She was deep in an alcoholic dimension, grim, perhaps facing a disastrous balance-sheet. She was ugly. Her green eyes – those famous ones – gleamed with fierce animal malignity. I had told a joke, better still a pun on *faire la queue*, and the manageress had burst out laughing, I had brought it off very well. Anyone could have laughed – but not Signoret.

'She had thrown a disapproving glance at the woman and her pearls which were clattering under her noisy laughter. I had the feeling that Signoret was granting me a moment of blind and irrational hatred, of a menstruating woman faithfully betrayed by an infernal being with no regard for anything – not even a special woman like her. She alternated brandy and pastis, anisette with a drop of water, anisette with a drop of water. If she stared at me I did not drop my gaze. One gaze went on and on and then she was not even able to act out her hatred for the imagined lack of respect. She lost with the look. The first morning that I found her in front of me on the set – and before bumping into her I had rehearsed a dozen times a scene in which with other members of the Czech secret police I got in and out of a period car and was worn out – she seemed not to recognize me, in fact, I had cut off my curls, and she paid no attention to me when I had to begin to go back and forwards from a staircase acting out a search until our eyes met and she certainly saw in me the witness to a couple of drunken bouts that needed to be hidden – but who knows whom she saw sober or drunk. She recognized me and embarrassed by the hatred which I felt was mounting in the green of her eyes, I said to her precipitately almost as if I were saying good morning: "Oh you know I followed your flop in *Macbeth* in London, performance after performance. Not long ago, was it?" In fact three years had passed but my remark must have plunged her into that precise moment, into that precise flop, which went on for a month. I saw flash out from her the humiliation she endured performance after performance. She turned round suddenly and went off. Partly I was pleased at the effect I had produced but I had no intention either of taking my revenge for her state of snobbish indifference to me in the bar or of offending her. I was sorry at once, really unhappy, but by now the damage was done.

'The second day my break was longer than usual. Montand was around, there was nice sunlight in the garden, he was outside smoking. I had begun to talk to him while Signoret had been busy for two hours in a kitchen scene with a little old woman dressed in black. I noticed that she was looking at us through the porthole in the door, she looked like an overcooked sunfish, I felt ill at ease, I was embarrassed, but all the same I did not want for that reason to stop talking to the *best-endowed* actor in France – oh, you know they used to say that this indiscretion must have come from Piaf's dirty talk, she didn't beat about the bush when it was a question of calibres and showing off – But what is going on here in the Columbarium? Don't you think there are more and more people?' I check on the map and see: Maria Callas. I leave Duncan's bare stone and mix with the little group of music-lovers. Each one is looking for the niche on their own, I too and Jeanne too, we go over a hundred or so and then we all look at each other. A Portuguese woman says: 'But it must be here amongst all this.' A couple of Spanish gays: 'We've been looking for it for an hour,' then an Italian trio arrive out of breath, very effeminate and stuck up, who unfold the map in unison. 'Niche 16257,' one warbles. 'It's down here,' the other says in tune. 'They don't say where it is so that you have to ask the caretaker and tip him!' the third intones. And we all rush down into the vault with the Mimis and Toscas and the Normas at the head, the operatic arseholes, all little one hundred per cent cashmere jumpers, canary yellow, deep red, celestial-Aïda blue.

'Montand was affable,' I tell Jeanne as we climb up again and make our way towards Section 97. 'I was carrying out a real interview/interrogation with him, seeing how I was dressed! I didn't care for Montand physically, too *mec*, too old, but I liked him a lot as a person – witty, quick in his replies. I knew all about his trips to Russia then. He too, like Gide, did a political turnabout, the renunciation of the basic Stalinism because of which they had had their moment of glory in Moscow. It is odd how for reasons which are inherent in tea-making, those who fall out with the myth of Communism end up by becoming what they were previously: a member of the upper bourgeoisie, demagogic to begin with and less covertly later. In Italy the same thing has happened with Dario Fo – he has been the victim of a sort of homologizing process that has finished him off artistically as well. Populism has to be paid for no less than integration when it occurs and those directly interested pretend it doesn't. From being revolutionaries they are reduced to transgressors, the same difference as there is between stealing high explosive from the Boss State and jam from a mother who is consenting and takes a long view of things where glucose derivatives are concerned. Montand, on the other hand, did not even ask my name nor what the devil I was doing, an almost beardless Italian youth, there on the borders of Belgium. He was very fond of talking about himself, of remembering his youth, of telling me things – even intimate ones – about the women he had had, which had perhaps unleashed a flush of jealousy in Signoret there at the little window. You know, many months later I met him by chance in Saint-Germain and he recognized me, and when I was near him – I was coming from the opposite direction – he greeted me: "Good evening, how are things?" I am still grateful to him for that greeting – so I existed, so I left a mark on the existence of other people even when I was behaving as lightly as an elf. And that is why I decided to visit Signoret – to erase the suspicion that I had ever wanted to be rude to her intentionally. And then, listen, what does a flop matter to someone addicted to the bottle? She may have been drinking because she was losing her husband, so much more courted and seductive than her who had plunged into a premature ageing process. Ah, if only I could remember properly that scene when he meets Marilyn for the first time! I think it was in the lift in the house of an American producer. He said she was a very shy girl. His eyes shone a lot; when Signoret came and with some excuse carried him off he put on the look of a nurse, or perhaps only of a husband. She loved him, he was fond of her. Here is Piaf, buried with her father and her last child-husband; for her who was terrified to pass a single night alone it must be a great relief now – these two guardians who no one can take away from her any more.' And some middle-aged tourists leave it all to us after having also laid flowers.

Scarcely a minute later a couple of men arrive – in their fifties – my God, they are the same ones as at the Fair! Shifty eyes – on me and not on Jeanne – they stand a bit away, one of them looking a little more stupid than the other day, the other with a weasel look – both fat, but solid, built like oxen. Criminal faces of armed pickpockets, they have a way of looking at us that bodes no good. I keep thinking that Jeanne's equipment is worth a few million and that in a cemetery suddenly with no one about, on a dull afternoon like this murders are committed for much less. But the two look hard at me, taking sudden turns – and suppose they were simply two farmers from Toulouse here for the Agricultural Fair who fell in love with me from behind? When one of them takes off his little black hat and the other his woollen cap and they turn down the collars of their waterproofs I recognize the marvellous feeling of terror. Did they both touch me up at least once or did they put the evil eye on me? Now I feel myself very flattered, the two of them haven't yet realized that shortly I shall be older than them. Unless they are two odd gerontophiles who like old men in good form. But in any case types who are not much to be recommended, taciturn, the kind of people who are even capable of running you through with a fork before carrying you off to the manger in a stable. A touch of madness kept in check etc. It is as if we were playing at pig in the middle, I do not know how to defend myself from the arrogance of their slavering look – besides, just here, but in summer with everything in full flower, I just managed by a hair's-breadth to escape from an attack by suspicious-looking tramps, whom I had met in the rustling bushes which I had entered out of hunger for sex at all costs and two of them were there, squatting to shit, and a third up in the fork of a plane tree as scout, and then at a whistle he came down faster than a squirrel and I began to run because they were literally at my heels. I have never fully understood this episode, how much of it is imaginary – very little, I believe – but for years I have been gnawed at by curiosity to know what those three were up to hidden like that among the foliage of the giant plane tree. A new grave to desecrate, a drug party, or were they waiting for a fresh supply of beer from a fourth good-time lycanthrope whom they had sent to do their shopping?

The smarter of the two says: 'We keep meeting,' addressing me, attempting a grimace of a smile, and if it is meant as a greeting it is still disgusting. And I say: 'Paris is a small place' and he says: 'Do you know that up to twenty years ago the keepers had their private gardens here? Great vegetables, how they grew, better than modern fertilizers! They pulled them up when Indian hemp arrived. Are you here for the Fair too?' he says while the other looks as if he were covering his back, on the lookout to stop me from running away. He isn't at all interested in Jeanne's camera and exposure meter and rolls of film, he likes me – that's what it's all about. In fact as I move off the one who must be the *boss* of this pair of sadists from darkest France says to me: 'Are you staying long in Paris?' – a question that disconcerted me because what answer can you give a man who has the audacity to pay court in a threatening way to another man who could also be the man of the woman at his side? 'Yes,' I say, turning my back on him by now, and he says: 'We are going to see Dalida's grave, it is the most impressive of them all . . . Are you coming?' Jeanne, who is game for anything, looks at me questioningly but without fear. 'No thank you, we're tired, goodbye' and he comes up to me, takes me delicately by the wrist and says: 'Would you be interested in a black Mass? Tonight? I'm sorry but ladies are excluded . . .' 'No thank you really – with this damp weather!' And disappointed he says: 'I made a mistake . . . and in any case it's in a flat! You don't have a devil in your body, we thought you had!' and he retraces his steps. Jeanne comments: 'Misogynists – but nice. In any case it's either that or nothing – otherwise what sort of characters would they be? The world is sinking because of people who are mad and normal. These are better.' I bow to her wisdom and sagacity and we arrange to meet next day.

At eleven o'clock the mud of the sky had changed colour and the ragged and contemptuous custodian of the cemetery in Montmartre is leaning on the fountain getting water and is spitting viscous stuff with a violet tinge. At the monument to Dalida two black boots emerge from the valley of vases of flowers and an extraordinarily beautiful girl is cleaning all round without raising her eyes from her rag and pail. Honey-blonde thigh-length hair, clad all in black, tight black trousers, a tight-fitting top, a contrite expression, a mourning look. Very dainty, as if in a ballet, the most living and passionate thing I have chanced to see in these buckets of rain and of humanity wading through the buckets. Dalida stands upright on the black marble as if on the top layer of a cake at a wedding that went wrong – the bridegroom having run off at the last minute taking a moment to commit suicide just so as to get on with the honeymoon. 'No photos, please,' says the girl with her weepy voice, 'I do it for her not for myself.' And I say 'A relative?' 'No, a friend, Dalida helped me a lot when I was an adolescent – she was very close to me.' 'Naturally I very much appreciate your gesture – your devotion to her memory, but there can't be anything wrong with a photograph,' I say, lying shamelessly. 'What is your name?' 'Mariethé.' 'And you come here on Saturdays to keep it clean?' 'No, every day.' 'Really!' 'Me in the morning and Barbara in the afternoon. There is so much to do and we don't trust the custodian, who takes away the flowers which she says come over the edge of the plot. She throws everything away, that witch – candles, cards, vases that have just arrived. A war. She says: "Who does Dalida think she is? a dead woman like all the rest" and she gets angry with us and the monument. We from the Dalida Society have to keep watch' and I say: 'What kind of society? How many of you are there?' 'Thanks to the 1921 law the society has been declared in the public interest and a public utility. There are lots of us, even a few men, all aspiring sucides.' 'Ah, it seemed a little odd to me that the State . . . and Dalida keeps a good watch?'

'She watches as well as she can. In a year three have slipped through her fingers. Barbiturates, the Seine, electric current in the bath. I pray a lot,' and I cannot but notice how much Mariethé herself could be an object of adoration. Her beauty is stronger than all the effort she makes to shroud it in black. 'If you like we can meet,' she suggests, 'and talk about Dalida more calmly. So many wrong things have been written about her because of her friendship with Mitterrand! They have even gone so far as to say that she was one of the first transsexuals operated on in Casablanca!' and I say: 'Was she?' 'No, she was a woman obviously' and I have to resist the temptation, more than Jeanne, to ask her if she ever had intimate relations with Dalida so that I can write my bit in the style of Pierre Louÿs. 'I should be extremely happy to invite you to supper,' I whisper to her, and leave her my address.

Next day she doesn't ring, on the third day I had to move from the hotel where I was and go to another. Then thanks to all the elaborate arrangements set up by me between porter and porter, Mariethé's message reaches me; but I was out and she does not leave me her telephone number. Every time I go out I am tense, she could at least give me the means of getting in touch with her. On the fourth day another message; but I wasn't in the hotel. Then I begin to go out less, even if I have to go out because of my engagements with a young boy from Guadeloupe, who grew up in a social services orphanage and who, in a bug-ridden little hotel, is giving me a course in sex à la Coco Chanel, Caribbean penury and African female dresses, because this is the passion which was passed on to him by the missionary sisters. Hairdo today, hairdo tomorrow, Eugène now even calls himself 'chéri' when reporting direct speech ('Chéri, said someone who was my friend and died of cancer of the bones; and one day my nurse said to me: "Chéri, you mustn't cry any more – chéri, your mother is dead and, chéri, your father too, chéri, and one day I'll die too, chéri" '). Yet the services in spite of the smell of nail-varnish, his up-to-date black briefs, his calling himself 'chéri', are savage and semi-permanent as one might imagine finding oneself on a little island of the Antilles with a very tall creole who is altogether too well proportioned all over.

And then in a dusk singed like a voodoo doll pierced with rusty pins, Jeanne and I set off to meet Zizi Jeanmaire. The maid in ordinary clothes shows us into a drawing-room which is all damask, the colour of a blood transfusion, with divans in the same haemorrhaging material and big cushions like spotted Dalmatians. Zizi is slightly late, she arrives out of breath: 'Oh forgive me, forgive me! The television, Roland is leaving for a ballet at the Bolshoi and I ought to make a disc at last, an important appointment . . . Forgive me.' I give her an idea of my intentions and, having got rid of her doeskin waterproof with mantilla, she goes on like a thoughtful little girl: 'But then I must go and put on a little rouge! Oh my poor hair, it looks like a mop. All this rain! But where will we end up if not in an ark – if Noah lets us in' and she flutters away like a Sylphide, a few grammes of tissue paper which take off from the ground as if they had caught fire. In the doorway Roland Petit appears, more handsome than ever, and greets us and disappears again. The maid brings us unwillingly what we had asked for: plain mineral water without ice or lemon so as not to be a nuisance. Zizi comes back and nestles down in the cushions, releasing a kind of gratitude at us who are so grateful. She is so tiny, so warm, but she is wearing trousers and nothing is to be seen of her legendary legs which made the fortune of the Casino de Paris. And she is just as much a *coquette* as – how long ago? two centuries? a century? No, ten years ago when on Italian television she was still doing those little ballets with her chair-lover which left me amazed.

She insists that I am making unfortunate calculations, she looks at me a little afraid, I set her mind at rest: 'Madame, I have absolutely no intention of interrogating you but at most getting a *numéro de charme*. I don't want confessions nor will I ask embarrassing questions, *charme* and nothing but *charme*.' And she says: 'Oh, in any case it is only like this that we can talk – by mutual seduction. The rest comes of its own accord,' and she sighs: 'I'm not too untidy?' and seems to be saying: 'It's not too much of a disappointment? Wouldn't I be wiser not to grant even this interview after so many years when I refused myself? Is it not madness at my age to let myself be photographed?' But it was not my unknown name that opened this door to me but a little word whose magical powers one has to go abroad to understand: Italy. 'You, see, a ballerina dies twice: once – the necessary time and that's all right with me. The other, and the harder to bear, when one has reached the peak of refinement, of technique, of the possession of one's expressive powers, when one knows to a millimetre the extension of one's muscles and of one's tendons, the final orchestration of one's body on stage: in short, artistic maturity which cannot be perfected any further. There you are – at that point one ought to die, leave the field or become ridiculous. Think of Nureyev – a genius and now just a human case. I, *bien sûr*, no longer dance on points, though I can still do so much by dancing, but the focal point has become the song. The musical has saved me from a precocious death. I have just finished a season at the Bouffes du Nord, six hundred seats all taken for a month.' 'I was looking for one of your discs . . .' 'Oh, there are some about.' 'And you're not sorry to have worked so much without leaving a trace of yourself?' She says with sincere modesty: 'But what I like is contact with the living public. What is supposed to remain? It is not important. Nothing is more important than a fleeting emotion.' And I say: 'Certainly in France there is a real hothouse of great stars of a certain age but still with us: Régine, Barbara, Gréco, yourself . . .' and Zizi says: 'Yes, but someone like Piaf is born once in a hundred years, there can't be thirty-six of them – we are the trimmings. I, for example, have my own timbre, my own style, I imitate no one: Queneau, Aragon, Marcel Aymé, I have a whole list of Nobel prizes – but Piaf is always Piaf. Like your . . . what's she called?' and she puffs out her cheeks and spreads her arms round her stomach and I say: 'Mina.' 'Yes, Mina, that's it – it is extraordinary – no one else will be able to come up to her maybe for decades. And they have to be made to die off before we realize it. But so it is with everything – humanity has to be forgiven' and she smiles frankly without the slightest feeling of revenge, envy, regret.

Zizi is a very lively creature because she always kept the feathers in their place – she never stuck them in her head: she put them on and took them off each time. No excuses, no induced failures, to flourish off-stage, to serve as crutches for a hobbling existence; she is so little like a doll in a museum that I am almost disappointed. 'Madame, and your legs? Your famous legs?' 'Don't tell me you want to see them – you can see my trousers. Tight at the ankles – it would even be impossible for me to lift up the hem,' and she bursts out laughing, adding: 'Things are the way we learn to use them – including legs – and love as well.' 'That is?' I urge her, and she says: 'Love doesn't just come to one – one builds it. Luck is a second, life is all the rest. To discipline one's inclinations. I met Roland when he was nineteen at the Opéra, where we both first set foot on the same day at the same time. Oh, the hard work it took me to seduce him! Years of apprenticeship. He wasn't the kind to . . .' and I say to help her 'to be in a hurry'. 'That's right. I knew that to succeed I had to awaken his admiration, I had already excited him, but I wasn't so easily pleased, what do you think? But you will know, will have noticed, you must be the kind who knows that things that are not encouraged don't come on their own, *n'est-ce pas*? It is not easy to make passions coincide, fifty years of intimate and professional life together are not a gift from heaven, they need a bit of work . . . Oh, the phone – I'll answer it' and she lifts a cordless phone from the cushions. 'Oh, oui . . . oui . . . oui . . . oui, Valentine,' she says very lovingly and then, lowering the aerial: 'It was Valentine, our daughter.' 'Did you never think of opening a dance school?' 'Oh, you know dancers are terribly like poor relations and I have no patience. No, too much of a perfectionist. Just because you can do something doesn't mean you can then pass it on. I would be a total flop. The most gifted teachers are often those who are not themselves extremely good in a particular discipline,' and I insist: 'But you are a star in flight. Fortunately the television services will have a few tapes . . .' 'I have learned that the ephemeral in order to be great has to accept that it is what it is' and I say: 'That is a law I would also apply to the Bible and to the pyramids – never mind the rest.' 'And then let's be realists – life is a discovery to be made, but once you have made it you have to settle down in it – there's of course always some last little medal to be won in the field, but the time for great discoveries passes. After sixty life is hard, one has to turn constant repetition into happiness. To do this it's best to begin at forty' and she laughs again, shrugging her shoulders. One certainly feels her acquaintance with Gide, Sartre and Cocteau. 'Do you know what Gide said? The secret of art is not so much to work with one's own intelligence as with that of one's friends. The continuity of the group is very important, joining in, tradition, shared ideas, everything that unravels and comes together again in the social fabric, thanks to determined work. Today people are more isolated – even the artists, it seems to me. They should be so much greater than us, instead they aren't up to much. To be alone is not a guarantee of true individuality, don't you agree?' 'Yes, it would be like claiming that sex is a guarantee of intimacy.' Zizi asks me not to exaggerate and then turns to Jeanne, who has been as dumb as a fish as arranged: 'But your hair – let me see it close up – *mon dieu*! it really is pink!' and Jeanne smiles and nods. 'Ah, one should either die very young or, in desperation, as old as one can! Taking great care not to do it by halves – it is such bad taste!' And after a *perlage* of *pas de deux* and bows we say goodbye with well-bred frivolity.

Back in the hotel far into the night the phone rings. 'Can we meet at once?' says Mariethé's somewhat mournful voice. 'Right – I'll wait here for you.' 'I have my personal album of photos with Dalida, the dedications, the shots on stage.' 'Splendid' I say without sincerity and without irony – I don't have any special thoughts about this macabre adoration – in fact I have no thoughts on the subject at all. I think only that Mariethé moves me and that I very much wanted to see her again.

So we left the hotel, she didn't want to walk, she said that lately two old friends had tried to rape her, and I burst out laughing, how could she think that of me? And every time I tried to speak to her about herself, Mariethé swooped down on Dalida, her unhappy love affairs, her Catholic observance, her housekeeper, her transvestite brother, the details of her suicide, the discovery of the body, the teasing she had suffered because of her squint, and how she had undergone an operation on her eye which had given her pain for two years, her loneliness, her three dead friends, but I asked her: 'But Mariethé, apart from this, what – '

'Apart from what, I'd like to know.' 'Apart from praying?' and she stops on the pavement in front of Monsieur Renard's doll-shop where I have brought her without noticing: 'I pray God to take me to her.'

'But doesn't that seem an exaggeration?' 'No – it is all that I profoundly wish – to die a natural death without forcing my hand any more. I wanted to go into a convent too, once, I hitch-hiked, a character gave me a lift, I won't tell you what he tried to do to me. I looked him straight in the eye and said: "God is watching you" and he opened the door and let me out into the wood. I didn't even know where I was' and I say, putting my hand on my chest like a distraught mother: 'But you really must be careful! Someone like you hitch-hiking!' 'What do you mean like me?' 'But you must have a mirror too, don't you? Don't you see that you're beautiful?' 'I am so small, even when I stretch my arm I can't dust the top of the marble.' 'Come on! there must be something else in your life besides the memory of Dalida!' And she who in herself has none of the creeping arrogance of Jehovah's Witnesses says: 'No!' 'Do you like dolls? If you like I'll buy you one.' 'No, I don't accept gifts. Dalida said . . .' and we continue to walk among the restaurant rubbish bins. I have instinctively put my arm round her shoulder but almost holding it in midair because I wouldn't like it to be too heavy for her, who is like the fiancée in a Peynet cartoon, apart from the fact that Mariethé is all black in the night and knows nothing of the pastel colour of youth – I, who knows what, perhaps an uncle on a European level. But I would have preferred to be anyone at all rather than a relative or a genius.

. . . it is a naked doll, Paris is a doll in mourning, Paris is a little golden doll. Perhaps it is the epitaph for a toast, a Western autobiography balanced between death and that other thing . . . Mariethé is trembling with cold and I too, for I have come out without a pullover. Two people can even walk as long as they want in the night, one of them being Gothic and the other telling her off, but if it is true that one cannot but be born, it is inevitable that there should be a dawn lying there. It will be a special kind now, but one there must be. The other colour of the dark – just so that we understand each other. We are not important enough for the synchronicity of the event to stop suddenly with us. It would be a legend. One has to be content with going on.

When I arrived in the Roma bar for the appointment with Someone who had asked for me by telephone half an hour earlier, he was at the other end of the room, alone and already radiant, black leather jacket, a folding overnight bag on the chair beside him, shirt unbuttoned and tie awry. Why at the moment when I put down the receiver did I think of a little truck setting out to deliver a kitchen? I sit down – a hearty handshake – I am unable to connect, is he a commercial traveller for handbags *and* for aeroplane spare parts? I do not insist. He had blue eyes, the big face of a gaga adolescent, high cheekbones, thick black hair, long at the neck but well combed and possibly lacquered, a way of making people look at him as if he knew he was a sequence in a photo-novelette. The truck has arrived, they are unloading; I see the sink, the fridge, the cooker, the dishwasher. A nice kitchen, it has to be said. He says to me, you are much better-looking than in photographs, and in the meantime Lina arrives bringing the two small grappas and says to me: 'Have you got over that attack of piles yesterday?' and I say: 'Not entirely – obviously the ointment you use isn't the greatest' and she says: 'What ointment? It's you that has the piles, not me!'

He laughs and laughs and laughs then he stares at me for a moment in ecstasy. I sigh to myself with relief. Then I have to get away.

The second time we see each other is at dinner in someone's house. I invited him. He was silent and attentive all evening, once he left the room, I thought he was looking for something, I followed him, I didn't manage to embrace him right away. He clasped one of my hands in his, like that, he did not shun my embrace but he could not reply with a whole one, he embraced my hand. The kitchen fills up, they have arranged the table and chairs, I feel as if my mind has left me without telling me to go and do the shopping. Later in the car at the hut on the autostrada where everyone has arrived with their own car he says: 'Those people are so used to being bought that they don't know any more how to set about selling themselves'. There is a certain beauty – a somewhat sinister one – there is the critical intelligence about society, there is the fact that he brushes his lips on mine and does not pull back but drives off just the same. I don't know when we shall meet again.

One night when I was awake even though I usually disconnect the phone I saw a tablecloth with red and white checks, like an apron, flying through the air to then appear laid with its glasses, cutlery, plates.

The third meeting took place in a deserted square in a little village where there is not even an inn open. We are facing each other on two low walls, I stretch my legs out in front of me a little, I am confused and grateful – really moved. We talk – about accidents in cars, a week in coma. An IOU that falls due in a few days. Then he looks straight at me and says: 'I tried to commit suicide with an electric saw last year. I had a wife who had several lovers.' My mind goes numb and, as if nothing had happened, goes out leaving behind it the shopping trolley full of every kind of goodie. Some terrible details about his past as an ambitious person with few resources apart from criminal ones – making up for losses by throwing cans of petrol into distilleries, furniture workshops, travel agencies. 'But now it's all over, I was under the thumb of a man and I wasn't sure if he was useful to me or disgusted me – perhaps both.' My mind goes back to the supermarket, pushes the trolley towards the cash-desk – there, let's add a bottle of champagne. I hear a noise of pots and pans, I did the shopping but I am certainly not the cook. It is a banquet that is being prepared, perhaps a free gift from the firm that makes the kitchens. His tongue slips into my mouth for an instant, and he gets back into his car – white, enormous, pricey. It will come.

The words on the telephone have a good smell of minestrone, cold omelettes with courgettes, black olives, the unknown gastronomy of seduction which I know is indigestible. He asks me how my piles are doing and if I insist on eating red peppers with garlic, he says he likes my cheeky breath. When will we see each other? He doesn't know – business, a young woman lawyer who is driving him mad. I pack up the whole kitchen and he says no, listen, it's just that I can't change my life all at once, everything is so sudden for me too, I could never ever have imagined that the man was just as exciting as the writer – that's what he says, *exciting*, the least exciting sexual adjective there is. The men put the kitchen back again – in fact I make them put in a cooker with an alarm because I am deaf and even if I did not hear the alarm the cooker turns itself off. Or so I hope. The telephone rings without any regular pattern, I come and go as always, but I carry everywhere with me the aroma of oil and vinegar, undoubtedly there will be a salad of plain lettuce at a certain point, to be dressed at the last minute. If the salt and pepper have got lumpy meantime all you need to do is hit them with a spoon for a moment. He always starts off with a subtle lack of reverence: 'Dear Dirty Doctor, how are you? I'd like to see you – do you buy it?' and I say: 'I buy it, I buy it, you bet.'

Magically, little cubes of exotic pulps begin to run into a crystal soup-tureen – that is to say kinds of fruit that by now are all ours. He tells me he had not hoped that I would agree to see him, that perhaps I was already tired of him, that he felt as if he were dreaming, that you can't have intellectual relationships with women, they always play cat-and-mouse, not like the distinguished Dirty Doctor, who is always available, even if he makes you pay dearly with his little poisoned darts which one then has to treat for a whole week. He says he thinks constantly about me. I have been caressing the back of his neck and his hair all through the journey, we are going to a famous restaurant in a little medieval town. He caresses my kneecap, says he is used to threesomes and that when all the rage has surged up in his body sometimes he goes off and climbs the cliff-walls of a mountain. I tell him that I don't give a damn for intellectual relationships, I try to move his hand elsewhere, he lets me but he places it there without tightening his fist as I had hoped. He tells me the opposite of what he told me a year ago, last year, ten years ago. 'You are so real, damn it!' 'For what goes into my pocket . . .' and he says: 'Sometimes you're as hard as stone, at other times you're a lump of cotton wool. You look to me like a lost child.' 'There's nothing you lack either.'

A bottle of wine has also appeared on the tablecloth, it must be a vintage one even if I don't manage to see the label, which is turned towards him. I think that the variety of the *antipasti* is really impressive – maybe the best bit of the dinner will be the service. *Antipasti* are usually eaten standing, but people's eyes keep going to the table in the centre of the room which is more and more splendid – and distant. Will there be a risk of not being able to swallow a single mouthful of the real dishes?

Having left the medieval citadel, which is brightly lit in the spring night, we return to one of the many huts on the autostrada where I usually leave my grey car. We stay there a little. 'I don't believe in rape,' I say, and wait for a reaction from him. 'I feel I'm being pursued by you,' he says, and I say: 'I recognize my weakness for you – apart from that I only feel what I am allowed to feel. I feel that you want me to feel up to the point that you wish. I can feel infinitely more and infinitely less. But I certainly feel more than you.' 'You're wrong, You don't understand.' Since I had run my fingers into his hair and was gently scratching his scalp, he lets his head go back and says: 'Your lips drive me mad. And the tips of your fingers, Your Honour.' 'Deeply grateful, sire.' I bend over and kiss him in a position that is killing for my back, I am uncomfortable. He says to me: 'Let me stretch out on your legs.' And he puts his feet out of the window and lies on my lap. He sighs, shuts his eyes, I do not move. I think it is love that has been put on the table. A little more and we will settle down and eat each other. A last little *antipasto* of hesitant touching with the hands, more on his clothes than on the bare skin, an embarrassing laugh. I make a gesture which I hate in the hope of coming to his aid: I stroke the crotch of his trousers, seeing that he is now leaning his cheek on mine, turgid but composed, I don't want to make concessions – it must be love, it cannot be sex again, I don't want either of us to be satisfied once more and only once more. Either like this or not at all. He says: 'A man who doesn't get it up is like a whore with her legs open. But kiss me just the same.' I do as I am told.

Then one morning he descends on me at home, a previous telephone call, he wants me to go along with him, he was passing this way because of the airport. (Or the travel agency? The handbags for organized tourism? Travelling bags for airline companies, the kind they give first-class passengers? Plane parts?) We go for an apéritif outside the village. He says: 'Your voice is so good for me, to hear you talk is the panacea for all my ills.' I detest the word panacea. He caresses me, but I do not respond to the caress, say instead: 'Now I'm going to make a compact disc suppository which you can stick wherever you like and listen to it when you feel like it, my voice that is.' 'This is the first week I haven't taken barbiturates in order to sleep. If it weren't for that woman I'd be happy.' 'Listen, you're happy because of that woman and nothing else! She is someone who unlike me makes you run. At least you are paying off your car for some reason, aren't you?' And he says: 'I like you – I have always been an unconscious gay – I used to make myself up when I was a boy.' 'Listen – all your generation used makeup – it doesn't mean anything.'

An appointment for an evening in the next three days. I am available. Now in the kitchen the meat is just ready on the grill, I am making his grilled chicory, there will be a risotto and spaghetti *al dente* and all the other details mentioned in the fittings of this kitchen, which is still as spotless as the first day: an uncut calendar, a crucifix asquint above the fan – I don't know where it came from – perhaps he put it there – and all the tranquillity that a spider's web on a beam without a spider in it inspires. That evening he decides on a vulgar place by a lake. There is a somewhat alarmed conversation by both of us – he seeks future guarantees and I have no intention. I say to him: 'Maybe I don't even like you enough to make love to you – even if at this point you were to have a mousetrap between your balls it wouldn't matter in the slightest to me. With its little piece of cheese that has already been nibbled at. But maybe it wouldn't go off.' 'So you're not buying?' 'Even if the box is shut, yes, I'll even buy – but one box – not the whole store . . .' 'To love cautiously . . .' 'You don't love me and are cautious just the same.'

He stops suddenly and take his diary out of the dashboard and hands it to me: it is full of poems dedicated to me, love poems. He has written one almost every day. The blood rushes to my head and beyond. And they are beautiful, complex and witty. And dramatically they don't mean anything simply because they have an unexpected life that is autonomous of me. I swallow hard. And then what is one to say in this kitchen which is confusion where nothing happens and fascination increases until it suffocates me? Meeting after meeting, less happens each time – we live a kind of exaltation of the senses without touching each other, hearing each other, feeling each other, looking at each other. As if every time we leap away from each other the better to court each other, cajole each other, seek each other. I am delirious, I don't understand, will the meat not be a little overcooked, the risotto (with truffles – a taste I have never been able to identify) already a little less *al dente*? But not even the stew can diminish the atmosphere of magic, of waiting, of my body which is ensnared and ready, ready. However if that is how he likes it – slow service – then patience. Everything is so fabulous in the kitchen, everything is sparkling. Aren't you hungry? I say once at the end of a somewhat mad evening when he talked to me about spare parts and handbag handles, what a wind, what cold, we were in a bar in the open and he takes off his leather jacket in front of everyone to put it round my shoulders. I gave him a shove that almost sent him sprawling on the chair. And with him feeling like fun and games and me cross, he comes to me and wants to kiss me in front of all the women and men and families, something very easy for me if I did not catch a whiff that behind the gesture there is the scandalous kiss given by an anonymous person haphazardly to a man who is only too well known. Everything is getting cold. His IOUs are falling due, he says suddenly. I make a sign with my hand – I smooth the tablecloth at one corner because it was getting crumpled. He says, just a minute I'll be right back and he gets up from the kitchen table – how beautiful that kitchen was, the fresh *grissini* and the smell of the cork that has just been pulled. The wine ready for pouring, I already saw the reddish trickle into the glasses. I wait for him, I look round me – what a good smell love has. I sniff and wait. I wait for waiting's sake – I know the kitchen has a door at the back. What is success for a man? The meeting point between pain and its study as a commodity. Then I began to help myself. But I shall not forget to have a good memory of it all just the same.

'Beautiful, torrid Madrid!' I had thought to begin the moment we touched down. But the captain tells us that in Madrid it is raining and that we shall find 17°. The person beside me is called Manolo and his huge smiles, thrown out as applause at the mere fact of existing, encouraged my curiosity at such a fine example of flesh, nails and hair. Manolo has been at Quarto Oggiaro to acquire very sophisticated lamps to a value of 5 million lire and the parcel has been passed from hand to hand among various hostesses, for it to be stowed away so as to guard its fragility. In Madrid he runs a shop for car spare parts and sport and aesthetic equipment – the lamps are ultraviolet ones.

But now I want to know who reaps pleasure from his luminous virility, which even a few carious teeth are unable to detract from. Manolo is divorced and now lives with a social worker; there is a little girl from the marriage; she is three. His wife was Iranian. 'A very beautiful woman, believe me, and odd. I met her in Tehran. After going back and forward for two years I got her to come here and we were married. We were madly in love. With her come her parents and a fourteen-year-old brother, because that was the age when they send them to fight. Then from here we were able to help an older brother and her sister-in-law to escape. And by now we were seven in my flat, which is five hundred and fifty square metres. I couldn't be alone with her and by nature I am monogamous. I began not to come home because of the overcrowding. She always took her family's side and wouldn't listen to me. Then she got pregnant and left for London. To protect herself from me naturally. She didn't want me to make love to her any more, said I would kill the baby with my banging. Madness. For twelve months, and for months after the birth, I was patient, waiting for things to sort themselves out. You can see me – I'm not sure if I am making myself clear – twelve months of abstinence beside a woman I loved madly,' and he sighs, remembering the obvious efforts of his humiliated explosive nature. 'Then I asked for a divorce. The moment I get back, since it is Sunday and it's my turn, I am going to swim with my daughter. As beautiful as her mother.' Length of divorce proceedings in Spain – three months. Global costs: less than 2 million lire. And I had been hoping he would take me to the swimming-pool. In his immense transport of affection and with the goodness of those rare persons who do not know how beautiful they are, Manolo does not know that daughters take after their fathers. I think that Iranian women must be stupefied by surface-to-air missiles to give up a native of Madrid like that.

Madrid is more beautiful than ever – it is alive. In Plaza de España on Sundays the Filipino maids meet as they do at Santa Maria Novella in Florence, and there is constant hard talking about new and old bosses. In the bars the money machines tinkle with cherries and bells and lemons; the most famous 'baby bombos' belong to the firm Recreativos Franco S.A. and a notice hung on a cured ham says '*Existen hojas de reclamación a disposición del cliente*' – that it to say there are complaint forms available. The baroque simplicity of Castilian! All this gives me a great appetite.

It is the third time I have come to Spain in less than a year, and each time I find the air lighter than in Italy, where the carbon monoxide of the party splits has made everything entirely hoarse: the carefree air of citizens in the public spaces. Old women with high grey chignons offer tickets in the Loteria Primitiva: first prize, a dinosaur. By dint of walking I arrive by chance in Plaza Tirso de Molina (*Gil with the Green Stockings* and *The Joker of Seville*, to name his most famous and malicious plays, 1583–1648). In the Bar Cruz what a helping of *mariscos* and what a draught of local beer among couples looking at each other with hostility, removing the hand that was put on their elbow as a signal of peace, continuing like possessed sparrows to eat from the same plate an unending series of different dishes. Two customers who were standing in front of the television set which is on – I had sat down *behind* it – were a little surprised that I had found a place at a little table without greeting them or rather without allowing them to greet me – the point is that in Italy we do not exchange greetings with strangers in public places and I am used, unfortunately, like everybody else to staring at the menu and then at my plate or the label on the bottle. Although late I make up for it by opening up with a smile about the focus of which I could not be sure – but I score a bull's-eye and the two habitués, who do not know each other and who are in two different spots in the rectangular saloon, take off in chaste conviviality, which compels me for a whole hour to simulate a toast with the one and then with the other each time we raise a glass to our lips. A real labour of sociability in minuet time. Meanwhile an unknown delicacy arrives for me – tripe, cow's tripe as they say here, perhaps to distinguish from sheep's tripe – wrapped round a little stick with bark on it (certainly from a vine) and roasted on a hot-plate. There is something coarse and savage about a dish like this, the material assumption of a gypsy Middle Ages, which for the first moment is repugnant. I eat it up with eyes shut as if it were a case of passing some test of virility. I do something with my tongue to reconstruct the taste which I had refused to take into consideration – irresistible. I order a second and then a third stick. And I finish up stuck into the Culinary and separated from the Tragic.

Outside in the square someone is playing hide and seek with a dog, a Nordic backpacker no longer has the heart nor the desire to refuse the pressing invitations of two friends who have the prospect of a room, a couple of old office-workers walk along, bumping their umbrellas, while the right arm of the one and the left arm of the other describe in the air, which is still damp from the recent rain, great amphitheatres of memory to give rhythm and choreography to a conversation composed of amazement, of *ralentis*, of exclamations of scandal and delight if a girl passes in blue jeans. And in fact now three are passing at once, with big hats like wandering clouds which sparkle with a crisp acacia-honey blonde under the street-lamps, which are already lit, even though there is still natural light, a kind of coloured wind among the varnished leaves of the damp trees. The girls laugh when they see me, because I have my shoes in my hand, for my feet had still been hurting me so much and sitting on a bench I had put them in the puddle in the gutter. They have thick hair, too thick and provocative even for little well behaved grandpapas, extra-ordinary earrings of different designs, these are locks of hair which in some lively spot will find fingers ready to make them even more unruly and pull them back in a clenched fist a little brutally, just enough not to hurt, until their neck is fully stretched and they pretend to beg for mercy with their foreheads perpendicular to the sky or to the ceiling of a discothèque, thrusting out the red of their lips. From one of the old men comes one of those compliments the building-workers used to pay – to which the girls reply in a chorus, each one adding a distinguished and silvery obscenity. Beautiful, beautiful, beautiful.

I cannot believe that with this night before me, with all these people in the street and now in the Plaza Mayor with this panic desire to give oneself, to squander oneself in talk and feline endearments, to laugh back at each other and to seduce or at least make even the little flies hovering above a kiss take part, I cannot believe that the Alitalia flight this morning was two-thirds empty. At half-past eleven at night the great arteries of the capital which continue with equal majesty to the most desolate suburbs, are bright, lined with gardens full of people and terraces crowded with people drinking wines and beer and eating *tapas*, chatting in groups of twenty which move about like reeds in the wind driven by a whim or some instinct to please or to experience pleasure. At the bus-stops, even at those most lonely and badly lit, women alone wait calmly to go home: nurses, cooks, cashiers, women policemen, many still with bags of shopping bought in a break.

The euphoria of the post-Franco period of 1975–7 being over, Spain has got off on the right foot and more cautiously in order to find stability in an active state of trust which has nothing in common with the aftermath of a post-Franco reaction. Besides the failure of Suarez on the right, the corrosion of the other parties by the PSOE, led by Prime Minister Felipe Gonzalez, who received no less than 52 per cent of the votes, the lack of a charismatic leader like Le Pen or Thatcher or Almirante or Strauss have ditched any serious attempts at a revival of the extreme Right, which has had to be content with (and will for a good few years, I believe) transforming itself into a Right weak in terms of thought, indeed downright *intelligente* as they say here; in fact the press in order to define the rightwing movement which is tied to technological and industrial development uses a depressing periphrasis for a true Fascist: a civil Right. The old culture of death linked to the myth of the *conquistador* and of victory for its own sake (over whom and what no one knows, otherwise what sort of a myth would it be?) no longer awakens any suspicion of an evil eye because it is covered by a pathetic patina of a faded Past. The new sociopolitical approach (new but a good ten years old) is allowing European intellectuals who are not specialists and the inquiring minds of the world to approach this inexhaustible Iberian phenomenon like any other source of wonders and surprises, which have to be integrated into the real European curriculum.

I say to the night porter: 'Am I wrong or are there very few Italian tourists in Madrid?' 'Ah, the Italians descended on us in masses for the World Cup of 1982, they saw the Bernabeu stadium and then they forgot us.' 'Mad – don't they know that the best goals are scored abroad and now? A bottle of mineral water, please.' 'You have a minibar in your room, sir.' 'I've checked it but I want it without gas. The little that is still natural is already in fact so artificial that to take it with carbon dioxide seems an extra effort to me.'

Next morning the sun throws a gladiator's net from the whole sky over a city taken by surprise for it had already come out with jumpers, umbrellas and waterproofs, which in ten minutes were a nuisance to everyone. At the Puerta del Sol the sun makes a huge portal of phosphorescent cream on an inlet of the flagged square. In the Calle Mayor I go into a shop selling classical guitars because in the soles of my feet, which aren't swollen yet, I have a *brio à la flamenco*; a classical guitar must be quite the opposite of that coffee-pot with its spout turned round towards the handle in that advertisement which says *'Cafeteria para masoquistas: objetos impossibiles'*. The proprietor who is also the maker of the products, Señor Manuel Contreras, has just had an operation on one eye which they removed because of a tumour on the cornea. But he overcomes his difficulty in speaking – he is all bandaged, even his nose so as not to breathe in dust, and in truth he should not be here now – and begins to show me his most recent inventions, which have revolutionized world technology. He has been making guitars for twenty-five years, and since he hated the microphones at concerts, by dint of trial and error has invented *'el fondon de resonancia'* – a kind of little hood outside the guitar proper which with this gadget emits a much more intense sound than traditional guitars. For wood he uses only the most expensive wood from Brazil, as well as the also extremely valuable Canadian cedarwood. The Hispano-American Pepe Romero in Rome was the first person to use the Contreras guitar with the volume which, being increased by 40 per cent, finally did away with the need for microphones at concerts. And Señor Contreras shows me international expressions of gratitude and then at a ring on the telephone goes to answer it and to contract – and it's not that he does it on purpose – for two examples of the dearest model (around 6 million lire each) for a father in Sidney (a friend of his) whose two little girls are the most amazing prodigies on the Australian scene. He and his two assistants produce an average of four to five models a month. 'Do you know the Guitar Duo from Ancona?' he says to me. 'No, I'm sorry,' and he says 'And Professor Carlo Catagna at the Conservatory of Santa Cecilia in Rome?' 'No, I'm very sorry.' 'Then you will certainly know the Bari Prize for Classical Guitar,' and I make off wishing him good luck with the other eye and leaving him amazed at my sincere good wishes.

Then I go to the Italian cultural centre, which is overflowing with people who have signed up for courses in Italian, in order to breathe the good smell of macaroni and anchovies and cod in the Basque manner which steals down the main staircase from a kitchen worthy of the Knights Templar with, as annexe, a library with bookshelves twelve metres high. The interiors in hand-painted majolica with blown glass set out here and there is always a frying-pan cooking something while glasses of white wine are handed round. It is obvious that with such a refined cuisine, Basque and Andalusian photographers' models at the ovens, a wine waiter imported from Genoa, relationships with the press are also wonderful. I ask the director, Marco Miele, how much a set-up like this – and let's admit it, one that functions well – can cost the Italian taxpayer and he turns his natural loquacity into a smile of a Thousand and One Unavoidable Ills. A famous poet arrives, neutral enamel on his nails, a bouffant foulard, and begins to sing the praises of Monsignor Lefebvre as the only person who can compete with Prince in the Nineties. Then two journalists arrive to interview me, and with the entry of a functionary of the State TV, the signal is given for a banquet in great style just to spite anyone who thinks it is not possible to be rich, famous foodies, generously salaried and content. In the foreground of Goya's picture in the Prado called *El Entierro de la Sardina* is Momus, god of Sarcasm, Madness and Scornful Jests –

Momus threw the other gods down from Olympus. But he is not perfect like me – because he forgot to throw himself down as well. For which reason I shall not snipe at this rare occasion when an Italian Institute was nice to me – but sooner or later Miele must tell me what it costs to keep up a Royal Salon abroad.

The road that runs along the side of the royal palace: I am sitting on a bench undecided whether to set out for miles of tapestries and china and porphyry when there appears before me a figure in a black cloak who looks like Franco come to life again – as like him as a drop of coagulated water. The dirt of the shirt – which is blue – and of the black tie is black, like fired clay. The face is austere – with a hint of suspicion and contempt. He brings out a crust of cheese and sits on the edge of the bench on the other side, turning his back to me. Bald, hollow-cheeked, he has nice hands, cooked by the sun in the fried and refined grease of his scanty sweat. He is about to go off and, since he has not asked me for anything, I take out my wallet and offer him 200 pesetas, which is a good deal for a beggar in these parts. He takes them and puts them in his pocket without thanking me. Then he makes a sign to me with one hand as if to say Wait now, I shall show you something you can't even imagine. He rummages a little in the inner pocket of his cloak and extracts a plastic envelope along with an aluminium dagger made with the handle of a filed-down fork. I notice in his grin the teeth with the gums dug out around them, the rotten crown. From the little cellophane bag he pulls out a brand-new passbook, well kept, and opens it under my nose at the last entry. I read the global sum deposited and give a start: 480,000 pesetas! 'These savings are my liquid capital. Then naturally I have the houses. I hate my family and my children. Away with them all. An ex-combatant like me cannot bear degenerate children like mine. I shall leave them nothing. Democracy only creates confusion. The dagger is for the night – to protect me from vandals.' 'Have you ever used it?' 'I prefer not to give an account of myself, far less justifications. And who are you? If one says nothing there is a further possibility that one knows nothing. Why should I say anything to you? Silence is a constitutional right to allusiveness.' 'If I were an assassin I would be much prouder than you, you know.' He begins to mutter mysteriously.' . . . it is a confused story . . . a legionary never knew if he was being sent to the altar or to bed. They stabbed the Catholic politician thirty-nine times, thirty-nine . . . Adios. Enjoy yourself while you can. If even the king is a traitor . . . the first traitor . . .' All I understand is that he is referring to King Juan Carlos, considered by the Fascists to have betrayed Franco and his *spiritual* legacy in order to transfer his allegiance to a whole people in extreme need of justice against a little caste in the South American style made up of High Prelates (Opus Dei), High Officers and Head Waiters.

Since I have taken my shoes off again and am walking barefoot I may as well make for the Monastery of the Discalced Nuns. It is the oldest building in Madrid and at present lodges 29 enclosed nuns out of 33 (the years of Our Lord whereas 'legs eleven' is women's legs) who can be accommodated there. Margarita of Austria, the little girl in Velazquez' *Las Meninas*, was shut up here at the age of seven because her mother had been widowed. Of Margarita there is also a picture as a young nun and another as a dead nun. The end of a childhood which seemed to promise a whole world and kept only rosaries, scuttling feet and daily memento moris along with the semblances of power in the form of those few cloistered intrigues possible for any nun of rank to whom virginity would give the necessary authority to take decisions on the lack of virginity in others. There is a statue of Mary Magdalene of the many tears and the sumptuous robes who must have thrown into a faint more than one unfortunate girl. How many reliquaries, how many baby Jesuses offered up here: ivory, lapis lazuli, china encrusted with precious stones, exactly seventy-two of them on show, the most valuable ones. Did the Discalced Nuns have a dialogue with the Carmelites? *Ora et labora, labora et ora*. In any case a life of hell, thanks be to God.

Outside in the full afternoon of far-reaching light two girls clad in leather from head to foot are kissing tongue in mouth on a scooter and shoot off through the traffic, which is at a standstill. On my way to the vegetable market in Plaza Ligazpi where there is a performance by the company La Fura del Baus from Barcelona, I see two black girls and a blonde one embracing – half-standing, half-lying on the grass – with black men who will at least be Nigerians and at most Afghans. If anyone dared to look at them with an air of disapproval the little black boy will deal with it – all three are well hung and in fact one of them was turning somersaults to make his ambulant erection change direction to the right and the left from inside his tight shorts. Well done, girls! For me too there are such things as mixed couples – is a couple of a man and a woman not already mixed even when they are of the same colour?

Fura del Baus in Catalan means 'The Ferret of the Stream', which does not mean anything. When the performance starts I notice with great pleasure that the word has been replaced by shouts and hoarse noises and that there are no lovers, no cuckolded husband, no merry widow, no gay, and not even anyone in search of an author. In a space of a few hundred square metres the spectators are crowded together; they have to watch out to see where the trollies and moveable platforms, which are continually moved about and taken down by the actors, are being pushed. At stake is the fate of man, caught in the grip of two Evils who are fighting to determine which of the two has the greater right to be described as Good. Flames, obsessive trumpet music, earsplitting drum rhythms, flour scattered by electric fans, incense, a legless actor who rages with his crutches, a mess of goo in a manger where men as if already dead are kept apart in coffins too narrow for them; the eight volunteers make an immense effort to carry out the usual charming lady who has fainted. The whole thing is of an indescribable violence and aesthetic quality, pared down to achieve demoniacal paroxysms. Lanterns appear, it gets dark, invectives, the noise of iron-rimmed wheels, spotlights pointed at a tomb of inner tubes, inflated and lumpy, the men lose all control and strip themselves naked and clamber about, attack each other, hang each other, throw themselves with gymnastic skill from drawbridges. On a crane a musician – he is extremely accurate in his playing throughout that pandemonium – has blown up a balloon which now crumples and folds itself over the microphone. I have not seen anything so theatrically inspiring in the last ten years – and in any case I have taken care not to go to the theatre apart from Eduardo di Filippo and Orsini, who bored me to death, and Lavia and Cecchi and Bene, who in only three sessions cured me of an insomnia which had lasted three years. Title of the play, *Tier Mond*, which I like to think means 'Third Moon'.

At the end of the play, the flame-throwers and the lights too being extinguished, I pick up a spectator who still has hair standing on end and scorched cheekbones and we go off to express ourselves in our own way. Every time I go and fuck a Spaniard I call to mind that co-pilot from the Iberian airline who came specially to see me in Verona, altering one of his stopovers. In the door he put a bottle of Calvados into my hand and pushed me gently into the bedroom because he had to do the trick in a hurry, and did it to me eight times without ever giving me time either to greet him or uncork the bottle. I remember going to the station with him to take the train with the sensation of having third-degree burns in certain parts and second-degree ones everywhere else. I counted the minutes and could not wait to get rid of him in the nicest possible way (after all he had flown 4,000 kilometres to – let's say – see me and that was still 450 kilometres per orgasm, although they were all his) and to run home and soak myself in a cold bath. Obviously I gave the brandy to the student on the floor below. In my frenzy to get rid of it I remember the slip of the tongue I made as I offered it to him: 'Here, get this bottle of *calvarios* down you!' Ah, the bad old times have still not managed to get any better.

In the morning I go round churches: Goya's tomb in San Antonio de la Florida. Goya's body newly brought from Bordeaux to the elite church was decapitated and the head purloined – the usual mad collector, I imagine. Then the Prado – I am looking among the Goyas for the cover of my next book which, being this one, is already printed and it is not easy to find by tomorrow the cover for a book which was due to be printed yesterday or never at all. And then to and fro by taxi and bus, and kilometres of walking, inside and outside passers-by and passengers politely indifferent and slightly caught up by their 'look' – the fashion which has seen its day in Italy is very fashionable in Madrid and even money is very fashionable here too.

At midday I go to get robbed in the Cinema Carreteras. Oh, it is an old whimsical exorcism of mine, not because it excites me, no, it is to make me start giggling and meantime to get into training for when I shall be old – if I still have the same fancies. This cinema is only famous for getting robbed. The pretext is usually sexual snuggling up. I don't have to wait too long, since I am wearing fresh clean clothes: at once a little man stinking of rain-water with the eyes of a ferret struck by lightning begins to rub against me behind a column and then, losing no time, takes me by the hand, drags me into a row, makes me sit down gropingly and then begins to feel me all over as if he had ten hands, he even tickles me. He quickly lets out a kind of hoarse Celtic noise, heavy breathing with choking thrown in, a whole botched performance, meantime he has unbuttoned my shirt, felt in my underpants, pulled down the zip of my fly. He caresses the nape of my neck, but merely a routine pass, and has taken the wallet out of my back pocket.

Since with one hand he was giving me a quickie (clumsily) and since he had done everything with the other hand alone, he must have fingertips extremely sensitive to watermarks in order to make his selection and also great skill, because he is now reinserting my wallet in the back pocket after having cleaned it out. Wonderful solicitude! In fact since at this point I might have withdrawn into myself (never having gone away) he triplicated his attentions so as to confuse me to the point of brushing it with his mouth and pulling out a couple of hairs with his teeth so that I almost begin to shout. Then giving a sigh of relief – I pretend not to have noticed anything – he gives a few strokes as if to say to it, come on, get a move on and come for I don't have time to waste. I say to him: 'Forget about it – you can't take it away with you' and he says: 'No, no, go on, come, come!' and I come – I always come when I decide, in this case to cut things short rather than risk a definite one – and he gets up, mutters something, goes off, runs, with me following him, I corner him in the bar although I don't think he intended to leave. 'With all that money you could at least offer me an orangeade,' I say to him smiling, joining in the joke. The ferret is probably thirty years old – even if he doesn't show his years, which he could wear in any other way and it would still be the same. And so it was – without making any comment he ordered me an orangeade.

Then Juan confided to me that he works only on weekdays and that on an average he manages to relieve two or three clients in a morning – however what with getting up early, taking the bus (he lives about forty kilometres from the centre) and paying for the ticket, it is a way of passing the time more than anything else to make two o'clock come and time then to go into a factory which makes pallets for trucks. The greatest possible punctuality – that is to say he's there at ten o'clock when they open because of the pensioners who have to go to their own homes or to their old folk's homes for their foodies at eleven forty-five, which is a breach of rules because no Spaniard willingly sits down at table before half-past one. With the proceeds he goes and has a high old time, a great weekend with his *novia*, but very few come here with more than two or three hundred pesetas in their pockets and sometimes you practically have to do a mouth job on them and then it is difficult to pretend because you know at once if there is saliva or not, *verdad*? Not to mention the quarrelsome ones who notice and begin to shout so that the usher comes every time to tell them to be quiet, that they are annoying people. If you know how to do it life is still tasty and piquant like an icecream with paprika. Then Juan says to me: 'Have you been to the Valle de los Caidos?' 'No, what is it?' 'It's near where I live, where Franco is now he's dead. Further on there's also the Escorial where there are the dead kings. A beautiful place to visit.' 'Have you been there?' 'Never, why? In any case they're not going to run away.'

Wonderful criminal behaviour with strong nerves which does no real harm to anyone; on the contrary, sometimes by giving an electric shock gratis it makes people grow up a little and shakes the calves of colossuses with feet of clay. In a bank, in a post office I would collaborate with the robbers certainly not with the loyal cashier who, also endangering my safety, refuses to open the safe, because he does risk his life but with an eye on promotion, I only risk a candle that lasts three hours twenty minutes. Certain idiots who rebel carelessly only on emotional grounds and what is in effect attachment to what is being taken away from them as if it were life itself, really do think at such crucial moments that a minute's violence is a greater violation than a political act of violence which lasts decades and strips you of freedom of choice, of dignity as a social person, of civic conscience, of the desire to fight and denounce prevaricating arrogance and to cooperate even subversively against the topsy-turvy State.

The release from prison of various dangerous criminals has brought about a state of civic depression in millions of Italians: it has been a further way of *suiciding* libertarian consciences, in order to make them feel more than ever impotent and stupid, ridiculous, and at the mercy of judicial cavils with which the hegemonic knowingness of certain members of the magistrature triumphs and grows fat. The degree of previous criminality which Italian institutions demand from the ordinary citizen is always too high. We are all criminals for nothing, one feels like saying, in order to be able to breathe and have a motion of the bowels as the result of favours obtained from right and left.

These Italian matters present themselves more clearly to me when I am abroad, and in fact I go there just to *feel* them and formulate them with greater daring.

I went to book a car with a driver but since there are no Citroëns available and the driver is waiting for his jacket to dry, I go to the Museo Bellas Artes San Fernando and for the second time go down into the Tailer de Reproduciones de la Real Academia. The director, Miguel Angel Rodríguez, receives me very politely and is astonished at my renewed interest in the plaster statues which fill rooms and corridors in their hundreds. He guarantees me that no one has ever come here to take photographs; I find this difficult to believe. In the basement life-size casts are taken of all the statues in the actual museum, which are then sent all over the world to buyers, normally other fine arts academies so that they can serve as models for young artists. This factory has existed for two centuries and boasts casts from as far back as the eighteenth century when Spanish artists who went to Rome sent here those of the most important statues in the Vatican and the Roman excavations. The tour round is like a submerged world coming gradually to the surface; I stand in front of the bust of a certain Gonzalo Fernández de Córdoba, Gran Capitán, whose dusty ermine stole looked to me from a distance like real fur. Don Rodríguez tells me that purchases are also open to private persons and thousands of examples are requested all over the world for gardens and columns, from the Venus di Milo to David (reduced scale), the statues of Donatello, the Nike of Samothrace; prices go from 2,000 pesetas (a souvenir like those one can buy in Florence) to 90,000 and about a million. Recently he has introduced synthetic resin to give the effect of the patina on marble while with other procedures they now succeed in recreating both the patina of earthware and of bronze – and it is always plaster. In fact I lifted a little statue preparing myself for the weight of an alloy and it flew from my fingers.

It is a world of captains, kings, queens, infantas, saints, madonnas, brown torsos without arms and dust. Don Rodríguez says that while there was a period in the Sixties and Seventies in which there was a demand almost exclusively for *modernism* (Moore, Miró, Modigliani etc) now there is a return to the grand style of the Roman, the Greek, the Renaissance and the baroque. It seems that even in the reproductions which a student aims to copy the human scale has become fashionable again – that is to say man as almost everybody deludes themselves that they see him. In any case there is nothing at the Venice Biennale which is not already in the Acropolis museum in Athens. I who have bought a few pictures by contemporary artists have always done so because I could not afford a little Flemish still life with pears and anemones, and little by little my acquisitions end up in the attic.

The place Juan takes me to at a quarter past three in the afternoon – he was late because a passer-by had his wallet fastened with string, and today things went badly at the firm – is a sauna-meeting-place where the youngest person must be seventy. At the entrance already a slight smell of ammonia and dirty underpants strikes me favourably: this must be the smell of the Old-fashioned Fascist. Because here there meet any number of those grandfathers whom it isn't thinkable to associate – apart from the arsing around of old age – with the Francoism of the old days. We go in and each one goes his own way with a towel round his waist. In the most complete silence I pass in review a row of old men with eyes that are burning or sad or full of great dignity, although their scrotums are hanging out over the edge of the plastic seat, and go into the steam department. Here too old men who on my arrival begin to caress me. I let them do it for a few moments as hospitality demands and then I get out. There is one who is particularly insistent, who follows me every step and offers the soap, opens the doors at random, shows me the various departments. He has only one eye, he explains that he lost the other in Germany, thirty years working in the same steelworks, then a splinter and zac! Would I like to make love to him? No, *muchas gracias*. Then finally I catch sight of my type. Tall, thin, a kind of Don Quixote with a little beard and moustaches, an interested look but not far short of a glassy one. His ribs well in evidence, an aristocratic bearing, his chin always a little higher than need be, his backbone assured. 'Señor, satisfy my curiosity,' I ask him, 'is it true that Franco put one hundred thousand men into forced labour to build the mausoleum in the Valle de los Caidos?' 'Who knows, certainly they were all thieves and murderers, that was what they deserved.' Good, I have hit the bull's-eye – I know where he stands. 'And is it also true that they all died?' 'Does it matter? They should do the same thing now – let us free the streets of the criminals with knives and we will rediscover another beautiful Escorial. But El Rey is too dreamy to think about serious things. A pauper's grave is what he would deserve.' 'You don't like him?' 'Like him? He is the ruin of all ideals, the puppet of Communism.' 'But to whom is the cult of the Valle de los Caidos dedicated today?' 'To the dead of all wars – otherwise they would have already razed it to the ground.' 'So also to the common prisoners and the political ones who lost their lives in the mountain.' He gets up, does an olé with the towel round what is left of his thighs, and goes off scornfully. I catch up with Juan again – he is complaining: 'Here they are all stingy' and he doesn't dream of using the shower. I give him some money and wish him better luck with the locks on the lockers.

At the Hotel Cuzco I watch the usual parade of ladies past their prime who meet at about five o'clock for tea and for the pounds and pounds of jewellery, real or false, which they display, imparting a gleam to the cenotaph of highly made-up faces and prosperous but never generously displayed busts. They look at each other's bracelets and earrings, weigh them up, and begin to paint their lips anew and look in the little mirrors while they brush on face powder; this is their entire social activity, I imagine. Poor dears, I suppose that a large part of them will follow their husbands on 20 November, the day when Franco's death is remembered at the Valle de los Caidos. Or perhaps they have become more cunning and will send their Filipino maids who also know how to stand at attention.

The car with the driver in a uniform that is washed, dried and ironed – he too given to nostalgia and insistent on saying the opposite to all the others, that is to say that the 20th of November is an appointment that is less and less observed and looked down on even on the Right – brings us to the square in front of the mausoleum after having zigzagged for several kilometres among woods of firs and yellow flowering bushes. The mammoth cross dominates the landscape from ten kilometres away. The Patriotic Monument, the decree for which was promulgated on 1st April 1940 to make a fine Easter fool of the Bolsheviks, took twenty years' assiduous work under the direction of several architects worn out one after the other by the imposing nature of the project. The site is truly impressive: what with the courtyard, the cathedral, the cross, the buildings alongside (where recently an interesting theological symposium was held), stairs and statues, the life of one hundred thousand men seems little to me; the 'gran esplanada' alone is 30,600 square metres, a St Peter's in the mountains. The first base of the cross measures 25 metres, the second and the cross 42 metres in all, another 150 above the level of its own base; the arms have room for two luxury tourist buses running in both directions. I go in – at the sight of the soldiers on guard I think what bad luck to be born *real* men. You walk and walk, you arrive at the main altar behind which Franco is buried, his tombstone right under God, who from the dome is making signs to the Madonna, who is bending over the tombstone of José Primo de Rivera, the founder of the Falange and ideologue of Francoism, got rid off, they say, by Franco himself. I find their juxtaposition fitting, since ideology is the womb of all the vices and therefore wishes to be immaculate, while power, which assigns ideology to procreation so as not to be removed from the action, is the scrotum of the Creator. José was also the designer of those blue shirts of Spanish Fascism – Mussolini, the innovative designer *ante litteram* of Made in Italy, at once copied it, turning it into the black shirt, seeing that little Adolf had already thought up the brown one. A reasonable number of bats in the vaults. I had just had time to read under God in the dome '*Ego sum lux*' when the electricity went off and the crucifix leapt out illuminated in the total darkness. Franco boasted of having himself cut the tree which now supports the sinister sacrifice.

I go back to Madrid and get taken to the royal gardens of the Buen Retiro – Velazquez' house, a glass pavilion, the little lake with the Pharaonic stairway with lions surmounted by an equestrian statue, another little blonde and black couple enjoying a perpetual erection, and under the statue of the Fallen Angel begin to scan the national press. Today Italy does not possess a politician loved even by the taxidrivers as King Juan Carlos is, who at the beginning of his reign was called a lame duck and is now recognized by plebiscite as being able to gather round him the progressive democratic energies to which the Fascist and warmongering forces – not so unbridled here as in Italy and other European nations – have had to take third place. The bloodshed in Spain has more to do with the Basque separatist movement than with diffused and indiscriminate terrorism as in Italy; it is estimated that there are about forty members of the Red Brigades stationed in Catalonia alone, all dedicated to financing their *activities* and their stay there by very frequent raids on banks in and around Barcelona.

Not only *El Pais* but *ABC* and *Diario 16* give full daily accounts of Italian political life and of Italo-Spanish meetings, and such is their anxiety to ensure that they have a trusty partner for the imminent ERM affairs that Craxi is given out to be a disinterested Red Cross nurse and De Mita a person of culture.

The statue up there is the only public representation in the world of the Devil: the passers-by stop and search for an impossible demoniacal feature since the winged boy – one wing spread to resume his flight and the other already broken at his feet – is of a beauty that is purely angelic and that is that. A fallen angel confronting an unlimited power is not the Devil but the minimum a man can be. Then I read an anecdote about Franco: 'It is well known that Franco considered himself to be apolitical and the story goes that when he was already head of State, *caudillo, generalísimo* of the armed forces and Father of the Fatherland, he replied to someone who asked for advice: "Do as I do – have nothing to do with politics." ' It would be as if Andreotti were to advise Marcinkus – for once improbably and sacrosanctly extradited from the Holy See in order to answer to an Italian tribunal for his crimes – to stick to the golden rule: 'You must say that you have always and only drawn inspiration from Divine Providence.'

I get up and take a long walk that brings me somewhere to a little lane full of small shops. According to Góngora (1561–1627), there is only one way to tell dogs to stop barking and that is to play with them. It would be like saying that the only way to defeat the mafia is to live with it. Just think! Fatalism is the wisdom of my worst enemies: winners dressed as losers. I put my head into a dairy full of eggs: a dozen normal ones 120 pesetas, extra large 130, super-large 150. This is for my mother, for it is all that interests her about my travels away from home.

The only way to translate *saudade*, an untranslatable word which stands for a state of perpetual melancholy in the Portuguese people, is *Weltschmerz*. The old taxidriver who takes me on board at Lisbon airport is melancholy, and melancholy too is the adolescent lift-boy who takes over my bag and the keys to my room which have been handed to him with an anguished gesture by the melancholy porter. Sunday, melancholy Sunday! Empty streets, closed restaurants, a hypochondriac rat follows me part of the way along Rua Castilho, turns off and disappears into a thicket of greenery and rubbish; I go on to a dreary terrace with glasses and plates turned upside-down on little deserted tables, I sit down feeling tired and after half an hour of absolute resignation, when my appetite is by now uncertain, an ageless waiter arrives at a shuffle – a fifteen-year-old boy whose eyes serve only for weeping. With unspeakable difficulty and a broken voice he recites the menu from memory, sardines, cod, meatballs with chips, swim up half-drowned out of today's *fado*. After another fifteen minutes, in which I felt out of place in a family of restaurateurs whom I do not know and who are in mourning, a beer arrives, the waiter makes off with great caution, cursing the distant day when he was born. The beer, on the other hand, produces a foam like a rabid dog, which makes it that less tempting to me. On a wall in the Rua Marquês de Frontiera no one has cancelled a graffito which must date back to the end of 1970 (the year of Salazar's death): 'Death to the PIDE', the secret police of the União Nacional at the moment when it disappeared. While I wait for the cod I make every possible effort to get interested in Mario Soares, who has many strong points to please me as prime minister (imprisoned thirteen times for opposing the ascetic and cultured and pitiless Salazar, banished in 1968, exiled in France in 1970, he returned here after the coup d'état in 1974), but I drop the newspaper with his photo: he really looks too much like someone who will never make it. The cod arrives dull, depressed, in a sad sauce, I would devour it even if it were only sadness cooked in butter and sage – I take the bones out one by one, in any case I know that I shall have to wait another half-hour before the sweet manages to come, a limp crème caramel from asexual eggs which don't want to be whipped up by powdered milk. I shall never risk a belch, a belch is too swift a phenomenon to take Portuguese nationality. Then the terrace began to fill up with the few citizens of Lisbon who haven't gone to the beach at Coparica and were too excited to renounce a bit of life away from home, in the open air, in the dark collective chamber of national sentiment. A slow pace here is slower than elsewhere, and if someone at a certain moment were to call out the winning numbers in the lottery he would do it slowly and one at a time, pronouncing them very distinctly and then testing them rigorously.

A mini-cruise on the Tagus, freshly polluted by Spanish industry via the river; we sail past the industrial zone connected by the 25 April Bridge, 2,278 metres, which Salazar willed: on this bank of the bay there are the steel and chemical works and at Trafaria the beautiful grain silos which seem to emerge for an aquatic Beaubourg: cranes, bridges, wharfs, ladders fussily and symmetrically painted in purple, red, white, green and grey. Torre di Belém, one of the few ancient remains after the earthquake of

1775 which razed the city to the ground, destroying castles, churches, monasteries, from the Gothic to the Manueline to the baroque; the towers of the Sé Patriarca (the bishop's palace) and the half-ruined ones of the Castle of São Jorge. The tourists on board today are almost all South Americans, with the exception of a young Italian couple on honeymoon who instead of kisses and signs of tenderness give each other pats on the back and digs with their elbows. There is an Indian girl – perhaps Peruvian – with the ecstatic look of a suffering madonna who is trying to smile, richly dressed in a modest traditional costume, and she too is on her honeymoon with a husband who is almost seventy. Perhaps she used to be a peasant, who not of her own free will married a moneyed old man who needs attention, a gringo whom age and infirmities have made affectionate. The face of the Indian bride – her flat nose and extremely high cheekbones above which her eyes seem to be a single eye or a black gleaming strip light years away from here – draws my attention like a magnet for the whole crossing. The old man says to her 'Smile', forgetting to add the name of his child-wife, then he takes a photo of her as she opens a mouth full of gold plate, a smile from a Maya tomb, to commend her soul for safe arrival in her native village whether it is one in the hands of the Sendero Luminoso or of an anti-guerrilla corps. I have never seen such a disquieting expression; it looks like the incarnation of a memory of life dreamt somewhere beyond the tomb, a pang which not even ashes will ever be able to appease.

Since the shipping company then offers a port-tasting to the honoured guests, two young Mexican boys, blond and punky, and a litle French flirt gave each other a knowing look, went off to the bows and, away from their parents, knocked back two glasses each and collapsed on the deck, from which they were carried below asleep and happy – they were laughing drunkenly, dazed by a combustible mixture of alcohol and heat. In a bay at the foot of a fishing village two boys are taking the sun, but suddenly one leaps to his feet at the sight of the boat, pulls his drawers down to his knees and, not giving a damn for *saudade*, begins to show us it grinning and shouting – perhaps to throw ourselves into the sea and join him. I very much like melancholy persons – for the first five minutes. And I also like timid people – if they are not more than fifteen years old. Beyond that I tolerate only the jokers and mockers. Melancholy is antisocial because it is resigned to the inscrutability of fate, and timidity is too flirtatious to offer much interest for long. I am sure that the Portuguese foreign legion in Angola, Mozambique, Cabinda, Guinea, Macao was made up of the most impenetrably melancholy people and that generally the most bloodthirsty mercenaries have been the most blameless of timid people and will continue to be so. Yet the most perfect timid person is the one who, feeling horror at the sight of blood, hires a killer to go and shed it, not from any concern with alibis but out of discretion or a weak stomach. Timid and melancholy people, like all splenetic people, have a predilection, in words, for the inner life, in which in fact they hone a lurking criminality; a decent person does not even have an inner life, and when the temptation becomes really irresistible goes to a chemist's. For the inner life: Clesidren, one spoonful after meals. We are tying up at our moorings.

In Alfama, the oldest and most picturesque quarter of Lisbon, there are no young people about; the old women are sitting in their houses at the windows or barely out on little rotting balconies half-hidden by very pretty mended blinds and let slip only a sphinxlike glance between wrinkles of cactus which have the warm tones of autumn. I catch a glimpse of interiors with candles, patron saints under glass bells, little china ornaments, faded photographs and a whole lot of plants in food-tins; the windows are often broken and held together with cardboard; a pink hibiscus has branched out of the window of a house that has lost its whitewash and is abandoned. Love-birds and canaries sit mutely in little cages hanging out in the morning; it is the avicultural realism of my village childhood. The shops remind me of Giulio Spurc's, where the mice nested in the sack of rice and the dried cod was allowed to drip on to the sugar sack with a phlegm that would have driven into a rage even the dying in the streets of Bombay, and he would mutter incomprehensible things because he kept the money, paper and nickel, in his mouth. They said he had never washed or changed his clothes in all his life – my mother sent me to get only big bottles of bleach. Now I am moving to another district.

In Rua da Emenda, Barrio Alto, I go into a restaurant. Since the men's toilet was shut from the outside (to prevent its use by people who were not customers and by drug addicts as everywhere in Italian metropolises) I slipped into the women's and the proprietor began to protest and a waiter started to knock madly, telling me to come out at once. I had shut myself inside not in the least disturbed – sardines, swordfish, sole, mixed salad and new season's plums. Then on emerging I told him, indicating the boss with my chin: 'And now tell him to come and put it back in if he can.' Moral: what's done is done. In Rua da Alegria I stop at a stand where the newspapers are kept on two fruit boxes, the newsvendor – a young girl with a face that was entirely like a hare's – except for the lips – a pony-tail with a clasp with little plastic pearls and very few teeth – is making things difficult for a fat, toothless old man who turns his head in one direction and in the other stretches out an arm to feel her bottom. In order not to appear indiscreet I buy the *Jornal de Sexologia – Lesbicas Portuenses*. In fact the most interesting title says 'A primera vez foi num Rolls Royce' (The first time was in a Rolls Royce). The newsvendor also takes a copy of the sexy review which has no glossy cover (here second-grade coke is wrapped directly in butcher's paper perfumed with garlic which along with the fact that it has never been assimilated to the rose in the poetry of *antan*, remains one of the greatest and inexplicable mysteries of heterosexuality, because I have stuck my nose in both and I have a delicate nose and I do not understand why one should do an injustice to garlic, roses and coke) and takes a look at it in front of the smelly joker: 'This is good enough for you – goodness, in here there must be that thing on the front of the Rolls with its wings open!' and they laugh. A moment then melancholy settles on both of them as if the world had suddenly come to a stop. They pass their days, you might say.

Lisbon is at present the chosen set for American fashion photographers: in Avenida Libertade a gigantic Russian model (who talks only Russian, explains one of the two assistants to the photographer, who is about fifty metres away, assisted in his turn by a girl) goes up and down with a suitcase and a trunk loaded on his shoulders while the instructions from the photographer have to overcome the decibels of the traffic. The boy has those thin pink lips which are as rare as a meeting with a hippogriff. A pigeon arrives like a rocket, flutters an instant two arm's-lengths above me and lets go. A direct hit between eyebrows and septum. A Lusitanian youth in a greasy torn blouse is in a bad way head-down on the steps of a side entrance to the Teatro Nacional. He indicates to me that he would like a smoke. 'Do you have cemeteries in Italy?' he says after the introductions. 'Cemeteries,' I repeat, fearing I had not understood. 'Yes, cemeteries for the dead,' he insists. 'Yes, yes, we have them practically everywhere,' I say, thunderstruck at the thought of having found for the first time something that north and south have in common. 'And hospitals for sick people so that they don't die right away?' And I say 'Yes' more and more ill-temperedly. He allows a pause: 'Here we have only cemeteries.'

Standing to one side of the entrance to the Confeteria Nacional – a century-old pastrycook's and one of the most famous – is a blind woman of about thirty, short chestnut hair, a short jacket in grey tweed over her beige skirt (it is also her wallet), pale white moccasins and a grey stick with an aluminium handle held tight in her fist, and on top of her fist, with the other hand, she holds a little wooden drawer fastened with a thin string that goes round her neck. Her right eye has been entirely removed and the eyelids sewn together, scarred one on top of the other; the left eye, although it has neither eyelids nor slits, has inside it a kind of ball which beats continually – every twenty seconds it gives a twitch, moves almost imperceptibly to one side and starts beating again in the centre. It is a soul mechanicallly asking to come out, one of those souls so profoundly wounded that they rebel without ever telling their bearer; every so often the girl adjusts her hair or touches the exposed hands of a wristwatch. When something falls into the drawer the voice says '*Muito obrigada*'. If something falls which cannot make a tinkling noise but rustles she says the same phrase but accompanies it with a nod. By dint of suffering without remedy defeat becomes something you get used to marking up. She feels the hands of the watch again: thinks that in an hour she will leave and go to eat. Tric-trac: today has been marked up too.

In the Castelo Sâo Jorge I lend vastness to the sea by looking at it through the open tail of the first white peacock I have ever seen in my life. I thought that white peacocks were an invention of Oscar Wilde's and instead they exist and, alas, they look like whitewashed turkeys. I squat down between two walls and wonder how to pass the time idly and with profit. The calcareous stone is ideal, if it sticks out sharply, for scratching one's back after taking off one's T-shirt. Sharp-edged stones here dating from 1147. Then I go up to the cathedral behind the apse of which a little market unwinds, poorer, if possible, than the usual flea markets. The children sell comics, the grown-ups sell everything short of the hair that got stuck in their razors this morning. There is one man selling ancient nails and pieces – rusty ones – of ironmongery. Suddenly I feel alone and don't know why I keep on walking. Not even this time did the aeroplane fall to the ground, and I should so much like to die in a celestial catastrophe. It must be the rarefied air of this city which gets at you as slowly as inexorably. I buy a couple of little nineteenth-century plates, for if you buy plates it is because you think you have enough time before you and the wish to hang them up. I sit down at a table where three English tourists are talking about women and lovers – conversations which the English only have abroad. It is an easygoing place and you sit anywhere. 'How do you imagine the ideal lover?' 'A hearty eater.' They drop the conversation while a plate of snails arrives for me – there must be at least two hundred of them – and a cork with no less than ten sticks in it. 'Did you never happen to want to have company when eating alone and to behave as if *you* were that absent person you'd like to have sitting opposite you?' I say to myself. Then I act something out: for every stick I imagine that I am a different person in terms of gestures, grimaces, simpers. Not even the three English tourists can maintain their composure faced by all this. I succeed particularly well at imitating Liliana's fussiness, Mary's diffidence, the snobbish questioning manner of Franceschini. Of the eight I produce, no two would eat the snails in the same manner. Aldo, I tell myself, make it all real.

Rua do Carma is a little hilly Calcutta where everyone exposes what he has – always more or less – to the charitable instinct of others: a foot turned up towards the knee, a little hand joined to the armpit, a horrific burnt face like a wax model which throws into relief the collection of muscles and nerves beneath, a skeleton heaped at the feet of a box of flowers, but nothing as extraordinary as the elephant woman I saw in Madrid walking with a sister, perhaps younger perhaps not, both dressed with all the petit-bourgeois proprieties, patent leather shoes and a little black purse with an old-fashioned clasp. Having got to the top of the hill I sit down in the Brasiliero bar not far from the statue of Pessoa with an empty table and chair next to him, all in bronze, perfectly incorporated with the little tables on the terrace. He was convinced that he was sitting in both of them – but he never convinced anyone – or that he was on the point of succeeding in doing so. Pessoa, Yourcenar, Kundera, Eco are part of that insubstantial area of good taste on which publishing has founded an empire to capture those who are anxious not to give a bad impression in terms of Fate and the House Beautiful.

Meantime evening arrives and I take myself off to Plaça dos Restauradores where I say hello to Eva and Rosa, two transvestites whom at home they wouldn't even want in circuses: tall, angular, covered with badly shaved hair, knock-knees, gap-toothed, nail-varnished tights, shoes shoved on outside in, two shit-holes dressed up as toilets. They are working, not to have an operation, because according to them you die if you are more of a woman than this, but to start a business as *cabeleirerias* (hairdressers) and so become moral or normal women, I'm not sure which. Late in the evening going towards the Plaça Marquês de Pombal, the pavements are an exhibition of secondhand foreign porno magazines and of streetwalkers, of whom all one can say is that they belong to the human species, with their possible and ghostly customers. A selection of really ugly women, all either skinny or wide-hipped, in crocheted cotton blouses which are losing stitches under the arms or at the waist because of pressure. There was a little man of about fifty leaning against the back of a bench tossing himself off gratis calmly and happily, putting it back in every so often and taking it out again, when one of the women came and walked past him – someone who was certainly at his ease, having found a do-it-yourself method at little capital cost to keep going till midnight. None of the women ever told him to get lost. A smell of gas from rubbish, of cheap lavender water, of grilled sardines. An elderly couple is waiting patiently for their puppy to do its business in front of a watchmaker's which seems marked down for the purpose because it has a whole aureole of previous shots. I imagine the melancholy of the owner every single morning in his life as a watchmaker, knowing what to expect from the inexorable passing of twenty-four hours.

One day I take a trip to the Madonna in Estremadura, a very sexy name for a province, and arrive at Fatima; another day I go to Cascais to see the blue convolvulus in the garden of exile belonging to King Umberto of Savoy; another to the monastery at Alcobaça; blessed are the monks who don't have to go with women and whom no one pesters by asking when they are going to get married! One evening someone holds me up on my way to the Rossio and says: 'Your purse or you.' 'Me.' But he took the purse anyway.

A phrase hammers at my head on a Sunday evening: 'Something agonizing'. A more perfect fiction, a better organized way of losing oneself – a childhood friend who knows I could kill myself from one moment to the next out of boredom and stages something to distract me. My elder brother comes in shaking off the snow: how imperceptibly he has remained the same for decades and everything that links me to him explodes in my memory. Another phrase which he uttered looking hard at me: 'Why go here and there the way you do? In the end you will have seen everything and seen it too quickly. You will be a squeezed lemon and still on the branch. Your life will be horrible, without emotions or feelings, without anything. All burnt out.' Then I had looked at him and said nothing. I was thinking: 'Better to burn too fast than never to catch fire like you.' This all-understanding friend of mine must naturally have a thorough knowledge of all my shades of feeling which cause my eyes to glow like fireworks an instant before they flare up. He must transmit this knowledge he has of me to the total actor whom he will put in my way and at my disposal. My friend knows what I do not know or have forgotten and is capable of reconstructing for me the detailed iconography of the ideal and slightly miserable love each of us carries with him: he knows the kind of man I would like, he rediscovers for me the colour of his eyes because this time they will have one and the colour of his hair and how his neck must be attached to his body; he will be an actor who will act in broad daylight and of whom each detail will come to be put together in a memory of love I have never had or have forgotten. My friend also knows the shape of his sex, he has made a selection from a great number to find that kind of Slav glans which could make me exult aesthetically, and he has imposed on him – on the actor – a voice with the timbre that makes me feel instantly weak and makes all existence fall away and hands me over to my enemy – the vocal chord. Everything must happen, is happening by *chance*. The chance meeting has been arranged down to the slightest detail, my saviour knows the kind of chance that fascinates me, he knows the clearcut silhouette, the objects or the structure of the walls which define the theatrical space for the *coup de foudre* – there I am getting out of a car, he has put a bag in my hand, he signs to me to cross the street. There's a station, I say to him, where do I have to go? – anywhere – not far from here, he says, it's all a pretence. Thank you, I know. Just as I know that the man I am going to fall in love with and with whom I am going to spend the evening without feeling a single moment of fatigue and a desire to sleep for ever is a perfect robot under remote control with a mind neatly constructed and an ordinary greed for money, a human robot, interested, without alibis, without ulterior motives. He is paid not to make sense of my life which has none and needs none, but to entertain it just enough not to finish it off, to go home and fall asleep again and wake up and reflect that yesterday was a dream like any other, and what the devil was I doing in the train? Or was it a travelling bookshop? I visit a couple a week, he could be there, on Saturdays, and leaning over the booth is asking about a new Ancient Greek dictionary. I do not know that I know the plot contrived by my friend for my own good. He likewise knows what I do not know about the following details: the age he must be, how he must preferably be dressed, the things in him that strike me at once and annoy me, and the mystery of his nose and mouth, what must they be like? What will they be like? This journey and this meeting arouse my curiosity – finally I shall meet someone who without knowing it I never knew really existed and had a matrix, however unstable, in my deepest and most unconscious desires. I know what his ears must be like, I told my friend: see that they are big and flapping, they excite me, I like to spit in them. My friend is very sorry for me – he takes trouble to save me from this, the worst kind of suicide: without cause. It is something that would leave him speechless for the rest of his life and he would not be able to endure not understanding something about me, would not put up with my escape from him precisely at my very last moment. In fact he does not want me *to save myself*, it would not be very important to him if I were to do away with myself after giving him the certainty that he will find a good reason. He will not forgive me for leaving him alone and in canvas trousers, he is too much of an animal and too hungry for life to allow me to abandon him, he would not put up with no longer having any spectator who is so interested in his bloody stupidity. He has made over – but out of my pocket because my friend has a hole in his and cannot permit himself the luxury of really organizing something from a to z – 5 million lire to this perfect actor, a down-payment on the part he must play for me personally. My friend has kept back 6 million lire for his general expenses and – because of his emotional worries that the expedient may possibly fail – a million in the event of suicide. He will come well out of it, he will call a band, will play a threepenny ditty, overcome with grief, as if he had been ruined by the last gift which I permitted him to pay me in advance.

Few people in the station, at the ticket office it is my turn now, someone goes ahead of everybody, stands on my foot, I give a shout of pain, the new verruca after the fourteenth operation, great God.

'I'm sorry, can I have a ticket, the train is at the platform.'

I look at him. Is this the one?

'I'm taking the same train.'

'If we're in time,' he says out of breath.

The train may be the one for Milan but it would be funny if it were the slow train to Parma which stops at every hen-house and wraps one in a pleasant relaxed feeling about things and men and the landscape of the Po. What could I be going to Parma for? It is the only bacteriological centre in the North specializing in the culture of chlamydia. But I don't have chlamydia and I don't even have the amoeba any more. If I turn up for the third time for a negative examination they will throw me out with a kick up my backside seeing what it costs. Then I could go to Parma for . . . A meeting with the Author, Civic Library, an appointment with the progressive councillor at seven-thirty for dinner in a hotel and the presentation to the workers, all included. Or because I simply felt like taking a train dating from the days of the Risorgimento with lots of water above and below, birches, fields of beet, grey banks, embankments of an English green, colourless bridges in the emptiness which is so beautiful out of the window. And he? What is he going there for?

'Parma,' I repeat when the other has barely disappeared. 'Return.'

'By the skin of our teeth,' I say, drawing a deep breath the moment I am in the carriage. There are only four passengers, I had no difficulty in discovering him. A pity that he has small ears.

'There's one every five hours. It would have been really bad luck.'

I watch him sideways without looking at him. Yes, my friend had guessed everything – it really is him, the ideal, anyone at all. It only remains for me to discover if the first thing he does will be to slip a hand into my pants and twist a finger in my arse. Now he – dark brown raincoat, style of last century, dark blond hair, almost reddish, thick, silky and greasy, a little dandruff, big lips, like ravioli, the smile of a lean lamb, a little sullen, not juicy – but no, there is a silvery drop of spit at the corner of his purple chilled mouth – he ought to ask me something at this point otherwise I can't justify the fact that in an empty carriage with all its seats wooden like a second-rung porno cinema, I went and sat right in front of him and not four naked pieces of joinery further on. 'Are you going to Parma too?' he asks, he is looking for something, his cigarettes. He is surely using the formal mode of address because he has taken in that I am bogusly youthful. I am not sure if I shall actually go to Parma, it was my friend who got the ticket for me in agreement with him. In fact neither he nor I was at the ticket office-it had all been arranged beforehand. Indeed an orange-coloured season ticket falls from his pocket. I take out my ticket and glance at it.

'No, I am getting out at Parola.'

'What a coincidence, so am I.'

'That's funny – you and I getting out at the same place.'

It is sure to be raining, I hear the rustle of discontent on the windows, not even the dearest, most thoughtful, most treacherous of friends could have foreseen this. Or else today he is foreseeing everything exactly. And the heating on this train only works in summer, I know that, I remember one August – but what's the matter with me, what's the matter with me, my cock was itching and so off to Parma, we didn't know where to put ourselves, all of us at the windows, I went to the engine-room, as you might say, and said to the fireman look we're boiling there, don't tell me, he said.

We are sitting opposite each other but not facing and it is me as usual who put my shoes on the seat. Now I could ask him a little question just to deflect the corner of his eye – yellow eyes, like those of a cat – towards my crotch which I am massaging with both hands.

Is he feeling himself fleetingly? Or is it I who am imagining everything and he is simply distracted by looking with concentration at the little trickles of rain on the window and is muttering a little with his beautiful child's lips perhaps because he is cold.

'It feels like going to the wars,' I say. The erection is total, only a blind person could not notice, I with my legs apart and with both my hands spread out hold it in by pulling at the cloth of my jeans. It is not a question it seems of going to the wars and yet he ought to distract me from my suicidal intentions. I am so ashamed to ask questions which don't interest me, to use words for ends different from those declared by the words themselves. For any end silence is enough, what need is there to debase the most noble stuff of man?

'And I have to take it every other day. I go over your way to practice,' he says sighing and hugging himself inside his raincoat.

'As a lawyer?'

'No, target practice with a pistol . . . As far as pistols are concerned you . . . And as far as I am concerned . . .'

But we have already arrived at Parola. He gets out, I stay where I am.

From Montichiari to Charleville, nine hours by car. For years I had wanted to visit the place where Rimbaud was born and lived until his first flight to Paris, on 29 August 1870, at sixteen, three years after mine, a flight organized by my father in a hotel in Manerba on Lake Garda complete with his friend's little Fiat and with his friend because he himself had no driving licence. Of these two men, the driver and my father, I remember that they dumped me in front of the entrance with my bag and that they did not even come in to talk to the horrible proprietor, a blonde squat woman, old and very made up, who always had her guard dog at her side, her daughter, an elderly dwarf, cruel and of few words – orders, nothing but orders. I still smelt of the third year of secondary school and of baby cheese, but already the untameable nature of my reek of sulphur had spread through the village. I was a little wretch, with no present, no future, no past, with an uncontrollable hunger for sex and books. The two men I saw again for several months because my father, who lived with a tight grip on his money, turned up long enough to pocket my wages and disappear. Before getting back into the car with the money I had just handed him – but it will last only a few months – he always found an excuse to give me a kick or a punch. With these precedents my infatuation for Rimbaud cannot certainly be attributed to the petit bourgeois projections of spoiled pupils in a *liceo* who can allow themselves something superfluous (school) and never what is necessary (adventure). When a little later I discovered Rimbaud, I discovered his poetry, naked and elegant, not the element however fascinating of the man with a particular existence of his own – at a century's remove his wild youth could have nothing about it so very different from my own, and then at that time, in the early Sixties, studies of Rimbaud were really very scarce in Italy and in any case it was impossible for a tearaway of fourteen to have access to them. Not even the Biblioteca Queriniana in Brescia had anything of the kind, except for a few spurious translations here and there, and it was really impossible to learn any more about them. Up through Switzerland, in Germany for a little, and here I am in France.

At fifteen I learned by heart *Une saison en enfer* and was so proud of my choice and of my memory that some evidence of it must exist in some newspaper from the province of Brescia because when I went to recite it at the Agricultural Fair at Chiari the 'personality' who presented me knew nothing about this poem, and when the whistles began to start up along with the insults he came back on to the stage and interrupted me and gave me a push to cut short my protest. To anyone who insists stupidly and out of excess of 'philological-textual' specialization on separating the work from the less important existential work of its author I shall say that in any case, for reasons inherent in me and which one certainly cannot demand of the common reader (who *is* the reader), I have always read and studied the writings of others in what I would call a 'scientific' manner without allowing myself to be influenced by possible autobiographical sympathies or antipathies caused by irrational, passionate, emotional reflections. Indeed until a few months ago I had done so little research into the human figure of Rimbaud that I (like, I presume, the overwhelming majority of those who love Rimbaud and are still forced to know something about *him*) have always thought that not only did he die in Africa but that his body never came back to Europe. In this respect I can justify myself by the fact that the contributions I gleaned about Rimbaud in Italy in those papers to which I had access as a child were so rare that I could swear that this conviction of mine was born from some vague literary article read like liquid gold not more than fifteen years ago. In other words, Yes, I did at one time make a thorough study of the works of Arthur Rimbaud as such and for a fundamental reason: because I have always thought the adventure of my existence to be more adventurous than his, including Abyssinia. To work the summer and winter season offering oneself as an underpaid dogsbody meant to put oneself at the mercy of such Beys and little monsters in comparison with whom Menelik was a Padre Pio and the desert and the robbers and the medical services at Harar in Abyssinia could certainly not be more pernicious than at Cortina d'Ampezzo for a hungry youth, angry and unemployed, who in order to eat had himself hospitalized.

Hence my more than neutral appreciation where Rimbaud is concerned, that is to say of his poetry; Arthur was never a myth for me and, if he was not such, one can understand that no one else ever had the power to be such and will never have it, either dead or alive. But new elements came to modify my memory of him as poet and above all of him as a man. I too, like all those who have been the victims of Rimbaudesque journalism in Italy (what appears in the dailies and weeklies – not the strictly inaccessible work of the university researchers), believed that I had been exhaustively informed about his mother, 'mean and petty' Vitalie, until reading the biography by Françoise Lalande, *Madame Rimbaud*, unleashed in me a profound anger at the *scholars* who complacently hand down to those who come after them little figures of cruelty only because they are not capable of grasping the secret passion, the emotive cornerstone of an atypical mode of behaviour, which is immediately branded as perverse or pitiless, because the great, the real generosity, is so hidden from indiscreet eyes that it takes on the mask of its opposite. Before this reading I knew nothing of the love and the proofs of love that all her life this proud and humiliated woman gave to her son from his birth on. No one ever revealed to us that this peasant woman of the Ardennes, tall and nervous, and always dressed in black, sets out for London when summoned by her son in difficulties and runs to his aid every time he calls (to London, Paris, Brussels and then to Marseille, and rarely through an intermediary); no one ever told us that Vitalie Cuif meets by post every necessity and whim of this son who is at odds with the Franco-Belgo-Anglo-Dutch colonial West (until he too allowed himself to be corrupted by the mirage of wealth and by making his fortune at the expense of the native populations with a cargo of weapons), sending him books, telescopes, medicines; and above all no one gives us a full account of her letters and of her gestures – often real feats – whether of unconditional love or inflexible authoritarianism.

The Ardennes resemble a landscape in Lombardy, more green because irrigated by natural and artificial channels, more beautiful because hillier and sweeter, more mysterious because less populated. Here within a radius of a few score kilometres in particular, the earth has been a battlefield since 1400, certainly the dung is a mixture of armour, standards, uniforms, bayonets, crests, hoofs, Norman and Ostrogoth hair, goat's hair and gilded Prussian insignia. The whole region is considered to be 'the Cemetery of the French' from Verdun to Sedan and Rheims: this sign recurs at the side of the road along with another with the heads of the two Poets in red: 'Route Rimbaud-Verlaine'. Because Rimbaud was 'the man with winged soles' – he walked for hundreds of kilometres and certainly made the old, drug-addict Verlaine – old more from corruption of the body than from age – walk a score or so (in fact he made him run). The huge size of the properties today and the tiny number of farmhouses lead one to conclude that people here must rise at dawn to get to the place for ploughing, sowing and reaping – at half-past seven, say. Sometimes there are expanses of fields of rape or grain or barley for kilometres and kilometres and no buildings round about, no silos, no human presence on a tractor or cart. Tall trees line the streams and ditches, rivers and dams, it is a spot where it is easy for a *Bateau* to get drunk on water. With the engine cut off at the side of a road, the waters with that noise of theirs carry along with them a geographical emotion of ineffable drowning in the vast expanse. I am at the gates of Charleville.

Often as a youth, and specially when very young, I thought of the couple of vagabond lovers with a certain envy: how was it possible that they had met and 'we' hadn't? I thought of their flights and pursuits – pursued in their turn by their mothers and Verlaine's wife – to Ostend, Brussels, London, Liège, Stuttgart, amid threats of suicide (Verlaine) and grazing pistol shots, and prisons and impossible farewells, of their passion which was that of turbulent down-and-outs full of lice and mycosis, of thrush and blennorrhagia. Because if it is true that the real sexual need was that of Verlaine for Rimbaud and not vice versa – Arthur turns out to have been sexually indifferent and therefore more passive or active as ordered – it is also certain that Rimbaud loved Verlaine for other reasons, and no less madly than he himself was loved. These two nervous systems so different and highly gifted, carnal and abstract, had been able – without cowardice and with all the arrogance that certain drastic choices require – in the eyes of the world to mix two visionary natures in one. Verlaine was also subject to a lawsuit brought by his wife, but the scandal did not prevent him from confirming his love for Arthur and this for him, a citizen and a bourgeois one, was certainly not easy. The two, finally, love each other with heads held high at every moment, the basic solidarity is never lacking except for intimate reasons – never out of respect for the public. In this sense I, a century later, have only met lover-boys ready to throw the stone, yes, but only on condition that they could hide their hands: in short, where was the Arthur or the Paul that was right for me? I have always admired them as lovers as well, when I thought of a friend I thought he ought to be clear and magnetic like Arthur or brave and tenacious like Paul, that sublime disgusting creature.

Here I am in the square in Charleville. Charleville was founded in the early seventeenth century by Carlo Gonzaga and it is only in the last score years that it has joined up with Mézières by a process of natural urban-industrial expansion to form a single city with a single real historical centre. It is here that Arthur was born in 1854 to the soldier Rimbaud – a father and then later a husband, and to all intents and purposes absent – and to the female proprietor, Cuif, to whom with foresight fate had given the name of Vitalie, and she did indeed have to be vital, in view of the fact that everyone around her – from her father to her brothers, her two sons, her two daughters, her husband and even her son-in-law, Paterne Berrichon – was inept, soft, lazy, ailing and often incapable of supporting themselves by their own means. All the human beings – the members of her family – who gravitate to Vitalie are affected by languor, dromomania, parasitism, intellectual aspirations. Her daughter Isabelle and her son-in-law, the third-rate painter, become the depositories of Arthur's memory and unfortunately of his papers, of which they burn everything that does not fit in with their aim of transforming him into a martyr of Catholicism no less. What I would call the physiological mediocrity which is dependent on the strength of her shoulders and on the authority of her character is such that it will be she, hardened by life as if she had been mummified for centuries and so semi-immortal, who accompanies almost all of them to the cemetery.

This spiky woman, vaguely sinister, toughened by work in the fields as much as by her petit bourgeois frustrations (which will lead her to move a dozen times from one district to another with the ambition of demonstrating to the community her phantasmic social ascent), is the real protagonist, along with Verlaine and the African myth of material 'wealth', of Arthur's most secret life, of his emotional dreams which will not leave him, not even in his last hours in the Hospital of the Conception in Marseille, where he dies in 1891. Mother and son love each other and hate each other, come together and part, seek each other, implore each other, accuse each other, absolve each other; he understands her definitive and unfounded solitude, no other tie apart from this sublimated incest, which is vulgar, without any sentimentality, will ever be able to capture their attention by its intensity, duration and charity.

In the Rimbaud museum in a case, hanging by a thread and framed, there is the original of *Voyelles*, newly acquired, then Arthur's suitcase, some cloth, a water-bottle, photographs, photocopies of Verlaine's editing in the margin of some proofs of *Illuminations*, and very little else. The sepia-coloured photo of Arthur, who is by now unrecognizable, skeletal, in a white tropical jacket, makes me start. He resembles one of those people with AIDS whom they photograph from a distance, so that in the end you can give them any face you like – even your own. As a youth Arthur is very beautiful, even if too feminine for my taste, and the oval is really exaggerated. But those eyes . . . There is also a photograph of Léon Rimbaud, son of the famous Frédéric. Arthur's brother, dressed as a sailor, the same look as his uncle but the Rimbaud stock is already extinct; there is a photograph of

Isabella, a little hat with a lace rosette, contrite, like a bigoted virgin.

The sharp-eyed cashier in the museum suddenly takes a liking to me and shows me some of the houses which Vitalie moved to – none of them has remained as it was, obviously, the best-preserved is just there at the corner where the chemist's is. The lady from the museum talks with enthusiasm about the book by Lalande:

'It has restored dignity to the Widow Cuif, who was a great woman, against whom all the most poisoned ink has been directed. You see Vitalie was not one to be put down by the authorities. In 1901 when the bust of Arthur was inaugurated at the Gare she even refused to turn up. You see she never ever allowed a word to escape her about her son to a stranger – and to her everybody was a stranger. Go to La Roche, go to the Cuif farm, it isn't very far . . .'

At La Roche Widow Cuif – the white widow – had her land; it is there that Arthur sets hand to his 'black book', to the *Saison en enfer* which he publishes at his own expense (but thanks to a 'loan' from his mother) in Brussels in the summer of 1873; so when he was nineteen. I shall go there, but now I am running off to an appointment with Gérard Martin, the very nice director of the library, who accompanies me by car to the archives of the region where for the moment the slim Rimbaud archive is kept. Before going into the room, which has a controlled temperature, I ask him not to let me out of his sight for a moment. He smiles and understands. Finding myself at such close quarters with these manuscripts I would not want to fall into temptation. The Rimbaud archive is shut away in a little grey box and can't weigh more than a quarter of a kilo. I ask him how much was paid for the bit of paper with *Voyelles*; about 70 million Italian lire. Today any paper in Rimbaud's hand starts at 40 million – and they are not to be found, and there are collectors, even Chilean, Japanese and American ones, who know all about them, who carry on the most friendly correspondence but only in order to be the first to be informed of reciprocal deaths and hence of the availability on the market of Rimbaud originals.

My emotions are strong: but every document bears the stamp

in biro or ink of the various careless librarians who preceded the present curator, who does not allow any catalogue marking on the documents themselves. I stay there about three hours: I hoped to find, at least by speaking about it, confirmation of a rumour which reached us (the few of us) from Paris in far-off 1870.

'Have you ever heard of the three rapes which Rimbaud suffered in Paris?' I ask the curator.

'No – I have never heard or read anything of the kind,' he says, a little surprised.

'I had heard talk of it in France at the beginning of the Seventies at Roubaix from a very old French officer and again recently in Milan from a friend. It seems that there is even an account written about it at the beginning of the century, which now is not to be found.'

'I have never heard anything of the kind,' he repeats, very uninterested.

'When I read *Les Confessions* of Verlaine for the first time about twenty years ago I very much hoped he would say something about Arthur, but as you know if I am not mistaken he is almost entirely silent. But is it not extraordinary that "gossip" should reach us at a distance of almost one hundred and twenty years? Is it not tremendous, this mythical sign which contrives to find its winding way from mouth to mouth to us?'

'I'm sorry,' says the director and gives a little cough.

Then I ask him to photocopy an extraordinary document – Arthur's case-history year by year, which Paterne Berrichon had set out by request, relying on his wife Isabelle's memory. When I had finished reading it it really seemed to me that Arthur Rimbaud was the first death from AIDS of modern times, which by convention begin at 1850. I even come across the word 'sarcoma'. And the sudden violent pains and the gangrene and the unstoppable wasting process and the great moral depression and the violent attacks of fever. This is what I came for, I know: to have in my hands this manuscript, the existence of which I vaguely knew about. Arthur's atrocious death drew me here, to his life. It is for this gloomy reason too that I have kept postponing this trip from year to year and it has taken me months to write these disordered, reluctant pages.

For years I have felt the work of Rimbaud at my own fingertips to the point where I might say that I became an independent writer only when I succeeded in understanding that *Les Illuminations* had lost a great deal of their poetic – that is to say their linguistic – enamel. Because Rimbaud's poetry had grown old like everything else. And if it has grown old imagine Baudelaire's! The reading of a rather stupid book by Henry Miller, *The Age of the Assassins* (I hope not translated into Italian), did however prevent me from falling – but I would never have fallen – into such ostentatious behaviour as to refer Rimbaud and his works to myself and to my own as does Miller, who is the big chief of a very bourgeois and American way of conceiving of life (read – sex) and literature. Besides even Saba and Montale fell into the same trap: they who in their lives barely dared to go out to buy bread now and then without their nanny felt themselves 'in intimate syntony' with Rimbaud, so brazen-faced are they! All the sedentary characters of Italian poetry and literature feel themselves on the same wavelength as Rimbaud. All those who get their backsides off their sofas only to take part in a literary jury or symposium of fine university minds and only go anywhere by wagon-lit feel themselves to be legitimate relations of Arthur! I have never thought that – also because I have never thought that Rimbaud had performed so many more feats than me, nor that my work is less significant in the twentieth century than his was in the preceding one. I have never brought Rimbaud to Busi but always Busi to Rimbaud as two very distinct and separate entities, even given the astonishing similarity in their respective wild youths; in fact Rimbaud, unlike Busi, enjoyed some privileges which I never had: more than one shoulder to weep on and at least a safe refuge where he could get over his numerous convalescences, which were typically chronic or purely depressive. Further I suffer the humiliation of having lived an irremediably long and compromising time – already four years more than he, and four years are a lot when faced by the risk, which is always imminent, of becoming marginalized and ridiculous, integrated and ridiculous, and then only ridiculously inconsistent, like grown-ups as young people who have the bad luck of then becoming centenarians.

At the central bookshop – whose manager confesses to me her dislike of Lalande's book – 'a little rhetorical and sentimental' – I buy a detailed map of Charleville and immediately pick out the way to La Roche, which is not altogether simple, because I have to take a motorway and then various roads and even pathways, it seems. Posters with the faces of the two poets proliferate and I shall never know with how much embarrassment for the inhabitants, since they look as if they were about to kiss (which is not at all true). Their spirits, perfectly stripped of any form of Catholicism, always appeared to me to be unique in the West, both seemed to me to have been born on an uncontaminated star far from here. From the point of view of poetic style I have always preferred Verlaine because his is a more complex and descriptive spirit, with a more stringent lyricism. The writerly world of Rimbaud could not be further from mine – his centres on the figure of analogy which because of its oracular dogmatism is related to neo-platonic esotericism; mine on the metaphor hidden as well as possible and unfolded in a social story about 'matter' and therefore political. Yet then as now my point of reference as artist has been Rimbaud not Verlaine; in Rimbaud art is life and the one tries to cannibalize the other with alternating results. For this reason I find loathsome the liberty which almost all literary people take with Rimbaud: they turn art into a discourse and therefore into a craft. They speak about an experience without having lived it and believe that the fact that nothing exists *that has not been thought* can make up for the fact that most has not been *lived*. If he had an experience that was unusual I have had mine: in me there is no need for projections ahead supported by an excess of *thought* and by an *existential* lack which can produce only texts on a (*the*) text. Miller, basically that sub-species of the damned, says this: 'Rimbaud c'est moi.' Poor dear – one of the thousand-and-one poor dears who enjoy scant artistic autonomy the moment they have drawn their last breath. If one can delude oneself into replacing consciousness by the proliferation of *thoughts*, no one can delude himself into believing he can take the place of the body which gave birth to it, and the body is the very consciousness of art which articulates a gestation or a creation. In this connection I shall quote a fine passage from

Alain Borer's book *Rimbaud en abyssinie*: 'Of a score of essays on Rimbaud's African years not one of the authors has gone to Harar to verify, to inform himself, wander about, live . . . They did not go there but have heard so much talk about it . . . No one could conceive of analysing a text without having read it, but these same people talk about an experience without having lived it – or attempted it in their own way, at least – as if life was not less singular than the text, as if experience was general, given to all, immediate.'

I have no desire to be Rimbaud, seeing that I am already Busi. I am always even with Rimbaud – he a poet, I a writer, he a man fleeing, I a boy in service, he writing in the attic, I in the basement of the hotel in rooms with a dozen employees, he in Africa, I in France, England, Germany, Spain, which for someone who left Montichiari in the early Sixties was as amazing as going to Arabia, Cyprus, or Egypt a century ago. For both of us, if one considers the respective historical times, I would be inclined to say that it took a great deal for Rimbaud to be Rimbaud and for me to be me. Rimbaud gets the better of me however for one reason only: he dies young, I repeat. He can permit himself the luxury of marginalization to the limit, I have to succumb to the greatest perversion of my time: to go to Channel 5 to do a number with a red boa may be less ridiculous than not to go there these days. I arrive at the point where I myself construct my ridiculous situations in order to affirm my inviolable seriousness. Rimbaud does not know the desertifying effect of success and enforced integration, he lives and dies splendidly absent – and nothing can guarantee me, in the end, that he did not go and hide himself. Besides almost all his letters from Africa show the capriciousness of a son from a good family with the same aspirations as a failed accountant in a bank – and had he remained in Paris perhaps he would not even have succeeded in becoming one – an accountant in a bank – or if he had succeeded would not have had the energy not to produce literature displaying the wisdom of an accountant. Rimbaud, unlike me, who am a successful writer, does not know the temptations to which I am exposed day after day by the world of politics, of television, of the textile industry; let us say it – Rimbaud does not give me the ultimate guarantee which Proust gives me, Proust, who would have written *A la recherche* with asthma or without asthma, well off or in penury, satisfied or frustrated, live – or moribund. Proust is someone whom nothing can stop or make go faster, like me: he goes on writing, consolidating his socio-sexual dimension for what it is and without letting himself be determined by it. Rimbaud, no – I am sure that if Rimbaud had been able to achieve his deepest desire (to get back to the countryside, cultivate his native soil, marry and have a child to make of him 'a famous engineer') he would have come to a much more miserable end than mine, which is something I do not know yet but certainly it is not this.

I draw the car into the side not far from a house – I should be there; outside in the garden there is a peasant woman tending a bed of cabbages. There are three buildings in all, nothing makes me think that this is La Roche. I have seen no signboard, and yet the crossroads is the same as the one on the map. I shout to the woman 'Rimbaud?' and what a strange sound hangs for a moment in the leaden air of this little valley. 'No one of that name lives here,' she says, coming up to the fence by the ditch. 'The poet,' I insist dubiously. 'Ah, a poet. Down here. Yes! yes! eheh! But no one has lived here for ages!' and my eyes follow her hand which is pointing to a little ruined house.

Among the undergrowth there is a broken column on which almost all the letters of *Une Saison en enfer* have crumbled. The little house had been constructed after the First World War and is in ruins. Very beautiful glass protected by gratings of wrought-iron on the central door and windows; odd that no one has yet made off with them, like everything else here. Even the trees – perhaps one oak is all that might remain of that sacred year 1870 whch changed the destiny of world poetry. I climb over the wall, and go into the bushes behind the house – there are irises among a mound of broken tiles. I climb back again, collect what is really a very old stone, rough-hewn by hand, which was lying beside the narrow gate of what must be a pigsty – obviously the original one – and with my poor dusty fetish get back into my car.

In the cemetery at Charleville Rimbaud lies between his mother and his maternal grandmother.

The attendant whom I get to show me the way (but there is no need, for the three stones are just inside) tells me that almost every day one or two letters addressed to Arthur Rimbaud arrive from every corner of the earth. Even with Easter greetings.

'Then there are still vandals today,' he says sighing.

I do not understand, I go on but he does not follow me. He knew I would understand by myself. *'Priez pour lui'* – someone after trying to outline it with paint has defaced the word *'priez'* on the stone with a sharp instrument so as to change the 'P' into a 'C': *'Criez pour lui'*. I leave happy that the vandal did it for the good of his soul which has no need of intercessions. Arthur has no need of anyone to lend him a hand at this moment. It was he who wrote, seeing far into infinity, *'mange ta main, garde l'autre pour demain.'* I have always thought that this advice was the only one to give to anyone who wants to become, it does not matter which, either someone who lives or someone who writes.

At the Fiumicino airport the living space of the Air Algérie counter is next to that of Air Tunisie and my number on the standby list is 25 and the plane which ought to leave in an hour has not landed yet. In this coming and going of young men from the Maghreb who do not know if they will have a seat or not (because all the flights of every company which lands in Algiers are said to be taken for the next three days), I am the only Italian, an obvious sign that my fellow countrymen, simply by insisting on Alitalia, display a distrust which takes off from a common, rampant racism to which not even tourists are strangers and only persons like myself who am in a state of need are disposed to clip its wings. There is an Italian lady who stayed for a very short time and who has a seat; in the course of these five minutes spent among their cheap stereos, spare parts for cars and boxes of jumpers and jeans from the Fedini sisters in Naples and huge boxes usually tied with string in incredible ways, she felt it her duty to seek my complicity by whispering: 'Just smell them.'

They always begin with the sense of smell – the nose, by measuring what is needed to keep one's distance, already traces an ideal *cordon sanitaire*. I replied with an understatement:

'If you were to clear off I am sure the smell would move away.'

It is the smell of carefully counted money in the pocket – I recognize it: the money of someone who has slept in his clothes for several nights in doorways and who, washing as best he can in the fountains, got his sleeves and fly wet, the smell of rusty and slightly mouldy zips, of someone who has sweated from walking for kilometres looking for a little better situation and then comes back to a room in a pensione, four beds (camp), 12,000 lire, outside tap, and has found the toilet with a sign saying: 'Out of order.' Of a person who, having been chased out of the airport at two-thirty at night – the latest time for untidy coloured persons to stay inside – has huddled with all his goods between one car and another in the dark to discover only in the morning that someone had relieved himself just there under what, after all, looked like a soft place to doss down. It is not the smell of dirt but that of a loyalty towards acceptance of the circumstances as they are without forcing them. Dignity rarely smells of *Bizarre*.

So the trip began a good time ago, here, waiting for hours; every so often there resounds among the announcements and the clatter of the trolleys being braked the same invocation concerning a place in the plane and the flight itself: 'Inshallah' – if God wills. A little Algerian arrives in a black track suit, a big close-cropped head, gangly, and on his thighs and chest the track suit, which is flashily coloured where it is not stained with reddish rings, he wears a white Valentino *griffe*. But he is not the only one; another two arrive with the same brand of track suit, one white and the other yellow, with badly washed stains of tomato and mud. Since one of them was smiling to me and once he started they all smiled one after another like little lamps which didn't expect anything else, I ask him how things are and what nice places he has been to.

'I live in Naples in the country, I gather so many tons of tomatoes! Ten thousand lire a day for ten hours. I am going to take this,' and he too points to his packaged stereo, 'and to see my family, then I am coming back for the potatoes and the artichokes. I live in Tizi-Ouzo, come and see me.'

Mouhlu and Mohammed, however, have invested their scanty gains in little Versace cotton suits for children, three pairs of jeans each, five virgin videocassettes, the usual stereo and five pairs of shoes medium size – and Valentine track suits made in country basements and no more ridiculous than the originals, I presume: the mania via the ether for little tunes broken by commercials and that for elegance as in Via Condotti can only be of interest now to the Third World and Sophia Loren.

Since (after opening my Michelin map) I was asking for information about places to visit and local hotels they gather round, more than ten of them, to give me advice, to direct me – preferably to their own village. Since they are all beautiful, I think I shall show up at each one of them – I begin to write in my diary: 'Algiers: Mohammed, Hamid, Abdelkrim; Tizi-Ouzo: Shéif, Muhdi, Hamed; Sidi Ferruch: Idriss, Johnny . . .' Constantine and the part of the region west of Oran is blank. When I say they are beautiful I mean to say that it will certainly not be their caries nor their missing teeth that will stop me; one smiles as best he can – in any case your tongue ends up down the throat, it seldom stops to count molars and incisors.

At last the glass at the counter is raised – they have drawn the lucky numbers. A great throng, but no pushing, no discourtesy, no instinct of prevarication, so many eyes shining with the same hope that each one respects in the other. How far away Italy is already. It is a calm throng which is born of infinite patience, cast because of ancestral nobility into a state of resignation that is stirred by the possibility of being lucky; no one will get there in front of anyone else; in the end, to leave or wait a little longer will not change the dates without precise appointments with destiny. If it is not the tomatoes it will be potatoes, in any case one must bend one's back to a destiny that is adverse but not unfavourable. We will remain human beings in spite of the scanty crops in their seasons.

Barking behind us, two Alsatians are making towards us, pushing us on either side; the two policemen with dark glasses and expressionless faces allow themselves to be pulled along by the leashes, the damp nostrils of the dogs tremble in spasms of abstinence, one dog shows its fangs to a little boy who has a slightly darker skin than the others in the group that is motionless at the end of the throng. The police look us up and down, they are unable to look without lenses like normal human beings: then they go off grinning.

Mahdi says: 'They do it always at least once when we arrive and leave,' and then he begins to pour out things he had not meant to display to me for fear of wounding my non-existent love of my country: 'Never a word – you go into a pizzeria and they are rude to you, go into a bar and they have problems about serving you, four out of five pensioni are full, to eat they give you olives and dry bread in the fields, and it's kicks if you are bending down a little less than usual, not to mention the girls, but we pay too, it's not as if we wanted things free . . .'

And one of the Mohammeds who, because he has spent two days in Naples as an ordinary tourist, thinks he has been in Italy: 'In the train I tried to start up a conversation with a woman, she jumped up to call the ticket-collector, I went away and got out at an intermediary station and I saw her at the window beginning to shout "It's him, it's him" and they jumped on me – look at this,' and he raises his right arm, which is fastened to his neck by a dirty bandage.

And Idris: 'No one looks at you, as if they didn't see you, as if you weren't there. If you ask for information they know nothing. But we are in good spirits just the same – after all we at least managed to come to Italy. You couldn't before.'

I know what they are talking about; about the Italo-Swiss eye that suddenly glazes when it meets a hawker, so that all the people from the Maghreb (Morocco, Tunisia, Algeria, Libya, Polisario) who have the misfortune to be illegal immigrants or to stop over in Italy are extraterrestrial dust, and since it cannot be got rid of one can at least accustom one's eye not to accept it in one's delicate Aryan prism.

Meantime the employee in the white shirt and blue jacket with tabs continues to call out loudly from behind the glass.

'What is your number?' I turn round surprised and a little complacent because the question at once repeated in French was addressed to me in Arabic. I already have the same smell too, as well as the same wide trousers, a dirty T-shirt, worn rubber shoes – or perhaps I haven't lost it entirely and it goes back to my wild but nice youth.

'You look like an Algerian,' Hassi continues.

'What is your number?' I ask him.

'There are three of us, a girlfriend of mine and her little brother – 26 27 28. I am taking them with me – that way I can take in more stuff per head.'

'For example?'.

'Everything – tea, coffee, Marlboros, apart from the knitted stuff and shoes and the toasters, batteries, electric heaters. On commission, sometimes I also take in little pots, headlights, special valves. In our country there are not even branch agencies and all the cars are worn out, apart from those belonging to the important officials. Obviously I have to pay for everything in lire, Algerian money isn't convertible, not even in the countries of the Maghreb. I go hunting for tourists from morning to evening. I'll give you a good rate if it interests you.'

They call my number and then the others up to 30; the two brothers from Tizi-Ouzo who gave me their addresses did not have any luck – and they had already withdrawn their luggage yesterday because they ran the risk of not having any more money to pay the deposit; I offer them 50,000 lire but they refuse, say they will find a way, that they will sleep there and that they still have bread. Both are university students. On the ground there remain about thirty emigrants without savings and little small-time traders as well as young tourists on two-day trips everything included (those who every four years have a right to foreign currency equivalent to 200,000 lire and don't have the means to pick up foreign tourists on the spot cannot allow themselves more). Many had been waiting for two more days before this – but from no one is there a note of rancour at the humiliations they have suffered, certainly not more serious than all the others they have learned to live with from the Turkish invasion to the French *colons* of the Organisation Armée Secrète to the present Socialist oligarchy.

On the plane during the flight amid stewardesses of rare beauty and politeness, there is a padded English atmosphere, in the sense that the Algerian passengers have a degree of politeness that has been forgotten in England itself; they don't get up, don't make a noise, don't press the bell once, are enthusiastic when confronted with the modest little tin of apricot jam – the peak of in-flight service. My neighbours are extraordinarily ugly, just as their manners are extraordinarily good, and the usual ignoramus who claps hands when the plane lands was the Italian lady who takes all my rude answers with a laugh and turning to me incautiously remarks:

'The more one flies the more frightened one is of flying. Did you feel how it shook? It felt as if it were looking for its target.'

I say, politely detached: 'Well, it must only have been your cellulitis.'

If one applauds when a plane lands what does one do if it crashes? Whistle? The last horrible flight I made (Manaus–Brasilia) all I was able to formulate as I was thrown against my seat-belt was: 'When it's your turn, it's your turn.' I don't believe that one dies of anything specific – one dies of death, that hyperinvention of Western thought which has become fossilized on itself . . . I therefore wish to live for life, not for one thing alone in life, even though it might be the literature I produce – the more I go on writing the more I realize that I have no equals, there is no point in your telling me some other version: this one – just as it is – is humble.

At the luggage conveyor belt – a good hour's wait in which the heat of Algiers is already penetrating your clothes, reducing you to a damp torch, Hassi fills me in on the black market:

'Four times the official rate of exchange. I want to get away from here, I'm waiting for confirmation of a visa for Canada or Australia, I need foreign currency.'

The belt begins to move.

'I want to leave Algeria – there's nothing for us here – neither work nor a house – I want to emigrate to Australia – I have a cousin down there.'

And Shérif:

'I don't ask for anything special, no life of luxury, just to work, to have a family, here it isn't even possible to find somewhere to live unless you can pull strings, and I can't.'

The Italian woman who has a husband here in the hydrochemical industry at last says something nice, very curious to see what piece of rudeness I shall manage to invent for her this time: 'Algiers is the city I love most after all. We have been in so many. Here a woman is respected, safe when she walks about, at least by day. And the fish restaurants are the best in the Mediterranean. In the restaurants in the centre, at the Pêcherie, you can get lobster for ten thousand lire and the wine from Medea is good too, for us residents there are no currency limits as there are for tourists, in the high-class hotels you have to pay in valuta, we don't have to, and even the flights, which are the cheapest in the world. Ah, there's my husband.'

Here is a woman who will never make the mistake of loving something that does not answer to her self-interest and her comforts. She waves to her husband, who is stuck on the other side of the barrier and who begins to chat up a guard in order to get past the ropes. She goes on:

'In any case there's no point in your changing much – there's nothing to buy. No carpets, no Kabyle pottery, and the silver is not as good as at home; the meat is delicious. Always ask for fillet, go and eat at the Pardo near the main post office.'

She is reunited with her husband who has had permission, granted with deference, to come and wait for his wife's luggage.

The conveyor belt unloads occasional parcels separated by metres of bare rubber spirals. I make an appointment with Hassan for him to bring me the dinars at the Hotel Saint George next day: I was thinking of something really offensive to say to the lady to give her the knockout but then I reflected that it is mathematically certain that nothing disagreeable can ever happen to someone like that – because nothing agreeable can ever happen to her either. Someone who changes her money on the black market, buys and then turns up her nose. She is one of the tribe who come back to their native country when they have made a fortune and left a desert behind them.

One after the other all the boys with whom I have exchanged a few words come to say goodbye and wish me a nice stay, and even the shyest put to me the only question that was close to their hearts: Didn't I have a sister? Blonde? Pretty? She is married already. What a pity – or a girlfriend to lend him – it doesn't matter if she is a bit of a brunette? The tourists get through like a flash after handing in their *fiche* which registers the amount of foreign currency imported (a barbaric legacy of bureaucratic ingenuity in matters of international finance) while I have deliberately got into the queue of Algerians behind Hassi and his two fellow travellers, to see the treatment the Customs officers reserve for them. The search of the first parcels and bags is meticulous, not a piece of string is overlooked, everything is opened and scrutinized. I guess at the subtle annoyances in Arabic, the whys and the wherefores, the irony, the hints, the invitations to come into the office, the pedantry of methods equal perhaps only to those which the Algerians have to submit to at the airport at Fiumicino where the photocopying and stamping of passports can last as long as the *Sura of the Granter of Pardons*, Koran XL. (Perhaps it could be pointed out to the passport office in Rome that since the need for a visa between Italy and Algeria has lapsed they should show more respect to travellers from Algeria and the Maghreb in general and that, even allowing for the falsification of every document, an Algerian or Tunisian passport has not got the sinister value of a Syrio-Lebanese or an Iranian passport and that the Algerian people is perhaps the last one left in the world which neither uses nor deals in any kind of drug, hashish included.)

Now the agents have gone on to tear apart the boxes of Hassi's extremely lively girlfriend and of her little brother. They undo big packages in such a way that it will not be possible to put them together again, they pick up little feminine trinkets of plastic and strass with the end of their batons or with a couple of fingers gloved in sweat-stained white. A good job for the girl that she has not been buying up female underwear. None of the three friends says anything, they give forced smiles, obedient but stubborn in terms of the ends they have in view; to get it over with at all costs and go and sell it this very day.

Damp heat, sweat, patience – and a vague kind of amusement round about, as if this were a little family drama rather than something staged by sullen power. There is no arrogance on the part of the Algerian police towards their fellow countrymen who have been abroad, in Naples, but a kind of passive carrying out of obsolete orders that have come down from a *high* bureaucracy which cannot cope with the needs and most modest aspirations of a population of whom 75 per cent are under twenty-seven, and the *high* authority still does not miss an opportunity to make itself felt. It is as if the young Algerians, abandoned to themselves and to the privilege of coming to let themselves be exploited in Southern Italy or in their disavowed mother, France, enjoy, after all, favourable treatment: the application of a bureaucratic process of Byzantine formality but void of any serious threat or substantial inhibition on the part of authorities which are dedicated to maintaining the state of protectionism. All of them will get their goods back after due loss of time (they will have to go through again to get them for a further check) without paying any fine or duty – although a little backhander is very acceptable here too. It must be the sheer number of the youths who are the well-behaved but determined nomads of the airports that makes the Customs officers and their superiors shut an eye and then both eyes – a number of youths which is growing visibly. Algeria had 12 million inhabitants in 1968, today it is between 24 and 26 million. The silence, heavy with reproofs, provides a certain laissez-passer so that the reproof disperses and does not risk turning into a real state of siege, into a new revolution. A week after I left the latest bread riot would start in the suburbs of Algeria. It would leave on the streets the corpses of about a thousand boys. I have traced one by one all those I knew and their families and everything is well with them, at Bellecourt, Boumerdes or Tizi-Ouzu. It is a youth without means or skills, plucky and polite, ready for many more sacrifices before taking hard strong measures of any kind; it is not for nothing that here patience and age-old courage is so concrete as to become a kind of rage. Just to begin with, in recent years these boys have conceptualized something that was impossible for their fathers, serfs of the desert and the kasbah: the indissoluble linkage between religion and politics, between Islamism and social repression, between religious oligarchy and economic oligarchy. If those sitting beside me, when asked with all due circumspection, are reluctant to talk directly about the economic system, none held back when faced with the subject of 'religion', all Muslims, but none of them 'says his prayers', that is to say none of them is a practising Muslim, far less *khouan*, bigoted. The 'Muslim Brotherhood', with their integralist faith in spite of political persecution (about two hundred prisoners in jail without trial, of whom no one knows anything – not even Amnesty International), do not enjoy any charisma or following here, they are simply considered politicians excluded from power who have recourse to Khomeini's fanaticism in the hope of installing themselves again in the upper reaches of the State. The government of President Chadli has nothing to fear from them but everything to fear from the blocking of the market which prevents the young men from buying a car at a human price, from the housing crisis and that of the aqueducts always promised, never repaired or constructed, from the laughable salaries even for those who have work, from the imposition of classical Arabic in the schools against the legitimate desire to use a standard written language which corresponds to contemporary Arabic, which is contemporary, a vehicle, living, of the people not the Koran. The boys make fun of Chadli, who insists on talking in classical Arabic on television and makes devastating howlers or uses phrases taken from the Koran and applied to the description of a reality which today cannot be contained by any possible *classical* linguistic parameter.

The programmes in schools (and on television) are thought up to put a brake on this linguistic awareness in revolt, which is obviously considered dangerous and subversive, however – alas! – unstoppable. No account is taken of the cultural patrimony of the various ethnic groups, above all of the Berbers, who are opposed to the attempt at homogenization which has been going on since the 'Socialist' takeover in 1962. The Berbers will never give up their language, and the basic paganism of their culture, and the presence in ordinary life – not only in the family – of their women, on whom no abstract process of Arabization will ever impose a veil which has always been scorned. In terms of religion and power, Algerian youth seems to me more advanced than the Polish workers who are forced, who knows to what extent mystically, to turn to Catholicism as the aggregating force to free them from a régime that stuck in their throats, only to fall at once out of the frying-pan into the fire. It is possible on the other hand that the Algerians are, after all, less oppressed by this 'Socialist' power, which is indifferent, ignorant and badly prepared, but less ferocious and militarized than certain South American régimes (but here too there is a certain amount of violence, as in the vast majority of Italian barracks), and which, as has been confirmed, has at its disposal no *special* corps for repression. It is a political management which is simply facing in another direction in terms of thought and acts, which does not believe enough in *the here and now* from which it draws its income: schools abroad for the offspring of the rulers and generals, private clinics abroad even for operations on appendices, the usual secret accounts in Swiss banks for almost all the 'serious' politicians who live with the Ben Bella syndrome of unexpected exile but with all Swiss comforts. In other words one is talking about a power in office to make not history or technological progress but above all lots of money to put in a safe place.

I talk about all this with *the person* (to whom I have given my word that I will not mention even their sex) who came to fetch me at the airport (on his/her own initiative) or rather, I alone talk, because this person rather than conversing with me gives me to understand that (s)he fears I might compromise him/her with what I write about this trip and that (s)he does not know me and would be obliged to deny everything and would end up in a sea of troubles if . . . I point out that I am not a spy nor am I interested in military secrets. It doesn't matter, (s)he blurts out, you are unfortunately famous here too in certain circles, your dispatches from South America caused a stir in certain embassies even here, they say that you take advantage of people's good faith and then come out with all the confidences they made to you, that you send up intellectuals, officers and priests and they are all recognizable, worse than if you said their full names, apart from the fact that you always give them, you talk on the phone as if you were in the street, forgetting that certain people listen in on the phone. I shall take you to your hotel but I shall let you out beforehand, you will get there on foot, a slight hill, but you scarcely notice it, you must be careful and you must give me your word that . . . Why the hell did (s)he come to the airport to fetch me? I shall never know, perhaps out of a dutiful sense of courtesy, seeing that in Italy I was very nice to him/her. My word is given, but the connection is immediately broken off; I detest people who live in a state of panic, they are ready to betray themselves and you and to drag you into a mess of troubles without even doing their sums like Judas, exclusively because of psychic fragility, or because of an exaggerated idea of their own social status, all the more stoutly defended with tooth and claw the more insignificant it is to all intents and purposes. Yet this person does not succeed in saddling me with any sense of fear, and I remain virgin when faced by the panorama of the city. It opens up to the left with the monument to the fallen of the revolution (called *Hubel*, the idol, as a sign of contempt for all the billions in petrol it cost and which everyone – except the political caste which provides its own incense – would look at in a more kindly way if they had been spent on the sewers and water systems and on the upkeep of the kasbah, which is in ruins, where people go on dying because of the collapse of whole buildings from one minute to the next) and to the right with the Hotel Aurassi, both on the ridges of the mountain which slopes massively down in a single flow of urban cement to the port. Of the Algiers one might have imagined seeing, not a trace is left. Now I only want to be set down as soon as possible with my bag, even here, beside the sea, to recover from the unexpected blow from the only person whom I knew as a *friend* in these parts. I pretend I haven't noticed – (s)he too offers to change my currency, I accept, at a rate of exchange that is very unfavourable to me, and goodbye, (s)he says to me: 'If you want to contact me don't do it by phone from the hotel. Go out and use a public phone booth. And don't tell me as you did last time that you want to talk about politics.'

I settle into my hotel, take a walk round the city, take the first taxidriver who brings me back up to my room, give him a bottle of cognac, a stack of cigarettes, so that he will stop asking for them and will go away without feeling obliged to keep up the hints. He gives me redoubled thanks because it is a day of abstinence and he could not in any case have done anything. He keeps on at me about the rate of exchange even in the lift and makes me consider how much he was risking for something like this. At most, I reply, you'll run the risk of sharing the presents with the porter. I insist so little these days, being almost grateful that I can after all do without what males have to offer.

It is comfortable at the St George, air-conditioning, swimming-pool, foreign cigarettes, drinks, discothèque, TV in the room with intercontinental channels by satellite. In the entrance hall however you can immediately sniff the presence of incognito sentries who pretend to be guests and keep an eye on the entrances and exits and watch you as far as they can when Hassi, my first private currency dealer, arrives. Tiny, chicken-breasted, a little James Dean face, he is busy from morning to night because he is the head of the family and has to keep his widowed mother and five younger brothers. Bright and loyal, proud and punctual, a real and very young gentleman, and like all real gentlemen afraid of nothing and no one, he follows his own conscience under the stimulus of necessity, and he is not at all worried to be seen going into the lift with me and says:

'Let them keep an eye on us – what can they do to us? Nothing to you, and me they can only thank because my efforts put precious valuta into their banks. Up to a year ago it was forbidden to have a bank account with foreign currency, now it has almost become a must and no one wants to know how you got it. And then I don't have anything to do with politics, I am busy trying not to stand about doing nothing like most people.'

He allows himself to be undressed as a pure matter of courtesy, excited and rational, well-mannered. I dress him again and adopt him at once – he will be my guide.

But the St George is too far from the centre and I am fed up with signalling to taxis that don't stop because they no longer feel the need and confine themselves to rushing around as they feel like it on their own. The denationalization which is taking place of even the smallest firms has had bad effects down to the roots: up to two years ago taxidrivers were State employees and were obliged to report to the radio centre their route, from the point of departure to the point of arrival, so they took one passenger, confirmed their destination and pocketed all the extra trips from the point of departure to the point of arrival and the State paid for the petrol. Hassi tells me: 'Now it seems that Chadli is waking up – very late in the day – and is loosening the disastrous grip of State control of everything including farts.'

At the St George things are not going well for me, because today in the swimming-pool I protested loudly to three waiters all busy prostrating themselves before a little group of local bigwigs and quite indifferent to my fourth request for a lemonade. I got out and told them that, given the way things are, I wanted to order not only the one now but another for tomorrow at the same time. The little group – they looked like provincials dividing up the world between them over havanas and whisky – turned every available eye on me, as if I had dared to commit the most shameful offence: to disturb the rite of their hegemony over the waiters and the entire service. The waiters turned pale – fearing, I think, more for me than for themselves. The lemonade arrived and the five figures never stopped staring at me coldly and whispering among themselves. I took a swim, letting them see that I did not allow myself to be impressed by their looks of veiled hate and going back to my room, packed my things and slipped away very quietly, as always amazed at my excessive boldness which manages to disrupt the boredom of being born a coward.

To get a room at the Es Safir I had to wait patiently for two hours. Because I had not booked in advance it seemed impossible, then the room is suddenly there – everything in it is practically broken but I have the advantage of being in the centre, near the restaurant La Pêcherie where I am now welcomed as an habitué. At night I stand at the window looking on to the harbour and the railway station. The oil gleams on the surface of the sea and I exchange a good evening with a guest who was sleeping on the next-door balcony, which has no railing, six metres from the fifth-floor terrace below. He is a young Palestinian who is here for the PLO – the hotel is the place favoured by ambassadors and politicians. I am calmed by the tranquillity with which he says something like that to a stranger whose face he can't even see clearly: the trust he instinctively has in me is equal only to that he cherishes in Arafat. I tell him to take care, that he could fall down, he is thirty centimetres from the precipice, he only needs to turn round once and . . .

'Oh, don't worry, thank you, we are used to sleeping without moving, and even to not sleeping, or not altogether.'

What an extraordinary sleeper! Calm, optimistic, with his pistol in the elastic of his underpants, I imagine. I send for the room service waiter and then another but don't like either of them, I don't even try. I can't sleep. Perhaps tomorrow in the restaurant I shall meet that unpleasant Italian woman. Surely she could invite me to dine at her house! Then it was day again twice in succession. Here the stairs and lifts are watched, I am sure they have extra reason to keep an eye on you, there is no point in exchanging a smile with some customers down in the hotel bar, they don't stay here and I have no desire to follow them home – the only thing they want to know is why Milan didn't sign up one of their fellow countrymen, problems with his meniscus, isn't that right? And one says the meniscus and another a tendon, and each one talks as if it were a catastrophe worse than the drought in the Sahel.

In Algiers I get a feeling which I hadn't had for years – the nicest of all: Love for people. I forget everything – the moist heat, the mosquitoes, the lemonades with their arbitrary colours and all with the same taste (there is no other), the chemists shut, museums shut, the absolute Spartan essential nature of the shops and the goods for sale. I find myself driving around by taxi for an hour and a half looking for a chemist's that is open for suppositories against catarrh and at least an aspirin for a cold that is coming on. Finally we unearth one.

In this crowded pharmacy there was someone listening to the attendant in a white shirt who seemed to be saying the same thing to another ten disappointed customers. 'We don't have this medicine, this is a special Belgian one, there's no point in talking about this one.' I follow this man with the prescription dangling in his hands (to me – I have a sore throat because of the air-conditioning – the pharmacist has given a little bag of torn plastic with little peppermint sweets since there are no suppositories; as an alternative I had to take one of the two existing antibiotics: penicillin or some terrible stuff that wipes out everything from mycosis to syphilis) and I question him. 'The medicine isn't for me' he says, 'but for my mother – it's the fourth chemist's I've been to, the trouble is that the doctors don't prescribe on the basis of what is available but on the basis of their international tables; if you protest they get angry, so it's best not to say anything and to hope, from among the medicines in the prescription, to come across one that can be found even here – maybe after a lot of searching.' And he said all this in a way that I would never be capable of: smiling sadly.

I walk about in Algiers, I even find male prostitutes leaning against the doorposts of worm-eaten doors. They have a little mascara round the eyes and apart from that are humble like everybody else.

In the morning at eleven in Place des Martyres, which is paved with flagstones, there is a game of football between children and an adult dwarf who runs about holding up the string round his trousers with one hand: I sit down between some spit and a turd on a stone bench, I watch a whole succession of ragged beggars and madmen with bristling beards and hair, a woman with a stupid swollen face and her crutches leaning beside her whom I had already seen outside a hut devouring some remnants of fried fish. No one asks for anything, they stand there, recognizable by anyone who wants to give them something – usually a dinar, which equals 60 lire.

I leave in someone's hand a sum that will astonish them, but in return I would like to see them at least show amazement. Instead nothing happens, no reaction, or the same as if I had given them a cent or had passed by them uncaring. And no one says thank you – apart from the woman who, suddenly frightened by the unforeseen wealth, signals to me by painfully deflating one cheek. They get up looking worried and run off towards some goal of the mind or stomach which had been there gnawing at them who knows how long.

The usual policeman demanded by ritual arrives and hurls threats, the children scurry away, the dwarf runs to lose himself among the crowd with the football under his jersey – they are all bleeding at the knees and legs and have scratched faces and they have taken blows to the head, but what if one of them breaks a leg?

'We live as slaves of the excessive power of the doctors – a real aristocratic class here – a State within the State,' Hassi will tell me. 'They look after only the friends of friends and whoever has all the necessary money. Someone break his leg? Ninety chances out of a hundred that he will remain lame for the rest of his life, he will put a splint on it at home and however badly it goes the family can count on one beggar more. It's no tragedy – on the contrary.'

I am in the detested *cité universitaire* where (well, who do we see again!) Otto Niemeyer, equally hated by professors and students, devised under Boumédienne a promontory of reinforced concrete which roasts people inside and outside, without planting even a single tree or rosemary bush and where water is no less rationed than teaching materials. But why does no one protest?

A university professor whose identity must remain vague tells me: 'You see, Algerian intellectuals are famous for their cowardice and for grabbing French nationality the moment they can get it. Traitors because of an Oedipus complex, they continue to adore the white man, they look towards Marseilles, not towards the Sahara. They don't want to know about what happens there, they cling like ticks to their little jobs and are uninterested in any libertarian movement that has not been officially sanctioned by the government. Do you know that there is not one political prisoner in Algeria, one single intellectual in prison? And what can we teach if not the discipline of the consensus? Anyone who has the means to denounce or even to give a helping hand to the ruling class does not do so, he is afraid to put himself on show, and in any case everyone would disown him, his friends first and foremost, those with whom he passes the years discussing the ideas he keeps secret. It is all a case of I who watch you who watch me who watch to see that there is no let-up in watching us, like in Russia, while the powers that be drive about in Mercedes distributing little presents to a mass of intellectuals who stand there, dead with fatigue, with holes in their shoes and yet all for political hygiene and Koranists out of fear. The Berbers, if they want to get an administrative job, have to take care never to be heard uttering a word in Berber, not even on the telephone, with their relations. You have no idea how many politicians with elections in sight make propaganda out of a degree or specialism they don't have just because the son, the cousin etc of someone else in power has one . . . And then if the elections don't go as foreseen in the provincial constituencies, then oops, the results are changed and no one says anything for a few more years. We have no free press, free television, no party other than the National Liberation Front, which has served the country well but is now a little behind the times and corrupt. And no art, no literature, a little government film-making, and now not even the oil revenues any more, which seemed to be the panacea for all ills. We are left with a few carbohydrates and polyphosphates, but it doesn't add up to much, the revolution was a catastrophe, harvests have been halved and halved again since the disappearance of the French colonists – some increment! Ah, Communist agriculture! As if there were anyone who could ever establish a bureaucratic-State relationship with 'the land'! Algeria, once the granary of Rome, continues to halve its harvest and the export of grain is finished too. The country is slipping back from month to month, irresistibly; there are thousands of urban districts in Algiers where there is water every three days.'

I want to go to some place by the sea. Nothing doing with the hotels – a booking is necessary to be accepted, booking is impossible. The secretary of the Es Safir tries day and night for me, but the telex doesn't work and no one picks up the receiver at the other end. I try just the same, I go by taxi to Sidi Ferruch. The manager of the hotel is very sorry – there is no room. I say I shall wait in the hall until one turns up. I feel I am in disgrace – then one turns up. But only for one night – then I have to go. Agreed. There is a young subprefect on the beach who never goes into the water – a lively character who strikes up a conversation with me when he sees that I willingly go off with boys to the thickets beyond the sand. He asks me first of all if I have a bottle of Ricard. No I don't. He shakes his head and reluctantly starts to talk about sex in a hyperliterary way.

'You could donate your buttocks to the tides, the boats would plough into them, you would enjoy as much libido as a whale.'

'When the hollow in your scrotum is stretched by the erection of the hair I'll put my tongue to dispatch radio messages to your prostate which is swollen with desire. I have a long tongue,' I insist.

'Be quiet,' he continues. 'You're driving me mad. Of course with a Ricard it would be better . . .'

'You'll howl at the way your armpits are licked while I drain the juice of your cock with the sphincter . . . a Ricard and a fuck, a Ricard and a fuck, an ice-cold Ricard and water and . . .'

'Just a tiny drop of water,' he groans.

'And an ejaculation, a Ricard.'

'Yes – go on – it's so good for the throat,' he gasps.

The subprefect has shut his eyes, intoxicated by the imaginary Ricard which meantime has inflated his whole bathing costume. When he sees that it is a mirage he looks at me disappointedly and throws himself into the water.

I fall in love with the naked gums of the attendant at the swimming-pool grill – speciality sardines. I make an appointment for midnight on the beach. He arrives with someone who looks like a undertaker's assistant and who is assistant in the kitchen, he says he is like glue, he follows him everywhere and is mad about sticking it up some arse. The attendant devotes a million attentions to me: I raise my eyes to heaven and curse him. We make a tour of the bars within a radius of five kilometres without arranging anything. Then we make for the sea, our shoes meet resistance on the sand because we have landed right in the midst of the sewage discharge which takes place at night, right on to the beach so as not to alarm the bathers who by day will end up with diphtheria or a sure case of gingivitis. We go to the end of an artificial isthmus of rocks, my beloved is very annoyed by his friend on heat whom we're unable to make stand away a little unless we promise him his turn. In the moonlight my marvellous cook displays in his melancholy way a mouth without teeth and a sex-organ without feeling – we blame too much beer. We go home after umpteen attempts on the way with the other guy who is nothing but a whispered supplication right up to the gate. Since I was afraid he would begin to weep I slip it between his thighs – only just before the gate with the excuse that his last lover was an American and I don't trust Americans in terms of hygiene. The little fellow protests – it was an American who only wanted to suck him off and swallowed it. I don't give in, and good-night to all the staff.

Next day the manager of the hotel is delighted to see me at his mercy, he rocks on the back legs of his chair, permits me a last night's stay. Why not, he asks me, go on a tour to Bou Saada accompanied by State guides and then go back to Algiers? Bou Saada is three hundred kilometres away and a night's stopover is included, they leave tomorrow at half-past six in the morning. No – there's nothing doing at Tipasa – don't even try to go there without having booked beforehand, all the hotels are full of Germans. I spend the day on the lookout in the wood where I now carry out a blanket patrol along two kilometres of coast. Encounters in bursts also because there was a building site nearby and the workers went here and there in the wood to do their business and with pleasure discharged this unexpected business – a real break.

At Bou Saada one gets out of the bus and enters the unlikely hotel surrounded by off-duty soldiers. Few women inside, some wrinkled women tourists. I'm sure I shall do very well too. Likely candidates: the pool attendant, the waiter, the porter. All in pursuit of a quarter of an hour's sex with the woman tourist gracefully made available by the husband who is all eyes or merely passive, a woman who will find provender, penis and pain, for her teeth and his – the tactic is well-known: after the first trimmings, the moment they have got it in they whisper *'Le cadeauauauau'* which for them is already the signal for orgasm. Never allow yourself to be taken unawares, saying 'Of course!' with enthusiasm, and meantime both the lady and the husband and I, why not, will continue to enjoy ourselves without being too ashamed or sufficiently so to achieve acme or acne.

Here there are the remains of Ferrero's Mill, called after an adventurer at the end of the last century who built it under the cliff of a waterfall, and now it is completely in ruins. Gina Lollobrigida came here to shoot *The Queen of Sheba* and unfortunately came back again. Now it is the set for Westerns. I immerse myself in the pool, taking the jets of water amid a dozen youths and adolescents, extremely beautiful and as lazy as lizards in the sun. I make my way on foot to the hotel, passing the mortuary chapel of a famous French painter buried here with his godson who turned his hand to everything. At a crossroads a very tall man, sensual as tall men never are, comes alongside me. He tells me he is a semi-nomad Touareg and asks if I want to visit his tent, which is just outside the walls (which are non-existent) and in the midst of the desert (and here the desert is a little island to be visited by tourists who will never go any further south), that his wife is by the sea with her children etc. I accept with joy and he makes me get up on to his brand-new jeep. An impenetrable mystery. He stops near two tents as big as circus tents, dark purple in colour, makes me go in, and the moment I have set foot inside, trying to avoid a she-goat and not fall over the 25-inch television set which gets CNN and RAI Uno, he catches me in flight and I am no mere handful, lifts me in his massive arms and, looking round at the various beds which pave the sand:

'On camel skin or sheep's skin, chéri?'

'Sheep's skin, sheep's skin.'

Desert of a kind – six hundred species of trees and as many of animals, men are unchanging in their nature. In Algiers once again. The Hotel Aurassi, the most luxurious, where there is always room. A hotel as broad as this cannot but dominate the landscape.

Up at the little wood which surrounds the monument to the fallen, mounted police are hanging about. Hassi, who now is my guide every day and has introduced me to his family and hopes to become my brother-in-law, explains: 'They go there to part the lovers. If they see a couple kissing they make them clear off. And you can't go into a hotel with a girl to make love and you have to take two rooms and there aren't even any gardens and no one has a house. To have her you have to marry her. Now the couples up there keep their ears to the ground to hear the tramp of the hoofs drawing near. What a life. Who would you marry – Sahra or Soya?'

Apart from that, endless little cups of mint tea. An assembly of inquisitive people in front of a house in the very centre of the town, people who whisper to each other, who ask for information when they arrive, all indicate yes with their chins. I ask Hassi for an explanation.

'The house has been taken over by beings that aren't human.'

I thought he perhaps didn't know the Italian for rats.

'No – not rats! Spirits!'

'What kind of ghosts?'

'Not ghosts like in France – spirits. They belong to the Muslim religion and are ambiguous.'

'And the police have the job of getting them to leave.'

'Yes. Squatting. But perhaps not being really bad they didn't know they were squatting.'

'And you believe in them?'

'I am not an unbeliever.'

Then we go to the cinema in Bellancourt to see how they piss from the balcony right into the stalls with squawks of delight and cheers each time they score a hit. But all bladders were peaceful. Then I go back alone to the hotel, take a shower and go back to eat at the Pêcherie. A girl with a black shiny fringe comes out of the foyer in great style, dressed in black white and gold organza, covering her face with a lace veil and presenting a perfectly arched nose, a high forehead, eyes of incandescent green, an expression of undisputed femininity, the whole – radiant. As she walks a split opens from ankle to calf revealing magnificent legs. Someone to whom the veil cannot be an annoyance of any kind, no more than a little hat, like a traditional piece of flirtatiousness in a 'rock' interpretation of the past. She has three men with her as escorts, all a step behind her, and obviously they do not lose sight of her for an instant. She gets into a powerful car and disappears. She will be going to some caliph.

At the Pêcherie there is the usual emancipated Algerian woman with a new lover and a new woman friend. She pretends not to know me and we have sat opposite each other for ages. Patience. I choose my bowl of fresh fish. Malhudj, my favourite waiter, tells me every time that he was worried that I had not arrived. By now the fish makes me feel ill, but I don't know where else to go. I look at the vulgar red-haired woman. I take a closer look, she does not once meet my eyes. But she knows who I am, of that I am certain. She looks shocking tonight – even squeamish. She is here against her will, naturally. Perhaps she is an émigrée with a room in Rome here on holiday. She would like to be somewhere else. She must be forty-five. Malhudj is thirty-five and has five children, he shrugs at my astonishment and laughs. Little moustache and red heart-shaped lips, the big eyes of a child – I come here, you may say, for him because he meets me every evening as if I had been there since yesterday and even the day before that. He always gives me too much to eat and then, in secret, gives me discount which I automatically add to the tip. I always need more time to allow myself to get fond of someone – I have been here for two weeks, I should like to know how I have passed all this time. Whole mornings and afternoons I have sat on the low wall of the Place des Martyres, looking at nothing in particular.

A little time ago, the father of a family walked along with a transparent plastic bag in his hand: in the bottom there were potatoes, above that onions, then watermelons, and above that tomatoes and on top of everything a bunch of parsley sticking out as long as sedges. When I think of the Apocalypse I think of the human trajectory which it would cost once more in millions of years to arange the lighter cells on top of the heavier ones and so on. I think about salad or of the parsley of conscience maybe, once again underneath everything, under potatoes and watermelons, crushed and damaged, and of a man who takes a hundred prehistoric years to arrive once more at the same conclusion as the father of a family: that salad is not peeled, but is eaten as it is. Then two hefty fellows arrive in the square, one – a black man – I recognize because he was staying in the Hotel Es Safir where I was last week. Both brush against me, I am sweating, sticky, indifferent, I am watching but no one would dare to say of me that I see anything – instead I see everything. They stop short in front of two wretched *fellah* (peasant) youths. Very amiably the black man puts an arm round the shoulders of one of them, as tame as sheep, they must be buddies, and suddenly when the white man too puts a hand under the chin of the other one I realize that this is a full-scale search. The couple are made to turn round and round and seem not to understand what is happening, the black policeman goes off with one of the unlucky youths (on whom not the slightest thing has been found) while the second policeman has put his arm round the other's waist affectionately as if the four of them ought to go to a bar and toast an unexpected meeting. The two boys allow themselves to be pushed gently in a direction which they don't know, both in slippers, without a word. By now I must have met a hundred or more, no one has ever asked me if I had or wished for a smoke, no one has ever uttered an opinion that did not express scorn at such a proposal and political scorn for Hassan II, who would have every advantage if he allowed a large part of Moroccan youth to become cretinized with hashish – and to me this firmness is pure music: having spent most of my childhood in inns I cannot even speak a word to anyone who is the least bit tight – never mind someone who talks when he is a prey to drugs. I don't know what they can do with them once they are in barracks – apart from giving them a good warm meal and a bed for the night. Perhaps tragically that is not how it is . . . Meanwhile I tell the waiter to take my plate away – I can't manage any more – this time too he has overdone it.

The Algerian woman has wilfully ignored me as if I were one of many left-over fishbones – I mean that precisely for this reason the opposite is true, I don't know. And it is not as if the conversation at her table is very brilliant. That red of her hair is not even real, it's false: at the roots are blackish-yellowish bristles which make it particularly vulgar. Her lips are thick, her shoulders important, her bosom overflowing in a modest nylon dress but décolleté with the little folds in the cleavage and a gold safety-pin, her oval face puffy, one nostril bigger than the other as if she had been punched when she was little, her nails pink-enamelled and from their length you can see that she is a woman who has a servant at home. And now what happens, while I am taking the change from the saucer and count it and put it back she is asking to be excused and gets up. She looks at me fleetingly, turning her shoulder to her admirer and her friend, who would like to follow her but she stops her with her hand, then she goes to the toilet. And she goes down the steps in haste and I don't know how or why I slip into the toilet between the kitchen and the stairs, lock it, she doesn't bat an eyelid, throws herself on the wash hand-basin and while she starts vomiting, stretching her neck out so much that she spatters the mirror which is full of verdigris, I get down behind her, push her dress up over her thighs, she lets me, I get to the crutch of her knickers and from the side extract her cunt with the chestnut hair as curly as straw and she vomits and pushes against me who am kneeling perfectly and I eat her for five minutes or so, mucous tissue to mucous tisue, a prey to this extraordinary and extremely dangerous overwhelming impulse of mine, I lick her and lick her again and then when she fills my mouth with a discharge of that glue which I had not savoured for ages and then as she comes gives a last sob, biting her tongue between her teeth so as not to cry out or say whatever comes into her head, she pulls the chain and goes off without saying good-bye or putting on her rouge again, just like any man.

I am sitting again in Place des Martyres. Evening has now arrived, the square is well lit, to find a taxi is not easy. There is a little queer, striking and thin, with a fiery glance, contemptuous, sitting on the low wall nearby; he stares at the men and puts out his tongue in invitation and calls them all sorts of names to their backs in French too. He is dressed in a worn red T-shirt but decked out with pins, I would say he is thirty but he cannot be more than twenty, black eyes and pouches beneath them, he makes his earrings dance and continually adjusts a flowing and dirty black lock of hair, nails long enough for an animal which has scraped the earth, I am sure that, in his own way, he is considered to be recherché in dress and 'look'. The way of being a queer is the same everywhere, the same way of gesticulating here as in Burundi or Desenzano, the same stupid jerks of the neck, same conceited quiver of the vertebral column to the point of arching it to show off an imaginary bosom, the same way of shrugging the shoulders to express conceit or casualness (which there never is), the same look of desirous damnation, perfect. There are also irreducible obsessions – reduce them and they become a pain that is imperilled. But suddenly this satyr-like creature gets up as quick as a hare and tucks under his right arm a crutch which he was hiding behind the wall and, under his left arm, the one hidden in the bushes and begins to run, hopping along because he has one leg much shorter than the other and affected by rickets. He goes and squats against a pillar in the porch opposite and begins his little act over again, obtaining in reply only insults but he does not change his expression in the least, which is hard, challenging, as if he had been brought there by a rock in order to lay down as sediment a fossil rage, black, the self-imposition of a kind of pride like a self-mutilation, no concession to pity. He twists the rings on his fingers, shakes the long crow-black fringe and then snatches up the two crutches and runs off like a horrible chimera to the other corner of the square, playing alone at pig in the middle with his little foot in the air, at the height of the other knee, with a certain terrible grace, in a moccasin of dirty red cloth. Since I was observing him and then from a distance began to contemplate him, he turns his little uneven buttocks to me, sticks them out as far as he can and blows a raspberry. Two people pass and say: 'Filthy syphilitic queer!' and he smooths his brow, flutters his eyelids, happy at this acknowledgement, which takes him far in terms of imagination. One of the two turns round, winks at him, he gets on to his crutches and follows him, a blackish ferret following two brown tumbler pigeons already in flight. Distraction is better at making the world go round than love. Contempt is the agreed signal of desire. I go back to the Aurassi on foot, through dark lanes and climbing one set of stairs after another, with little groups of men who by the light of a lantern or a torch are playing chess on the landings in the open air. In Algiers it doesn't take long to tell the tramps from the normal citizens: three hours. In fact since only 9 per cent of the population has a job, all of them are at their leisure day and night with an infinite gamut of fine distinctions from idleness as sport and idleness as marginalization, bearing in mind however that in general sport *is* marginaliztion itself.

Ouargla: even the taxidriver, between a curse at the starter and another at the silencer, in the dawn, which is withdrawing across the airport, sings to me the praises of Transat and he will put in a word with the secretary in the hotel who is a friend of his. He sings and sings its praises and I expect by now a host of odalisques who will fight to get hold of my bag or give him a push to set the jalopy in motion again. He drops me outside the gate – so no word with the clerk; in the courtyard there is only a car on three wheels and a prism-shaped piece of cement to act as quadrant under a roof of withered twigs. A rusty iron gate, peeling paint.

The employee looks at me from inside more by chance than out of pressing duty to know what the devil I can want in this place early in the morning and with luggage.

'I should like a room for the night,' and here the fateful question is fired off: 'Have you booked?' and he puts his head to one side as if to say: Now I shall deal with you, let's just see what you have the courage to say in reply.

'No, I haven't booked,' but I look around and there is no sign of life, a home for retired ghosts.

'Wait, I'll call the manager. I fear it will be difficult.'

The manager arrives – a corpulent man with a little beard and a neat blueish vest, a severe look, statuesque – cold? He examines me with cynical detachment, in an insulting manner, then he bends over a register, leafs through it, leafs through another – from the board there hang all thirty demystifying keys of rooms that are never occupied.

'There is a room, there is. Only for tonight.'

The hall is deserted, Swiss in its cleanness, sinister, down the stairs appear some elderly army officers, bottle-green uniforms on the brown of a moquette carpet where it looks as if goats have been grazing.

I carry my bag up to my room, come down the external stairs which give on to the back of the house, and I find myself in the garden: sacks of rubbish torn by cats which are thin all the same, palms which cannot decide whether to dry up and turn entirely into fossils, various kinds of grass looking like drooping boiled vegetables on stalks of frayed cellophane and rags, like shrubs in a ditch. The primordial remains of a bonfire of dry leaves. I see the edge of the swimming-pool, I approach it hesitantly as if not to disturb the process of decomposition that is going on there: detached tiles in ten centimetres of gangrenous water dotted with drink cans which crown the rotten throne of the springboard which is broken in two, and alternate with the aluminium steps leading down into the water. The rails are attached to the side like two thick canes running into the ground which has sucked everything up stealthily from morning to evening – many years ago. Everything including the bathers. I want to leave, I see the two railings wandering about at night stretching out and closing like the arms of an octopus, patrolling the rooms in search of the only guest here – myself – to suck him in and squeeze him into the porous, thirsty maw of a subterranean beast made of earth with mad earthen roots, lazy and insatiable, then merely inconsolable until the next guest spends the night there. And even the faces of the two old squinting staff, of a waiter with senile cataract, don't promise much – let alone anything special: I have decided that this time I shall work on the men retail and not wholesale, and how can I shut an eye with all these blind people about? I go out – I shall see if there is another hotel nearby – even with three stars it will be less sinister than this one.

A well-proportioned little man is coming from the other end of the street with the improvised goal of someone who doesn't know where to go and who is searching in a hole in his pocket, a low-built youth who keeps his eyes directed high up and looking wounded – the eyelids move very little – looking into the air or watching the gambolling of the little flies or on the lookout for some novelty he has waited for too long. I cross the road and stop him, in monosyllables he says that there should be another hotel somewhere nearby but he has never been there. He does not speak French well and I am already off in a different direction on the beaten earth road when I notice the bitter wateriness of those eyes. He replies with a grunt to my goodbye, as if to say you are off already and what will become of me?

The hotel further on is full, packed, and they will not be able to put me up before tomorrow evening – they have groups. Out of pure spite they urge me to visit the restaurant and the pool which is full to the brim with running sky-blue water.

'There are two taxis to Gardia every morning. If you hurry you will still be in time,' says the manager, who has had enough of my expressions of appreciation and my disappointment at not being able to have a swim among lemon trees and palms.

Outside the little man was leaning against the corner of a wall, and the moment he saw me withdrew as swiftly as a little ostrich. I will not turn round so that he will follow me. I turn round and he still has not appeared but on the top of the point where the two walls meet his hand was sticking out. There are moments when one is no longer anything or else a little lie moving about in the iris of another person who is even less important – pure space to make space for the first one to knock. To go or stay till one hand that has become part of the arm of a chair or the corner of a wall becomes an act of disappointment and of sovereign power. Like this old married couple which is coming along, he on the back of a mule and she on foot, covered in white and keeping within the veil the perfect triangle which only her left eye leaves uncovered: they have understood justice and injustice, if now that they are old they should want to go turn and turn about it would be the mule that would not allow them to do it any more. I go back to the Transat in a state of confusion, quit my room which I offer to pay for just the same – but the manager, indifferent, lordly and haughty, does not accept – and I make off for the unknown taxi station.

The little man with his tufted hair cut in an artless way was outside kicking at a stone unconvincingly. When he decides to look at me I ask myself what on earth he sees in me, perhaps only a privileged person who can arrive and then go away just like that.

'Will you go with me to the taxi here? I have to go to Gardia.'

'Yes, yes . . .'

We walk along in silence, I am thinking of something else, I hand him the string bag, if it transforms him into a page-boy it will be so much easier for me. Every so often my glance catches the corner of his eye, I smile at him, he doesn't smile at me, he doesn't know what to do and doesn't smile because it is not called for. I say to myself: There's no use your starting to take an interest in him, in half an hour you will already be far from here, there are children galore for you and your crazes as a patriarch manqué.

'What are you doing going about at this time of day?' I say, knowing that I am asking the stupidest question I could manage to find to let him understand that he is wrong, that I am stupid, that he hasn't lost anything.

'I am not doing anything. There is nothing to do here.'

'Do you live here in Ouargla or somewhere nearby?'

'Yes.'

'With your family – I mean brothers, par . . .'

'Yes, yes,' then he thinks a little and repeats 'Yes', which is shouted out like a 'No!' to the mirror.

We turn off in this direction and that, a few bicycles, some oxen pulling carts with watermelons and pumpkins, some little girls outside among the rubbish inventing a complicated game for themselves but with nothing to play with. Every so often he takes a little run to keep up with me and I feel rising within me the tenderness for everything that is stripped to the bone but real, without feelings, as harsh as the impossible trace a whiplash would leave in the air. Carrying my bag – it is very heavy – has made his vest come out of his trousers of heavy moth-eaten wool and I see his navel, as white as a newborn child's. I touch it with one finger to see if he smiles and he parries me and looks at me with a still more tragic expression, he makes a move to take my bag as well but I don't let him. I try to make him speak, to make him tell me the names of the various public buildings, but he says: 'I don't know – I don't know – I'm not sure' with his voice and with his eyes says: 'You had just arrived – and now? And what about me?'

'Have you ever been to Gardia?' I ask him – after all it is only a hundred and eight kilometres.

'No.'

'Anywhere else?'

'No.'

'Were you born here and have you always been here?'

'Yes.'

'Did you do your military service?'

'Yes, here.'

He is wearing sandals of artificial leather, he comes up to my shoulders, every so often his eyes bore into me a sadness against which I have deployed my usual veil of salt. I am letting him suffer and do not even wish to know why.

'My goodness, this station is a long way away. Shall I still be in time to catch it?'

'I have gone in neither the Transat hotel nor that other one. They have told me that there is a pool full of water.'

'It's not true – only at the second one.'

'If I had a house you – ' he stops.

'But don't you have a house?'

'No, I – '

'Ah, here are the taxis,' and I leave him behind to go and find out about things.

There are three taxis in all, the one for Gardia fortunately is not yet full, in fact I am the first traveller. When there are four more we shall leave. The owner-driver is wrapped in a caftan which is in one piece with the turban, and his face widens in teasing smiles; a strong snub nose, big very black eyes, moustaches turned up at the ends, a statuesque figure, on his neck a kind of scarf with gold threads which make him gleam at every movement. I and my nameless companion sit down against the wall of a lemonade stall, both draught and bottled, as well as apricot juice in milk by the half-litre: orange juice – finished. I offer him a drink and he shows some resistance, it seems too much to him; he sits beside me on the ground and I feel that this novelty which he expected so much is something so odd that it does not even have time to become a disappointment. Could I take him with me – and then?

'I don't even know your name,' I say and look at my watch.

'Ahmed – and yours? And yours?'

Round the taxi there is a little crowd of colleagues of the driver and perhaps, I hope, a few more passengers.

'With this,' I say, putting two bank notes in his hand – ones that are worth something, 'you can buy Coca-Cola for six months.'

'I don't like it,' and he firmly pushes away my hand. I don't know what to do.

'We're leaving, signore,' the taxidriver shouts to me, and he puts on a pair of welder's glasses which turn him into a kind of Red Baron ready to go round the world in eighty minutes or thereabouts. Besides the driver there climb on to the taxi a pregnant woman, her husband, her brother-in-law, all coloured and distinguished, and next to me in the back an extremely thin boy, his hair dirty with dust, and newly shaved.

'Goodbye, Ahmed, who knows!' He has already sprung to his feet and holds out a hand to me, three fingers of one hand, perhaps he doesn't even know how a handshake works. He stands there watching me leave and I so much wish he would go away, I feel my stomach close up like a vice, the more I look at him the more I fear I have done him a great wrong. The motor starts and

Ahmed appears at the window and hands me a tin of apricot juice which I shall never be able to open. I feel like saying to the driver, forget about it, stop, I'm getting out, but a great cloud of dust alongside and behind makes any vague desire to live on like this evanescent and remote.

In the stony desert the taxi runs along the well tarred road, missing by a hair's-breadth colourless old trucks a score of years old; every so often a group of motorcyclists with helmets and leather overalls shoots towards the legendary trails for restless, reckless tourists who do not indicate either destination at any starting place because they do not know them. In the taxi the driver, at the request of the almost-mother, has poured water from the little demijohn covered with plastic and is now passing her the tumbler of pink bakelite. The three have it refilled every time, my neighbour drinks what is left by the young coloured husband – and holds it out again without passing it to me. I could be thirsty too but I don't dare to ask. If only I could open the tin of apricot juice with my teeth! My neighbour has tried to start up a conversation but I can't hear anything because he is on the side of my deaf ear and the engine is making a great noise like a plane. I ask him not to talk to me any more, a real effort.

Five camels sitting one beside the other, mountains of rubbish of plastic and industrial waste from electrification, oil pipelines, carcasses of cars overturned and completely stripped inside, a small boy in the far distance bending over to look for something among gleams of metal sheeting and a big skeleton. Then having come round a hill, Gardia is upon me like a beautiful dream and a shout of joy rises up in me. 'At last!' At last what? I don't know, at last a real city, something unlike anything else, a total view. The passengers get out at two different addresses. I tell the driver to take me to the Hotel Rostemides and get up in front. He has taken off the curved glasses and now his face is no longer as daring as at our departure, and since he must be my age he laughs heartily and doesn't worry about my hand which has slipped under his caftan while he is changing down for a hill that risks being the last. I take my time and withdraw my hand with great difficulty, then when I say I am not French but Italian he turns toward me and his face is lit up and although the road is now flat keeps at the same snail's pace.

'I worked in Paris for fifteen years and got to know an Italian called Spartaco, we became great friends, he lived in Milan, he came to Paris every so often to work, he always came to see me, he took me out to supper, he always paid. Once he said to me: Come and see me in Milan so that we spend Christmas together with my family. I really went there. He fetches me from the station and introduces me to his fiancée. Be-a-tri-ce! She wore a red dress that was all pleats and never said anything, she was very pale. One evening I say to Spartaco as a joke that I had given her a hug when he wasn't there. He says if that is true I'll kill you but he was joking too. She always went about with high heels and showy dresses but she looked like a little girl dressed like a grown-up. Then I found out that he made her dress like that. She was always there that Christmas. I stayed in Milan for four days, Beatrice, when we were in Spartaco's house and he had got up to fetch something, she looked at me in a way that felt like a punch in the stomach. Then I went back to Paris, I drove a taxi there too, and for three years I did nothing but think about her without touching a woman. I never saw Beatrice nor Spartaco again, never even heard whether they had got married. I did though. I haven't been back to Milan. But some day I must, I must go back. Here we are at the Rostemides! One ought to be of stone when one is young, not now that we are getting old, now it is natural.'

'Well, as far as stone goes congratulations!' I say to him squeezing his penis and go off to try and arrange a room.

I have heard many stories like this: two close friends fall in love with the same woman because they cannot confess that they love each other. If not I cannot understand why with all the beautiful women available, two close friends must perforce fall in love with what the other loves already. The woman is a terminal for secret – and taboo – pulses transmitted to the two friends, it gives them off, transforming them into a passion which is unhealthy but permissible. If I were in her place and if my greatest desire were *to be loved for myself* (a fantasy of which a woman is rarely the victim) I would be on my guard against both of them or I would take part in the game knowingly because the queen of many hearts is almost always a two of clubs. 'The room is only for tonight,' says the porter, 'you should have booked. Come back at noon.' So punished but refusing to stand in a corner until noon I leave my bag there and go to see the Mozabites, the inhabitants of the M'zab, which is here. They are the founders of an age-old city and of a flourishing trade all over Europe, whose astuteness and parsimony is matched however by a protestant culture based on lucre, which would serve not to allow them goods and luxuries but to produce more capital to reinvest in the next son to have just attained his majority. Gardia has long emerged from its enclosing walls and for decades has known the lunacies of tourists to whom it even opens its own mosque in the morning provided dogs stay outside the sacred steps. I wander about everywhere drunk on the cordiality of the faces, the sex-appeal of the men, and feel I shall experience something beautiful; I look in the market pursued by money-changers on mopeds, stopped by old traders who have little of value to sell, and just to get things going, I buy a dried camel's udder, hand-painted, which opens like a box and contains fragments of strongly perfumed amber. At midday the porter is forced to give me the room promised and refused and now in the labyrinth of corridors I have a kind of vision: a young fruit vendor who was taking a sprig of mint and holding it out to me as I walked so that I could smell it but I was distracted and only now realize how perfumed it was. The point is that I have been in Algeria twelve days now and between Tipaza and Tizi-Ouzo and Bousaada I have got tired of men and go in search of carpets which are also hand-made to those who cannot see that they are machine-made. But, for goodness' sake, there's nothing to complain about: everything went very well with everyone, some tremendous encounters in terms of sexual power and co-participation but unfortunately through the exhaustion of all desire the symbolic system that keeps the flesh upright becomes slightly limp and there are even long periods (two, three days) when you touch them and all you want is for them to be sausages for frying *alla puttanesca* wth garlic and oregano.

After losing my way and my floor a couple of times I manage to reach C212. A kind of little goblin of about sixty in a livery on which the red strips can be the black ones and vice versa stands in front of the door and says, looking me up and down 'Good day, it's hot today.' 'Yes, very hot – I like it,' and I open the door and am about to shut it when the little man with the goatlike face and a tuft of hair standing on end pushes the handle of the door and enters with me and begins to spray the air. 'Deodorant,' he says; with one hand he deodorizes and with the other scratches his crotch, taking a look every three seconds at my reaction. 'But deodorant disgusts me,' I say and open the door for him to go away. He slips into the door of the toilet. 'If you want toilet paper . . .' and I notice that there is already an unbroken roll, 'I'll go and get some.' And I say: 'No, no thank you,' and at last he goes out staring at me with big blue eyes. I go and take off my clothes, turn on the shower: knocks on the door, I can't hear what is being said to me, I come out of the shower and go to open the door, putting only my nose out: 'More towels for you,' says the gnome with a neutral voice and a look like a startled hare and he sticks a wizard's foot inside the door. 'Thank you, but you shouldn't have bothered,' I say, taking some heavy threadbare things that are still damp, and try to shut the door. 'I'll put on the air-conditioner,' he suggests, there is no putting down this randy little oriental monster – who knows how many strange Aladdin's lamps he has managed to get going during his life as a waiter. 'No, no, air-conditioning gives me a sore throat,' and I slam the door shut without worrying about his aquiline nose which dips itself in his sharp and violet lips. I dry myself smiling at the downcast look he threw at me, this rejected wooer – certainly he has not noticed that he must have got old *in the meantime*. I am sure that his advances at over sixty are no different by a jot or tittle from those of his twenties, and he does not understand why before he had so much luck with the guests and now every other one flattens his nose. I take a quick glance in the mirror at a body which is flawed and very plump, still very good at carrying all its own suitcases and walking for kilometres every day in spite of the stabbing pain of the twelve-year-old corn on its big toe.

But now I go out again and on the stairs at the entrance there he stood, this morning's fruit seller, serious and, like all Arabs when they are devising something or dreaming of something, with the most absent-minded and distracted look in the world. When our eyes meet his glance wanders to the left and mine to the right towards the mountain and then they meet again on the mosque and finally are lost in each other in a lightning stroke which makes his heart leap at the fact that I greet with a nod without using my voice. I stop for a moment, a couple of words. He is wearing a T-shirt with white and blue stripes above typical trousers with a low crotch which reaches to his knees, a stretch of road together, stairs, he in front of me, I notice his calm step and aristocratic bearing, the composure of his upper body, the determination of his walk, he turns his head to right and left, he raises a shutter, I feel it my duty to enter wriggling and find myself being kissed at once against bunches of mint hanging on the wall.

In the hotel swimming-pool in the middle of the night the diving of soldiers who have permission to come in and refresh themselves at any time. I swim, drained by the love which was the hardest, the most sensitive, rhythmically attuned in its synchronous violence and hunger and reciprocity, that I have made in these last ten days – or ten years, I really wouldn't know, I forget so quickly and this mnemonic zero-setting is part of the memory of time, of my time, where the instinct for survival, which is universally imperilled beyond words, brings us imperceptibly to get rid – not as before only of the nasty things – but of the beautiful ones as well, because they are too few to have any chance of remaining afloat in the sea of those that must be discarded, forgotten, never lived through. At this time Gardia presents us with huge moons, breezes that are still warm, little lights in the palms, silence – and still a fierce desire for sex with him, the same one; strange, very strange for me. Issir told me the story of his house – five hundred years old – from the great-great-great-grandfather to his father, carefully preparing the mint tea, wearing a pair of underpants of a periwinkle blue that throws into relief the beauty of his strong and muscular thighs, his barely indicated but firm belly, the well-divided scrotum and his beautiful cock which I could scarcely fit into my hand, curved slightly downwards, like all of them here, for they have the habit from childhood of carrying it folded under the testicles . . . and I swim without seeing where I am going and bump into one of the young soldiers who says to me in the dark, good evening, as if he were adding a few suspensory dots. 'I am going to the shower now,' I whisper to him, 'follow me in a little.' Three more came after the first one, I wanted to see what remained of my desire for Issir once I was awake and overtaxed. Then I pick myself up, it is half-past six in the morning, and wander about a little in the entrance hall, strike up a conversation with the man who doctors the cars – he is the State mechanic in charge of repairing vehicles, especially jeeps, which break down and have to be traced on the desert routes. He is under thirty, not very tall, unshaven, a sardonic little smile – a farseeing one – the smile of someone who has in his hands the fates of many rash destinies. 'There are lots of tourists who disappear for ever. A tempest, a dune uncovers a skeleton and perhaps goes on to bury another who is still half alive and keeps him in there for an indefinite number of years. They have just found a motorcycle, but of the driver no trace. The desert is five times as big as France!' But these are not all accidents, in my opinion some people come here to find an easy death, they go off the map routes on purpose, they venture towards the Nigerian *erg* where it is forbidden, there only a touareg could come out alive. He makes a blunder, takes only a little water as if saying to himself, let's see how I get out of this, and he enjoys his suicide second by second, by dehydration or exposure, crawling on his knees inch by inch towards a mirage in the worst taste, a little picture of happiness denied, that something which always moves a little further off and is called life – life that coincides with the arm stretched out towards safety or fulfilment only when it is giving up the ghost.

Issir: how he threw himself on my emotions, how he met me shorn of all fantasies, how close he was to *me* without letting either of us lose our heads for a second; and the things he said were measured, chosen from a thousand others, clear, without hyperbole, a way of making love that was elegant and decided, a dance in the reality reciprocally captured in our minds. A man like that is rare because he is like me: when I truly feel something I feel nothing and nothing that is *mine*. I and another (Rimbaud). I feel Issir and Issir feels me.

'It's hot, oh! it's hot today.' Here comes the satyrlike elf who hasn't been seen for twenty-four hours. 'Why are you up so early? Come here, come and I'll give you DDT.'

The appointment is for one, after the meal, in the afternoon he doesn't work. Issir will take me to El Ateuf, to a private zoo, to see the vipers from Mali, but I am already down here, fifty metres further down, in front of another shutter so as not to be too obvious, waiting for him to arrive to pull up his. I shall pretend to buy half a kilo of muscat grapes and then with my mouth sweetened, I shall astonish him.

Haj Assia hunts scorpions and serpents, he has also caught a horrendous, gigantic hyena in the desert. Issir looks at me out of the corner of his eye as if he loved me in the space between his retinas and no other part of his body was aware of love. *Farewell now my love/farewell till I see you again*. In a cage there is a tangle of motionless colourless snakes – some newly born ones already dead and shrivelled. The snake from Mali is long and fat, stupefied by its last meal, with its eyes closed; a little stray dove has landed on its neck. The snake from Mali ate six days ago and for six days the dove has been living on this strange perch which is putting on weight and of which it has perhaps become fond out of habit. Their life together lasts nine days in all; on the tenth the snake makes a sudden movement that shakes the whole cage and swallows the dove which does not know it and will never know it.

I must have been eight and Marisa, who was twenty-two and lived in the little square by the theatre and always ironed in her vest and was out dancing till midnight, said to me while I was wondering whether to undo the cork of the little bottle:

'Of course, write that letter to Lollobrigida. I'll deal with the address, don't worry.'

Marisa put on airs because of her tits being all over the place and said she would go to Cinecittà herself one day and of course she knew where Lollobrigida lived. She made a couple with Signora Altolà, who was a teacher and – so people murmured – had taught her a thing or two.

I pulled out the double centre page from my lined copy book and dipped the pen in the ink. 'Dearest Gina . . .'

'And say hello to her from me.'

'How shall I address her?'

'Be familiar – she'll be used to it. Actresses, you know . . .' Enchanted I watched her wipe her armpit with the piece of sheet she stretched over the clothes so as not to scorch them. 'Not even Silvana Mangano shaves them. Give me the envelope.'

It wasn't as if for me it was the letterhead for a myth, and I don't know why I wrote to her – not only, I fear, to ask her for money to subscribe to the magazine *Grand Hotel* or for a small part but because I really wanted to see what it feels like to write to someone so important. There were two posters for the local Cinema Gloria on the walls between the mill and the square with the butcher: *The Most Beautiful Woman in the World* and *Trapeze*. I was amazed that the most beautiful of women should have had to risk her neck for a living.

Marisa gave me the twenty lire for the stamp and the envelope addressed by herself personally.

'But are you sure?'

'All the actors live there – in the Colosseum,' she said, giving to understand that she was not prepared to argue about it. As if she didn't know this when she was just going to get a certain offer and then would take off! She would go and shoot a film. Strangely enough, not only for me who was a little boy, but for her too to shoot a film meant an implicit movement – a real physical one – of the thighs and feet. Marisa was beautiful, provocative, and she liked city men who had a certain way with them, so long as they weren't from here, had a car, and knew the casinos either in Campione or Venice.

'I'll only make films with high heels, what do they think? Besides I can dance.'

One night she was so late that she never came back at all. She had 'moved to Rome' along with a trumpet-player who was well known in a local nightclub and with 'the whole orchestra behind her' I heard two of her friends at the bar say 'and in front of her'.

So as a child I had the myth which fits the poor and bewitched childhood of the Fifties: the life of the new saints, the actors and actresses. When she went out of circulation I felt that it wasn't her I missed but *Grand Hotel.* And then she didn't even send me a postcard. It took me a good few days to strike up a new acquaintance who would buy it for me every week. What luck! Ivana also bought *Bolero Film.* I wanted to write to Sophia Loren this time but Ivana said to me:

'It's no use – she's always travelling, she goes abroad . . . She'll never get it. Write me a nice letter because no one ever writes to me.'

'What am I supposed to write to you?' She was skinny and bony. She went to work in a tyre factory on her moped, ten kilometres there and back, getting up at five, in fog, rain, wind.

'Pretend you are Prince Charming and then go on. Put "My adored Ivana".'

I wrote to her with her there, she insisted that I should not read it to her, in the confusion I went and posted it without a stamp. Then she told me off because she had to pay the postage due to the postwoman and I who am touchy didn't go back there any more. In any case I didn't like the new format of *Grand Hotel.*

Other myths were slow to arrive – I did not like to go to school, apart from writing essays I didn't like anything in class. I had a weakness for the world. I began to collect postcards. There were the families of airmen who got postcards even from Indian reservations. Then I fell in love with running water – I went to places where there were streams and waterfalls and fountains. Then suddenly I fell in love with a fourteen-year-old boy like myself. I tried to get him to the river, I contemplated him – without once looking at him – in the mirrors of the water. Love, unrequited love, involved my mind in a process of self-destruction for ten years, and this was the Myth of youth: water, silence, the pretence that nothing was happening, a ripple of burning heat.

One day I came home and my mother, who was fed up with me, had thrown my whole collection of postcards into the fire. It was not easy to remain attached to anything that existed: on the one hand you were not allowed to hang on to anything, on the other, it was violently taken away from you. From destruction I passed to distraction and from the myth of love to the myth of sex with my metal suitcase in my hand. It was not as disturbing as waiting for months for Lollo to reply to me but it was better than nothing. And I was strong and passionate and the mystical atmosphere in which I had nestled for so many years without uttering a single word of love to my contemporary was such that the slightest thing threw me into a mad bout of sexual promiscuity so absolute that I see it now as a form of subliminal mental chastity. I went about with only one aim: to dream, to ejaculate, to suffer. So it seems to me that I stretched out to infinity a childhood which does not generate that other age adults expect from a child. I, who was in London at the time of the Beatles, never bothered much about their songs: I had no myths, except that of becoming independent and ice-cold, degenerate and angelical, an incorruptible but inquisitive mountaineer scaling my own peak. Then I did not want to become a fanatic about anything, mad about anything, a bigot about anything. I had a single belief: to breathe in and out. With full lungs. Other people had very little to do with these decisions and then I am someone who has really done very little bad, almost none, apart from some momentary psychological troubles which, when some years have passed, will be seen very differently by my numerous victims of those days. I could not help it if I unleashed more passions than those unleashed on me: I was an accomplice but never tolerant. I am sorry, however, that a few shits, both male and female, did not commit suicide, as they had threatened, when I abandoned them. In any case what is more boring than someone who feels everything while you feel nothing, apart from patience, contempt, the worries about how to get the price of the ticket for the next train out of them – or at least of a snack?

I was so tempted by my thoughts, by how they formed and fell apart – I could invent them, abandon them, take them up again, superimpose them. Remove or add a comma in total privacy and change the sense of the world without even letting it know – not right away, not entirely. Clearly I could not fall into the myth of the car, of wealth or of hash, of the East, of politics, power, fashion, religion – even if later I got my driving licence at thirty-two and took part in the whole first part of a concert by Talking Heads and even if once I bought myself a fur-coat of red fox which was stolen from me almost at once by an emaciated sailor, completely toothless, who wanted to take me for a ride in his car for half a mile and I found myself in the open country wearing a vest and it was snowing – I think it was somewhere in the Lunigiana. And the Myth of a state of marginalization or of Bohème made me shit blood more than any other. I quickly got tired of the world of the cinema and never recovered from it. Because I wrote as well and familiarity with writing cancels out all the rest. It becomes a vampire, male, female, love, sex and affection, becomes what is lacking and without which what there *is* would no longer have an existence. I have always taken great care not to have proper myths, apart from children and little girls in particular. I had a general myth which engulfed every specific object capable of external mythification: not to accept a single identity of this phenomenon called life which had lifted me up with the absentmindedness of a gust of wind – and yet not to commit the irremediable error of refusing that part of me which I knew only because I was saddled with it like a crime, rather, to hold it even more dear because of its slight sliminess and in its marvellous yet insidious nastiness. In this blind injustice of the moment I divined a far-sighted justice, unfailingly rejected but no less blinding for that. I would have become a giant for the very fact that I started off from my insufficiency and from the precariousness of my state. I would have become something much more than superhuman: I would have become human. The true giants know they are made of clay.

Montichiari, Lower Po Valley. 'A parcel has come,' says my mother without raising her eyes from her crocheting. 'It's as big as a chest of drawers and doesn't weigh anything. I'm not going to open it. Suppose it's nitro or something nasty?' I am to blame for her distrust, it was I who drove home to her to suspect TNT and a cautious approach to mouth-watering surprises which then turn out to consist of powdered faeces. 'Go on, you open it!' she continues in a maternal way, 'outside.' It is very light, a washed-out red colour, with no indication of where it comes from. I put it on the terrace uncut. The last time I had to wait for the usual funereal depression to make up my mind to get it over with and open a box sent to me by a woman reader in Turin, I discovered chocolates filled with liqueurs wrapped in blue paper with a pattern of stars; I even ate one against my rule, which is to say thank you for all food sent to me and to throw the whole lot into the rubbish bin. But once, when I was going through a period of particular euphoria because not only was I not coming across the usual mythomaniac psychopath who was mad about me, but I was not coming across anyone else either, a little cellophane bag full of shit remained untouched for more than two months in its Easter dress under the cement sink.

The next day my mother to whom I have played second fiddle more or less since she was born says with one of her rare looks: 'Another one has come – no, not a parcel – a big envelope.' And this at nine o'clock: at midday there was another. I open the trio of dispatches: in the red box there is a purse and a sleeveless vest with compliments from Bava, in the big envelope a maternity dress with pretty girls in blue uniforms on the front and men also in the national colours on the back, the signature says 'Trans-trans', perhaps a firm that produces maternity dresses for athletes who come back from Korea pregnant with a physiological build that is suitable or has been made so; in a big box a fine cotton vest with the words 'Italia Press Seoul 1988' and a little tricolour around the neck (marvellous!) and a plastic bag: I undo the Stracciardi label and put the vest on at once. 'But it's not a maternity dress,' says my sister who, unlike me, is seven months pregnant, and has come to try it on, 'It's a miniskirt,' and she hands it back to me as if I could after all put it on. 'No, it isn't,' my niece Wilma explains, 'it's an XL, you can make a knot at one side and show your thigh.' 'Ah, of course, if you can make a knot at the side that's different,' I agree, and put it away in the drawer for better times when I shall be really *mad*.

'It's some firms who are sponsoring the Olympic Games, they're wanting you to do a little publicity for them,' says someone who knows about such things. 'They get away with very little,' I answer back, 'but no one asked them for anything . . . well, they know what they are about. A peremptory but discreet mail-shot. If it works it works and if not Amen. Who knows how many people in the press, who are used to being bought, pocket it all out of snobbery and pretend that nothing has happened.' Then

I decide to do the opposite in order to underline my capricious inability to be bought (what would be the use of buying a wild character like me to sell himself?). Thank you, people of old Italian stock who sponsor so many powerful Italian lungs playing away from home.

And the same goes for the parcel of about ten kilos which a carrier from Bergamo personally brought to my house and which sent my relations, who shammed poverty, into ecstasies: an infinity of stylish delicacies which were at once sampled and unanimously approved – not even the crumbs or the fragment of chopped basil in the bottom of the tin remained; my mother said that croissants are quite simply the best she ever allowed to dissolve on her palate – also because they don't stick to her dentures. Now I am waiting for a track suit and a pair of shoes because a polite employee rang up from the firm to find out the size of my shoes and the suit and I think another firm wants to send me 'cables' which are not more clearly defined (I didn't take the telephone call and my mother can remember only the word 'cables', which according to her – plurals apart – is not a single word but a whole lot of them). I wonder how many millions I could have asked for just to boost the name of one of these firms – so many that not one of them would have accepted it. The Italian dress designers know something about this, for they have been thinking for a while that after becoming a writer the next little step up is to be immortalized as a coat-hanger, but like this it is different. Faced by the cunning kindness of the various firms it is like when I am put up against the wall by other people's talent: I take down my tutu and bow, for it is the same thing – or else the second is the natural consequence of the first.

Television: 'I can't take any more podiums' I shout and turn off the sound.

I can't help it: the *circenses* bore me whether live or recorded. I understand the well-intentioned organizational efforts (behind them are the private funds of industry, not the public ones managed by the ambassadors, the cultural attachés, the bureaucrats and imbeciles who are appointed on a party basis by the Foreign Ministry and who organized the Frankfurt Book Fair without any thought for the book nor for whoever is supposed to write it), and the mania for peace between the people who are healthily at war, but it seems to me like sending a scientific team to Saturn to put the finishing touches to a new Aspirin. The sports commentaries are unbearable, a flood of insignificant facts which are imposed on images in order to interpret them with the usual anacoluthons. But there is nothing to read in an image and often nothing to see.

When the teams begin to parade with the flags I prick up my ears: no one shouts 'Na-ked! Na-ked!' I turn it off. A least once upon a time the Olympic Games were played by men and they were naked: women in sport are like women in literature: they are often women who are no women – too ambiguous for my complex nature – and if they are it is all the more serious. As for the naked Greeks it is to them that the tradition goes back which makes one in every two trainers a homo with the vocation of *paterfamilias*, men of few words, a lot of claps on the back, basically going back and forwards between the *veiled* carrot and the *lace-trimmed* stick like the one in *Rocco and his Brothers*. The sports prostitute is supposed to be ennobled by the Pygmalion role inspired by industrial sponsorship which aims to extol 'the values' of youth and to keep it away from drugs and alcoholism and bring it closer to the magical cure of a turbo-drive with stereo and headphones thrown in. But sport *is* a drug with devastating effects on the mind, the body and the autostrada! Antidoping apart I have never known a normal sportsman, and now the youthful crazes for 'kisses, chests, and legs' are past I don't intend to attempt to get to know one. The pair I met were neurotic, with their cunt here on their foreheads (and from there it has never moved on to a real one), sexually inexpert, they even turned a toss-off one melancholy winter evening into a ski-race. And, constitutionally antidemocratic and reactionary (and because the brain of their head office has been substituted for their own), they shrug if you mention politics – has anyone ever heard a footballer say anything about the way social and political life are going? They would be perfect even when they speak if only they would avoid doing so.

Take the maiden priestesses who attend the Formula One racing drivers: they tremble in the boxes, those all-peroxide blonde ladies with dark mirror-glasses, mute and apprehensive. In a state of ecstasy at their great good fortune at being able to suffer at Montecarlo or Monza, they believe there is such a thing as champagne just as there is French lingerie. What existential models do they toast for us, these ace-drivers, these motor-women, apart from tenacity, which is something that the people have who collect syringes in Milan and Naples?

I have never gone to the stadium to see a game of football under any letter of the International Olympic Committee's alphabet – they say that in the popular ones you hear more din than in the upmarket ones and that if you want to understand something about the political silence of Italy's citizens you have to start off from the savage shouts at the little clouds of dust that rise there for ninety minutes: Byzantine expressions of the uncircumcised shouted at the characters who are exorcising the danger of being called upon one by one to answer for complicity in the civic cowardice in which they graze discontented and blissful. In short, one must go to a stadium sooner or later to do exactly the same as in the theatre: look at people in the same way as one looks at and strains to hear not the actor but the comments of one's neighbour on those actors who are not on the playbill.

The day after the inauguration, always at two in the morning, I turn on the set again and find the eliminating round for female swimmers: the most interesting moments are the false starts – as the rules have developed, cloaks have been introduced – apart from women – and therefore also bathing trunks to cover the male pudenda because the first divers in the Aegean, for example, must have protested a good deal because of blows in the balls, which were avoided even in Graeco-Roman wrestling, but not from a diving-board a metre high.

The false starts being over and having learned the world record that must be beaten – ten minutes or perhaps ten seconds – I turn off. I have put to one side a ream of supplements which have appeared in the papers and weeklies and am still waiting to begin to want to get interested in the Olympics and therefore to *read up* about them, as people say who also use another word – *professional* – having three in all at their disposal. Up to now nothing doing. What on earth am I going to do in Seoul, apart from

Tokyo? Who knows – once there I shall be able to make up for lost time and galvanize myself with the interviews I do with those concerned on their way to the showers. Meantime I have persuaded my mother to put on the track suit and to go about the house like that to give me a feel of the Korean atmosphere. Tomorrow I shall fill the rubber bath on the terrace with water and will try to persuade her to carry out the trials for canoeing or at least those for the breast stroke . . . But I have no questions for a sportsman – take the centre forwards who one Sunday after the other reply in the same way to the same questions as on the previous Sunday.

Is there any difference between *La Gazzetta dello Sport* of Monday 8th three months ago and that of a Tuesday 9th three months from now? – apart from the fact that at half-past eight in the morning there still isn't a copy to be had in the newspaper kiosk.

It is the people who sit there who make the marathon runners sprint and the latter are going to retire as soon as possible and give a metaphysical sense to some other unfortunate who runs, boxes, or stands gangling like a monkey between two wooden posts with a net at his back to keep out hell or repel paradise while the sky falls on everyone and no one notices. The illusory superstructures of the sports fans, in the bar or the factory or in the office block every possible ideal of *true* human progress, just like any possible serious attempt by the trade unions to bring into step the labour force and the rise in the cost of living. Wherever the talk is of sport, political stasis is guaranteed, revolution avoided (even a false one!), the system is strengthened immensely – as with love: to avoid speaking about it is the only way to come to blows, one must not lose time saying or not saying 'I love you.' It is demonstrated by allowing the hormones to speak. It is sport, immediately after the sense of guilt we have from Adam, which makes the world go round – in its own way, alas. I know I must go against my will to the very place where this world goes round more giddily than ever *for what it is*: a sponsored circus with reductions for teachers and students – the more people that get in the more animals one sees! No! And since I have always been bored by the infancy of the villager or shepherd or little crook who, after years of apprenticeship in his family with fifteen mouths to feed, his mother off her head, his father off altogether, gets up into a ring as a joke and achieves *fame*. How many painful biographies of boys irredeemably lost in the *favelas*, who then became goal-scorers and became successful and have wealth and their mother in a private clinic and their father, who has come back like the classical prodigal father, and at thirty as a point of reference to this day and age they have: a Topolino Villa with Swimming-Pool, Mercedes and her namesake *the* Mercedes if things are going well. That is what people call liberation from poverty! And he deserves it. And tomorrow on the 22nd of September Milan-Zürich-Seoul. If only they were holding the championships for Erections for Him and Her from 100 metres to 100,000 metres with mixed teams since in any case no one notices and may the best woman win!

In the meantime, competition after competition, the mighty native Italians have become mighty useless displaced persons. Time to leave!

A hostess of the Italian airline on leaving Linate to hand me an *Olavita* bag, two jerseys and a waterproof jacket, and a hostess from the Olympic Family on our arrival at the airport of Mimpo to hand out to me a preferential and systematic search and here I am, in the press village punctuated by delicious barriers and detectors painted in various colours and made nicer by garlands of plastic flowers. I saw nothing of Seoul, or perhaps what I did not see was Seoul. I am put in a flat with grey wallpaper and a photographer who has been settled in the next room for three weeks and who has therefore seen everything there was to see, that is to say, he confirms to me, nothing, or rather some millions of Americans with almond-shaped eyes and corresponding dance-halls for 'dolls' and sailors in whom Americans with normal eyes are specialists.

In any case at Seoul as at Rimini at the Communion and Liberation congress I have no intention of talking about sport nor about the mixed bag of God and Socialism but always and only about tiny details. With all the more reason now that even the last number of *Time*, which I found on the plane, has explored in depth the last socio-political areas which had remained undiscovered under the heading 'Korea'. For months they have been stuffing our heads with the XXIV Olympics, and in Italy the feeling was one of tolerant lack of interest. Had it not been for the defeat of Italy at the hands of the Zambian team – which caused the little Italy of the football fans to go into mourning – normal Italians would have continued to do the same as the Americans – switch channels and prefer family soap operas to the numerous Italian defeats. Seoul today has been changed into a garden – for kilometre after kilometre, on the obligatory routes to the sites of the games, it is an abundance of beds of white and yellow chrysanthemums with insertions of red plumes, giant balloons which move in the wind, flags as big as parade grounds with the spiral symbol of the Games taken from Korean iconography to signify peace-harmony-progress, everywhere – above alongside behind – policemen of every age with eyes like croissants poached in a sinister way in the turtle soup served up in the groove of a sword camouflaged in their irises. Ah, the baroque Korean system of public order! Their politeness which no one has asked for, the fiction of brotherhood continues, the frenzied boy-scout behaviour which, with their submachine guns under their arms and a baton in their belts, they let loose on you so as to make you feel at every moment like a little old lady being helped over the street.

Here I am in the Olympic stadium just in time for the semifinal for the medal of medals – the 100 metres. There are to be two heats: in the first there is Carl Lewis, in the second Ben Johnson. Here and there, meantime, there are young ladies jumping over a crossbar and trying not to knock it down, while in the distance to the left, too far away to be seen with the naked eye, there is a volley of javelins unnoticed up to now, and Czech, Finnish, Bulgarian, Russian gentlemen, impressive in their bulk and everything else – the huge screen set up not far from the Olympic flame seems to shine with extra luminosity when it pokes about in the intimacy of the clinging track suits of the javelin throwers.

Since I have the sun in my face I hope I won't get sunstroke. And at half-past ten a hubbub rises from the crowd: first heat of the 100 metres and Lewis, first with 9.97, raises an arm, salutes without smiling (as if he hadn't enough skin left to do so), and goes back down the steps pushing aside a television journalist who had been lying in wait for him for goodness knows how long. Second heat: here he is, the big black man with the dare-devil look, with the white of his eyes red with unpunished insolence, the unbearable simple-minded man, the lecher. A real ovation welcomes Ben Johnson, who up to now has always had better times than Lewis and who now pulls his track suit over his head like no one else and you feel you want to go over and give him a hand, two hands, everything, and to pull off as well that little he is left with: yellow and black shoes, red pants, red T-shirt, a gold necklace which makes him look like a Neapolitan mastiff, and a slip. A false start – and his fault without doubt, sly one that he is. There he is taking up position again – off! Another false start. At the third attempt he wins with 10.03, with the gap as usual too big between him and Lewis. But what legs! But there is nothing to be said against Lewis either, a big girl, a bit too thin for my taste, always with that psychedelic look that the Americans put on when they beat men. We are all grateful to Johnson for having beaten every record, for otherwise we would not have realized from the summer photographs – of him standing on a boat with a bevy of vivid bronzed girls at his feet – how irresistible he is in a bathing costume, even if I would pull it over his head, and how attractive the calves and the Egyptian waist is of a black man who is not famished.

The black men break one record after another – these are their Olympics – because they have learned to organize their anger, not because they are 'more motivated'; whereas the whites now have only stress and fear of not managing, or perhaps they are slowly beginning to think that sport is not a particularly charismatic activity, a little like politics, which even in Italy is handed over by the industrialists to personalities who, in short, are without influence and have an intellectual and socio-political profile that is far from outstanding.

Now the women finalists in the 100 metres are coming, heats: there is Evelyn Ashford, the champion of the 84 Games, with 11.10 here and precious little chance of beating Joyce Griffith, the star with the Star Wars head-dress, who in fact at once sets a new Olympic record with 10.88. There is Rossella Tarolo too, with a very intense expression, Italian women should only take part in beauty competitions. There is Merlene Ottey, 11.03, Jamaican, florid, a beautifully bronzed velvet, luminosity like the northern lights on her face in ecstatic concentration – how they jiggle their buttocks to a frenetic rhythm before taking up their positions. They look like mad egg-whisks, they could base another special event on it on the podium from beginning to end, but the javelin throwers! They are pricks who throw their darts into the sky to meet up with God before they decide to settle for ending in a hole. Great sport, like great art, is either sex or patience.

Final of the men's 100 metres – great suspense, a silence of the tomb in the stadium where shortly before the screen had announced that the president, Roh Tae-woo, had entered with his lady. A proper start: Ben at once gets ahead, he sticks out a piece of red tongue to his left, a desperate attempt by Lewis who did not expect it, Ben pulls ahead, a white pigeon appears suddenly and measures out the full length of track accompanying the fleeing competitors in slow motion, victory for Ben with a hand raised from which his forefinger stands up and thrusts itself into the sky. That finger! It will always remain impressed on my memory.

Provided always that that finger does not crumble from one minute to the next, seeing that we are still waiting for Johnson to turn up at the press conference and only ten minutes ago they informed us of the cause of his tremendous delay – he is undergoing anti-doping tests. It was like learning that he has been transubstantiated into a divine erection by an anti-piles suppository.

Carl Lewis on the other hand arrived almost at once after his unforeseeable defeat and, in his turn, the bronze, the English Linford Christie. Unlike the latter, Lewis turned up on the platform alone without any technical Mephistopheles alongside. Not yet free from the tension after the race and his capitulation, which is relative but no less tragic, his face looks like a trackless map, his eyes, sucked into their cavities, make an effort, which is not entirely successful, not to pop out. Some journalists protest, they want Ben to appear as well. Lewis looks at the Korean referee below the platform, frowns questioningly, what procedure should be adopted? He taps the stand of one of the microphones, opens the palm of his hand, he is ready to answer questions; the jacket of his track suit hides his neck up to the chin, his two hands and long narrow head emerge as black as bits of tortoise from the white of the Terylene shell and do not prove that the rest of his body is in there; what one sees of Lewis is abstract, disturbing. The temple which is exposed to my gaze is beating strongly, from his cheek to his ear, his skin suffers from pimples and he is altogether a marionette of embarrassed endurance: the confusion among journalists and cameramen and referees is total. No! Johnson has no intention of showing himself, he has decided to be temperamental, to make himself desired, the usual teaser, so let things begin with Carl.

To questions of basic inanity ('What do you feel like after your defeat?' 'Did you expect it?' etc) Lewis answers calmly and quietly, above all when the pro forma curiosity of the journalists touches on their favourite topic of his personal rivalry with Johnson, which he replies to with heavy embroideries.

'I was very relaxed in both heats,' Lewis replies in a very gentlemanly way and without any resentment at the sharp prods he is subject to. 'I don't think it is disappointing to come in second – I trained as hard as I could, and I ran with the utmost energy, I am satisfied with myself; I have beaten the American record and still have three other events to come.' And when someone tries to get out of him some nasty remark about Johnson, Lewis replies with a natural tone of voice: 'I am happy for Ben, there will be other chances for us to compete.' When at the end of the race he went over to Johnson, who turned his back to him, and patted him lightly on the shoulder with his left hand and was already holding out his right, Ben took a long time to turn round and when he decided to do so it was with such downright rudeness that I would like to ascribe it rather to a surprised reaction than to real resentment, then looked him up and down with a smug look, before accepting the hug of his enemy who before the whole world paid homage to his superiority. Would Ben in his place have been capable of this gesture of congratulation, which was obviously diplomatic and therefore all the more difficult to allow to overcome his real feelings? Lewis leaves the microphones open and our wait for Ben starts over again, punctuated by the arrival, no less, of the winners of the hop, step and jump, headed by the gold medallist, the Bulgarian, Markov, a gypsylike cowboy, astounded that his arrival gave rise to loud disappointment. The conference stops again, people want to know why the committee doesn't bring Ben along bodily, a piss has never taken up so much of anyone's time, whether mortal or immortal.

Two hours later, I decide that his insolence will make me feel tenderness for him, seeing that his slips make me drool at the mouth; I am cross with him only because in the meantime it was his fault that I missed the gold medal won by that lovely bean-pole, Jacky Joyner Kersey. In the bus to the Press Village some ten kilometres from Seoul, a city which I imagine, given its vast size, could never be taken, for it is always ten kilometres away from itself, I look at all the hundred metres in the moviola of my imagination: when Carl came on to the track from among the crowd there at once rose in a rustle what I would instinctively have expected to be an ovation, which was given to Ben Johnson immediately afterwards. The two share a comparative table of those points which in the eyes of the masses represent their virtues and defects: the crowd is more interested in Lewis than in Johnson, he is more articulate, more reliable in his results, more monstrously a superman than Johnson, but they do not love him; he can even run the 100 metres in 5 seconds just as I can get the Nobel prize for literature or aspire to become president of the Italian republic if uprightness, civic sense, complete identity of thought and action for a whole lifetime in which there is not even a slightest possibility of blackmail were the requisites. But I am homosexual, and we homosexuals bear witness in the results of our social flesh to a power and a morality which is not altogether human and therefore we are not representative even where, with less laziness and common 'received ideas', we could easily be emulated even by those who want to play the game of him and her and set up house and family. Johnson is rough-hewn, vulgar, raw material that is not at all refined, is not – taken all in all – a great athlete like Lewis (the greatest of the Eighties), but if he wins it is ordinary humanity that people recognize in him, that humanity which falls often and willingly, the kind that gets up again, the kind that, boasting of the fact of having barely excused itself a minute ago, dashes towards a repetition of the same mistake, the human nature of males who are brutal with women and of women who dream of having their cake and eating it – that is to say males who are brutal like Ben and all in all are infantile and tameable like him with a smack of the vagina.

Lewis does not want anyone alongside him; no technicians, no trainers, no guardian angels, not his mother like Ben; he has killed all the fathers; doctors and technicians are at his service, not he at theirs; Lewis never has recourse to *captatio benvolentiae*; if he wins he pockets the proceeds, if he loses he pays. He never loses sight of the real terms of the social contract between the challenge of himself, the stake and a certain fixed waiver which is simple when he wins, double when he loses. Johnson represents the static ecstatic dream, the earthly paradise with homologized apple, the innocent animality which cleanses the world of its sins, putting his tongue out at it with a malicious smile: Lewis is alone and knows it, Johnson is alone and does not know it. Lewis sacrifices himself to himself; Johnson sacrifices himself to success, which is infinitely more easy to quantify on a human scale – he has just started building a seven-hundred-thousand-dollar house and does not hide his own happiness at his billion-dollar contract with an Italian sportswear company which has just begun to broadcast commercials in a publicity campaign on a Western scale with a budget estimated to be about six hundred thousand dollars. Lewis leads a monastic life, home and track; Johnson is in the discothèques in the small hours and would fuck a mosquito if it turned up saying it was called Lady Diana. But once again I see the gap between his thighs, the bright red of his pants which form a groove between the two superpowers ready to leap off in unison, his arched bust, the ox-like neck which supports the head that stretches forward giraffe-like, the little close-set eyes where a bloodstained calm boils, the smile of triumph at eighty metres from the tape, the certainty of triumph which explodes in the raised arm and the forefinger sticking out of the fist which certainly cost him some hundredths of a second. Once again I see the dove flying over the six runners on the track, one after the other, very slow and sacral – or was it a pigeon?

The village catalyses a ghostly twilight, like artificial light on artificial quarters which are vaguely reminiscent of the Sahara, with little artificial trees and little artificial birds which whistle on in a sinister way in the milky haze of night, which is an artificial one, because I do not sleep and my real dream gives way to an insomnia which is also artificial, because it cannot be true. I am too tired to rest and my heart is torn between Johnson and Lewis, I am surprised and depressed by the ardent ways it beats for Johnson and the suspicion he harbours towards Lewis – the deep and hysterical distrust of every other self.

At six o'clock I do not find it difficult to get up, in the course of two cycles of sun and moon I have become a fanatical sportsman, tough enough for all the races in the programme. With some Italian Stakhanovites, who for three weeks have been photographing everything from eight in the morning to ten at night and who still have not found the time or the courage to try Veronika's famous 'lotus flower under high vacuum' in Tao I Won 7th floor 24 hours full service, at first light we meet in the cafeteria to leave together for the artificial lake dug out of the highly polluted Han River, where the boat races take place. Yesterday I tried some Korean vegetables in the early morning and for the whole day was unapproachable – like any Korean. Here they put garlic everywhere and there is no nice young woman, all bows and smiles, who does not give off a whiff at sight, impregnating the air for metres and metres: it is the most typical smell of this Olympiad and you find it everywhere, even walking in a park, because from the kitchen chimneys comes nothing except essence of garlic and boiled cabbage in foul vapours. Cloves and heads of garlic take body in the sky, they cluster together and dissolve, and – it is terrible for hair and clothes – they pour down in the form of garlic rain. We get into the first bus for the Press Centre and there they count us when we get in and and when we get out, just in case anyone might have got lost on the way or climbed up into the luggage rack. However, *chapeau*: if there has to be a check this is checking at its best. I mean that no Japanese or North Korean terrorists would get through – neither would a firearm camouflaged as an umbrella. A pity that in order to smile and count you and pass the detector over you each time you have to get in anywhere they have to breathe, and it is well known that if you breathe in sooner or later you breathe out. The photographers have by now lost patience and blaspheme every time. For me it is all new, and then it is the first time I have been felt all over in the Orient.

The sports journalists, fat, with big tits, semi-solid, are like members of parliament who, since in youth they specialize in taking bribes, are, when they come to maturity, nominated Ministers for Posts and Telecommunications – hence prose on the lines of 'it was as a team with its feet on the ground, its head in the air and its heart on the ball' – that is to say complete literary stasis. I already feel bad at having lowered myself to the inexpressive expression 'first light' just to be quicker.

Meantime the fourth heat for the women's pairs – from the grandstand the Americans are shouting as if possessed USA USA USA even when the scoreboard shows that the American crew is last, and a Neapolitan voice shouts: 'USA piss off' and begins to wave the tricolour. They are supporters of the Abbagnale brothers, for ten years or more they have been following them everywhere: after the coxed eight with a woman cox it is the turn of the pair with a male cox, that is to say Carmine and Giuseppe Abbagnale and Giuseppe di Capua, who immediately pull away from their most feared rivals, the English, and after six interminable minutes and a bit they dash to the finishing line with a lead of several metres. I too shout enthusiastically and for the second time in my life find myself singing 'Alé oó' – the first time was a week ago during a voice test which included a song called 'Mad' and another 'A Day By the Sea', a dialogue between me, that is to say, between wives on the beach and a chorus of husbands in the stadium. Ah, the sublime patriotic kitsch of victory! I let myself go completely to celebrate the trio, shouting and jumping up and down on the iron grating, carried away by the joy which Di Capua splashes with full hands, dipping them under the surface to splash the two rowers, who are still in shock, their heads bent back, their chests relaxing, staring at the void of a marvel, uncertain what to do now with their eyes.

In the meantime the women rowers are given their prizes: the band of the marines plays the national anthem of the gold medallist (almost always that of the GDR) while another extremely funny band of Korean trumpeters in costumes straight from a Viennese operetta blow their trumpets and seven pages dressed in white raise the flags on the three flagstaffs. Everything is so unreal that you feel you are looking into a sweetbox full of beans disguised as sweetmeats. Then three girls in national costumes on stiletto heels, led by a haughty and distant court lady, come forward, holding in their arms cushions with the medals and bunches of pink gladioli and chrysanthemums so that I am moved by the agonizing inwardness shining from their beautiful serious faces which every so often break into a smile provoked by a wiggle by Di Capua, who is like a joyous jester, who is thrown into the water immediately after the ceremony and fished out without the medal and put back on to the podium by the two brothers who scarcely move a finger. Great jubilation from the managers and the co-nationals of the eights which did not get into the final. Then the Italian fours also win the second gold medal of the morning. What holds true for the blacks who come up everywhere is also true of the Italian medallists, it is no mere chance that they are almost all Southerners dedicated to sports which are truly romantic and not very lucrative, like rowing and fencing.

A pity that the community of Neapolitan football fans is little or not at all disposed to take something from Maradona to invest it in the rowing skills of these philosophers of the oar. Their message is not sufficiently *éclatant* and the life of ordinary men – workers, employees, students – which they lead is too sensible. Rowing is a sport lacking in any malice, it presupposes harmony and blind faith in the other, a deep-rooted social sense in their character from which any narcissistic sharpness is sandpapered away on the character of the other in the years of apprenticeship until any sham tolerance is transformed into profound acceptance.

After the ceremony, off at a run not to miss the finals of the women's 100 metres: there is the black gazelle, the extravagant and slightly melancholic Florence Griffith-Joyner. I arrive at the stadium just in time, the names of the competitors have already appeared on the screen, the stadium is packed, not a place free, not even in the gangways between the steps. There! A free place! I drive my way through the standing crowd and with authority make for the mirage just in front of the tape and sit down beside an old Swedish journalist with a stick, a hearing aid and glasses, false teeth and a gloved left hand. He is saying something to me but I don't listen to him, if he tells me it is taken I'll finish him off. My eyes run across to the pitch where my idols are still at work (my God, how many of them I have, what shameless lycanthropy, insatiable my need for idols to clothe in order to undress them like well-proportioned hundred-kilo dolls): the ones who are throwing javelins, discuses, or hammers – a pity there are none who specialize in the screwdriver, pliers and pincers, which the International Olympic Committee hasn't so far thought of. 'Saint Sebastian,' I beg mentally, 'allow me to meet Ovalenko, USSR (in a dacha on the Ticino on the hop skip and jump between one ditch and the next or Protsenko)' and St Sebastian in a very loud voice says: 'Why not Bofki, Hungary, weightlifter?' The Swede doesn't give in. 'What are you seeing?' and I tell him what I am seeing – the athletes who have come on to the track, Florence in a more sober get-up than yesterday, all black and red, with the number 569. 'What are they saying?' and I tell him what they are saying, starter, proper start. 'Who is that?' and I say brusquely: 'Will you shut up?' Florence immediately ahead of them all, at fifty metres she opens up with a radiant smile, but I am grateful to the patched-up Swede for it must have been precisely because of the nuisance he caused earlier that I found this place free, in front of which Florence cuts the tape followed by Evelyn Ashford and by Heike Drechsler. She bends down and kisses the ground, a compatriot approaches her and hands her an American flag, my hands are skinned and I have two lumps in my throat. I am happy if the blacks win because thus they are Americans, if they lose they immediately become coloured people in that nation which, as far as certain basic aspects of the interracial social pact go, is perhaps still worse than England.

The Swede: 'What will her husband do for her to celebrate her victory?' and he is lost in a wicked smile. He pronounced 'victory' as if it were something out there. Suddenly it is the turn of the gold medallist in the 400 metres hurdles, Phillips, to make a circuit of the track waving the star-spangled banner, improvising a strip-tease beginning with his shoes and then continuing with his T-shirt, advancing majestically and sticking out his chest, as if he needed to. I wink at him and he winks back. 'Did you see those buttocks! A full cup could stand on them,' says the Swede, and I say: 'You know this isn't Griffith any more – it's someone else.' 'A man? I take it back.' 'But it would stand on them just the same.'

In the Italian House, on the 34th floor of the Intercontinental Hotel, I went to take my place at the Abbagnales' dinner of honour. After a good half-hour spent in establishing my presence, I say to a youth, thinking he too came from Pompeii: 'So after Benedetto Croce Naples has the Abbagnales,' which was meant to be an opening compliment, but the boy opens his eyes wide and, taking it for a trick question, says: 'I'm sorry – but what category does he compete in?' then by good fortune, to draw a thick veil of grated cheese over my gaffe, the maccheroni alla bolognese arrives served up in half an entire Parmesan cheese. People are talking – I talk – about the clumsiness of the trainers who aspire to be fathers, the pathetic ridiculous figures they are, how they ruin the consciousness – never mind the bodies, because that is what they are there for. Someone confirms what I say: 'I had an earring, I had to take it off otherwise I was a queer; then if someone has long hair he has to cut it, if not people think he is queer.' And I say: 'They all have the complex about being buggered, they all think like housewives with the *idée fixe* of rape, terrified that something so extraordinary only ever happens to other women.' The atmosphere becomes heated in my favour: the unexpected hatred which rises against the sports technicians is choral and liberating. They listen to me fascinated, the Abbagnales, a little sceptical but amused, detached in a gentlemanly way, more concerned with the maccheroni than anything else. 'I have killed all the fathers, godfathers, sponsors, who dared to lay their claws on me but my problem now is what to do with those in the shadows, the subliminal ones,' I explain. 'The ones who know how to exploit even your instinct for self-destruction, as well as your insistent desire as a professional Phoenix of Araby to at least cheat the tax-collectors.' Words, whether oral or written, either explain nothing or do not wish to say anything. Words that are worth something do not serve to exhaust reality but make it vibrate. Mesmer, who says too much while thinking he explains everything, should learn from me, or better still, from the resoundingly laconic behaviour of the Abbagnales, who win their gold and smile like wicked cats and have understood that no words from the mountain can ever reach where their silent canoe does not arrive at on the river. So, all displaying very white and very healthy teeth, they talk with refined caution which expresses more freedom of spirit than a person who talks at a gallop like me, whose time is limited to a few minutes and who must amaze people on a grand scale in order to collect the greatest possible number of reactions in the little time I am allowed.

We are interrupted by a journalist from the RAI who asks questions so trivial that, were he a man of ordinary intelligence, they could be mistaken for surreal ones. Then the Italian ambassadress and the female cultural attaché enter: they are very chatty, either because of their hats or because of a husband suspected of pushing or already in prison, and since the Koreans have everything except this (which is indispensable) both raise their elbows and are very easygoing and easy to feel – only in the very first moments.

I am enchanted by these southern oarsmen, by the lack of any macho vulgarity, the hint of desire in the looks as they wink at the busy hostesses (who, they confessed to me, receive three hundred and fifty proposals on an average per day, and for a little went along with it but now are really fed up: 'You see they are all sex-starved here, once the races are over they become wild animals, more polite than ever, for goodness' sake, but only because we are in a skyscraper and there's a lot of people about, but they don't realize that there are three of us and five hundred of them, and it isn't included in part-time employment. Here a sclerotic hunchback would have a busy time of it!'). They are polite hot-blooded young men who, after two months of abstinence, are still able to look at a woman and to sigh without coming out with the hallucinations of brutal gynaecologists about orifices. And then they are Neapolitans and used to patience; if it isn't in 1988 it will be in 1989. Meantime most of them go to rest in Bangkok and then in Hamburg, places famous for thermal mud with massage.

On 27 September at five past six in the morning I am getting something at the self-service in the cafeteria when I notice that many of my fellow guests are getting up from their chairs and unhurriedly gathering round the television: the journalist is saying incredible things, obscene words like 'anabolic steroids, 'anti-doping committee', 'after the two Bulgars'. 'The clinical urine test after the race leaves no possible doubt. Ben Johnson risks having his gold medal withdrawn and being disqualified from all events for two years, which means the end of his career.'

I lose my appetite, I go out into the fresh air, ah! there is the false and so-called 'first light', as false as the Rolexes for 30,000 lire, as false as the little tarts of thirty who put on a little falsetto voice and say they are twelve – as false as these Olympics, as their gold-plated medals. I am tossed about with contempt in a state of incredulity. I try to find something to remember – apart from Florence's smile, so feline, feminine, that she could not put more ardour into in the race, for a woman . . . I go into my room: the confirmation of Ben's disgrace is official. I feel deeply wounded: never love from afar with eyes shut, behind a puma a farmyard turkey is always hidden. I feel that this news is terrible and apocalyptic only for me, once I have gone down again among the photographers and journalists: their swift indifference seems to be already directed towards another scandal to be transmitted in order to make news. The point is that they are professionals and have seen every possible hormone.

I was mistaken about Lewis; telepathically I wallow in excuses and mea culpas: he is certainly the greatest Jesse Owens redivivus and the most worthy of our love – certainly the one most in need of it. Perhaps I do not love him because I am reflected too much in him and in the secret martyrdom of his overturned spirituality which so dramatically fills his eyes, so charged with panic, with shameful effeminacy, with martial solitude because of an ideal that does no one any good, which changes nothing apart from yourself, which eats you up inside with a rage that becomes colder and colder, perhaps a little stale. There is nothing

Mozartian about Lewis apart from the lightness he shows in his self-destruction, as if it were the only possible project for his ephemeral genius. He had no choice, that body around that mind, among the many beautiful things in life he had to choose the least pretty: to be extraordinary. As for Ben, who at this moment, with his baggage already packed, is leaving surreptitiously by the service entrance, I still feel great pity, but a pity that is avowedly physical. He has never been an archangel to suddenly become a fallen angel. Lewis is an angel. Ben is a man. I would take him in my arms to console him and meantime I would turn him round. He is normal.

On the flight to Tokyo determined to check what the Emperor Hirohito intends to do if he suddenly wakes up from a coma and says: 'What a hunger, what a thirst – otherwise I am well,' and watches a quarter of an hour of a samurai soap. I fish out again this indelible detail so as to refresh my memory, which has been emptied: it was in the Casa Italia, an oarsman was paying very timid court to a big blonde, my eye falls on his little red woollen pullover which was coming out in all directions. An old pullover from a stall in a back street, with him not knowing any advantage that might overcome the resistant and extra-beautiful blonde: on the left shoulder of the pullover the moths had left a hole. Not only the medal – he too was all gold, why did she want other guarantees? Ah! who could forget the roll of porno-photos a swimming team took of each other only to leave them on the bedside table?

At the airport at Narita one single taxi. I run to stop someone from getting there before me, but here everyone seems to prefer to take things easy and wait for the bus, who knows why. As I say to the taxidriver 'Plaza Hotel please' he leaps away from the mudguard against which he was leaning, begins to whistle and then quickly takes the wheel. But it is well known that taxidrivers whistle, sing to themselves and look in the rear mirror with scrutinizing curiosity, which is a little unhealthy, like someone shaving you. I don't know why he has to look at me so much. But am I mistaken or have we been travelling for a good twenty minutes? I take a quick look at the taximeter. 'Well I never!' I think, even if I haven't yet had time to check the rate of the yen to the dollar and so to Italian lire. But there are a lot of yens coming up like so many clicks of the tongue. He keeps on looking at me and instead of bending forward to check the taximeter I listen to the clicks: he must have noticed and turns on the radio. Who knows if it is possible to see an ear which is more and more pricked. He turns up the volume of the radio from which there explode exultant crowds of hotheads, with in the foreground the voice of a journalist who is singing the praises of some brutal moment in rugby or cricket, I imagine; since, besides stretching my neck, I stick it out, he turns up the volume of the radio and strikes up over it a twelve-tone tune with a few sibilant noises added through his teeth. Forty minutes under way. I put my head out and look and fall back against the seat as if I had been hit by a hammer. I changed one hundred and fifty dollars at the airport and Tokyo cannot be that series of low factories. How long these outskirts are!

In the centre of the freeway finally a notice 'Tokyo – 40 kilometres'. I throw myself back stunned and since here they drive on the left and now there are two lanes of traffic I almost end up under the seat because, as we overtook, the sensation that we were going to crash into a truck was like a shock. And now what is happening, because this rascal with his face squashed like a knave of spades, having got on to a raised highway, is immediately stuck in a jam which goes neither backwards nor forwards. He jumps out of the seat and begins to shout an arrangement for the machine-gun which goes 'Kakaka-kakakaa! Ka! Ka! Ka!' I feel more shaken than usual, and the damned radio and the damned horns, and why is he waving his arms crazily, what is he indicating and to whom? Am I perhaps feeling more jelly-like than usual just because I am vainly going to and fro from taximeter to wallet? And he turns and looks at me and his glance, meeting my defenceless annoyance, is saying I am a fool and now he thrusts his right arm out of the open window and begins to fire a burst of 'kakakakkka!' but I hold out, I don't pay undue attention to this sudden desire for conversation given that he could have used his tongue to tell me that no one – I swear no one – takes a taxi from the airport to Tokyo. And why is the traffic jam taking so long to unjam for only a few centimetres? Absentmindedly I follow his hand and at the tip of his finger I see a flag waving and then, my God, the flagstaff as well and a crane too . . . and a skyscraper! We are caught in the midst of an earthquake shock which no human being can scale down and the car stands on end and the whole bridge shakes under us and the truck ahead is coming down on us, put on the handbrake, you bloody nippofool! The little man at the wheel shouts something back at me, perhaps to stay calm, and I am completely unruffled – the important thing is that if I have to sink under the earth among hardware and sacks of sand I should first have time to ask for a receipt. When we arrive at the hotel the meter stands at 19,700 yen (about 215,000 lire) and I am forced to get the porter to give me his tip because I can't manage it with what I have, and in exchange I carry the luggage up to my room myself.

I have never taken a shower after a journey: I lay down my things and run to show myself off. The most notorious district is precisely the one a few streets away: Shinjuku, and I consult neither maps nor porters, I dash out. My nose is my compass. Seoul = abstinence. I go into a chemist's, the woman shop-assistant does not speak English, I try to tell her without managing to make her understand. She shakes her head; then I draw it. She gives me a box with a geisha on it with her hair already undone. I go along underpasses and under the underground, big shops overhead where a road goes from one floor to another, I stop and look at the Japanese. If I concentrate I can just about even find them sexy. Not many of them are walking about, most of them run in rivers in and out of something, they come together and pour on to the streets, they disappear swallowed up on one side and reappear on another, perhaps they are never the same people. I go up some iron stairs which cross a railway line and smell the odour of special flesh, raw and naked. The notices are all in kanji characters. I wander about as if floating on a cloud of transparent resin, for a couple of square kilometres I feel that up there or down there they are performing erotic rituals, in hotels with rooms by the hour, video-clubs, saunas, but the moment I presented myself at a couple of doors with strange and incomprehensible lighting I did not meet with expressions of welcome for a client – in fact I took a step back. Perhaps I am making a mistake, this is not the district of the Japanese mafia and of prostitution on tiptoe and with the tip of the tongue, here no one does the obvious – and there are no tarts in the street apart from one who, the moment she sees me, turns her back: she must be expecting a sweetheart. From the restaurants a nice smell of fried food in soya sauce and, at last, a porn cinema. I stand there for a minute and watch who goes in and out. Another woman who sees me and turns on her heels. I am beginning to understand – I am beginning to understand that I am unwelcome – that is it. Perhaps if I try another district. But that will be for another time; now, seeing that I shall have a good deal of difficulty in getting involved anew I shall go back and telephone a couple of addresses I have managed to get. I feel the little box in my pocket and since it runs the risk of being unopened I go into the first toilet on the road and try one on. *Try* to put one on – the condoms here are on the scale of the local man, they are *smaller!* Oh they are so nice – if it weren't that today little boys of eight have quite other things in their heads I could give one as a present to my grandnephew – but he is as well endowed as he is innocent.

Taka Banda, a pianist who attended a conservatory in Brescia and is one of the many orientals whom Europeans do not forgive for having a knack for music and the piano (considered to be the Italo-German prerogatives, which every so often are granted to France, England, and perforce, at most to Russia and America), is very happy to come and see me today, since tomorrow he has a concert in Yokohama. He comes and introduces to me Salute, his fiancée for nine years, who is in Japan for the next great step. Both of them with sufficient flesh to get married and of medium height, she has even contrived to be shorter than him to please him and not disorientate him too much; she is dressed like a child from a foundling hospital with some jumpers and at least one extra vest, it is not clear whether because she was afraid of the cold or did not want people to see that she had nothing else; he, on the other hand, is even more sober but only because he has only one item of clothing for each limb and does not have to wear no makeup in order to present a well-scrubbed look. Salute is really *too* natural – is it possible that she does not see that here there is at least the repressive paw of a mother and of the couple of maiden aunts who got sloppiness mixed up with the serious look of a good little girl who will go to catechism every Sunday all her life?

'Where do you want to go?' Taka asks me while I am enraptured by Salute's infinite capacity to smile, a tiny little loving person who needs someone to make her laugh, I feel, a litle girl who has blossomed with all possible respect for Mummy and Daddy and the nuns who one day, since the child, having been rejected at the altar in Italy, was getting on for thirty and certainly wasn't going to take the veil, summoned a family council and decided she could go to that country over there somewhere to get married, of course, to a pianist! With almond eyes! Who knows what habits the men have in these parts! Will he not hurt her too much or do nothing at all? She is happy. 'Anywhere – even the imperial castle – let's see if my arrival will enliven Hirohito's periods of coma. For how many months has he been coming and going?' Hirohito, in fact, by steering his middle course between here and the beyond is holding up the political and ceremonial life of the whole country, to great rejoicing on the part of the nationalistic extreme Right, which is exploiting the event minute by minute, dominating all the television transmissions which are forced to bring medical bulletins every quarter of an hour. 'I suspect,' I say to ingratiate myself with Salute, 'that he can't make up his mind to emigrate because that great son of the Sun, although self-dethroned in favour of a son of his dear ones, has not yet found a dwelling to his taste and is drawing things out with the celestial estate agents.' Salute bursts out laughing, pulling her head down into her shoulders a little, like a blackcap. My God, women like this really do exist, graduates in chemistry and brought up like vestals for marriageable young gentlemen cheesemakers, and are then, it goes without saying, promptly struck by the diligent apathy of a gentle pianist who could hide behind his bows his membership of a sect of sadistic neo-Confucian 'students of the mind'. The little couple is disturbing and one of them is certainly the victim of the other.

'What nice things are you playing tomorrow at Yokohama?' I ask Taka in the underground, because I don't even know if he composes, performs, or does a cabaret act in one of those famous nightclubs for single but energetic little ladies who have not much time to be loved and pretend not to be majority shareholders in Mitsubishi or General Motors. 'A sonata by Clementi,' he says, which to me is as if to say that he carried about a zither in water to amuse himself by passing through it little violin-shaped submarines. 'Ah,' I exclaim with great admiration, 'the famous Clementi.' 'Yes, completely unpublished – I found the music at the Queriniana in Brescia, it was under a layer of dust.' 'Three fingers deep,' adds Salute. 'What excitement!' I imagine the great joy of the lotus flower housewives at the concert when he tells them that they have listened to an unpublished sonata by Clementi no less – I don't know who Clementi is, but I would be enthusiastic too, what have I to lose? But I know Verdi by reputation and I know there were at least two Bachs, father and son, that one of the two was either a candlemaker or a sacristan, but I don't know who is who, the Sixties wigs with a permanent wave both of them wear are tremendous, besides the father of a son is not his son, and hence the real father, only because of a quibble over timing of you first, not at all, I couldn't possibly, you first, I wouldn't dream of it, after you etc.

At the imperial castle there is an endless queue of subjects with little umbrellas and plastic overcoats waiting to be able to add their own propitiatory signature on the umpteenth register made available by the State chancellery. (The ceremony has been broadcast on television with every detail about the paper – old rice – the binding, the sewing, the number of good wishes expected tomorrow, when it will be replaced by another brand-new one later to be laid beside the pillow of His Celestial Highness, whose expansionist celestial nature cost Asia some twenty million dead not much more than twenty years ago.) I tried to start up a political conversation with Taka but he very amiably let me talk without ever interposing any sort of remark. In that he really is a *classical* artist. He confines himself to observing that 'no one expected such exhausting tributes in modern Japan to an Emperor who people thought had disappeared to all intents and purposes decades ago' and that that 'brings with it dangers', but he does not specify which. Salute turns the conversation to my observation about the new and considerable height of the young Japanese. 'They no longer carry on like my mother-in-law, sitting cross-legged for hours, with their backbone compressed. Every so often I try to keep her company but oh, my joints! oh, my poor knees! I feel sick. Young people play a lot of sport today and also do a lot of motorcyling to and from work and the food isn't based on rice any longer,' and I bite my tongue, which was getting round to forbidden territory, condoms, until such time as there are no Japanese men present and no engaged couples. The castle cannot be visited, it is closed to ordinary visitors and there are no parties to be seen to slip into, thanks to some foreign embassy. If you stand on tiptoe you can just see a couple of sloping roofs of the Edo period. And today too old Hirohito has used up his 400 cc of fresh blood. 'Even if he dies,' Salute tells me, 'it can be three months till they have the funeral,' and here was I who had flown in to enjoy the spectacle.

We leave behind us the double bridge leading into the palace and the gardens which, if sold by auction (one of the few green zones left in Tokyo), would be bought up in the course of five seconds at a hundred million per square centimetre. Walking along under a yellowish drizzle, I am seized once again by the feeling of being the only one to know that I am here and am breathing. The eyes of passers-by slide over you and if I don't stand aside they might go through me or walk over me. The massive anti-AIDS campaign has turned into a real anti-Western campaign: everything I live and get to know in this city will be from the outside – the certainty that I shall not have access – I don't mean to an orifice but to a house, to a family, to a confidence, a gratuitous inkling of existence. That I shall remain a tourist whether I stay here a week or ten years (in a little lake which, from the colour of the water, could strike me dead if I dipped a finger in it, grey and red fish are feasting on bits of bread thrown to them by some citizens) so long as there are no limits on opening hours and on bows for getting into a big shop, into a bank, into a factory, seven days out of seven. I propose we go into a pastry shop with a very exclusive and recherché look. Furnishings modernized classical, a lot of white and a little gold, waiters in dinner-jackets, waitresses in a black and white uniform with geometric designs and a little white cap over their hair, linen tablecloth and peach-coloured upholstery, an orchid hanging over each table, lamps with crystal pendants, silver-plated tea-pots and a little display of pastries. A waiter arrives exhibiting a tray with numerous little slices of different kinds of cake, I choose the tray with them all. The single portion of cake arrives for Taka and Salute and ten pieces of cake for me, plus a cup of American coffee each. I do thus with my fork and the orgy of cake is finished. They are still halfway through their only piece, or rather, little slice. The couple manage to lower their fork so many times and bring it up to their mouth with something on it that I am amazed at their skill and their love of detail, of crumbs. It cannot have been easy for Salute to adapt herself to these infinitesimally little pieces; peasant girls are greedy and devourers of compensatory sweets, she must have spent exactly nine years to reach this rhythmic and gastro-intestinal symphony with him. Certain mouthfuls one learns only either in a concentration camp or with a view to a marriage which makes of frugality an art to defy the state of conflict between finite matter and infinite time. There is a silent musicality about the way they peck at intervals in unison. The bill arrives, I blink a little at the peach-coloured furnishings, an extremely dear colour. We go out into the air which I shall call open out of laziness. The sky is a chaotic tangle of electric cables and poles and cups of dark green glass and signs and long strips, and looks like a prisoner who has hung out his washing in his cell. The drizzle, the sky darkening and the signs lighting up, drip in impure colours.

In Mitsukoshi, down in the food department. A great stir of male and female salespersons offering at each step snacks of raw herring, dried seawed, dried eel, steamed eel, Chinese mush-rooms, rice dumplings, dried anchovies cut in half, quartered eggplants as black as pitch, gleaming little biscuits, so after the sweet I throw myself on the antipasti and say 'Arigatô!' at each stall. Meantime I am comparing some prices, trying to find adequate expressions of amazement: a melon a hundred thou-sand lire, an apple four thousand, a mandarin two thousand five hundred, a pear thirty-three thousand, beef twenty thousand a kilo; it may even have been whisked around in beer to remove the fat, but not even sacred cows cost as much in India – I don't mean to kill but to keep them on young carrots and salad. What wonderful prices, what wonderful prices! – the adjective 'wonderful' is the only one that comes to mind.

I leave my two extremely nice chaperons at the entrance to the underground, I tell both of them to think again, that marriage is not all cherry blossom and Buddhist temples. It seems to me that before settling down in Tokyo a woman from Brescia ought to know that even Cracow risks being more amusing for shopping and flirting, and in the farewell smile of both of them there is a shadow of obvious second thoughts. I get into the train duly accompanied and duly instructed because either I get out at the right station or not at all. It is rush hour in which everyone has come out of their work places and the pedestrian subways or those in the underground release and swallow twelve thousand expressionless people passing through at the same rate. I am the only Westerner in the convoy, and not even by mistake do I come across a single glance on the same trajectory as my own.

Having arrived again in Shinjuku I cross streets and lanes in the evening. I ought to go back to the hotel and get in touch with my cousin Modesto who has been living here for ten years, and instead I once again try the descent towards something living, however touristy, and fleetingly astonished. I stop to smoke a cigarette on a low wall, I watch the employees with grey suits and briefcases who swarm like schoolboys in grown-up uniforms, I sit in a café asking myself whether I or they exist least: I am not made to exist for nothing. I go into a junk shop simply to strike up a conversation with some assistant. They do not talk English, they bow twice, once at the entrance and one where you get your change, and I think there is no more original way of telling people to piss off. The notices are in Roman characters only where there is something to buy, the rest look like a host of little gnomes huddled together in Indian file or in flight. Now more than ever behind the multicoloured plastic lanterns I feel more strongly the smell of secret sex for money, of unmade beds with sheets of tattered paper, of women with a delicate gamut of gestures in the extremely complicated rite of a hand-job which has to look like something else, the smell of ponces and perhaps a thread of smoke with a trace of opium rising from a linoleum stairway – and then it is impossible to be mistaken: in the two telephone booths in the immediate vicinity of a bus-stop there are labels stuck up with the telephone numbers and the corresponding little faces of blonde Heidis or other caricatures of female characters from animated cartoons, and the instructions in characters which are already less mysterious. I make for the park in front of the Plaza where for three minutes today I saw a band of employees bending and twisting and then they disappeared. The noise of running water, empty benches, a tramp with an absent look in garments which give the feeling of being frozen and stiff, his beard with a parting in the middle which gives him a saintly look, an old woman taking an incredible dog for a walk.

At night I wake up not altogether with a start, lulled by a rustle which is like the wind – impossible, the windows are hermetically sealed and cannot be opened. The lamp in the ceiling swings a little, then the whole bed moves a little towards the bathroom – I find myself at 25 degrees on the 25th floor of a skyscraper. This is the second earthquake in less than twenty-four hours! 'It's a bad habit then!' I say out loud, turn over and fall asleep. But about half an hour later there's a little shock which is nastier than all the others, I put on the light and take the little *livre de chevet* – entitled *It's A Good Idea to Glance at This*: 'Do not smoke in bed.' All right. 'The Keio Plaza Hotel was conceived of with every precaution to confront catastrophes; in the case of fire it is fitted with doors and doorframes with tin sheeting, with special stairs for evacuating the building, with fire detectors, with automatic sprays to extinguish the fire set in the ceiling. The fire station in Tokyo has actually given us a prize for excellence. If there is a fire, at the same time as the sprays begin to function the fire sends a signal to the emergency centre. In the case of an earthquake, the resilient structure of the building is capable of resisting a seismic intensity three times greater than that of the Great Disaster of Kanto in 1923, so there is no need to allow oneself to be seized by panic. Welcome to Japan.' There remains the question mark which in the midst of the night I allow to float out from the window over the city which is sleeping even if shaken: has there ever been a tremor two or three times stronger than that of 1923 to see if human, but above all technical, satisfaction follows these just hopes?

Modesto married a Japanese woman called Shoko – I remember at the beginning my aunt Romualda and her difficulty in calling her by her name in front of the neighbours, she thought she was calling her stupid (for in Italian her name means just that). The Nippo-Italian couple has a daughter and a son whose photos have gone the rounds of the relatives from since they were born up to a few months ago. Modesto is an intellectual passion of my youth: considered a genius by the clan, son of a Carabiniere NCO from near Como and one of my mother's sisters, he had completed his studies thanks to one bursary after the other and when he left university he had on his table sixty-four offers of work from the biggest Italian and foreign firms. He immediately chose the Turin firm of Diotallevi (literally God-care-for-you) and since then he has not changed god. When he was at the University I, seven years younger, was clearing the tables at the Hotel Terminus in Milan and was someone who exuded poison. Some years earlier Modesto had given me a collection of comics as a present and I had read it twenty times one after another. Then one day he turned up at the Hotel Terminus and asked for me: I was eating my nails to the quick, writing poetry and pieces. That day I had the afternoon off (in those times there was a free halfday every week) and he took me with him up into the mountains; he stretched out to take the sun and do his odd 'isometric' exercises (the kind that at that time people did in their offices, placing their hands or feet against something and pressing with all their might). I wandered off, captivated by a flora I had not seen before and some kind of little fruit which I did not know until I showed them to him and he told me they were blueberries and that they were good to eat. Since he was reading – he was always reading, if he was not reading he was studying; he never referred to women nor did I refer to men to him – I continued to nibble and swallow them, forgetting every other pressing matter and even myself. I have been grateful to him all my life, even if there were three things about him which I did not go along with: that he was ashamed of his own mother, who was illiterate and simple like mine; that he never allowed me to get a word in, neither then or any other time; and the third most serious of all, the definition he gave me one day of intelligence: 'Intelligence is the ability to interpret the needs and the demands of society and satisfy them' – he did not add: 'before someone else gets there first' because he was too much of a priest to expose himself to as much as a suspicion of craftiness. However, I saw in him the purity of the scholar and he vaguely seemed to me one of the few people who, when talking to me with a certain attention, assumed a certain intelligence in me which made up for the diffuse mythomania of my way of life, which was drawn to lost causes, the opposite of him, who aimed so rationally at hitting the mark with his undoubted energies, which naturally sought the approval of the élite of high finance applied to technological development. While in no way despising ordinary people I felt that his consciousness of his own superiority (which was subject to iron rules) led him to be a democrat out of tolerance and a basic sense of human weakness, the correctness of a person who can permit himself anything except outspoken Fascism. Moreover Modesto, like me, read and spent all his meagre university allowance on books – even literary books. He was a little less good-looking than my brothers, but like them was tall with sharp eyes behind his glasses, the look of someone who has eyes only to carry out radiography. My two brothers' eyes have always been dreamy, a little glassy, with a watery look that is poetically pastoral and which in fact hides the real insensitivity of their characters. Modesto fascinated me beyond words, my brothers did not. In them I saw the infantile nature of the instincts, in Modesto the desire for order. Today when all the boys have eyes like Modesto and no one the eyes of my brothers – who lost by the wayside their desires and emotions without being able to do anything about it – eyes like my cousin's no longer interest me.

I rang him hoping he hadn't got fatter just like my brothers who spread themselves round the only sins to which they are reduced: those of greed. And I am fated to bring my body to the same state, for it is stuffed with the psychic flab of accidia which stands guard over a fridge that is opened and closed every time the fairytale of life comes to a halt – and it comes to a halt as much as five times in an hour at night.

'You've struck a good day, I'm not working today, I am coming to get you, tell me where you want to go. Even though it is Saturday I have to look in at the office at about three to pick up some faxes, then either you come for dinner here or we go out, as you prefer. Tomorrow on the other hand I have a delegation arriving from Turin – but late.'

'Any place is fine with me – I don't even know one. Hirohito has had his 300 ccs today too – '

' . . . it's no problem, I shall deal with it quickly, if not there would be the theatre if you like but . . .'

'For goodness' sake, don't programme anything.' I chat away into the telephone now because later it might happen that I have only to listen.

'Oh, I don't follow these transfusions. I'll be there in half an hour.'

In the hall of the Plaza I see him coming towards me and thank him for his kindness as I embrace him; I had expected to see him with Shoko and a child.

'I'm sorry to take you away from your family on a Saturday – how are the children? And your wife?'

'The children are swimming and Shoko is where women should be – in the kitchen,' he remarks ironically.

I ask myself whether a Western wife would have been able to deal with this husband who works twelve hours a day, goes off to every corner of the earth for weeks, looks into the office on Saturday (and perhaps on Sunday) and truly does not even have a lover who would excuse his lust for business. He has got fat, or at least his chest and stomach have expanded in an abnormal manner; he vaguely resembles Perry Mason in television or a sumo wrestler. On the other hand, his face has remained the same, apart from the cheeks, puffy and full of small hairline veins, that is to say, in proportion he has become smaller. A man, one might say, without what is commonly called 'a life of his own', the man for any company chairman, the man who must be rock-hard in his job, the man whom very few out of some tens of thousands can keep up with, the man who out of the office is always deep in his work and so much the worse for anyone who doesn't want to realize this (a wife, for instance!), the man who is, in the end, an example for all and one whom all can end up hating were it not for his health, which allows him to affirm: 'Work isn't everything – it is something more' and never to have run up a day's absence in twenty years. And now in the car it is unthinkable to ask him private and confidential questions: he has already started to talk about subjects exclusively chosen by him without asking me whether they interest me or not, driving with unperturbed determination, careful to respect the traffic rules; entirely on purpose he almost runs into the back-wheel of a moped which, at a stop, tried to get in between him and another car. Quick comments.

'The Japanese are not intellectually brilliant, in fact all the most refined principles (viz. of hyper-technology) are discovered by we Europeans or the Americans, here they are simply applied on a large industrial scale. They haven't invented anything, the Japanese, neither hard nor soft ware. They are good at copying and at mass-production, but otherwise they are stupid and unable to think for themselves. Look how they drive – but for the fact that the road is in front of them it would only take one to drive off to one side for them all to follow. I like driving – just now I'm taking in what is happening sixty metres ahead, I anticipate the lights, I take in the passers-by, the arrows of the road signs, the acceleration and the brakes. It becomes a collective game. Apart from the damned motorcyclists who pop up on all sides and even invade the pavements, I anticipate everything. But I run them down without remission of the fine. Those that remain are still too many.'

At the temple of the goddess Kannon of Asakusa we take a long walk among booths and sellers of wax candles. 'Look, there is the counting house alongside; every temple has its fine administrative department, the monks work hard in there, everything has its price, pardons, the desire to be heard, thoughts for the dead. They sell little wooden tablets or paper tickets with your horoscope on them as if they were fried squid. They have arrived at the point of computerizing all three of their alphabets, up to three thousand kanji ideograms with the possibility of composing another four thousand in the word-processor, but they still have to believe in superstitions a thousand years old to justify the shitty life they lead. Look at the orderly way they are leaving the office where they issue good hope. And now they don't even have trees on which to hang their scraps of cloth with good wishes, they use plastic wire. Idiots. Then when something goes wrong in their programming there's a fine mass suicide. Does the husband die and there is no means of support? The wife takes the two kids and throws herself from the thirtieth floor or takes rat poison. Here the convention of non-solidarity rules: everyone for himself and everyone for no one else. Barbiturates & Co.'

I feel like saying to him: 'But do you realize that your children are at least half . . .' but I let it drop. Besides if someone talks so badly about the place where he lives and the people he has had at his side for ten years it is to exorcise the fact that he cannot do without it – and Brianza, where he has invested some savings, is his real bogey – not the little residential villa where he has the privilege of living and which is shut off from any kind of Japanese influence. As for me, I do not understand temples and don't want to see any more. But he takes me to another, more or less different, and like the previous one now built in reinforced concrete painted to look like wood, because the Japanese are fed up with having to rebuild the same temple every thirty years because wood rots but the tradition is preserved. There is not a scrap in all Japan that is original and the mania for restoring (because a man could not do without the history of the men with whom he no longer has anything to share) is the mania to restore an authentic copy.

'During the war, you know, they should have dropped the atom bomb not on Hiroshima but on Kyoto. They say it was an American general, a great connoisseur of Japanese art, who pointed out that to raze Kyoto to the ground would be like destroying Florence for Italy, or Rome. Go to Kyoto if you have time on the Shinkansen railway: you can go there and back in a day.'

I feel like telling him that the American generals are only snobs and see problems everywhere even where there is none, but obviously Modesto has already started up on another topic and I am not able to pay attention to him. It must also be his pleasure in speaking as much Italian as he likes – he has kept the most eloquent and precise expressions and no modern term is unknown to him – to impel him to this frenzy of information, which is very rich in details. Now he is talking to me about the annexation of Hokkaido, the island furthest to the north before Russia, about the Russo-Japanese war and about at least three dynastic periods all at the same time, and I feel like fainting: I hate culture! I hate people who let me know what they know out of disinterested pleasure in making me know as well. But I suffer a tornado of facts and only stretch out a little more in my seat, hoping that he understands that I am not such an urgent *programme*. But as usual my gratitude remains infinite because of the fact that he has put himself entirely at my disposal or put me entirely at his – my God, he seems like someone who only this morning removed a gag after half a century. I haven't even had time to tell him that his mother is with mine and that the over-seventy sisters at this moment are carding wool – on my mother's orders – and talking about what they will cook tomorrow. Each of them takes a year to visit the other, neither would ever want to leave her own house, so that the real sacrifice for both of them is not having convinced the other for the second time in succession that she has come and spent her holidays with the other. A tug-of-war and excuses and (presumed) aches and pains, which last for months, before – as every year – each has to abide by the convention of turn-and-turn-about. This matter seems tremendously more interesting to me than Pearl Harbor and so highly didactic on a strategic and military plane even for him, given all the head-scratching he must do to observe the international conventions and hierarchies.

At home, in a little villa among other little villas shut away in a park where ambassadors and airline directors live, we meet a man whose job is – Modesto informs me – to offer condolences. Ever since that plane crashed near the Maldives many months ago he has been going one by one round all the families of the passengers who plunged into the Indian Ocean with it; each of those who perished can have at least three condolences: one from the parents, one from the parents of the wife etc. If someone dies and has four children scattered across Asia this gentleman must visit them all and bring condolences and the apology of the airline which is flying a mourning flag.

Shoko is at home, just back from the hairdresser. She has the drawn smile of all wives who have seen their husbands on the day of the marriage and then never again. The walls are lined with books and the shelves are reinforced, and so is the ceiling weighed down by the tons of paper in the bedroom. As Modesto is going up to the first floor Shoko says to me: 'He keeps on buying books but he doesn't read them. It's a lot if he even looks through them.' My two second cousins arrive, plump and robust, and at once set themselves in front of the television with their mother. I bless the television because it does away with the obligation to hold a conversation, then Modesto offers photo-albums and shows me where he took Barbarella and Seiki in recent years: to Greece, to Texas, to Australia. The children come closer, curious and bored at one and the same time, and do not understand their father's tourist enthusiasm. They do not remember anything, they were too small. He insists on reminding them of this and that landscape; they shake their heads and go back to watching television. 'Oh, now I have to look in at the office, come on, then we shall come back for dinner . . .'

Once in the square where the firm is, Modesto exchanges a couple of words with the watchman and goes up without me. From its look you would imagine it was a dairy products firm or an old textile mill; nothing on the outside to make one think of the seat of a multinational. Perhaps that is why he did not insist that I come up into his office, because it will be tiny and ugly, no match for the post he occupies. He comes running down with two faxes in his hand: 'It's arriving tomorrow at six in the evening – the delegation – I have to go and meet them.' 'That's fine. Don't worry.' 'I'll organize an evening at the theatre with Shoko, who is always complaining that I never go anywhere with her. You can go with her.' He had thought of everything already. At supper the children eat with the greed of caged animals who know no other pastime, animals in a cage that is lined with cotton wool. Modesto asks them if they have done their maths and

English homework, then, since brother and sister go over to the television, conversation turns to the education one should give one's children to guarantee them 'a better future'; all the schools are private and very expensive here as elsewhere, but the expense is worth it for the results. 'Well, I don't believe much in education nor in the power of school, if you except certain depressing careers like the civil service. An ordinary school is more than sufficient, in any case it is life that decides, the stupidest are those who have studied abroad: they come back and with their *American* methods, which cause firms which were flourishing up to yesterday to fail. Here I don't know how it is.' And husband and wife are a bit upset to see that their financial sacrifice does not impress me and that I see in it rather the exploitation of their social neuroses than a real need of their children who, even if they are the children of industrialists or big managers, should have the right to be hairdressers or street-cleaners after a little compulsory schooling. I feel like adding an argument in their and my defence – will their heirs swot away to get on, and will the results be the same as those painted on your pale and anxious faces? Was it worth while? But nothing is ever worth while for anyone who looks behind him: everything is a waste of time, especially what has not even served to make us look back and shake our heads, disillusioned and incredulous, at the well-heeled and tortured vanity of the roles we have attained to.

The dinner is typically Italian, spaghetti al sugo and cutlets alla milanese, because Modesto has formally forbidden Japanese cooking and gets his supplies from a local trader – besides oil, parmesan cheese Italian wines, fresh *stracchino* amd even *mascarpone* as well. A man marries a Japanese woman, lives in Tokyo and, apart from a few antique pieces his wife wanted, recreates in his house and around him the hearth and the kitchen of an interior at Brianza. Modesto married a Japanese woman because he could not allow himself to make a mistake and made a dead set at a vestal instead of at an ordinary mortal; he has denatured her enough to create in her feelings of guilt worthy of the Milanese hinterland and now lives like a pasha; he knows that it is exactly *for ever* and that in any case she does not ask to exist –

she will never have time to become completely Milanese and demanding.

Taking me back to the hotel he adds the last touches to his contempt for the Japanese and their way of life. 'Why don't you get posted somewhere else?' I ask, and he says that for the good of the firm he cannot. And then for the children it is a heaven-sent gift to learn Japanese and English and Italian at the same time, the year 2001 takes off from here and Japanese will become an international language as English is today and Venetian was yesterday. 'But 2001 isn't here yet,' I say laughing. And wrong-footed for the first time, he has a sudden rethink, does not reply, clenches his jaws and then pulls his lips into a rather crooked smile. That is all I was able to say today: '2001 isn't here yet.' In itself it means nothing and like all upsetting truths is made of nothing. I run into my bedroom, tumble on to the bed and fall asleep at once on top of the little bag of books on Japan which Modesto recommended to me during our visit to three bookshops and which I shall never ever open. I do not even know if I shall be there tomorrow – just imagine whether I want to take on an *imprint* capable of lasting beyond the end of the century. How odd certain fathers are who manage to justify their own lives if they claim – through their children – to take possession of the future in which they themselves will not be. How absurd is the claim of the present to be an antechamber to a perpetual place somewhere in the future; if the place will never be there what are we all doing here waiting for a turn which does not exist and which we pretend to surrender politely to anyone else except ourselves? Is it not better to jump up and walk about wherever we like?

I go out – it is raining. I walk haphazard once again towards sex – a memory of other times, a spring which has lost its tension everywhere except in me, without peace, fortunately, who knows for how much longer. Then I take courage – although the signboard is as incomprehensible as any other I go downstairs covered with plastic raffia to see where they will take me – for a quarter of an hour I have been standing here under a gutter surmounted by a peeling lacquer dragon and have seen only men going up and down, as alike as a school of grey sharks with overnight bags under their fins. Once down I am just in time to see some clients choosing a porntape from a shelf, then the proprietor arrives and shows me the door and welcomes me uttering a 'Goodbye sir?' very drily.

The meritorious organization Madoguchi – which literally means 'come in by the window' – is that mistress of ceremonies to which we give the name of Mafia. A real parastatal power – untouchable, it makes and unmakes the necessary castles in the air of crime in a modern society of respectable people who, persisting in their naïve view of the taboo as something routine, succeed in elaborating desires and satisfactions only outside the law.

Were I a prostitute I would fight for my inalienable right to be taxed like any gentleman on the basis of very ordinary items of income and expenditure – the one always in a reactionary way exactly the same as the other, like an object and its image in a mirror. If you arrive in Japan without a specific relationship to rely on, you risk spending your time wondering if you are invisible or what on earth has happened. If you cannot get to first base with a Japanese person you will remain on every doorstep. The friendship network functions like the system of presents: you give me a present so that I give you one, you introduce a friend and I will introduce one to you and you will then introduce another to me and so on. It is difficult to get to know a Japanese person from scratch, very difficult, almost impossible; I who have no connections and perhaps did not even want one because of my craze for walking and nothing else, have in these days had a little *disinterested* chat only with an old Methodist lady who, seeing me on a little wall watching tens of thousands of human beings in and outside an underground station, addressed me (I was importuning an Indian there on the wall) to put in my hand a leaflet carrying propaganda for some sect and said to me: 'Come and see our church, it is very pretty,' and I said: 'But my dear, I have so many already in Italy if I felt like it!' But I was not cruel, of course she had a lot to do with foreigners because probably she had bored the pants off all Tokyo at their lunchbreaks sitting on the low walls eating sandwiches. Not only do I not understand anything about oriental culture, I don't even pretend that I find it important to understand it. I come to the point without effort –

and I stop there – of sharing the distress of Madam Butterfly who is so obstinately faithful to her Pinkerton: because having put up with that Yankee lieutenant she goes on for five years without losing anything. Suzuki – another faithful one – says too: 'If he does not return soon we are in a bad state.' Yet according to certain discreet information I have had from a Japanese teacher of French literature, today there is a whole group of Japanese women who from techno-macho acculturation embody Pinkerton's sadomasochistic character rather than that of little Butterfly; for he has been reduced to pure slavery, what with coercion to interstellar industrial production and the labyrinths of the bedroom and to slavering for a whipping and frustration at the hands of the cruel masterful woman – really cruel, not playing a game as in the specialist German brothels. A recent number of *Time* focused on the reason for the economic supremacy of the Japanese: they have – among themselves, strictly among themselves – an intense and happy(?) sexual life which is among the most frenetic in the history of the world. It may be the seaweed, it may be the radioactivity, it may be the raw fish and grated turnip, it may be that because they do everything in a hurry they have to do the same thing more and more often to convince themselves that they aren't doing something else, but it really seems that, with not infrequent bloodletting, they enjoy making love every quarter of an hour in their free time. All that is left for me is to go back to the hotel and hope for another shock to fill out the day.

'I'm coming to get you before I rush off to the airport and we'll take the children to Akihabara in the district for domestic electrical appliances,' Modesto tells me next day. 'Barbarella wants to spend the first money she has earned in her life right away – she wants to buy herself a Walkman with headphones,' and I say, struggling to get back my joky code: 'Surely you didn't get her to be a part-time geisha?' Nothing doing: 'She went and played a street urchin in *Turandot* at the Scala – three days as an extra!' 'Ah, and did you go too?' 'Yes, with Shoko and Seiki, but because we had free tickets. I don't spend four hundred thousand lire a head for a seat – I solve riddles myself for nothing.' In Akihabara Barbarella at once falls in love with a little pink box, but it seems to be too dear; her father advises against it. We end up by rushing around like a whirlwind in four different skyscrapers until we find more or less the same box as before, while Seiki looks at the latest electronic games and wants to give a friend a birthday present: he looks at some plastic monsters, some model cars of the future, videogames, and decides on a little black clockwork car which costs a fortune and annoys his father. In the car once more, the two children fall asleep. It is no doubt because of their extremely laborious digestive processes; they look to me as if they had put on a couple of kilos since yesterday. From their mother they have taken only their almond eyes. It's odd, but I feel neither liking nor dislike for them, they look to me like hand-reared children, tame, overfed, superfluous – an alibi. They have gone round half the world and lack any scale of values to know what position they occupy *here* – they mix only with children of their own class, dance, swim, play tennis or make pottery, every hour of their week is planned a week in advance, they play games where you don't get dirty. Shoko has the job of taking them about and picking them up; apart from that she is bored at home, working away for the three of them, is interested in interior decoration, has some knowledge of tea. Neither she nor Modesto has many Japanese acquaintances – he, of course, has no acquaintances except at work: if a meeting crops up at the last minute – when he has perhaps just got back from the office – he is off again like lightning; if they have to go to their in-laws for dinner or an afternoon of relaxation he invents a thousand excuses, says he prefers to stay at home and read. 'But he falls asleep right away,' Shoko confides to me while, as arranged, we are going in to see the Kabuki theatre where they are doing *Chusingura*, a drama full of wariors and noblemen who kill and commit suicide, set in 1702, a slaughter in slow motion which even today can kill the incautious Western spectator who isn't used to it. We went in at eight and at about eleven Shoko in a black costume with a string of pearls, and a somewhat embarrassed look, wakes me with a slight jab with her elbow and I have time to see that the sword which began to be drawn three hours ago is at last on the point of leaving its sheath. At night I wake up completely and deliberately shout, overcome by sleep but even more by Kabuki: 'Noh, Kabuki Noh!'

Hirohito continues to have tantrums – there! he's breathing his last – not the last, the last but one. Another 500 cc of blood. He is using up the available supplies, I can see them, the nostalgic samurai with wives and offspring who instead of signing loyal addresses now offer their arms, never mind the blood group. Hirohito laps it all up and with what is not suitable for his royal stomach he gargles. The important thing is to shed it.

I shall go to Kyoto, although I would rather be going to a porn-cinema to take in the latest adventures of the porn-star Marina Lothar. I take the supersonic train which does six hundred kilometres in less than three hours and after a few kilometres the waitresses arrive and make little ceremonious speeches about the varieties of American chewing gum and the little bars of chocolate-coated rice, then it is the turn of the guard who stands at attention and he too holds forth in falsetto. My neighbour has not even looked at me, I look out towards Fujiyama for a while, a while in the direction of the remote possibility of a conversation. Then since, while opening the little paper container for milk, I splash him he gives a start and gives me a big smile and we begin to speak, but after ten minutes of inhuman work we give up. I don't know a word of Japanese nor he of English.

At Kyoto there must be three hundred temples. I go into one and come out of another, I arrive at the imperial castle, then the previous imperial castle, both shut, thank God, so I don't have to visit them. I sit on a bench in the central imperial palace, take off my shoes, make a face that says ciao! to the blister on my big toe and then put on my socks again. And now that I am here? The temple of the goddess Kannon: it is more or less on the way back, near the station. I go into a little restaurant, ten minutes later – and there are two other customers besides me – I manage to acquire a certain physical substance and the waitress comes to take my order, which one usually does by getting up, going to the window and pointing to the dishes reproduced in plastic. An unpleasant goo arrives, I take advantage of it to open the map of the city with all the tourist attractions: the girl with the electric black hair which could reach down into her neighbour's soup, so long and wandering is it, shakes her head. No, she does not know where the temple of the goddess Kannon is: then I open a proper guide, I show her the interior of the temple with its three hundred statues all the same and all gleaming with gold. The girl is more puzzled than ever, she quickly smiles, no she really wouldn't know: if she had known English and, but this I rule out, were interested she would have asked me what all these little figures with tits and pierced pointed hats were. I go out, turn a corner, and there it is – the temple of Kannon: which is thirty metres away as the crow flies from the restaurant and the silly girl, although not directly opposite. And when I insisted she had even shown the guide around the kitchen! Obviously I don't go into the temple, I turn around and timidly go into a little shop to bargain for a fan, to see if I manage to experience the thrill of a little meeting with human beings. I meet humanoids: one hundred and ten thousand of them. I take the Shinkansen again. I shall fan myself.

On the telephone Modesto says to me: 'Yesterday I went to meet the three people from Turin, had a meeting, they left again this morning. Did you have a good sleep, eh?'

'What do you mean – they can't have even had time to rest and they're off again?'

'They'll rest in the plane. Why not?'

'But you don't rest in a plane from the fatigue due to the previous plane.'

'It's normal,' he says in a neutral way, and I realize that I am talking to an ancient and authentic samurai, to the only remaining entirely Japanese samurai left, to my cousin.

'I wanted to say to you yesterday – did you feel the earthquake shocks?' I ask him in case it was the fruit of my nocturnal imaginings, since in bed I mentally make a few investments with my amazingly little cash and at midnight usually find myself unable to decide betwen suicide and property investments.

'Yes, of course, really big ones. Every sixty years there is an earthquake somewhere that razes everything to the ground. Give or take ten years. It seems that it is Tokyo's turn this time,' and I haven't time to say: 'We ought . . .' before he adds: 'We should be there.'

She's at home there, my Mistress Maria, and now after what are more than four decades since we went through that business of bringing us into the world, that pretext that joined her placenta to my blood seems too distant to bother about. We decided to drop it and have put a stone on top of it. I mean that, if there could not be points of contact between us as generating mother and degenerate son, since I became a famous writer and she, who authored me, mother of the writer too, our life as a couple has become not only possible but interesting, and sometimes I have the feeling that she begins to tell stories to give a hand with my sterility, almost as if to make sure that my prolific production continues to be less suspect. She knows obscurely that novels are also made up from things you can't know all about right away, especially if they are things about other people, and especially even more so if they are things to do with herself, and seeing that she is certainly not a woman who indulges in confessions or goes in for gossip it is never a mother that talks but a pulpit or a pyre that stands out from the false haze of memories. A woman who hates all nostalgia and who before saying anything jolly has calculated every syllable and every intonation, has foreseen not just any sort of expression but a *form*: and she wants to make a big impression and often to make a lot of money.

Since up to a few years ago I had no other title than 'son', and moreover son 'who goes on the prowl at night', imagine the profound contempt where I was concerned – abnormal, with no job, no money, no future, the blackest of black to have given to the light of day. Instead now it wouldn't only be she who would have a role (which, I believe, above all is beginning to stink for her and to be seen with all the violence suffered because of it) but I would have one too. So she has ended up by considering me worthy to be on a level with herself, with her age-old dignity as an austere daughter of the land who was even capable in certain circumstances of laughing and making others laugh. Now, for some time, the clashes have been less frequent and bloody, we consider each other with more curiosity, the documentary cunning of investigators on constant and secret missions, with before us always the same investigative plan. And these two guests stuck there in the kitchen chat away peacefully and often without any inhibitions apparently but in reality using even the dent on an old cooking-pot or the recent tuft of hair left to me in my comb as elements of counter-espionage. They chat, but without taking on excessive familiarity. Only certain confidences are possible and only at the right moment: the person who listens to you at dinner-time could be your enemy at supper – this too a matter of calculation.

The day is strewn with legal nuggets which she drops in sparingly and with great shrewdness – Mistress Maria makes no reckless moves but dishes out justice no less than memories and proverbs, some of them so old that I have never heard them before. Recently, referring to a husband who left his wife and daughter to take up with a 'ne'er-do-well' she passed judgement that he was an idiot because 'the great thing about skinning a cat is not to make it scream'. She does not pardon anyone who puts at risk a social reputation, a contract, for something so base and fleeting as 'an attraction', which in any case lasts a short time, too short, and does a whole lot of harm to a whole lot of other people who are not involved and says that the real madmen who really get away with it are the ones who know what 'discretion' is, not the ones that do everything in public. In this she is a depository of a way of thinking about *decency* which is much more virile than many males who run a race on the mare of *passion*. In any case the words 'feeling', 'emotion' and 'heart' are not part of her daily but age-old vocabulary: she knows that such words exist, but to her they seem like weaknesses or tics of glib tongues which are all right on TV, not outside of it, and she uses the expression 'to have a passion' or 'to feel passion' for the dreaded moment of leaving a person, through death for example, never for the desire to grow close to someone for any reason, which in any case is 'always backwards and forwards and fine for him but you are left with a big belly'.

Thus the day before yesterday, at coffee time, six in the morning, she is more chatty than usual because she had found three hundred and forty thousand lire in a pocket of my trousers and, having decided to keep the money, did not raise her eyes from her bowl. One would have to describe that bowl, which must be fifty years old, the relic of all her wakings, to guess that Mistress Maria was once a little girl: a little coffee to reproduce the old poverty – not even her own but her ancestors actually, I imagine, because she was well off – soaked up by an abnormal amount of toast which overflows from the chipped galleon of her youth. And she crushes the bread against the side, crushes it with the same decisiveness with which she would break the neck of a rabbit, in order that that little drop of coffee, under pressure, will moisten the remaining bread – there is always too much – and finally she manages to swish about a whole spoonful of coffee without the slightest crumb of bread. And one ought to see how she gathers up that one spoonful of pure liquid, of wealth, luxury, play, lightheartedness, eve of St Lucy, a whole sea of intoxicating nectar: then she says, with a glance – a sky-blue one – as if she were halfway there: 'Once I saw the King.'

I looked at her terribly curiously, as I do every time that she begins to talk about 'carriages', for example.

'Where did you see him, which one?'

'Victor Emmanuel the Second or Third, at the Mille Miglia car race, in 1921. It was in September. I was eight, he was on a stand – he was as small as me. But the Queen wasn't with him. Nor Mussolini, but Mussolini came to the Mille Miglia later. Each time the peasants, at the end of summer, went mad with ladders to paint in the biggest letters they could and as high up as possible "Silence!" on the fronts of the houses and farmsteads. All the stands on the parabolic curve were put up on my father's land.'

I stay with my spoon in midair, amazed at the precision of detail and that she was able to say 'parabolic' flowlessly whereas she calls the Capitol 'Capriol'.

'The track went on towards Santa Giustina too, then it came to the sports field at Montichiari. It was eighteen kilometres long and everywhere there were bales of straw with the people behind them on the road. Under the stands there were the kitchens because they served food. They made salamis, tripe, pastasciutta, so much grilled stuff. They had to take the stand down every year, the moment the Mille Miglia were over they stole everything, from the beams to the seats, you know the green ones that folded. My father was host to the wine merchants, his friends who dealt in milk and flour in town, and then there was always someone just born to be baptized, and the person who had the baptism was always a very important gentleman.'

I felt that the story was taking as long as the surrender of her booty, and I always found fascinating in her the narrative layout of the material, without frills, strong, dry. She puts in a personal comment only when it is unavoidable, like a hinge between one pause and the next. A pause can even last some days, and in fact this morning she returned to the theme, producing with the most impartial magical methods some daguerreotypes – never seen before, because my mother has an iron memory and has never once told the same episode, also because *before* she would have considered it an unpardonable frivolity 'to confide'. But now she is anxious to let it be understood that, in spite of work in the fields from the age of seven – she went to school for four months in all – the housework with ten brothers and sisters, then the husband, the sons, the inns with kitchen and rooms, she too had had a *personal* life just as good as so many other 'once upon a times'. When I say 'before' I mean up to four years ago, because she was only seventy then and was still not sure if she was really old enough to let herself go and talk about private things with someone who was, after all, always a son. And then this morning she says – the business of the money is still not cleared up – while she was mixing filling for ravioli which she gives away to relatives who come from as far as Deseo to take them home:

'My mother laid a white tablecloth even in the morning, even for the servants. She treated them like her own children and on the sly gave them all a dowry – also to their daughters, just as with me and my sisters. I never once heard her complain, apart from labour pains. She said one oughn't to get too close to men, otherwise they don't respect you any more. That was all our education about this sex that is everywhere these days. We were lucky. Your father when he was wooing me on the farm at home was with me but surrounded by three of my brothers. But we weren't innocents either, what do you think? Between a mass and a funeral or a wedding we also managed to find five minutes. Then we got married. Now he is dead. If I really think about it I loved him for a while but it all lasts a little while, too little. When you have nothing to eat . . . you eat love for a while but then . . . then you have eaten him up too. Help me to fold the ravioli.'

'And your grandmother?' I ask her; I know so little about her. 'Ah, my grandmother I worshipped. She was tall, thin, wore a big petticoat under her skirt. I was always holding on to her apron. She made me a doll once from her long drawers from when she was young. I followed her everywhere, even when she went into the garden to do her business. I stood near her and she would say to me. "You'll hear some fine ones" and she would laugh. I held my nose and waited till she got up from the beams over the privy. The privy had bushes all round. New bushes, new shit, she said each year. She had light eyes too, she was always smiling just a little; she spoke Venetian, every so often she called on some saint from paradise. She was proud and wanted to buy the land. When she was still a tenant once she turned on the Owner saying to her "Countess of my two . . ." because they were almost putting her and the whole family off the farm; I had to wait a week before I was married to learn what she meant. Once she had even been on a railroad, from Vicenza to Padua, to see the saint . . . She didn't call it a train, she called it a tram. That had been for her honeymoon. She never saw anything else, like me.'

And now why do I remember the noise of the door that gives on to the little terrace, the door that banged shut this morning? We always leave it open, usually. This morning a neighbour called, Giovanna, who since she lives just down from us comes dashing in with her *manicaretti all'origano*. She gets up at dawn to make them. I think that if she counts them there must be a hundred. I heard the dialogue between the two women but Giovanna was in time to hear me singing at the top of my voice, I always do so the moment I open my eyes. Usually they are not songs but mad shouts in a bass voice, or in falsetto like when I shout 'We are women!' which doesn't mean much but it amuses me. Giovanna says: 'He's happy this morning, Aldo, listen to him singing,' and my mother, noticing that the door is open, running to shut it, probably pretending nothing is happening. 'The bird in the cage sings out of passion or rage.' I had never heard that proverb before, and even this 'passion' doesn't mean a passion of love but a dull pain. If I asked her why she shut the door she would say: 'Who – me?' and would not understand. Much of my lost instinct has gone to find refuge in her. And now she adds: 'She was called Maria too, Maria Regina.'

I left her the three hundred and forty thousand lire.

I am at Milan Central Station on my way to Rome on my own business. But here is the famous Giannina, one of the first to have *that* operation! She is speaking to a male jacket laid out carefully alongside her. She says to the jacket: 'You must think about it in time. Take your teeth, for example. If I had put aside something for the future every day you wouldn't be toothless now, you have to think about it while the caries isn't there yet. And the house – if I'd been good you would have a roof now, instead you wander about under the tunnels or come here to ask me for help. But I can't chew for you and my bed is a camp-bed, and, Gianni, two of us – at our age.'

The escalator on the right is under repair, the crowd waiting to go up the one that is working reaches almost to the entrance. Giannina, who has lived for years in the bowels of the station, arranges her transparent blue plastic hood and continues: 'The trains, the trains are wonderful but they hurt your back a bit. And then there aren't any unused platforms any more, you've seen that too, they're getting rid of them all, in any case they are out of use and every time you need a leak you have to get a day ticket otherwise they don't let you through. And woe betide if you wash in the wash hand basins . . . It's not like it used to be . . . If we had . . . Here, do you want a pad? I found it this morning, it's almost new, you can manage until the evening without changing it. He pisses himself at his age. It's the bladder – I was always telling you but you never listened to me.'

A few metres away on the icy travertine bench three Southerners are handing each other watches; they turn them over and over, one of them pulls out a little chain, a bracelet.

'Not that it's bad here – you see so many people going up and up, goodness knows where they come down. But of course you being so short-sighted, and glasses today, my dear, cost an eye. If instead of drinking you had taken a job, a taxidriver, say, do you know how much a taxidriver makes? Look at him! Always going to and fro, in and out of the arches, a Toy Town. But you don't see anything, Gianni, you see nothing. You have the lining hanging out and as for your laundry . . .'

'Shut up, you old cow!' shouts one of the three with the day's jewels.

'Do you hear them, do you hear them? All Libyans, Southerners, they have taken over Milan. What, me a racist? Do you know how often they have taken my shopping-bag? With nothing to put in their stomachs, vagabonds, tramps, thieves. The young people today. Are you listening to me or not? If only I hadn't been so idle, lazy, now I would have a fine beaver fur and you a new jacket . . .'

Every so often she begins to laugh, craning her neck, like a little girl. Then she stretches out her diaphanous hands on to her little bags overflowing with stuff. She takes a nail-file and with the air of a great lady adjusts her colourless dressing-gown.

'This evening I am making myself beautiful, for you, Gianni, we'll go to the Teatro Nuovo. I don't know what to put on, you would look good in a Prince of Wales check with a dark tie. Eh but you can't afford the theatre and I can't keep a man, it wouldn't be proper . . . I shall go alone, I shall find an escort, there! Why don't they have a train for going to the theatre? But of course, stupid, it's called the underground. How are your feet? Still sore? It's the gout that makes them come out of the shoes. Ha ha! That's good. You're not laughing? Can't you be just a little bit nice . . . Gianni, hey, Gianni, what varnish shall I put on? My God, I'm late . . .'

Suddenly she pulls up her sleeves, takes off her dressing-gown, underneath she has a puke-pink jumper, off with that too, she takes the jacket, slips it on, and in its place drops with a certain careless elegance her feminine jumper. She coughs, puts on a loud voice: 'Signorina Giannina, allow me. I wouldn't like to intrude . . . I see that you have no front teeth. Allow me. Gianni Godot, Godo to my friends. I have been waiting so long . . .'

In Rome the business is no longer altogether mine. The weekly *Epoca* buys part of it after a telephone call: 'Why don't you go to confession and then say what it is like?' What a bloody awful idea: of all that I possess only my 'sins' are ill-gotten gains.

At the Iglesia National de Argentina in Piazza Buenos Aires, at half-past ten on Saturday 3 December there is no one. I run my eyes over the blue and white flags of the country, which since yesterday has once again come under military pressure, and go away relieved. It is not easy to go to confession after not doing so for thirty years, and to do so out of ignorant curiosity is harder still. Besides I can send up an institution because of the sacrosanct right to state how certain sacraments function these days, but I don't feel like sending up the unfortunate confessor who, at the right moment, will find himself in the way of my heedless blasphemy. Nor do I go along with having to reel off amazing nonsense to put him fully at his ease: I have been thinking about it since yesterday but I can find no sin in me, neither in terms of the Church nor of my conscience. To invent them doesn't excite me. The pantomime of an act of contrition which I do not feel for sins I do not have does not excite my sense of duty if applied with a minimum of seriousness: investigation on the spot. I find it repugnant to invent, there are already too many Goody Two-Shoes with cultural columns, well written and abstractly free from any contamination with 'reality'. I am not interested in a scoop on God. I will go and stick my nose in, seeing that I have one and that it is more important than any incense from a writer's desk. But no caricatures.

I begin to wander about looking for another church, clenching my teeth because of the pain which has afflicted my sciatic nerve for two weeks – what a coincidence! I am going to defy God limping, which is already a way of asking him for mercy, and that annoys me a lot. But it is fate that even in Rome, when you look for it, you do not find a sacrament within a radius of a kilometre – I am tired, by now I am dragging my right leg. The district is very quiet, there is no traffic, the weather is good and my only wish is to go back to the hotel and lie on my bed: if I concentrate, I see more clearly that I shall never be able to see what I do not want to see. But it is useless, I settle down on two chairs in a bar, I drink my umpteenth coffee and all I see in the depths of my soul is a crème caramel round which I make a sort of knot in my handkerchief to remind me of gluttony and the sin that goes along with it. Certainly I would be tempted to start off with: 'Father, I haven't had it up me today again. Given the distance covered is that not a sin?' but I am not sure that it would sound really like a call for help and perhaps a confessor needs this agreed signal in order to hand out his sense of solidarity. I really do not need anyone, any longer, in any sense – I wish only to work so as to be just economically independent enough for me to stay shut up at home alone for the rest of my days. Anyone who does not set up a working relationship with me sets up nothing else. To hell with humanity and its monstrances of stupidity and crudity – including the sexual kind. I don't deny that I should like to talk to someone. But in the end, if I am not mistaken, I must arrive at an 'act of contrition'. Change the subject. I grope about here and there, I push and pull, but sin does not pop out.

Yesterday, with a determination which filled me with admiration, I ordered back to some country or other – Yugoslavia or Hungary, I imagine – four gypsies in a row who took turns to get alms while I was sitting reading on a step. I too have the right to walk about sometimes; it is too easy always to play the antiracist and confine oneself to handing out a miserable sum. And all these twenty-year-old beggars about the place with their nice placards at their feet written in capital letters, who ask for money for the train to go home – but what if they don't even have a house! And what use is a house at twenty? There are other people's – it has always been like that! And all these young Polish women with their white complexions armed with rolls of toilet paper at the traffic lights – can it be that they are unable to think up something more enticing in order to make a living on a grand scale? A little bodily prostitution chases away so many of these whims and can only do them good for the rest of their lives. Young people today are so twisted and already respectable that they cannot even score tricks . . . By thinking and thinking I arrive at a kind of sin – the contempt of the sour and lame libertine – but it tastes too much of the boudoir for me. No.

I started to walk again, I have at my disposal another quarter of an hour of lumbar autonomy, a real calvary. Telephone in a booth torn out, telephone in a bar with the notice 'Out of order' – I go back to the hotel. I have always been so involved with myself that I am not familiar even with the commonest feelings: I know neither envy nor jealousy, good bases for committing an almost infinite gamut of sins, many of them mortal. Too proud to have robbed, to astute to have killed – even if, in the latter case, I have regretted it, and the suspicion that I invented the astuteness to hide from myself the cowardice of not having done so. There are so many people who should be done away with and no one would notice – beginning with them . . .

'Near where you are,' says someone I know on the phone, 'in Piazza Ungheria they confess non-stop,' he tells me in the same way as those in the know pass on to each other the new places where people are on the game. I get up from my bed, drag myself down the stairs, try to find my bearings out in the street when a particularly murderous pang stops me short and makes me give up once more paying this absurd tribute to Signor Pope. I turn round, go up to my room again, try some moves from isometric gymnastics, massage the place with painkilling ointment, but the pain is already moving elsewhere, playing cat-and-mouse with my attempts to dislodge it. There must have been ten, but I don't think I can remember more than a couple; the last time I allowed a priest to challenge my freedom of spirit, which was anti-dogmatic and anti-ideological, with his commandments, I was ten years old.

On this subject – there is a circle of gay priests around Brescia and Cremona who confess to each other their weakness for a young gerontophilic policeman who approaches them on the road, naturally, and gets together with them in the sacristy. But I don't want to start off with the sins of the flesh – apart from those of the people who breed hormonized calves the others have more or less disappeared. Human flesh is all tinned too these days; a man is more likely to give you botulism than the clap. In a leap I dress again, I pretend not to notice the piercing pain or the curly hair which has come out of my left nostril and which wasn't there this morning: it must be the Devil peeping out. But growing is not a sufficient sin, it is barely venial, even if everything suddenly becomes hairy and painful – the non-acceptance of the fact of growing old, of having to die, that seems to me to be a sin worthy of the exorcist. But Moses does provide for it – in those days they lived for ages, there in the Bible, and died only because the chroniclers wanted to get on with the story. I arrive in Piazza Ungheria clenching my jaws. The church is shut. I let myself fall on to the steps, I contemplate a mammoth piece of shit under a low palm stuffed with plastic bags, I read the posters under the doorway arch: the 'With Us' movement invites everyone to the 'Floral Homage to Mary Queen of the World'. The space in front of the church is a parking place like any other. At one in the afternoon the light is full of twilight and I watch it for a little as if it were a procession in pink and gold, but after a single instant I see only traffic lights, cars, Polish and African windscreen-cleaners who wink to this or that driver and who, while the light is red, come on to the pavement to squeeze out the sponge of the long-handled mop. They sell packets of paper handkerchiefs, offering them with a certain grace; they no longer insist, they have learned a certain technique of approach for the metropolitan nomadic market. And if it had been open and if I were now kneeling in a confessional – presuming that I manage to assume that inhuman position – what could I tell him to get it over with? And how could I play my part, finally, without thereby 'pretending'?

What must be underlined is my strong sense of smell as a recalcitrant; of two churches, one is deserted, the other is not open for services. I have no more time for a third, I have an appointment – the usual swindling film-people who catch me without even being smart enough to get out of me something of myself at 'their' price – so my business is becoming nobody's business.

The only thing is to confess that I can't go on with it – can't invent everything from the ground up, I repeat, in a comically paradoxical style, with the scapegoat priest all sulky and shocked and me confessing the wonders of the world. No. And then I cannot pretend to myself to believe in a 'sin' washed clean by the Church and not in public; it would be an aesthetic prostitution with devastating effects on the rest of the conception and completion of all my work. I shall telephone, I shall invent an excuse – I shall say that for me a communion wafer is not sufficiently enigmystical.

Sunday 4 December, at a quarter to six I am already up – it

might as well be an event rendered solemn at least by the place. St Peter's is gleaming with frost under the ambered light of the lamps and the door of the taxi is the only noise to echo in so much empty space – apparently; but down there is a tiny figure of a lay sister with her hair coming out of her cowl, a little shopping bag, a quick step, and then another little figure in black, midnight black, the uniform of a carabiniere, a girl in jeans who makes for the staircase at the other end of the world. I make for the colonnade; a Swiss guard with a little black winter cloak puts out his head at the shout from a policeman in a doorway. There are guards everywhere, a security system already well in place – a rider on horseback also arrives, this can't be the way to go and dunk a brioche in your cappuccino! It is really a beautiful biggish square! Human figures are diminished not so much by the distance as by the concentric perspective; when one arrives from any point at an individual nothing is left . . . It seems impossible to me to get up there, to a door – I hope one doesn't have to ring a bell or produce a document. You have to try to guess which barrier will open to give you access to the steps.

The first and last time that I was here was in 1966. I was with my jeweller lover who later dropped me because I cost him too little and that didn't massage his self-esteem enough. I remember we did the rooms in the Vatican and the Sistine Chapel – I only remember State gifts in glass cases like the ones for food in luxury restaurants and that there was no toilet the whole way round. Maybe now they will have opened some nook which was uselessly there in order to relieve the customers . . .

A policeman in a uniform never seen before – something between a fireman and the gasfitter – once he casts a glance at me through narrowed eyes as if to say: 'I'm keeping my eye on you, you have a hammer in your pocket and are going to smash the noses of the marble statues.' I push a door and go to the left. No smell of incense, in fact, no smell, apart from a vague one of detergent and cooked toenails, like the one that hits you at the entrance to the autostrada at Agrate where the Star silos are smoking. A voice behind a curtain – I peep in: an employee in the grey uniform with a red trim on jacket and collar stands in front of a microphone reading a passage from the New Testament to some ten of his like seated with the faces of fathers of families who have put the Mass first on their work timetable – not extra to it – after a trade union battle that has lasted at least two thousand years. At each altar they are celebrating early Masses in a long line in absolute silence with at most two or three listeners. There is one where the priest is celebrating all alone, moving his body to right and left only from the pelvis, as if to indicate that since there isn't a crowd the intention is enough.

A group of enthusiastic Catalan faithful arrives to break the spell with joyful exclamations headed by a young nun with ample gestures which make her look like a soubrette busy showing off a newly opened nightclub. I see no confessionals, and in front of me appears the girl from before with the little knapsack, grimy, dirty gym shoes, blue jeans which sweat dirt, her hair very black and curly, thick tangled brows, sky-blue eyes, a foreigner from the East, I could swear, a filthy woman who has spent the night goodness knows where and now is carting her unwashed cunt from shrine to shrine and looking at me open-mouthed and leaving behind her a nasty-smelling wake. And she undoubtedly thought she was interesting. I am sure that the church itself received her only as a building and by an oversight. In fact when she approaches a holy water font – it could do for everything from shampoo to bidet – she is approached by a charitable and alarmed sister and the two go out by a side-door, probably for the department where they disinfect the faithful. Ah, here is a double row of confessionals in a square round a particularly big altar. A priest is coming out this moment from one of them, he is very fat, the right type for an advertisement for some liqueur featuring a friar. No, I do not dare to call him back. Another confessor candidate approaches and looks hard at me, wrapped tight in a kind of shawl of black felt, white hair, hard features, a nasty look in his eye – that of an educated peasant, an inquisitor. I pass him pretending not to notice. At the far end, a Mass with two women standing there, one dressed in a little flame-red coat, the other tall, from the countryside, with trousers, a man's trousers, that look like elephant's feet, a dirty shawl on her head; I draw near to look at them from the side without being seen. The little flame has glasses with thick lenses and holds her hands together like a little bewildered girl at her first prayers, she is very old; the other, about fifty, suddenly turns her head towards me and fixes on me two bulging madwoman's eyes, which quickly return to the richly embroidered back of the officiating priest. Places of worship do not give off anything poetic in my state of mind: I think that a human being who has taken God in his own image and appearance is a monkey and that a man who has taken a monkey in his own image and appearance is a man, and the latter are the ones I fall in love with and they are very rare and don't go to church. God has room only for an embellished imitation of the human being, and where he is installed I am certain that we are talking about a zoo decked out with the most common and commonplace animal chimeras.

One of the confessionals has a little lamp lit inside it. I draw near, if I want to this is it. I hoped to get away with it this time too, now I have no excuses. I glimpse the priest sitting waiting for the first-comer, I move to one side to see him better: deep in the reading of a book which I presume is not *True Romance,* or if it is, it is very small. How come that a volume one never finishes reading is called a 'breviary'? The priest is middle-aged, grizzled hair, his concentration looks sincere to me, he does not have a loutish look, not one of fermenting gastric juice, of tempered spirituality. I go for him. The important thing is that he should not have a face that says 'Jesus, My Spouse!' A little man arrives, one of the kind that go and tell their dream the moment it is deposited. He looks at me for a moment as if to say: 'Are you going or not?' He is about to pinch my place, I hurl myself sideways and say in one breath: 'Good day, Father,' and am kneeling and immediately see stars rising from my side right into my brain. The light goes out at once, I hear the slight sound of the book being shut. He has been taken by surprise but has quick reflexes – so well-disposed. I don't know if he sees me, nor whether he finds it important. The grating is called that because if you come too close it grates, I imagine. In fact I draw back at once but get stuck a moment too long to arrange the position of my calf – a burning pain fit to make one yell has started up again – as well as possible. I change my position again, I hear a sigh, perhaps he is looking at me, certainly he has noticed that I did not make any sign of the cross and that perhaps I am uncomfortable in this tight piece of joinery where there is no room for Bluebell legs. 'I am,' and he says 'Yes?' I clear my throat well, deeply embarrassed by the sweetness of that 'Yes?' which is not honeyed. 'It is about thirty years since I confessed.' 'What has happened?' He has an English accent, the voice is warm but on the alert, perhaps he has noted the insincere tone of mine and has already changed key to one of availability that is more of the intellect than of the heart. You don't do it with priests – the policeman apart. 'I don't know precisely, perhaps I wanted to recall to mind what it was I used to do as a child, I mean . . . the Church has always considered me a reject and I am not the kind that takes things on board so easily. I have tried to pay back in kind, and yet make it understand what it was losing, losing me and millions of homosexuals, maybe not exactly like me but, if there are a lot one can also shut an eye to the quality . . .'

We spend five minutes discussing my indisputable overall superiority over the rest of world, whether it be homo or hetero: I really have to kindle his interest at least by my pride, otherwise he will notice at once who is confessing to whom. But he rouses my liking and in a natural way breaks down my resistance to any form of sincerity. 'But for me that is not a sin!' I reply weakly to a sentence in which he uses at least twice the academic, obsolete word 'lechery'. 'It is not up to the individual to decide what is good or evil. Like the young mothers who kill their infants in the womb, they too say it is not a sin. But only God can establish the Truth and calls on the Church to mediate it to all men. And God is very understanding with sinners but cannot but remind them that sin is sin each time the sinner tries to disown it as such. Do you have a relationship?' 'No, never have, in this sense I detest the men as much as the women with whom I have had one.' 'Love of evil makes men fall, but love of good raises him towards God. God forgives the weakness of the man who mends his ways and asks his forgiveness.' 'Look, I have nothing specific that I need to ask pardon for, I am unable to see all this evil the Church administers, I do not understand the secular meaning of the concept of sin.' 'Yet you came here, why?' And I say, cornered: 'Help me. I feel completely innocent, how am I to blame?' 'Do you remember the parable of the Pharisee and the Publican? The Pharisee said to Jesus: "I am a just man," and Jesus sent him away. The publican said to Jesus: "Forgive me because I have perhaps sinned and submit to your judgement." And Jesus accepted him in his mercy.' 'Jesus is a bit like King Lear, or am I wrong? (I am on safe ground because outside there is a little card hanging with written on it 'English, Italian, Maltese'.) He is unable to tell who is more sincere, he pays attention to the official status of the statement, to who utters words of affection or not. In short, true feelings don't count, what counts more is the crime of lèse-majesté of the person who remains silent or does not comply with the need to have a judge other than his own conscience. And suppose the publican was a son of a . . .' I stop, a few moments of panic evaporate on either side of the grating; he says, drawing his voice from a greater depth: 'Knock and it shall be opened unto you,' all of which smells of carpentry and I, who by now am at the pitch of lumbar pain, say: 'And if someone only wants to get out, where should he knock?' and the voice, by now reduced to a hoarse patience, at best to vibrant oratorical art, says: 'Man can fall a hundred times and rise up again a hundred and one times if he asks God for forgiveness for his sins.' 'But I don't call this repentance but hypocrisy or the daily acquisition of indulgences cash-down . . .' And I make an effort not to insert an excessively emphatic exclamation mark. The priest begins to explain concepts to me which have remained the same from A to Z ever since I went to catechism, because the only chance I had to have a pair of new shorts, my own and not those discarded by my bigger brothers, was to go to my first and almost last communion. 'Father, thank you for your patience, now I really must get up, I am suffering from a strained back.' 'You have St Anthony's fire in your soul, I am always here. But to get absolution one must first set fire to one's own sins.' Absolution for what? I wonder, and am on the point of leaving.

At seven-thirty the big lamps shed on to the square a crimson aureole which floods from below the blue of the sky which is now fully awake. A taxidriver shouts for some reason at a young Filipino motionless on the pavement. A drug addict with a fierce air comes towards me holding out his hand. I suffered so often from doing without as a youth, having nothing to fill my stomach, but I never held out my hand – I preferred to hold out something else. The taxidriver starts to drive towards the Filipino as if to attack him, sees me, my signal, I dodge the hand held out to me, say Bravo to myself, deferentially the taxidriver turns in his tracks and opens the door. It may have been a spurious confession but yet it will be momentous: there will never be another. God is a cliché and the Church too old a dictionary to have it all. A pity.

But, Lord, don't have more than a modicum of pity.

En route to Sanremo. On the autostrada I throw glances to right and left, and it must be an instinct that leads me to encounter only cliffs or walls on which I catch sight of stagnant water or thin streams, cobalt, grey, hellish green in colour. My God, everything above the sea is putrid and runs off, or like just now when it is not raining, ferments while waiting for the right moment to rush down. An enormous white cat in the middle of the road: it looks to me as if it were licking a paw: since there is little traffic, I avoid it easily, I hoot, turn my head but it does not move. Behind me in the tunnel there was only one car, a powerful one; I watch in the mirror: she is at the wheel, he at her side, they are dawdling along and having fun, caught up perhaps in a banal love affair, the kind that amuses for a little and then unleashes the tragedies of ignorance and hysteria typical of people who do not read great narrative works. I watch them approach the cat at an easy speed and then what happens? It is as if she swerves suddenly and the other gesticulates excitedly as the wheels change direction, take aim, a slight bump, the red pulp that squirts from the white skin. They overtake me now at full speed and I see them laughing, she less, as if she had tested a new, more modern cynicism, and she is scarcely smiling with her jaws clenched – it is the only detail that remains of this story. I, on the other hand, never thought that cat had a different fate. But that couple too – man and woman so carefree – with a little blood of something else behind them, gamble better at the casino. In an hour's time they will stink of fruit-machines, piss, makeup and nicotine – and of what are (after all) ecological pop songs.

They will stink of Festival, of humanity's true origins, of him and her together for ever, and, being incapable of feelings because they do not know the use of the subjunctive or any formulation which is not basely at the service of needs and appetites which are all to be found in a pronoun and a verb in the present tense. They will end up by confusing their good intentions, their good will, their laughing fur-clad stupidity, signed and beribboned, with 'the feelings'.

In the air there is the smell of little plain envelopes with bribes in them. Here I am in front of the Teatro Ariston in Sanremo, which this evening will house the great sacrificial rite which will humiliate the Italian language for all the rest of the year, will humiliate journalism for a minimum of two weeks, will humiliate those people who disassociate themselves from their nice well-behaved family at home, silent in front of their TV, and don't worry about anything else because I'll see to it. But everything else is life, and only pensioners and people who can't get out of their wheelchairs can renounce it, deluding themselves that the Festival is merely entertainment.

In front of the Teatro two illuminated signs: a very feminine guitar and a very phallic saxophone – even though it is covered with appliqué. Under it all a couple of youths are waiting for some idol, but I have no idea who it is and who will be worthy of them. But they aren't very many.

From the accreditation office I go into the foyer and then down into the press room in which the first conference of the day is taking place: I learn that the humiliating number of invited guests comes to 900. Here on the steps there must be at least three hundred. Not many really stupid faces but even fewer really intelligent ones. At the table of power sits a certain Envelope No. 1 who resembles what is left of a man after he has lived at least three months in Naples or in Rome; alongside him another, a certain Envelope No. 2, organizational boss at the RAI, the government television network.

The journalists are unleashed in a convulsion of bogus questions followed by bogus, trifling answers – all of them known beforehand – which give way to the bogus polemics of people who think of nothing else, who do not think.

Are the journalists who cover popular shows perhaps more stupid than fashion journalists? Is it really still so difficult to understand that where there is no respect for the Italian language only State terrorism can thrive, even if it is sugar-coated? That where there is linguistic imprecision precision ends up by being only of the bloody kind? That whoever pollutes the historical evidence of his own language is capable of polluting anything else? I get up, go to get a mouthful of fresh air outside. In a little the rehearsals start, I shall have to approach a goodly number of singers whom I don't know, what shall I ask them? Nothing interests me in their lives or their profession, I shall catch them off-balance, it can only do them good. On a wall of a little yellow pub a few steps from the theatre 'Festival of authors' true lies'. I go back in with my ideas clearer. Rehearsals begin. Six or seven youths arrive and I don't know whether they are singers, strong-arm men, chuckers-out/in, all very hefty, with a nice look – perhaps even a human one. I am told that among them there is a certain Jehovah, someone who does one of these new jobs of today like putting on discs in discotheques, gives himself some airs for the brief space of a morning and then disappears for ever. I go up and ask: 'Excuse me, which of you is Jehovah?' Let the heavens open! Contempt, hilarity, panic: I must have confronted him in a single moment with the whole of his imminent future. When three of his entourage get up looking vaguely menacing, I see that it is better for me to go away at once so as not to create irreparable problems. I was no one to anyone and it doesn't even enter my head to make anything of it; to come here for a writer like me who is after all famous, is the proof that one ends up by being really famous for one's own Mamma and the village.

We all live in separate tribes, in diverse ethnic linguistic groups, each one wears his own identifying tattoos within his own ghetto: let's say so and Amen. In fact from a certain point of view I feel like introducing myself as Primula Rosi just because I know I am me, someone else, someone who turns up, a chameleon no one can suspect . . .

My most important question after having heard the tone of the songs is: 'Is this festival important to you?' No one who replies No to me. I shall not understand why Sanremo can be important to anyone apart from the political desire to get the people, that ox, used to bad faith, rhetoric, the thought mafia which will send out its message: 'Let's all lurv each other but you must lurv me more.' Wherever I turn my head I collect stupidities in full bloom and pink make-up: children of big shots, bastards, sons of whores, sons of God, the mammas of the sons of big shots. I go back to the hotel which is also in a state of stress because of maintenance work which was promised but never happened, and begin to pack. But then requests for interviews begin to pour in and my vanity is greater than my nausea. I shall see things myself live, at least for the first evening.

A little presenter who darts about like a mouse is wandering in the theatre foyer: he is notoriously provocative, bumps into me a couple of times but takes good care not to extend the microphone to me, which for me is the mark of a triumph. I am still hated, not even he trusts me. A doyenne of a journalist beside me applauds a singer who is past it because 'We have to support each other, we old hands.' She is really too kind. I spend most of my first and last evening away from the auditorium, I am waiting for it all to be over; I am bored by the Neapolitan songs, the Piedmontese songs, the Venetian and Lombard songs. I so much wish that it were a Festival of Italian Song. But what is Italy, where has it ended up? An eternal refrain now sung almost only in dialect.

In the auditorium and on the stage there are more silly geese than big shots – I have never seen so many ugly women, shoddy, men with indescribable faces – each one, simply to come here, must have left behind him something more than a cat (in the sense of a corpse). Because for them, one feels, as for the majority of these wretched journalists, to be here is an 'achievement', a goal. Old women gamblers have brought with them from the casino the smell of tepid tripe and stewed caries typical of the winners, that is to say of the losers; their hangers-on, supposing them to be theirs and that they have one, address them in Italian that is macaronic, sweet-meaty, pasta-loving. I am convinced that if the television cameras were to shoot the stolid faces in the auditorium in slow motion for sixty seconds, the nation of TV-addicts would be so shaken that TV would very soon become the memory of a barbarous age, even if a slightly nostalgic one.

From behind the wings in the corridor I hear every so often the emotion-laden uvulas which are incapable of transmitting emotion singing of feelings no one has any more. Not like this: these passionate feelings are more stated than felt, and it is not possible that the guitar, the shepherd's pipe, after century after century of rehearsals, should turn out to be rendered worse in duets than as solos. A Festival of Schizophrenia set to music. I would send all the composers to write their texts hidden in a booth in a ladies' hairdresser's or in football stadiums or in the parks with their syringes or among the inhabitants of the Val Bormida who have been fighting for years, without success, against the chemical factory belonging to the Ferruzzi Montedison group.

The trio Imitation Of arrives and another I cannot now recall with one member who plays the part of Andreotti's daughter – they pay homage to him even here – and goes off without leaving any trace except a pseudoscandal fired by religiosity (entirely synthetic) which quickly reveals itself for what it is. When even demagogy no longer manages to find the form to present itself as something else one can only say that the degradation of institutions has touched rock-bottom. This I understand, as do a whole lot of poeple who are not particularly cultured or perceptive where the representations of 'reality' by the media are concerned; in fact a waitress in the theatre bar says to me: 'So they rob us – OK – but to make fools of us – No!' The message is more or less this translated into big money: dishonesty for dishonesty, amorality for amorality, if they cannot carry on politics without criminality then let them at least respect the forms. If even demagogy takes down its trousers to show us its skeleton, how shall we manage to shut an eye, two eyes and then all the others, so as to continue to let ourselves be beaten to pulp like in the good old days?

The second evening I watch in Rapallo in a hotel as inefficient as the one in Sanremo: the usual pre-68 pout by a singer whose success has always been a mystery to me, a very nasty song by another (who perhaps was on yesterday evening or twenty years ago, I don't remember which), a grand finale with a famous couple, him singing, her coming down the steps very nicely with a little skin on her décolleté and less elsewhere. The Festival must be seen on TV, not live, that is dead, and has every reason to resuscitate itself.

I leave Rapallo too at once, it still seems too near Sanremo for me.

In a curve of the autostrada a truck is unloading a mass of colours which roll down one inside the other without ever getting mixed up. I draw up inquisitively, I signal hello to the driver, I lean out over the embankment: but they are flowers! Orchids above all, very fresh ones and roses and carnations and lilies and anemones which look newly gathered.

'Am I mistaken or are all the flowers good?' I ask.

'What?' the noise of the trailer has overlaid my incredulous question. I repeat it. 'One minute,' he shouts without turning his head. I have rescued a splendid rose of a velvety-orange colour and, my goodness, strongly perfumed, like the old-fashioned ones. And in bud.

'But of course these are good flowers. In fact very good indeed.'

'And why are they being thrown away?' I ask, still thinking in terms of the surplus of citrus fruit sent to be pulped under the rollers of what is to me the incomprehensible relationship between production and market.

'To keep up the usual prices. But not these ones,' he says mysteriously without even looking at me. 'These have not come right. They're wrong.'

'But to me, I'm sorry, they seem so – so real.'

'That's it, they haven't come out right. You see, with this funny climate this winter they turned out more beautiful, even scented, simply better.'

'And that's why they're being dumped?' I say, trying to hide my consternation.

'It would upset the market, which isn't used to that any more. It wants standard products, does the market. If we give it these ones here then maybe people will see the difference and won't want the others any more. Bye-ee.'

And the truck starts up again. I gather two armfuls because beauty has never frightened me, and the monsters sent to their deaths because they are too beautiful are the only ones to have a little life as I remember it.

Cleto Pomicino and his friend Ermete will come and collect me to take me to Tunis with them by car. We are going to Genoa and sailing this afternoon. They have been going to this paradisaical oasis in the south for a good thirteen years, and from what Cleto tells me about it, it seems they are real ambassadors, welcomed by now as living institutions. Greatly loved. In every sense of the word. We end up talking about the only thing that interests us. I don't know Ermete; Cleto told me on the phone: 'He weighs forty-three kilos, he lives on an orange and a portion of cheese daily. Just think – an old decayed aristocrat rings him up ten years ago to tell him that he is going into hospital to have a bypass put in. It isn't as if Ermete is a very great friend of his but he goes to visit him during those two or three days before the operation. The old man, who has no one, dies under the knife. A couple of weeks later Ermete is summoned by a lawyer: the old nobleman has made him his sole heir. An old palazzo in the old town, with an immense garden behind, furnished like a real museum, and even liquid cash to pay the death duties. Just to tell you what Ermete is like, for a good month he doesn't even go to see the palazzo, and when he arrives the maid is loading the last truckload of stuff, ancient and modern. Unfortunately the place was opposite the police station and they kept it under observation because of the coming and going of boys. A fixation of his – can you imagine? He sold it for next to nothing and with what he got for it bought a basement he calls his house by the sea – I call it the Marine Biology Centre – you have to go down eleven steps. It is below sea-level and sooner or later it will be buried by the sand. He is sixty and still lives with his mother of eighty-two. A good person. A bit on the mean side. He keeps alive on rennet apples. He knows the most distinguished families in the oasis, cultivates the most beautiful offspring and then once a year we go down and harvest the ripest ones. You know – those who are crossing the divide between boy and man, which makes them irresistible and unique only once in a lifetime.'

Cleto, on the other hand, weighs exactly a hundred kilos and is

Venetian, janitor at a high school. And to top up his wages deals in leather, in pedigree dogs, brings people together. Provided a young and vigorous boy is part of the retinue, takes mothers in invalid chairs in his truck to Lourdes and to Fatima and in his spare time sharpens kitchen and army cutlery on his great-great-grandfather's pumice whetstone to round up his month's wages and his human contacts. In all these jobs of his there is a wealth of turbulent stories of seductions and of sex with young men, none of whom seems to be homosexual or ever to be reluctant. Cleto is the picture in white and red, in the flesh, of happiness which waits patiently and then like a bolt from the blue falls on and envelops every victim he has marked down. The victims, the swine, set up with him a secret relationship which can last for years and usually is strengthened shortly after they have become husbands and fathers – Cleto strips whole families bare of males. There is no point in saying what the characteristic is that is shared by these beautiful ignorant mounts. Cleto seems to pursue no other aim in life than to unbutton a fly and find there something splendid which comes two centimetres above the navel. He can have people in until three in the morning those evenings when, incredible but true, he puts out at the window that gives on to the square his little vase with red plastic geraniums. He puts it out and in practically until the dawn. Everybody knows about it and everybody keeps quiet about it. He has never committed the mistake of officially declaring his weakness for the weakness of others and people ask for nothing better; since the only irreparable and unpardonable sin is not a specific sin but what leaks out. Cleto is the sublime reliever of pricks for a whole province which is very catholic and very schematic in bed. Cleto is a whirlwind which has become methodical: unsentimental, without passion or emotional weaknesses, or intellectual pretensions, with his lovers he does not use words to say something but to deny the whole thing, before, during and after.

'Sometimes they are already shoving it up me while we are there talking about cunt. They're pleased and I am more than pleased. I have a couple, Southerners, who are as thick as two planks, but they have certain tails! Now I have got used to the fact that you have to stay there and listen for at least an hour before they get it out: about football, about cars, about motorbikes, about Madonna and wives. It's always worth it afterwards. I tell most of them beforehand if they have problems in public, I tell them that if we meet it's better not even to say hello. That we are more at ease and what does it matter to me if they say hello or I say hello? What interests me is . . .'

Cleto is descriptive and lucid and with me extracts from his amoral stance fruit in the shape of knowledge of the human soul of the social male without fear of discovering something new about his own condition: he already knows everything and has crossed the threshold of consciousness which coincides with self-disgust. It is the clearest and most linear barrier I have ever come across since the Marquis de Sade. It is not his fault if he carries about with him all the damned liquids of male sexuality conceived of as an underground sewer. For me Cleto makes available a comfortable vessel in which to sail about at leisure and to tie up when I begin to get tired, or too mentally excited. He is, I believe I know from real knowledge, the human being most determined to match cunning with intelligence I have met since Celestino Lometto.* Odd that both of them, now that I think of it, resemble each other physically and that I share with them the feeling of travelling, of moving one's arse; in one case to sell pantyhose, here to buy at a good price a bunch of North African orgasms. It has all been written down already. *Repetita juvant*. And the enormous leather bag is already stuffed full of discarded clothes to take to the best-looking natives. I no longer feel like leaving. I shall breathe deeply, who knows, perhaps the date-palms are in flower and they at least have a perfume which I do not already know. Why didn't I think of it before! Liquid Vaseline as an antidote to AIDS. Here is Cleto's diesel-engined Ford appearing over the top of the hill. And my mother who is asking me at this moment, looking me up and down and putting her hands on her hips: 'And how much will it be by the line?'

And the two friendly misers have, without informing me, booked three bunks down in the hold in the lowest possible class! Where Cleto, at midnight precisely, not very far from the latest

* See Aldo Busi, *The Standard Life of a Temporary Pantyhose Salesman*.

patch of vomit scattered there in curves, has taken up position in T-shirt and drawers, peeping here and there in the cracks of the cabins where so many young Tunisians, turned back by the Customs in Genoa, are lying awake, playing up and down with the elastic and offering two breasts like women's. Behind his butter-won't-melt-in-his-mouth mask the vampire lies in wait. He will insert his fangs and will suck and wriggle his hips all the way, scandalized by one of them who tried to give him little kisses. Ermete is sleeping, apparently as fragile as a doll made from crinkled parchment, his profile sharp, his eyebrows recently trimmed and plucked, his mouth which has disappeared inside itself. I too eye a couple of sleepless and well-disposed boys as well as the crew-member of the *Habib* who looks like Charlie Chaplin, always with a broom, sawdust and a pail in his hand for drying up the vomit, his little squinting eye which underlines a certain ironical availability, a little game between a toilet blocked by a giant pad in the women's and a piece of Roquefort which has ended up goodness knows how in a flood of urine along with cigarette ends in the men's. For tonight I choose to transfer my unease to the deck and look at the difference between the blue night and the black sea. Only the wind is inspiring.

In Kairouan Ermete, burning with haste to arrive at our destination and meet a youngster whom he has secretly loved for three years and who won't play – what a rarity! – takes a bus and Cleto and I take a room in a hotel. The car is followed on its haphazard route by a moped with a couple on it who signal to come closer. The driver, a little, rather plump fellow in blue overalls says to us in Italian:

'*Amore*?'

I look at Cleto in case he should be interested in the one on the pillion, with a tawny beard and widely spaced, strong teeth.

'No.'

'Beautiful tarts too,' the driver insists. 'Cigarette, please.'

I offer the packet. Cleto says No again; the two behind us making signs which do not interest us. I at once go off on my own. I must find Shala to give him the clothes I promised him two years ago. I met him at the Gare Routière, when I was coming back from Sousse in the company of a jealous young soldier who was holding my bundle of carpets. And Shala, who looked like a young Robert Mitchum, thin moustache, the very first hair on his cheeks, a radiant smile and a rebellious tuft of hair the colour of petrol, begged for a kiss on the runnning board, in front of everyone. He was with a comrade in arms, very ugly and scrawny, squinting and with bare feet. I could have kissed both of them and could even have sent the soldier away, stopped over for a night, consumed Shala, but I did not do so: I knew he would remain my most exciting memory, perhaps the only one. When I got back home I put together a parcel of old-fashioned things, and in the post office they told me that it wasn't worth while, they would never get there. I kept the package in my wardrobe all this time, very easily seen, and my goodness, how many memories did this parcel whose contents I had completely forgotten force me to have. Sometimes I was afraid the moths would eat it, which the Customs in Tunisia had not been able to do. I also had the wrapping and the seal. It called to mind for me an emotion close to a love that was both impossible and possible, capricious. Pure light-heartedness.

I give the address to the first taxidriver, who knows it, knows it, I'm not to worry. He takes me all round the walls of the holy city, consults on the way with some traders, some students, some customers sitting outside a café, no, no one knows him – Shala. I insist that he should note all the details of the street and the official number. No, no: and he doesn't even add that he is sorry, sets off again, even if I had paid him to take me on a wild-goose chase he is not going to be the one that gets tired. I let out a curse, and at the starting-point in the big square I get out, shoving into his hand an exasperated sum. I go over to two policemen, they call another taxidriver, I get in, the taxidriver begins to slow down at the same place as the other, at the Grand Mosque, asks two boys on bicycles, another five come running up on foot, I myself go and consult a man selling soft drinks. I get in again and begin to protest. He puts me down very far from the two policemen, determined to look impressive and not like some madman, which I would if I presented myself with my face in the state it is in now. I go to the tourist office, ask if this street exists: they say it isn't a street, it's a district. No, says another woman employee, probably it isn't even a district. So what is it, I ask. The two young women lift the chiffon ever so slightly from their shoulders and smile at me intensely in a definite farewell. Third taxi. I explain the route already taken, he reads and rereads the card with the address, takes the seal and puts it in his pocket, says:

'I just left Shala's brother, five minutes ago.'

A complete turn round, and another. He drives with determination among carts and bicycles and potholes. He stops in front of a door, gets out, knocks, reappears and runs out again immediately, jubilant: 'Come, come. It is here but Shala is not at home. There's his mother.'

I go into the house welcomed by a pleasing scent of mint. An old lady with smoked glasses and a bandage under one lens comes towards me and smiles sorrowfully. She doesn't speak a word of French but behind her there is a very timid girl who explains that Shala is not at home, but in Monastir. I say it doesn't matter, I have promised him clothes, I shall go back to the hotel and bring the parcel, I'll put a note in it with my greetings. They thank me warmly but there is something in this that doesn't convince me, the lady seems really too old to be the mother of my Shala. I ask how old her son is now. The two women look at each other and the girl says: 'Twenty-eight.'

I make my excuses, dart a glance that is a curse at the taxidriver and go out. On the door I read the name and only as an anagram could it resemble the one I gave him well-written in clear letters on the label. Again in the taxi, the driver says he is called Nodir and that he too has a family if by any chance I should want to give him the parcel . . . I tell him to get a move on and let me down. We go about for another indefinite time and then I remember that Shala had said there in the Gare Routière: 'I live just behind here.' And there he lived where I myself lead the taxidriver: name and street and number finally match – one only had to move them elsewhere. His mother and a sister come to meet me, already grateful and obsequious. I compliment the girl on the splendid purple varnish on her nails, which are as strong as claws, and leave a note for Shala for him to meet me in the hotel as soon as he can. Meeting mothers upsets me, it makes me feel melancholy. I see the beautiful body of the son mixed up once again as impure matter and running back in time to reinsert itself where it emerged from. I see a chain of suffering and putrid things called human beings which, foetus after foetus, have preceded this boy who is nothing other than a mortal son. I escape from the mother, who is deeply grateful. If she knew.

She knows.

And Shala descends on me in the hotel, I recognize him while he is passing the porter's lodge at the entrance. He is with another companion, if possible still uglier than the one two years ago. I recognize him but, I should add, with difficulty. He descends on me, as I say, with his swaying load of listless melancholy, of missing teeth, of skin that has already grown old. I could count the tourists that have passed over him. In two years he has become someone else: he has difficulty in smiling, his hands are clammy, no little moustache any more, a sickly hue, his hair full of dandruff. And too thin. I don't know how, perhaps unconsciously, because it is forbidden for Arabs to go up into the rooms, we find ourselves naked, on my part more from a sense of duty than anything else. He hesitates, summons all his energies to play along at least a little, but can't manage it. 'Don't you want to give me the kiss of two years ago?' I ask him, and hope to myself that he will smile naïvely and turn his head away. We kiss with shut mouths. He does not get excited, does not know what to do with his hands and arms, I caress his backbone. I take a chance, he moves my hands away. 'Seeing you are naked try on the clothes,' I say to him, jumping out of the bed and slipping the string down the side of the parcel. 'No one will be as elegant as you here in Kairouan.'

Faced by the shirts, the trousers, the jerseys, the socks, the T-shirts, his eyes give a flash of surprise which is immediately quenched. I try to improve his morale, seeing it is not possible the other way. I dress him, make him go to the mirror, make him look at himself, escort him to the door.

Since evening is falling I make for the Roman reservoirs; here there is a house under construction and two rendezvous already set up. How quickly one grows old as a young man. Since I first began to have a pot-belly I have a kind of feeling of having come to a halt, of never having been so fresh and capable. Cleto is emerging from the same house under construction with his trouser belt in his hand. He sees me, he is in festive mood, he shouts: 'Shall I be a black photographer's model one day? Y-e-e-s. Please,' he adds, 'it's your turn. But please not more than two dinars each or else you'll spoil the place. We'll see each other in the hotel bar.'

Entering under an arch, taking care where I put my feet, I check the state of the small change in my pocket. The two friends on the moped who got in my way all morning until they dragged the appointment out of me are sitting on a little wall. I glimpse their silhouettes, they are both tall and robust and are smoking a cigarette between them. I begin with the one that I feel has the lowest tariff. Then I go on and repeat the programme, shooing away with my hand a third who was standing there hoping for a turn. Then burst out laughing by myself and the two of them laugh as well as they accompany me back to the hotel, but they will never know why.

It is because before I left my mother was asking me where I was going because 'I was going get cold in bed' in these parts – here. So to reassure her I told her I was taking work I had to do with me, that I would write something called a 'preface', and she instead of asking what it was – she doesn't know the difference between a newspaper and a novel – asked me how much they were giving me. 'Not bad!' she commented as I was getting into the car. And since I came running out again because I had left on the bed the little box of ultra-strong Fiatvoluntassua, she followed me into the bedroom and in those few moments wanted to know 'how much' I would have to write for that sum, and I broke the sum down into pages for her. I have never been falsely embarrassed to talk about money, and with Wilde am convinced that is better to have a steady income than to be fascinating. Besides the only way not to be greedy for money to the point where one writes for money is to have that little bit more or that little bit less than nothing which allows you without awkwardness to willingly do without it altogether. And since art is priceless, the price may as well be the highest possible. The only way in which a great artist is *himself* is that he has a lot of buyers competing with each other. He will not have to please anyone in a particular way and will do exactly the same as me, as if he had to please or did please only himself. In a few ordinary words and in dialect I told her all this. She listened with admiration and not even the little box had escaped her – she who has never seen them out of the packet when she finds one in my pocket says: 'I had to do a whole programme on the washing-machine for another of your American things.' And once I am again ready to cross the threshold she, fascinated by the mysterious tricks of a whirlwind of numbers and divisions and multiplications, spits out: 'And how much would that be a line?' I tell her, and almost breathless she says: 'You really know how to dot your commas! You have every right to piss the bed and say you were in a sweat.'

The boys, one on each side, do not even dare to ask me why I am laughing. Hiding it from each other, they each take a hand and place it on their fronts, then, as usual, they chatter away in Arabic, confiding in each other. I should like to tell them 'Thank you' as one does to two waiters, or 'Good shot' as to a champion at a clay-pigeon shoot. The hotel porter ceremoniously takes me over, staring at them greedily. I give him my last coin.

Now we have arrived in . . .

'But do you really have to give the name?' Cleto insists. 'Put the name of another city, of another place, in any case it is the same everywhere in Tunisia. Do roses really change perfume just because they change names? But at least they won't all rush here. There's an invasion already. Look at her – it's Giuliana di Puegnago, look how she's got up!' Cleto has noticed that during the journey almost every time I was sunk in thought as quick as lightning I took from my bag my little notebook and began by noting place and date at the top of the page. Guiliana di Puegnago, seen from the back on the half dug-up pavement and busy making promises to someone, looks like one of those shopgirls in a perfume department, bleached blonde (in pink kid bootees and a crimson frilly blouse), with the repertory of gestures typical of an youthful oldish woman who has invested all the expressive power she has left in her hip, which she moves from one thigh to the other as if she had only one. Meantime Cleto with his magic whistle built into his horn began to sound it the moment we entered the city and is waving his hand out of the window; youths run joyously behind us. Cleto calls them all by name – it doesn't need a great memory, the recurring names are no more than five in number.

'I had that one when he was fourteen, that one there was eighteen. Old stuff. But now I'll have each one once out of good manners and then I'll go on to the new ones.'

The old stuff can't be more than twenty or twenty-two. We arrive in the main square, and here the rejoicing turns into a national celebration. With the engine running, Cleto gets out of the car and begins to offer his cheek to a dozen ex-lovers to be added to the list. I am introduced, but my glance is too cold and detached, and then I feel like an extra, unworthy even to play second fiddle to such a monument of flesh and desire. I don't even think that what I feel is envy, it is much more: a real migraine. And the heat really is excessive.

Ermete is sitting down there at a table in the Café Central, and since there is the market this morning and so many vehicles are sitting there he has not seen us yet. He is listening to distinguished gentlemen whom everyone hastens to greet with a half-bow as they go up and down the steps to the terrace which is framed by carpets for sale in the shops. Ermete is silent and smiling like the Sphinx and says Yes with a movement of his big chin, like a minor authority from whom people do not want to have an opinion of any kind but do not wish to be without his assured and mechanical consensus with their own. Besides Ermete can easily pretend to be where he is without effort, since his head, in which no one is interested, and if at all then only in the chin which goes up and down with a regular rhythm, is certainly following his secret love who is due to leave for Italy in a few days, so he has been saying, to marry a cow of a tourist who gave him a sniff of it after their first ten minutes of acquaintance and decided, after another ten shots, to keep him for herself for some months by promising him a legitimate resident's permit through civil marriage. And the boy is packing, off goes the source of his sufferings, of his hidden desires as an adolescent old man; his boy, who has a surname as well, is the only one who does not go with queers, he and all his brothers throughout Tunisia. He is proud of it; Cleto has told me in private that he might have something to say on the subject but, you know, as one friend to another, it is better not to disappoint him. After all what does Ermete want at his age? With his guaranteed cornucopia of Arab pricks? Someone who won't play about to keep always in his heart while he is down there in his basement mouldering in brine. They write to each other, Ermete sends him all the boy and his family ask for, and he is happy that way; he is received with the honours reserved for a relation, almost a daughter-in-law. Now the procession of kisses and embraces is at an end – until the next crossroads, I presume – and Cleto gets into the car again, sees Ermete and hoots:

'The only thing he can distingush now is one car-horn from another. Apart from that he doesn't hear anything any more. He's a good person.' And Ermete turns round and sees us and greets us blandly with his hand, but he doesn't get up, signals 'Later' as if nothing had happened, as if this arrival of ours too was already over, already known, besides being foreseen, and so too with any possible messages it might bring with it. But as we are getting into first gear and setting off at a walking pace among carts and bicycles there is a shout:

'Cleto!'

Cleto turns his head towards the bench from which a huge tramp is coming towards us, running clumsily in a pair of old shoes.

'But it's Choukry!'

I don't recall anything about Choukry. He has told me so many stories about himself and the young inhabitants of this oasis that I can't make head or tail of them. And then quite apart from their number I would not be able to remember the year of entry and departure, the long periods between relationships approached, half-broached, half-closed. They embrace. Choukry gives him a resounding kiss on his nice puffy cheeks and Cleto on the other hand gives him a big clap on the shoulder and once again a minuet begins of 'How are you?' and 'How are you?' and 'How long are you here for?' and 'When shall we meet?' and round the pair there is another cluster of friends of Choukry, ex-national volley-ball champion, now trainer, I call to mind, the same person as takes up much of the car boot with wedding presents. Choukry greets me, turning serious, it seems, or embarrassed. Everything here is already too completely tied up for my taste.

'Who is Choukry?' I ask, as if I really knew nothing about him. In fact I do not want Cleto to realize that I remember all the details of something shameless which he presents to me with gleaming eyes as happiness and which really is so for him. I know the perfidious game of showing, as if it were of no importance, one casket of pearls after another to a poor bastard who has got no further than the slimy oyster shells, and I am taking great care not to satisfy him. Is he not already sufficiently rewarded and gratified, must he also enjoy my possible melancholy as one who is both frustrated and incredulous? Our types of sensuality are profoundly different, I am all for the means, he is entirely for the ends. I am all instincts and thoughts about instincts, he applies the psychology of others, which is the weapon of gamblers who do not wish to hazard much. Everything goes well with him always, and everything always goes wrong with me – I am not happy evidently, but if things went well for me in the way they go well for him when conquering men I would be a fish out of water just the same.

'But I told you! He is the one who bumped into me in the street one night, wrapped in a cloak, and I was tired, I was coming back from the oasis where I had been steaming my arse for twelve hours and at least sixty had been in and out and I was blissful, with my arse just out of the water, which was so nice and warm, I was a novelty – they competed for me – and there were those who queued up again to wait for their turn, and into the bargain there was I having to sing them Italian songs meantime, and at last I'm going home and one of them is following me, I had not even looked him in the face, I told him without looking at him to go and sleep because he had drunk too much, and he wouldn't give up saying: "I amn't like the others, misié, look at me, misié, I amn't like the others, look at me, misié, talk to me," and in the end I looked him in the face and I saw this magnificent creature almost two metres tall, all muscle, he had opened his cloak and under there was a naked statue of bronzed steel, with an erect prick which came up higher then his navel, and he takes me by the hand and takes me to his house, one of the finest houses in the village, with a porch with four vaults, and inside there was no one and what does he do? He lifts me in his arms and even then I weighed a hundredweight, like now, and carries me in, makes me cross the threshold like a bride! And we made love till the dawn and he even made me have an orgasm in my arse without even touching me in front. He is the one who is getting married. But he tells me that he loves me alone, you know at that time he really wanted me to come and live with him, I had even got to know his father, his mother, his brothers and sisters. My God, what big guns he fired off at me! For more than three years; you know what I'm like when they come up to twenty – I begin to look at their younger brothers. And so it was with Choukry – we see each other in private once in all the time I'm here – but more out of habit – I toss him off and that's that – but he is very jealous – it is terrible if I have an affectionate relationship with someone, he doesn't want that, he has me followed, always knows everything, where I've been and who with, I can set up decoys as much as I like, but if he knows that I'm taking another person a little present . . .'

The other persons to whom he has brought a little present cannot be less than ten in number, but nothing to what he has in store for Choukry: a bargain set of Upim plates, a cellophane bag of assorted cutlery with acrylic handles, a box of Nutella glasses (free gift), and that is supposed to be the astronomical wedding present. Putting it all together I am sure it costs half of a single pair of my trousers, or will we be exactly the same as one of the shirts I shall give away. But he is like that: he knows how to give a feeling of value to the things he gives because he knows it depends only on how you present them. I shut my eyes and pull something out haphazardly, I do not weigh anything, I want nothing in exchange – to the cast-offs I add neither more nor less than a modicum of tips, whereas custom calls for either the clothing or the tip – never both. And he is much richer than me, even if he is a janitor and, in his spare time, a civil servant.

'So let's choose an hotel,' says Cleto sighing. 'There's one just here. But you won't like it. We always go there. It costs next to nothing.'

'What's it like?'

He describes it.

'Let's go to the best one there is,' I say out of spite.

'It's a bit out of the way.'

'Well, let's see.'

We look at them all, the best ones: he says Yes to them all, he'd be happy in them all but naturally he tends to be thrifty. In the end he has to resign himself to one which at least is furnished with a bathroom. He sighs, says the price is absurd, but if it's what I want . . .

We stay there a night. The next day we go to his, to the Bon Repos, and he is once more cockily happy. There is a wash-hand basin, the room is too small, he alone takes up three-quarters of it with his bulk, strolling about in his drawers. He doesn't stand on ceremony: he gives himself a fix in the toilet and sings away. Because when he was going downstairs to greet one of the innumerable owners of the hotel, which is an ex-French army barracks, he had to stop again on the landing and go stealthily into the loo and satisfy the little new waiter.

'Stupendous! Yes – yes – I am a model in all respects!' he cries while the syringe sucks in directly from the tap. 'There's his cousin with him too. I wouldn't want to turn up dirty from before, you know. If you want to have a shampoo I won't take long. Bacteria of the colon against dandruff! That's it – done. Which is your towel? I don't remember. But of course, one or other . . .'

I don't know what gets into me. I begin to talk in a vaguely moralistic way about sex, about putting up with men's hypocrisy so long as you get them into bed, which is really all they want, all you need to do is respect that hypocrisy and go along with it and allow them the moment after to blot out from their memories anything done before with another man, and whether instead it wouldn't be a good idea to tell them to piss off: you come but you make them come too. Is it worth while – provided you come yourself – to make these idiots who don't deserve it come too? And I conclude:

'Sex celebrates the bodily functions, love does away with them.'

And Cleto, giving himself the last rub with the towel between his porky thighs, says:

'Long live sex! The only thing that matters to me is . . .'

'That they have ones that come up above their navels.'

'Right! You're a black photographer's model too. I'm off, I have an appointment at eleven and another at half-past. Now the troubles are beginning. If I like the one at eleven too much and I don't go to the other one . . .'

'But if you don't go to the other one . . .'

'Oh, they don't say a thing, if you go occasionally it's already pennies from heaven . . . They wait and wait. In any case they haven't a damned thing to do all day. Then we'll see each other in the Café. Go and see if our little ambassador is awake.'

Ermete sleeps next door in a room that is considered to be luxurious. He was talking to the old waitress who wants to introduce him to her son. He invents excuses then gives in. The old woman thanks him and disappears. For what? For the protection assent of this kind can mean for the good fortunes of her son. Another one trying to emigrate to Italy.

'But what shall I do with them – the mammas?' says Ermete with his little hoarse voice which has an Emilian cadence. 'They all want to put their sons in my bed and I'm not interested in that.'

'So have you found out when he is leaving?' asks Cleto, appearing like a naked Buddha.

'The day after tomorrow. He's mad. It's a good job that cow lives twenty kilometres away from me. He has said he will come and see me without telling her.'

'Maybe this is it!' says Cleto, putting his hands on his hips round which he now wraps two towels, the only two. 'I'm off. What a bore – so early in the morning. But I've already had a nibble.'

'With the new waiter? A pretty boy! He didn't interest me, he gave me the eye the moment I arrived but he's so young he looks like a child.'

'Just feel him down below – they are *two* children in one. Ciao, till later.'

Ermete invites me into his room. I dry my hair with what remains of the towels. They smell of newborn babies.

'What do you think of it?' he says very frivolously.

'Well, is this really a hotel?' I protest.

'But they shut their eyes to things. We've known each other for a lifetime. They let us take them up to our rooms if we want. They shut their eyes, elsewhere you have to take care. So to say . . . Oh, what a bore! I'm fed up already.'

'How long are you staying?'

'A month, two months, it depends, I have so many people to visit!'

'And how do you spend your time with them?'

'Lots of tea, tea and more tea, fifteen of us sitting in front of the television, without saying a word, that is after the first ten minutes of politenesses. Like that. I don't manage to arrange anything – you see by now they are too respectful. Yesterday I was on the point but then . . . Ah, it didn't interest me, it was so quick . . . And then I have to go and dine at least once in each hotel – you see I have seen almost all the proprietors grow up. I must stay in the restaurant with them and then with their families at home. They don't leave me a free moment. They need so much of that stuff from Italy. They even deposit cheques, valuta, they trust me, that's what it is.'

'And you?'

'Well I – three or four times a year they send me up a nice boy, very nice, he stays with me . . . You know they all say two or three days, but sometimes it's two or three months. But you see they are young and my mother is used to it by now – she cooks for three.'

'And what about your mother when you go to bed together?'

'Oh her! The most innocent woman in the world! She doesn't know anything!'

I have heard this too. Now he is taking a rachitic little apple and is beginning to bite it cautiously because he has no front teeth. He carries on like this till evening.

'Go to the Belvedere – you can walk there. A stupendous view. There are still German hippies. They are a bit off-putting, but no more than they used to be – but they are picturesque. They have their wolfhounds, their motorbikes, their skinny little whores. There's a whole lot of peasants at work round about. In all senses of the word. It's up to you. Ah, that's all I needed – the maid's son, now! He will arrive any minute. In any case I'll leave the door open – I don't want to compromise myself or let her think all sorts of things. It's better if she doesn't have any illusions that I'm taking him along with me.'

At the Belvedere there is nothing to be seen, apart from hippies round a tent and surrounded by a trio of silly mangy dogs. A car arrives, well! There was a guy down in the hotel bar who started to look at me as he knocked back beer and to feel his prick with his whole fist, bald, little sparkling eyes, a solid belly, moustache, a gentle belch every now and then, he looked at me, trying not to let his boon companion see, a tall skinny negro with the watchful face of a diffident giraffe. The negro did the same, staring at me without letting his neighbour see. When the little one got up to go and have a piss he turned his head and I followed him – he turned his head in front of all the others, I mean, and many of them raised their bottles or glasses to me, as if toasting what I was going to get up to. In fact we settled on outside and I went ahead of him and he left the negro in the lurch. But not out of discretion. He picks me up after I have been walking about a kilometre with him behind me in a car, hooting. In fact I was already regretting it and didn't want to get in. Then . . . A pity about his querulous voice: he is a Customs officer on the Algerian border, married and a father, he is twenty-eight (looks ten years older) but says: 'I want to live life all the same. But with a condom.' The car turns round in the centre of town, a fairly new car, and then roads and side-roads, it is maybe doing 3 km per hour. I understand! He is showing me off, forgetting that I might look more like a native of the Maghreb, like himself, than a European doll. Then among the palms he makes me walk a kilometre, no, not here, too much in the open, not there either, people go past there, we find ourselves in a cylindrical well which drains off the water and rises up above a ditch. He brings his mouth close to mine but does not press on it; he produces a whole muscular little tongue and a little away from me whips it once to the right and once to the left and withdraws it like lightning, like the tongue of a salamander. At the moment of final withdrawal three oldish men show themselves at a window – evidently they have followed us on hands and knees through the bushes and now are watching us in an attitude of repose and great interest, as if they had been there for hours. My beauty takes flight down an embankment, I am not disturbed, I salute the trio amicably. They show me their hands going up and down in their trousers and look at me with wide but sweet eyes and I run after the Customs officer, who to identify himself gives a whistle every now and again. Then we find ourselves in another round building, very far away and cool, a branch of the first aqueduct: condoms all around. He doesn't want me to press my cock against his thigh. Instead he takes me by the neck with two fingers and pushes me down and with the other hand masturbates into my mouth. I who after all do have a bit of a backbone meantime look at the beautiful beige of the sand-dune. I read the names of the brands on the torn packets. But here is Cleto's car turning up towards the Belvedere, I run to meet him down the little hill of smooth stone. He sounds his horn joyously and even the notes of that horrible song spreading through the sunrise, so detached and metallic, seemed to me to be a summons to which not only Ermete is sensitive. In fact the horn is saying: '*Until the boat leaves let things go*. Until . . .' and suddenly a din rises up from the ditches and streams of people washing and a group of young half-naked peasants come round the car and I run more slowly, held back by all these embraces. The problem of life is really to be loved for what one is not and to be despised for what one is. I should have paid more attention to the dream and less to the nightmare which it hides.

Thank God, Cleto did not see me. I shall not insinuate myself like a thorn into his arrogant, icy, happy happiness. I shall pretend not to notice and will wait until he has sorted them all out to the last, then I shall turn up and comment on the course of the day as if I had just arrived. A writer does not have existential problems and only in part those of others, including his own. A writer cannot confine himself to living like anyone else – he must decide once and for all to exist and that is all – like a sea. And the sea does not know what a sea is, nor does it matter to it.

One is born homosexual and becomes heterosexual and the

effort one makes to become heterosexual is not any less than that to remain homosexual. For this reason I have never been able to consider heterosexuals to be different. Different from whom? From themselves, perhaps, but nothing more.

Cleto on a sofa in the bar is telling tall stories to half a football team on its way through, who are listening to him, rapt. He is the only European capable of having beer bought for him in a place in the Maghreb without having, as in the south of Italy, to repay at least threefold. And he doesn't even speak French.

'Cleto!' I say to him, standing in front of him. 'I've found it!'

'If that's what you mean so have I. Just look here. Do you know what I say? Let's skip supper – they'll put the protein into you. In Indian file, messieurs-dames! And to think that if there's someone who hates it standing up it's me! *"But not my love, my love cannot . . ."* ' and he gets up, throwing an all-encompassing glance beginning with the first on the left. 'I don't know about you but I am going to go and pose. The third mimosa in flower just outside there. Shall I be a model?'

He does not know that I am already on the point of leaving and want to get back home as soon as possible. Meantime I give a little unattractive laugh for him, so as not to cause his inextinguishable enthusiasm to be somehow extinguished. But then I give an all-devouring laugh at myself and the symmetrical tightrope-dance which is the way things travel: the car was already moving loaded up with us like blood sausages and with second-hand clothes to trade for absolute chimeras and my mother is stepping out on to the doorstep and then on to the street and – still a few lines imprinted on the imperturbable wateriness of her pupils – and crying radiantly, waving her beautiful hand:

'Write in big letters!'